From Hatred to Heat

LACI MAE WYLD

ISBN: 978-1-7642098-3-0

Contents

CHAPTER 1

The Bookshop Chronicles

THE KEY SLIDES into the lock with a familiar resistance that Jetta's wrist knows by heart—a quick twist to the right, then a gentle push against the old oak door. Morning light spills across the threshold as she steps inside, her running shoes silent against the worn floorboards. The bookshop greets her with its particular silence, different from the empty streets outside—a silence full of stories waiting to be disturbed, of pages eager to be turned. She inhales deeply, letting the mingled scents of paper, binding glue, and yesterday's coffee fill her lungs before flipping the light switch.

FLUORESCENT TUBES FLICKER reluctantly to life overhead, illuminating dust motes that dance in the slanting beams of sunrise filtering through tall windows. Jetta stretches upward, her athletic frame elongating as she reaches for the ceiling, feeling the pleasant pull along her spine—a remnant of this morning's run still lingering in her muscles.

· · ·

"ANOTHER DAY, ANOTHER DOLLAR," she murmurs to the empty shop, her voice absorbed by the thousands of books lining the walls. The words are a ritual, spoken each morning like a spell that transforms the space from dormant to expectant.

SHE MOVES WITH PRACTICED EFFICIENCY, a choreography perfected over years. The broom first—sweeping behind the counter where loose paper clips, receipt fragments, and the occasional paperback price tag accumulate like literary debris. Her movements are economical, nothing wasted. The register next, buttons clicking beneath her fingers as she counts the float, mouthing numbers in a silent tally. The drawer slides shut with a satisfying ping that echoes through the quiet store.

JETTA PAUSES at the front display table, running her fingertips along the spines of last week's bestsellers. They need refreshing. She selects new titles from the cart she prepared yesterday—a thriller with a die-cut cover that reveals a blood-red interior, a romance featuring two silhouettes against a sunset, a memoir with an austere black and white portrait. She arranges them with an artist's eye for balance, tilting some forward to catch the light, letting others recline in casual invitation.

THE SHOP UNFOLDS around her like a three-dimensional map she's memorized by heart. To the left, fiction spreads across six tall bookcases—contemporary literature giving way to classics, then genre fiction organized by type. Crime novels with their stark, bold fonts stand sentinel beside horror's dark, atmospheric covers. Fantasy's elaborate illustrations bleed into science fiction's sleek designs. Romance occupies an entire case near the window, where natural light flatters the vibrant covers.

NEAR THE BACK, beneath a stained-glass pendant lamp that casts pools of amber and blue across the floor, sits the reading nook. Two armchairs face each other across a low table, their upholstery worn thin at the armrests where thousands of hands have rested while turning pages. The right chair—the one with the slight depression in the cushion—is Jetta's favorite. During slow afternoons, she sometimes steals moments there, knees tucked up beneath her, a new arrival open in her lap.

THE COFFEE STATION occupies the corner farthest from the books—a concession to modern bookshop expectations that Jetta had initially resisted. Now she's grateful for it as she fills the machine with water and grounds. She flips the switch, and the machine gurgles to life, sending tendrils of rich aroma curling through the air, chasing away the last wisps of morning stillness.

THE BELL above the door jingles, announcing Brandi's arrival in a chaotic flurry of movement. Her blonde hair is caught in a messy bun, strands escaping around her face as she hurries inside, her oversized tote bag swinging dangerously close to a stack of new arrivals.

"I'M LATE, I know, and I can't find my glasses," Brandi announces, already digging through her bag, pulling out a wallet, three pens, a half-eaten granola bar, and what appears to be a small potted succulent. "I had them when I left home, I swear." Her voice rises with each item extracted from the seemingly bottomless bag.

JETTA LEANS AGAINST THE COUNTER, a crooked smile tugging at her lips as she watches the familiar morning drama unfold. "They're on your head," she points out, nodding toward the reading glasses perched atop Brandi's head, nestled in her blonde hair like an overlooked tiara.

BRANDI'S HANDS FLY UPWARD, fingers connecting with the plastic frames. "Oh!" Relief washes over her features, followed immediately by self-deprecating laughter. "That's the third time this week." She pulls them down and slides them on, blinking as the world comes into focus. "What would I do without you?"

"PROBABLY WANDER the streets in a perpetual squint," Jetta replies, pushing a steaming mug across the counter. "Coffee's fresh. I've already done the register and front display."

"YOU'RE AN ANGEL." Brandi accepts the mug, wrapping both hands around its warmth. She takes a sip and sighs with pleasure. "Any special plans for today? New shipment? Author crisis? Mysterious customer seeking rare first editions?"

"JUST TUESDAY," Jetta says, but her eyes track to the calendar pinned beside the register. "Though the book club

4

meets tonight. Ms. Harmon promised to bring her infamous lemon bars."

"THE ONES that taste like furniture polish?" Brandi grimaces, setting down her coffee to shrug off her cardigan.

"THOSE ARE THE ONES." Jetta's laugh is soft but genuine. She watches as Brandi begins her own opening routine— checking the day's online orders, adjusting the angle of the children's display, nudging the reading nook's rug until its fringe lines up perfectly with the floorboards.

THROUGH THE WINDOWS, the street outside is beginning to wake—early commuters hurrying past with travel mugs clutched in hand, a dog-walker juggling multiple leashes, the bakery across the street flipping its sign to 'Open.' Inside, the bookshop holds its breath in these final moments before customers arrive.

JETTA MOVES TO THE DOOR, key in hand to unlock it for the day. Sunlight catches in her brown hair, highlighting strands of copper and gold that only show in direct light. For a moment, she stands perfectly still, taking in the shop—her shop—with its neat shelves and inviting corners, the coffee scent mingling with paper and possibility. Then she turns the lock, and the day begins.

MID-MORNING LIGHT SHIFTS through the bookshop windows, less golden now, more white and direct. It catches on the dust particles that rise each time a customer pulls a book from the shelf, tiny constellations briefly illuminated before settling again. Jetta adjusts the newsletter display by the register, half-watching the elderly woman in the mystery section who has been deliberating between two novels for the past twenty minutes. The bell above the door chimes, sharp and insistent, announcing a new arrival. Something about the sound—more commanding than usual—makes Jetta look up. The man who enters doesn't so much walk as stride, his expensive suit out of place among the casual browsers, his polished shoes clicking against the hardwood with purpose.

He carries a brown paper bag, held away from his body as if it contains something distasteful. His silver hair is swept back from a high forehead, and wire-rimmed glasses perch on a nose that seems designed for looking down at people. Jetta recognises him vaguely—a local lawyer or banker, someone whose name appears on building plaques downtown.

He approaches the counter directly, ignoring the handwritten sign requesting customers to browse freely and ask for assistance if needed. The paper bag lands on the counter with a soft thud.

"I need to return this," he announces, his voice pitched to carry. Two customers browsing nearby glance over before politely returning their attention to the shelves.

"Good morning," Jetta says, her smile professional but not ingratiating. "How can I help you today?"

. . .

HE EXTRACTS a book from the bag—a dark green leather-bound volume with gilt lettering along the spine. Even at a glance, Jetta recognises it as the first edition Hawthorne they sold last week, priced well into four figures.

"THIS ITEM IS NOT AUTHENTIC," he states flatly. "I've purchased enough rare books to know the difference between a genuine first edition and an elaborate fake."

JETTA'S FINGERS flex against the counter, once, a small release of tension that doesn't reach her face. "I'm sorry to hear you're unsatisfied with your purchase, Mr.—"

"CARSON. HOWARD CARSON." He says his name as if it should mean something to her.

"MR. CARSON." She nods. "May I examine the book?"

HE PUSHES it toward her with one manicured finger. "The binding is all wrong for the period. And the paper quality—" He makes a dismissive gesture. "Amateur work at best."

FROM THE CORNER of her eye, Jetta sees Brandi by the front window, arranging a display of brightly coloured paperbacks beneath a "Summer Escapes" banner. Her friend glances over, raising an eyebrow in silent question. Jetta gives an almost imperceptible shake of her head. She can handle this.

. . .

"OUR AUTHENTICATION PROCESS IS QUITE THOROUGH," Jetta says, opening the book with careful hands that belie the quickening of her pulse. This particular volume had been part of an estate sale collection, personally verified by their most trusted appraiser. "Every rare book we sell comes with certification."

"CERTIFICATIONS CAN BE FAKED," Carson retorts, his voice rising slightly. "I want a full refund. Today."

A TEENAGE GIRL browsing nearby edges away from the confrontation. Jetta notes the motion and lowers her own voice, forcing Carson to lean in if he wants to hear her.

"MR. CARSON, I UNDERSTAND YOUR CONCERNS." Her tone is measured, neither submissive nor challenging. "However, this first edition was authenticated by Malcolm Reeves, who's been appraising rare books for over thirty years."

CARSON'S MOUTH TIGHTENS. "I don't care if God himself signed off on it. I know what I'm looking at."

ACROSS THE SHOP, Brandi drops a stack of paperbacks, then bends to retrieve them, her reading glasses sliding off her nose in the process. She fumbles for them, squinting, before locating them beside a display stand. The small commotion draws Carson's attention momentarily, and Jetta uses the opportunity to carefully turn to the front matter of the book.

. . .

"SIR, the authentication certificate is right here in the cover," she explains, turning pages with careful precision. Her index finger indicates the small bookplate affixed to the inside cover, with Reeves' signature and the date of authentication. "You'll note the watermark and registration number."

CARSON LEANS FORWARD, scepticism etched into the lines around his mouth. "That doesn't address the binding issue."

"IF YOU'LL LOOK at the spine construction," Jetta continues, gently turning the book to display its binding, "you'll notice the irregularity in the fifth segment. This is actually consistent with Ticknor and Fields' bindings from this specific print run. It's one of the authentication markers."

SHE DELIVERS this information not as a challenge but as a simple fact, her voice carrying the quiet confidence of someone who knows exactly what she's talking about. Her fingers trail along the spine, indicating the subtle details that verify its age and authenticity.

CARSON'S EXPRESSION wavers between doubt and interest. Jetta presses her advantage, but gently.

"WE ALSO HAVE the provenance documentation on file." She reaches beneath the counter and produces a folder. "This traces ownership back to a private collection in Boston, with an unbroken chain of custody since 1923."

· · ·

SHE SPREADS the documents across the counter—photographs, letters, auction records—creating a timeline of the book's journey from printing press to their shop. Throughout her explanation, she maintains eye contact with Carson, neither challenging nor deferring, simply presenting facts.

BEHIND HIM, Brandi continues arranging the summer display, periodically misplacing her glasses as she works. She places beach reads with vibrant covers in an eye-catching pattern, occasionally glancing toward the counter. Where Jetta is all contained precision, Brandi moves with expressive warmth, smiling at customers who pass, offering suggestions with animated gestures.

"THE PAPER QUALITY YOU MENTIONED," Jetta continues, turning to a specific page, "shows the characteristic foxing of the period. See these small brown spots? Modern reproductions can't accurately replicate this pattern of natural aging."

CARSON'S SKEPTICISM is visibly eroding, though his posture remains rigid. "And you guarantee its authenticity?"

"ABSOLUTELY," Jetta says. "In writing, with a buyback provision should any expert of your choosing prove otherwise."

SHE WATCHES his face as he processes this—the reluctant reconsideration, the calculation of whether to persist. His fingers drum once on the counter, a tell she's seen in customers who know they're wrong but hate to admit it.

"I SUPPOSE," he finally says, "that I may have been... hasty in my assessment."

JETTA DOES NOT SMILE in triumph. Instead, she nods professionally. "It's always wise to verify such significant purchases. Would you like me to provide copies of these documents for your records? Many collectors find it enhances the value to have the complete provenance on hand."

IT'S A PERFECT EXIT STRATEGY—ALLOWING him to retreat with dignity while reframing his complaint as the diligence of a serious collector.

"YES," he says after a moment. "That would be... appropriate."

WHILE JETTA PREPARES THE COPIES, Carson examines the book more carefully, his expression softening into appreciation. By the time she returns with the documentation, neatly organized in a folder embossed with the bookshop's logo, his demeanor has transformed from confrontational to collegial.

"OUR CONTACT INFORMATION IS HERE," she says, indicating the card paper-clipped to the inside cover. "Please don't hesitate to reach out if you have any further questions about your collection."

. . .

"Yes, well." He tucks the book and folder under his arm. "Thank you for your... thoroughness."

After he leaves, Brandi appears at Jetta's side, replacing her glasses after having found them perched atop a stack of cookbooks.

"That was impressive," she says, bumping her shoulder against Jetta's. "I was ready to come over and kill him with kindness, but you didn't need rescuing."

Jetta's smile finally emerges, the professional mask slipping away. "Sometimes knowledge is the best defense against assholes in expensive suits."

"And sometimes those assholes just need someone to make them feel important," Brandi counters, straightening a row of bookmarks by the register.

"Different approaches, same result," Jetta says with a shrug.

"Teamwork makes the dream work," Brandi sings, already moving back toward her display.

. . .

JETTA WATCHES HER GO, feeling the residual tension from the confrontation dissolving. She flexes her fingers once more, then turns to help a customer approaching with an armful of books and a hesitant smile.

THE AFTERNOON SUN slants through the windows at a drowsy angle, turning the bookshop into a warm, quiet cave. The lunch rush—such as it ever is in a bookstore—has faded, leaving behind that peculiar midday lull where time seems to stretch like taffy. Jetta sits on the stool behind the counter, one foot propped against the bottom shelf, inventory sheets spread before her. Her pen makes soft scratching sounds against the paper as she counts and records, a rhythm occasionally broken by the gentle turning of pages from the sole customer browsing in the travel section.

THESE ARE the hours Jetta secretly treasures—not the bustling Saturday mornings or the vibrant book club evenings, but these pockets of stillness when the shop breathes around her. Dust motes drift through shafts of amber light, and the scent of coffee mingles with paper and binding glue. She rolls her shoulders, feeling the pleasant ache of a morning spent reshelving returns.

BRANDI EMERGES from the back room with an armful of hardcovers, her cheeks flushed with exertion or excitement— with Brandi, it's often difficult to tell the difference. She deposits the books on the counter beside Jetta's inventory sheets, her bracelets jingling softly with the movement.

· · ·

"So," she begins, in a tone that immediately alerts Jetta that this isn't about books, "I'm going to that gallery opening on Saturday." Her hands are already in motion, smoothing dust jackets as she speaks, a nervous energy radiating from her fingertips. "The one at that converted warehouse on Maple? They've hung these massive fabric installations from the ceiling—all blues and greens like you're underwater—and there's going to be live music and those little fancy appetisers that look like modern art but taste like heaven."

JETTA MAKES A NONCOMMITTAL NOISE, adding another title to her inventory list. She can feel the conversation gathering momentum like a wave preparing to break.

"AND," Brandi continues, her voice lifting with anticipation, "Owen's going to be there—you know, that guy from my yoga class with the amazing laugh?" She adjusts a book so its spine aligns perfectly with the edge of the counter. "The one who does that impossible crow pose without even shaking?"

"AH YES, CROW POSE OWEN," Jetta says, her mouth quirking into a half-smile. "The one with, and I quote, 'forearms like a Renaissance sculpture and eyes that actually twinkle.'" She affects Brandi's dreamy tone for the description, but keeps her teasing gentle.

"DON'T MOCK THE TWINKLE, Jetta. The twinkle is real." Brandi points an accusing finger, but she's laughing. "Anyway, he specifically mentioned he was going, and then looked at me with this... expectation. Like he was hoping I'd be there too."

· · ·

JETTA SETS DOWN HER PEN, giving her friend her full attention now. Brandi's enthusiasm is infectious, even when Jetta wants to maintain her immunity. "So naturally, you'll happen to show up looking casually fantastic, pretend to be surprised to see him, and then accidentally-on-purpose end up discussing the same art installation in some dimly lit corner."

"IS IT THAT OBVIOUS?" Brandi grins, not at all bothered by the transparency of her intentions.

"JUST TRY NOT to ruin another first date by planning your wedding before dessert arrives," Jetta quips, reaching for her pen again. Her tone is playful but holds a subtle edge, like a paper cut—sharp but almost invisible.

BRANDI ROLLS HER EYES, unfazed. "That was one time, and for the record, Marcus and I would have had beautiful children."

"MARCUS WORE socks with sandals and called his mother three times during dinner," Jetta reminds her, tallying a column of numbers. "Your children would have been well-behaved phone addicts with terrible fashion sense."

THE LONE CUSTOMER approaches the register with a guidebook to New Zealand, and Jetta straightens, sliding seamlessly into her professional demeanour. Her smile is warm, her small talk effortless as she processes the sale. As the door closes behind the customer, the shop falls back into its comfortable silence.

． ． ．

Brandi resumes their conversation as if there had been no interruption. "You should come with me," she says, leaning against the counter. "There's this other guy who sometimes comes to yoga—Daniel—who'd be perfect for you. He's got that quiet, intense thing you like, reads actual physical books, and I've never seen him wear socks with sandals."

Jetta's shoulders stiffen almost imperceptibly beneath her loose-knit sweater. Her gaze drops to the inventory list, and she begins recounting a shelf she's already tallied. "Thanks, but I've got plans with my Netflix queue and that bottle of Merlot I've been saving." She doesn't look up as she speaks, her pen moving a fraction too quickly across the paper.

"You and your Netflix queue have been exclusive for months now," Brandi says, her voice softening. "Doesn't it ever get boring? The same old shows, night after night? No unexpected plot twists?"

"I like knowing how my evenings are going to end," Jetta replies, still not making eye contact. "With me, comfortable in my own bed, no awkward goodbyes or morning-after regrets." She attempts to keep her tone light, but there's a weight to her words that settles in the space between them.

Brandi studies her friend's downturned face, the way her brown hair falls forward to shield her expression. "Not all guys are like Ryan, you know."

． ． ．

16

THE NAME DROPS between them like a stone into still water. Jetta's pen pauses mid-stroke, a small blob of ink spreading on the paper where the tip lingers too long. "I know that," she says finally, her voice carefully neutral. "This isn't about Ryan."

"ISN'T IT, THOUGH?" Brandi asks gently, reaching out to touch Jetta's wrist. "It's been almost two years."

JETTA FINALLY LOOKS UP, her expression composed but her eyes holding something guarded. "It's not about him specifically. It's about knowing myself well enough to recognise I'm good on my own." Her fingers flex against the counter, unconsciously echoing the gesture she made during the confrontation with the difficult customer earlier. "I like my life. I like this shop, our book clubs, my apartment, my routines. I don't need to complicate things with someone else's expectations."

"NEED AND WANT ARE DIFFERENT THINGS," Brandi observes, straightening a stack of bookmarks.

"VERY PROFOUND," Jetta says dryly, but there's no bite to her sarcasm. "Save the wisdom for Crow Pose Owen. I'm sure he'll find it enlightening." She deliberately lightens her tone, sliding the conversation back to safer ground.

BRANDI ALLOWS THE DEFLECTION, recognising the boundary. "So that's a no on the gallery opening?"

· · ·

"THAT'S A NO," Jetta confirms, her smile returning. "But I want every single detail on Sunday. Especially if the twinkle turns out to be glaucoma."

"HEARTLESS," Brandi accuses, but she's smiling too. "Absolutely heartless."

"REALISTIC," Jetta corrects, resuming her inventory count. "Someone has to balance out your rampant optimism."

BRANDI MOVES AWAY to help a new customer who has entered, her attention immediately and completely focused on their needs, her reading glasses once again misplaced and found perched atop her head. Jetta watches her for a moment —the animated way she gestures toward different sections, the genuine warmth in her smile—and feels a familiar mixture of affection and envy.

THE AFTERNOON LIGHT SHIFTS, casting longer shadows across the wooden floor. Jetta turns back to her inventory sheets, to the comforting order of numbers and titles, to the predictable rhythm of counting and recording. Outside, life rushes by with all its messy possibilities, its twinkles and disappointments. Inside, between these shelves of stories with their guaranteed endings, Jetta finds the certainty she craves.

CHAPTER 2

Party Surprises

THE BASS THRUMS through the floorboards, a persistent heartbeat beneath Jetta's reluctant feet as she steps into the apartment behind Brandi. Heat greets her first—the unmistakable warmth of too many bodies packed into too little space—followed by a wave of chatter that crests over the music. She tightens her grip on the bottle of wine she's brought, its glass cool against her palm, a small anchor in the sea of unfamiliar faces turning briefly in their direction before the current of conversation pulls them away again.

"ISN'T THIS GREAT?" Brandi shouts over her shoulder, already shedding her light jacket and revealing a flowing top that catches the light when she moves. Her reading glasses perch atop her head, forgotten as usual, creating a makeshift headband for her blonde hair. "So much more fun than Netflix and Merlot!"

JETTA FORCES her lips into what she hopes resembles a smile

rather than a grimace. "Absolutely thrilling," she murmurs, though her words disappear into the chaos around them.

THE APARTMENT SPRAWLS BEFORE THEM— INDUSTRIAL chic with exposed brick and ductwork, the kind of place featured in design magazines but seldom actually lived in. String lights crisscross the high ceiling, casting pools of amber that do little to illuminate the corners where shadows gather. Bodies move through these alternating patches of light and dark, creating a disorienting effect that makes the room seem both larger and more claustrophobic than it actually is.

JETTA RELINQUISHES her wine to a makeshift bar in the kitchen—a granite island crowded with bottles, glasses, and a punch bowl filled with something unnervingly blue. A lanky man with a patchy beard offers her a plastic cup of red wine in exchange, his fingers brushing hers in a fleeting moment of contact that makes her withdraw her hand a fraction too quickly. If he notices her discomfort, he doesn't show it, already turning to the next person in the informal line.

WINE SECURED, Jetta navigates the perimeter of the room, her back nearly pressed to the wall as she searches for safe harbor. The air tastes like perfume and spilled beer, with underlying notes of something herbal that might be expensive candles or might be something else entirely. She finds her corner—a small alcove between a bookshelf sparsely populated with hardcovers that appear chosen for their spines rather than their content, and a tall plant with waxy leaves that offers a thin pretense of concealment.

. . .

FROM THIS VANTAGE POINT, she surveys the room with the practiced eye of someone who has perfected the art of being present without participating. Her fingers drum a restless rhythm against the plastic cup, the cheap material flexing slightly under her touch. The wine is exactly as mediocre as she expected—tannic and a touch too warm, but she sips it anyway, grateful for the occupation.

ACROSS THE ROOM, Brandi has already integrated herself into a circle of conversation, her hands gesturing expressively as she speaks. She has a gift for this—for slipping into social situations as easily as trying on a new sweater, comfortable and at home within moments. Even from a distance, Jetta can see how the others respond to her, leaning in to catch her words, laughing at all the right moments. Brandi's reading glasses still sit forgotten atop her head, and she occasionally squints slightly when trying to make out someone's face in the dim light, but the small imperfection only makes her more approachable, more human.

JETTA'S SHOULDERS tense as a couple backs up near her corner, their bodies pressing closer together as they share some private joke. She shifts, trying to make herself smaller, less intrusive on their moment. Her gaze darts around the room, seeking escape routes should her hiding place become compromised. Front door: blocked by a cluster of people engaged in animated debate. Hallway: leads deeper into the apartment, unknown territory. Balcony: currently occupied by smokers, their cigarettes glowing like fireflies in the darkness beyond the glass.

SHE TAKES another sip of wine, longer this time.

TWENTY MINUTES LATER, her cup is empty and her attempts at human connection have resulted in three aborted conversations. The first died when she couldn't hear the other person over a sudden surge in music volume. The second evaporated when her carefully crafted comment about the recent art exhibit downtown was met with vacant stares. The third— a promising exchange about true crime podcasts—ended abruptly when the woman's boyfriend appeared with fresh drinks and a territorial arm around her shoulders.

THE MUSIC SHIFTS to something with a heavier beat, vibrations travelling up through the soles of her boots and into her chest cavity, as if the sound wants to synchronise with her heartbeat. The crowd seems to pulse with it, bodies swaying, voices raising to compete with the increased volume. Someone jostles her elbow as they pass, wine sloshing dangerously close to the rim of her cup, and she presses herself further into her corner.

"I COULD BE HOME RIGHT NOW," she thinks, watching a man attempt a dance move that nearly ends with an elbow in his partner's eye. "Comfortable. Quiet. No strangers invading my personal space." But even as the thought forms, she spots Brandi across the room, now talking with a different group, her face animated with genuine enjoyment. "This is why I came," Jetta reminds herself. "For her." Because Brandi has spent two years respecting Jetta's boundaries, never pushing too hard about Ryan or the walls Jetta has carefully constructed, but always leaving the door ajar, just in case.

. . .

THE SWEET-SOUR SMELL of spilled drinks mingles with perfume and sweat as the temperature in the room rises. Someone turns up the air conditioning, sending a brief chill across Jetta's skin before the press of bodies neutralises it again. She examines her empty cup, considering whether a refill is worth navigating the increasingly crowded path to the kitchen.

HER PHONE VIBRATES in her pocket—probably her mother's nightly check-in text. For a fleeting moment, Jetta considers using it as an excuse, crafting some minor emergency that would necessitate her early departure. The lie forms in her mind: an issue at the shop, a leaky pipe in her apartment, a migraine coming on. Any of them would work, and Brandi wouldn't question her too closely.

HER FINGERS CLOSE around the phone, but she doesn't pull it out. Instead, she watches Brandi laugh at something someone has said, her whole face lighting up with it. The woman deserves this night, this fun, this chance with Crow Pose Owen if he shows. And she deserves a friend who can occasionally step outside her comfort zone without manufacturing excuses to flee.

WITH A SMALL SIGH that no one else can hear, Jetta pushes off from her wall, empty cup in hand, and begins the delicate navigation toward the kitchen. She'll get another drink. She'll stay another hour. She'll try one more conversation. For Brandi, she can endure this temporary discomfort, this press of strangers, this noise that fills every corner of the room like water rising in a sealed chamber.

. . .

As she edges past a group of people debating the merits of some television show, her practised smile firmly in place, she reminds herself: "Just because I'm not good at this doesn't mean I can't survive it."

Jetta cradles her second cup of mediocre wine, having found a new observation post near a potted fern with dusty leaves. From here, she can see Brandi holding court near the makeshift bar, her blonde hair catching the light each time she tosses her head back in laughter. Brandi's audience has grown, the gravity of her charm pulling more people into her orbit as the night progresses. Then the front door opens, admitting a blast of cool night air and a tall figure who steps into the apartment with the easy confidence of someone who expects rooms to welcome him.

Jetta recognises him immediately from Brandi's breathless descriptions: Owen Cooper, the yoga class Adonis. Even from across the room, she can see why Brandi has been fixated on him. He carries himself with a natural grace that makes his height an asset rather than an awkwardness. His dark hair is styled in that carefully careless way that suggests both effort and an unwillingness to admit to it. The sleeves of his button-down are rolled precisely to mid-forearm, revealing tanned skin and the hint of a vein running along his wrist as he reaches out to greet someone.

Unlike Jetta, Owen doesn't hug the walls or search for hiding places. He moves through the party with the fluid ease of a fish returning to familiar waters. His path seems random but somehow inevitable as he navigates toward the makeshift bar—toward Brandi—pausing occasionally to shake hands or clap shoulders, leaving people smiling in his wake.

BRANDI HASN'T NOTICED him yet. She's mid-story, her hands painting shapes in the air as she describes something to her captivated audience. Her reading glasses have slipped from their perch atop her head and now hang precariously from one ear, though she seems oblivious to their plight. Then she turns, reaching for her drink, and sees him. Jetta watches the moment unfold like a scene from one of the romance novels they keep near the window in the shop: Brandi's eyes widening slightly, her hand automatically rising to tuck a strand of hair behind her ear, her body angling toward him as if pulled by an invisible thread.

OWEN NOTICES her at the same moment, and his face transforms with a smile that crinkles the corners of his eyes. He says something to the person beside him—a quick word, a pat on the shoulder—and then he's crossing the remaining distance to where Brandi stands. He doesn't hurry, doesn't betray eagerness, but there's an intentionality to his movement that speaks volumes.

JETTA CAN'T HEAR their initial exchange over the music and the ambient roar of two dozen simultaneous conversations, but she sees Brandi laugh, genuinely laugh, her head tilting back to expose the line of her throat. Owen leans in, speaking near her ear, one hand gesturing expressively. His voice carries just enough for Jetta to catch fragments about "client" and "presentation" and "complete disaster."

· · ·

"—AND THEN THE PROJECTOR JUST DIED," his voice rises momentarily above the background noise, "right in the middle of the most important slide. Murphy's Law in action."

BRANDI TOUCHES HIS ARM, her fingers lingering a moment longer than strictly necessary. "What did you do?" she asks, her body angled toward him, creating a private space in the midst of the crowded room.

"WHAT ANY SELF-RESPECTING CONSULTANT WOULD DO," Owen replies, his distinctive laugh bubbling up, rich and genuine. "I faked a coughing fit to buy time while my colleague frantically tried to reboot the system."

JETTA SHIFTS HER ATTENTION AWAY, uncomfortable with how much she's witnessing and how little she's partici-pating. She spots a group nearby discussing what appears to be a book—she catches the words "unreliable narrator" and "plot twist"—and decides to make an attempt at social integration.

"I JUST FINISHED something with an incredibly unreliable narrator," she offers, stepping toward their circle. Her voice comes out a touch too loud, too eager.

THREE FACES TURN toward her with the blank politeness of people interrupted. A brief silence follows, during which Jetta can practically hear the gears turning as they try to place her in their social context.

. . .

"OH?" says a woman with statement earrings that swing when she tilts her head. "Which book?"

JETTA NAMES THE TITLE, a recent psychological thriller that's been flying off their shelves at the bookshop. She launches into what she considers a thoughtful analysis of the narrative structure, but halfway through she realises their eyes have glazed over. The woman with the earrings checks her phone. A man in a turtleneck nods with decreasing enthusiasm.

"ANYWAY," says the third person, turning back to the original group, "as I was saying about the film adaptation..."

JETTA STEPS BACK, her words evaporating into the air like steam. The conversation closes ranks, continuing without her contribution. She retreats to her fern, feeling her cheeks warm with a flush that has nothing to do with the temperature of the room.

ACROSS THE SPACE, Owen and Brandi have drifted closer together. He's talking animatedly, his hands painting pictures in the air as he describes something that has Brandi captivated. As he reaches the apparent climax of his story, he touches her elbow lightly—a casual contact that nonetheless seems charged with meaning. Brandi leans in, close enough that her shoulder nearly brushes his chest, tilting her head to hear him better over the music that's grown louder as the night progresses.

. . .

THEIR BODIES MIRROR each other unconsciously—when he shifts his weight, she adjusts her stance to maintain their bubble of intimacy. When she laughs, he inclines his head toward the sound as if drawn to it. They move in a subtle dance of attraction, telegraphing interest in a language written in angles and inches, in maintained eye contact and matched smiles.

JETTA ATTEMPTS one more social foray, approaching the drinks table where two people are debating the merits of different whiskeys. She waits for a natural pause, then offers an opinion on a local distillery she's visited. The words come out stilted, her timing just a beat off. One of them nods politely but turns away mid-sentence to greet a new arrival. The other responds with a monosyllable before resuming the original conversation as if she hadn't spoken.

WITH A SMALL SIGH, Jetta refills her wine. The plastic cup feels flimsy between her fingers, the liquid inside now room temperature and increasingly unappetizing. She scans the room, finding no safe harbour, no welcoming circle where she might dock her sinking social ship.

HER GAZE RETURNS to Brandi and Owen, drawn back despite herself. They've shifted positions, now standing near the window where the light catches Brandi's hair and turns it golden. Owen says something that makes her throw her head back in genuine mirth, her reading glasses finally losing their tenuous grip and falling completely. He catches them with quick reflexes before they hit the floor, placing them carefully back into her outstretched hand. Their fingers touch in the exchange, and even from a distance, Jetta can see the spark that passes between them—not just chemistry but something rarer: ease. Comfort. The simple joy of finding someone whose conversational rhythm matches your own.

A COMPLICATED TANGLE of emotions knots in Jetta's chest. Happiness for Brandi, who deserves this moment of connection. Wistfulness for her own solitary state. A sharp, unwelcome pang that might be envy or might be longing—not necessarily for Owen himself but for what he represents: the possibility of finding someone who makes difficult things seem effortless.

SHE DRAINS her wine in a single swallow, grimacing at the sour aftertaste. The party swirls around her, conversations rising and falling like waves breaking against a solitary rock. She stands alone in the midst of dozens, watching her best friend bloom under the attention of a man with a laugh that carries across crowded rooms. The bass line of the music reverberates through her chest like a second, irregular heartbeat—persistent, insistent, a rhythm she can't quite match.

AN HOUR INTO THE PARTY, Jetta acknowledges defeat. The third cup of wine sits untouched beside a potted plant, abandoned after two sips revealed it to be even more vinegary than the previous glasses. The music has edged from background presence to foreground assault, each beat driving into her temples like a small, persistent hammer. Three failed conversation attempts have left her voice unused in her throat, words backing up like cars at a closed intersection. It's time to go.

. . .

SHE CHECKS HER WATCH—A gesture that feels both old-fashioned and defiant in a room where everyone else tracks time by the level in their cups and the changing playlists. Ten-thirty. Not so early that her departure would seem rude, but early enough that she might still salvage an hour of reading before sleep claims her. Perfect.

THE PARTY HAS SWELLED in the last thirty minutes, the apartment now hosting at least twice the number of bodies it was designed to accommodate. The resulting crush forces people to stand closer than social convention typically allows, creating false intimacies born of architecture rather than choice. Jetta feels her personal space contracting with each newcomer, the invisible bubble she maintains around herself in public spaces now compressed to the width of her shoulders.

SHE EDGES away from her latest failed conversation attempt —a strained exchange with a woman who kept checking her phone mid-sentence—and begins plotting her route to the exit. The path requires navigating several conversational clusters, a makeshift dance floor where three couples sway with eyes closed, and the treacherous territory near the drinks table where spilled liquid makes the floor sticky beneath her boots.

HER JUSTIFICATIONS for leaving early line up in her mind like dutiful soldiers: early opening shift at the bookshop tomorrow, the beginnings of a headache forming behind her left eye, the stack of advance reader copies waiting on her nightstand. None of these are lies, precisely, but none are the whole truth either. The unvarnished fact is simpler: she doesn't belong here, in this press of strangers finding connection through proximity and alcohol, in this ritual of performed sociability that others seem to navigate by instinct while she fumbles with the map.

SHE SCANS the room for Brandi, knowing she should at least signal her departure rather than simply disappearing. The search takes longer than expected—the apartment now seems impossibly full, faces blending together in the shifting light. Finally, she spots her friend near the kitchen entrance, still deep in conversation with Owen. His hand rests casually on the wall beside Brandi's head, creating a small pocket of private space within the public chaos. Brandi gestures as she speaks, her reading glasses now properly worn, catching light when she turns her head.

JETTA HESITATES, reluctant to interrupt what appears to be a moment of genuine connection. She watches as Owen leans closer to hear something Brandi says, his smile revealing a flash of white teeth. Brandi touches his arm in response, her fingers lingering on his sleeve. They look right together, Jetta thinks, two people fluent in the same social language, their comfort with each other visible even across a crowded room.

SHE CATCHES Brandi's eye during a natural pause in their conversation. A silent communication passes between them— the shorthand of long friendship compressed into a few gestures. Jetta tilts her head slightly toward the door. Brandi's eyebrows rise in question: Already? Jetta offers a small smile and touches her temple: Headache. Brandi's expression shifts to concern, but Jetta waves it away with a subtle flick of her fingers: I'm fine, stay, enjoy.

. . .

BRANDI HESITATES, clearly torn between friend duty and the magnetic pull of Owen's attention. Jetta makes the decision easier, mouthing "I'll text you" before turning toward the exit. It's enough—permission granted, obligation fulfilled. She knows Brandi will check in later, probably with a string of excited texts about Owen punctuated with too many exclamation points.

THE JOURNEY to the door requires a series of "excuse me's" and sidesteps, apologies murmured as she navigates through clusters of conversation. The music swells as she passes the speakers, the bass so heavy she feels it in her chest cavity, vibrating against her ribs. Someone's elbow catches her side, a drink sloshes dangerously close to her sleeve, a burst of laughter erupts directly beside her ear. Each step toward the exit feels like wading through increasingly dense water.

FINALLY, she reaches the door, her hand closing around the cool metal of the knob with a sense of triumph disproportionate to the achievement. She pulls her phone from her pocket, quickly typing a message to Brandi: "Heading home. Slight headache, but nothing serious. Have fun with Crow Pose—he seems great! Details tomorrow. x"

HER THUMB HOVERS OVER "SEND" when she hears it—a male voice from the hallway beyond the door. The words themselves are indistinct, muffled by the barrier between them, but something in the timbre, in the particular cadence of speech, sends an electric current racing along her spine. Her finger freezes above the screen as goosebumps rise on her arms, flesh responding to a threat her conscious mind hasn't yet identified.

. . .

SHE KNOWS THAT VOICE. The certainty settles in her stomach like a cold stone, even as the identity remains frustratingly out of reach. Her heart rate accelerates, blood rushing in her ears, nearly drowning out the music still pounding behind her. Her pupils dilate, an instinctive preparation for fight or flight that dates back to ancestors who learned that certain sounds meant danger.

JETTA PRESSES her ear against the door, straining to hear more. The voice continues, now moving away down the hall, the words still indecipherable but the rhythm achingly familiar. It tugs at her memory like a half-forgotten dream—recognised but impossible to grasp fully.

SHE HITS "SEND" on her text and turns the knob, pulling the door open with more force than necessary. The hallway stretches before her, empty save for an abandoned red cup on the industrial carpet runner. The voice is gone, or has turned a corner, leaving only the faint echo of its presence in her racing pulse.

JETTA STEPS INTO THE HALLWAY, letting the door close behind her. The sudden reduction in noise is almost physical, like stepping from bright sun into shade. She can still feel the music through the soles of her boots, a distant vibration, but her ears ring in the relative quiet. She looks left, then right, searching for the owner of the voice that triggered such a visceral response.

. . .

NOTHING. Just an empty corridor in both directions.

SHE TAKES A DEEP BREATH, trying to calm the adrenaline still coursing through her system. "You're being ridiculous," she whispers to herself, the words sounding hollow in the deserted hallway. But her body disagrees, still humming with tension, still ready for a threat her mind can't identify.

HER PHONE VIBRATES in her hand—Brandi's response: "Feel better! He IS great! Will call tmrw with ALLLL details! .

CHAPTER 3

The Third Wheel

THE ESPRESSO MACHINE hisses like a warning, punctuating the Sunday morning chatter that fills Roasted, the café with its exposed brick walls and hanging plants that drip occasional moisture onto unsuspecting customers below. Jetta watches a droplet gather on the leaf of a pothos directly above Owen's left shoulder, wondering if it will fall before their food arrives. Brandi leans into him, her shoulder pressed against his as she points to something on the shared menu between them. Their heads tilt together, creating a perfect angle of intimacy that makes Jetta shift her chair an inch farther from the table, an unconscious adjustment that gives her lungs more room to expand.

"THE AVOCADO TOAST here is practically a religious experience," Brandi says, her reading glasses sliding down her nose as she studies the menu. Owen's finger touches the bridge of her glasses, pushing them back up with casual familiarity that speaks of a week filled with similar gestures. Seven days since the party, and already they move around each other with the ease of longtime dancers.

"I'm more interested in this chorizo benedict situation," Owen replies, his voice carrying that rich timbre Brandi had once described as "melted chocolate poured over gravel." Jetta can see the appeal now, watching how other patrons' eyes drift toward their table when he laughs.

Jetta tugs at the sleeve of her cardigan, pulling it over her wrist before wrapping both hands around her coffee mug. The ceramic burns slightly against her palms, but she welcomes the sensation—something concrete to focus on besides the way Brandi's fingers now rest casually on Owen's forearm.

"What about you, Jetta?" Owen asks, his attention shifting across the table. "Any recommendations from the breakfast expert?"

The question startles her. She's been so focused on observing them that she's forgotten her role as participant. "Oh, I usually go for the cardamom French toast." She offers a quick smile that doesn't quite reach her eyes. "Though fair warning—they're generous with the maple syrup."

"Jetta and syrup have a complicated relationship," Brandi explains, her expression warm with affection. "She wants it, craves it, but then complains it makes everything too sweet."

. . .

36

"THAT'S NOT—" Jetta begins, then stops when she sees Owen's amused expression. "Fine. I have syrup issues. We can't all be perfect."

THEIR SERVER APPROACHES—A tall woman with an intricate tattoo of botanical illustrations running down her arm. Jetta orders exactly what she always does, while Brandi and Owen engage in a playful negotiation that ends with them ordering both the avocado toast and the chorizo benedict "to share." The concept of sharing food with someone outside immediate family strikes Jetta as strangely intimate, a thought she pushes away as she focuses on straightening her silverware.

THE CAFÉ PULSES with Sunday energy—couples hunched over shared newspapers, groups of twenty-somethings dissecting the previous night's escapades, solo patrons absorbed in books or laptops. The sunlight angles through the tall windows, catching in the hanging plants and creating dappled shadows across their table. A barista calls out completed orders over the constant percussion of steaming milk and grinding beans.

"SO THERE I AM," Owen continues a story he'd started before their server interrupted, "standing in front of fourteen executives, when my presentation slides suddenly switch to what can only be described as karaoke backgrounds." His hands move expressively as he speaks, painting the scene in the air between them. "Complete with floating musical notes and a bouncing ball."

. . .

BRANDI DISSOLVES INTO LAUGHTER, her head tilting back to expose the line of her throat. "What did you do?"

"THE ONLY THING a professional can do in that situation," he says solemnly. "I started singing quarterly projections to the tune of 'Sweet Caroline.'"

EVEN JETTA FINDS herself laughing genuinely at this, the image too absurd to resist. Owen catches her eye and winks, a gesture that feels inclusive rather than flirtatious, and she appreciates the effort he's making to draw her into their orbit rather than treating her as an audience.

THE FOOD ARRIVES ON MISMATCHED vintage plates—Jetta's French toast dusted with powdered sugar and accompanied by a small pitcher of maple syrup (on the side, as requested), Brandi and Owen's selections arranged between them with an extra plate for sharing. The scents of cardamom, butter, and coffee mingle in the air, a combination that would normally make Jetta's mouth water. Today, though, the food sits before her like a still life she's meant to appreciate visually rather than consume.

"OH MY GOD," Brandi moans after her first bite of avocado toast. "I told you." She cuts another piece, lifting it to Owen's lips with easy intimacy. He accepts the offering, his eyes not leaving hers as he chews and nods approval. The exchange feels so private that Jetta looks away, focusing instead on cutting her French toast into precise triangles.

. . .

"HOW'S THE BOOKSHOP DOING?" Owen asks, directing the question to both women but looking at Jetta, again creating space for her in the conversation.

"WE JUST GOT in a collection of signed first editions that has Jetta practically levitating with excitement," Brandi answers before Jetta can speak. "Tell him about the Fitzgerald."

JETTA GLANCES up from her methodical dissection of breakfast. "It's a first edition of 'Tender Is the Night' with an inscription that suggests Fitzgerald knew the original owner personally." Despite herself, enthusiasm creeps into her voice. "The provenance documentation alone is fascinating—letters that trace ownership through this American expatriate circle in Paris."

"SHE'S BEEN SLEEPING at the shop to guard it," Brandi stage-whispers, leaning toward Owen.

"I HAVE NOT," Jetta protests, though she has been arriving earlier and leaving later since the collection arrived. "I just want to make sure the humidity controls are working properly."

OWEN'S EYES light with genuine interest. "That sounds incredible. I'd love to see it sometime." The sincerity in his voice surprises her. He seems to genuinely care about things that matter to Brandi—and by extension, to Jetta.

. . .

BRANDI REACHES across the table suddenly, her fingers wrapping around Jetta's wrist in a warm squeeze. "Thank you for coming today. I know Sunday mornings are usually your sacred reading time."

THE SIMPLE ACKNOWLEDGMENT of her sacrifice catches Jetta off guard. She hadn't expected Brandi to notice, to remember that Sunday mornings typically find Jetta curled in her reading chair with tea and whatever new release has captured her attention that week.

"IT'S FINE," she says, her voice softer than intended. "This is nice."

AND IT IS NICE, in its way, to see Brandi so luminous with happiness. Her friend practically glows in Owen's presence, her gestures more animated, her laughter quicker. Jetta watches them share bits of their respective breakfasts, exchanging private smiles that speak of inside jokes already established, of text messages sent late into the night, of possibilities unfurling before them like pages in a new book.

THE ESPRESSO MACHINE SCREAMS AGAIN, steam escaping in a violent hiss that momentarily drowns out nearby conversations. Jetta flinches at the sound, but Brandi and Owen don't seem to notice, absorbed as they are in each other. Jetta takes a bite of her French toast, the flavours muted on her tongue despite the quality of the ingredients. She swallows with effort, then washes it down with coffee that's grown tepid in her neglected cup.

. . .

AROUND THEM, the café continues its Sunday symphony—dishes clinking, conversations rising and falling, the bell above the door announcing new arrivals seeking caffeine and comfort. Jetta sits slightly apart, her chair angled just enough to place her adjacent to rather than fully present in the tableau of new love unfolding before her. She offers appropriate responses when addressed, laughs at the right moments, but her attention drifts to the window, to the people passing by outside, to the rhythm of the day moving forward without requiring her active participation.

WHEN OWEN RESTS his hand atop Brandi's on the table, their fingers interlacing with practised ease, Jetta feels a peculiar ache beneath her ribs—not jealousy exactly, but recognition of something she's chosen to live without. She pushes the sensation away, focusing instead on the practical joy of seeing her best friend so happy, so seen by someone who appears, against all odds, to be worthy of her.

STRING LIGHTS SWAY GENTLY OVERHEAD, casting honeyed patterns across the evening farmers' market. They remind Jetta of stars brought down to earth—too perfect, too arranged to be natural, but beautiful nonetheless. She trails several steps behind Brandi and Owen, maintaining a careful distance that allows her to appear part of their group while giving them space. The market buzzes with activity despite the late hour: vendors call out final discounts, couples meander with canvas bags heavy with produce, children dart between stalls with sticky fingers from sample tastes. Jetta adjusts her pace, slowing when the gap between her and the couple ahead grows too narrow, quickening when it threatens to become conspicuous.

. . .

WEEKS HAVE TRANSFORMED Brandi and Owen from new acquaintances into something that resembles a single entity. They move in unconscious synchronisation, their bodies oriented toward each other even when examining separate vendor stalls. When Owen points to a display of heirloom tomatoes, Brandi's body turns toward his gesture before her attention follows. When Brandi pauses to admire hand-painted ceramics, Owen's steps falter mid-stride, as if connected to her by an invisible tether.

JETTA WATCHES this dance from her self-imposed distance, one hand clutching the strap of her crossbody bag, the other occasionally reaching out to touch items at nearby stalls—an alibi for her lagging pace. She traces the rough surface of a wooden cutting board, then the slick glaze of a pottery bowl, pretending interest in objects she has no intention of purchasing.

"LOOK AT THESE," Brandi calls back to her, gesturing toward a display of artisanal cheeses. "They have that lavender goat cheese you loved at the wine tasting last year."

JETTA MOVES FORWARD, closing the gap between them momentarily. The cheese vendor offers tiny wooden spoons with samples, and she accepts one, feeling the tangy creaminess melt on her tongue. "It's good," she confirms, "but not quite as herbaceous as the one from the winery."

"FOOD CRITIC JETTA HAS SPOKEN," Owen teases, his smile including her in the joke rather than making her its target. "Should we dock points for insufficient herbaceousness?"

"ABSOLUTELY," Jetta replies, finding herself returning his smile despite the stiffness she feels in her shoulders. "At least two points. Maybe three if we're being strict."

BRANDI'S HAND slips into Owen's, their fingers interlacing with practised ease. Six weeks of dating has erased the hesitation in their touches, replacing it with a comfortable certainty. Jetta notices how Brandi's thumb absently strokes the side of Owen's hand, an unconscious gesture of affection that speaks of accumulated intimacy.

THEY MOVE on to the next stall, and Jetta allows the distance to re-establish itself, falling back a few paces. The market surrounds her with sensory input—fresh bread from the bakery stand fills the air with yeasty warmth, while nearby someone plays an acoustic guitar, the melody weaving through conversations and vendor calls. She breathes in deeply, trying to ground herself in the present rather than feeling like a perpetual observer.

"OH MY GOD, Owen, look at these!" Brandi's voice rises with excitement as she spots a flower vendor selling elaborate bouquets wrapped in brown paper and twine. "Aren't they gorgeous?" She tugs him toward the stall, their joined hands creating a bridge between them as they navigate through the crowd.

. . .

THE MOMENTARY REPRIEVE gives Jetta permission to step further aside. She finds a quiet spot beside a pickle vendor who's busy wrapping up his remaining jars for the evening. With the couple temporarily occupied, she pulls out her phone, the screen illuminating her face in the gathering dusk. Her thumb scrolls through work emails—distributor updates about delayed shipments, a request from their event coordinator about next month's author signing, a customer inquiry about a rare edition they've been seeking.

THE FAMILIAR PROBLEMS of the bookshop offer comfort, concrete issues with clear solutions. Order forms and inventory counts don't require her to navigate the complex emotional terrain of watching her best friend fall in love while she stands on the periphery. She taps out a quick response to the event coordinator, her attention fully absorbed in the task.

"EARTH TO JETTA." Owen's voice breaks through her concentration. She looks up to find him standing before her, Brandi still at the flower stall, deliberating between bouquets. "Work emergency or strategic escape?" he asks, his tone light but his eyes observant.

JETTA POCKETS HER PHONE, feeling strangely caught. "Just a quick question about an author event," she says, straightening her posture. "Nothing urgent."

"COME ON," he says, not challenging her excuse but not fully accepting it either. "There's a honey vendor over there who's giving out samples on these little wooden sticks shaped like honey dippers. It's adorably pretentious, and I think we need your expert commentary."

BEFORE SHE CAN MANUFACTURE a reason to decline, he gestures toward the stall in question, not touching her but clearly inviting her to walk alongside him rather than behind. The small kindness—acknowledging her isolation without making her feel pitied—catches her off guard.

"BRANDI SAID you have strong opinions about local honey," he continues as they walk, matching his pace to hers. "Something about wildflower versus clover?"

"SHE EXAGGERATES," Jetta replies, though she does indeed have thoughts on the subject. "I just think if you're paying artisanal prices, you should actually be able to taste the difference."

THE HONEY VENDOR, a bearded man in his fifties wearing a denim apron embroidered with bees, offers them wooden sampling sticks. "This one's our spring harvest," he explains, pointing to an amber-colored honey. "Notes of apple blossom and clover. The darker one's fall harvest—you'll get more molasses and goldenrod."

OWEN ACCEPTS BOTH SAMPLES, handing one to Jetta with exaggerated ceremony. "The sommelier recommends the spring harvest with your morning toast, madam," he says in a pompous accent that draws a genuine smile from her.

. . .

THEY TASTE the honey in unison, the sweetness blooming on Jetta's tongue with surprising complexity. "It actually does taste like apple blossoms," she admits, sounding impressed despite herself.

BRANDI JOINS THEM, a small bouquet of wildflowers and eucalyptus clutched in one hand. "Did I miss the honey tasting?" she asks, sliding naturally into the space beside Owen, her body fitting against his side as if designed to complement his angles.

"JUST GETTING STARTED," Owen replies, his arm lifting to make space for her beneath it. She tucks herself against him, her free hand coming to rest at his waist.

A COOL EVENING breeze sweeps through the market, setting the string lights swinging and bringing goosebumps to Jetta's arms. She crosses them over her chest, hands rubbing at her sleeves while Brandi nestles deeper into Owen's embrace, protected from the chill by his body heat.

"TRY THIS ONE," the vendor suggests, offering Jetta another sample. "It's infused with lavender—pairs well with those goat cheese crostini you might have picked up earlier."

AS JETTA TASTES this new offering, Owen leans in to read the description on the jar. "'Harvested beneath the waxing gibbous moon from hives nestled in pristine alpine meadows untouched by modern agricultural practices,'" he recites, his voice dropping into a theatrical baritone. "Do the bees also perform Gregorian chants while making this, or is that extra?"

A LAUGH ESCAPES Jetta before she can stop it—not her usual measured chuckle but a genuine sound of amusement that surprises even her. "Don't forget the part where the jars are blessed by artisanal glass-blowers during the vernal equinox," she adds, entering into the game.

"UNDER A FULL MOON," Brandi contributes, her eyes crinkling with mirth.

THEY MOVE from the honey stand to a display of handcrafted soaps, where Owen's deadpan readings of increasingly pretentious labels ("Infused with Himalayan crystal energies and the essence of contemplative silence") continue to draw reluctant laughter from Jetta. Her posture gradually softens, arms uncrossing, shoulders lowering from their defensive hunch.

FOR BRIEF MOMENTS, she forgets to maintain her careful distance, drawn into their orbit by the simple pleasure of shared humour. When they pause at a vendor selling hot apple cider, steam rising from paper cups in the cool evening air, Jetta finds herself standing beside them rather than a calculated step behind. The string lights overhead blur into soft streaks of gold when she looks up, and the market noises—the last calls of vendors, the murmur of departing shoppers, the faint music from a distant busker—blend into a pleasant hum that feels, just for a moment, like belonging.

· · ·

Shadows dance across white tablecloths as a server passes with a tray of desserts held above her head. The Italian restaurant—Bella Notte—occupies a converted brownstone where each room holds only a handful of tables, creating pockets of privacy despite the full house. Jetta sits with her back to the exposed brick wall, wine glass poised between her fingers as she watches Brandi lean toward Owen across the table. The amber lighting from wall sconces softens every edge, casting a golden haze that makes the moment feel suspended in honey—sweet, sticky, preserved. The flame from the small candle between them catches in Brandi's reading glasses, reflecting twin pinpoints of fire when she turns to include Jetta in her smile.

"Try this," Brandi says, twirling pasta onto her fork and extending it across the table toward Owen. The noodles glisten with olive oil and flecks of red pepper, steam rising in a fragrant spiral. He accepts the offering without hesitation, his eyes closing briefly as he savours the bite.

"Amazing," he pronounces, then spears a piece of his veal scallopini, returning the gesture. Brandi takes the bite directly from his fork, an intimate exchange that makes Jetta glance down at her own plate of mushroom risotto, perfectly intact, no portions missing or offered.

Two months into their relationship, Brandi and Owen have developed a language of small touches and shared glances that makes them seem like longtime lovers rather than new ones. When the server refills their water glasses, Owen automatically moves the candle to create space without Brandi having to ask. When Brandi mentions a book she enjoyed, Owen's expression shifts with recognition, revealing previous conversations Jetta wasn't part of. These accumulated intimacies surround them like a soft aura, visible to Jetta in the way their bodies orient toward each other even while including her in conversation.

THE RESTAURANT HUMS with muted energy. From the kitchen comes the rhythmic chopping of knives against cutting boards, the sizzle of garlic hitting hot oil, the occasional command called in Italian. Closer at hand, neighbouring tables offer fragments of conversations—anniversary celebrations, business discussions, friends catching up—that rise and fall like waves breaking against the general murmur of dining sounds. Silverware clinks against porcelain, wine glasses tap together in toasts, chairs scrape against hardwood when someone excuses themselves.

JETTA SWIRLS HER WINE GLASS, watching the deep red liquid catch the light. The Chianti coats the inside of the glass before sliding back down in slow, viscous tears. She's been nursing the same glass throughout the meal, maintaining the clarity she feels she needs in these three-person outings.

"THE WOMAN at table twelve is definitely about to break up with him," Brandi whispers, her eyes flicking toward a couple seated near the window. "She hasn't touched her food, and she keeps checking her watch."

"MAYBE SHE HAS A LATE APPOINTMENT," Owen suggests, his voice equally low.

. . .

"No one has a ten o'clock appointment on a Thursday unless they're a spy or an emergency room doctor, and she's wearing too much jewellery for either profession." Brandi adjusts her glasses for a better look. "Besides, she hasn't made eye contact with him once since they sat down."

"Brandi should have been a detective," Jetta says to Owen. "She creates entire backstories for every customer who walks into the bookshop."

"It's a gift," Brandi agrees without shame. "Last week I correctly guessed that the man buying all those sailing books was planning to live on a houseboat."

"He literally had boat keys hanging from his belt," Jetta points out, but she's smiling.

Owen laughs, the sound warm and genuine. His hand finds Brandi's on the table, fingers interlacing with the easy familiarity of a gesture repeated hundreds of times. "Speaking of detective work," he says, "did I mention my friend Ethan is finally coming home? After two years of mysterious international business, he's returning to grace us with his presence."

Jetta's fingers tighten almost imperceptibly around the stem of her wine glass. Something about the name sends a flutter of unease through her chest, though she can't immediately place why.

· · ·

"ETHAN COLE, RIGHT?" Brandi asks. "Your college roommate turned international man of mystery?"

"THE VERY SAME," Owen confirms, his eyes lighting with obvious affection. "He's been doing security consulting in Europe—mostly for corporate executives and occasionally for diplomatic missions, though he's vague about the details. Says if he told me everything, he'd have to kill me, which, knowing Ethan, is only half a joke."

JETTA TAKES A SIP OF WINE, using the glass to hide the slight furrow that has appeared between her brows. The name tugs at her memory, a loose thread that, if pulled, might unravel something she's carefully woven shut.

"WHAT KIND OF SECURITY CONSULTING?" she asks, keeping her tone casually interested.

"PERSONAL PROTECTION, threat assessment, that sort of thing," Owen explains. "He was military for a while after college, then moved into private sector work. He's got this intensity about him that apparently makes wealthy people feel very secure." He grins. "Though to me, he's still the guy who once tried to make ramen in our dorm room coffee maker."

THE RICH AROMA of garlic and tomato sauce wafts from a nearby table as a server delivers a steaming platter of pasta. Jetta inhales deeply, using the sensory input to ground herself as her mind continues to pick at the name Ethan Cole, turning it over like a stone that might have something hidden beneath it.

"ANYWAY," Owen continues, "I'm throwing him a welcome home party next Saturday. Nothing fancy—just drinks and food at my place. You both should come." His gaze includes them equally, though it lingers on Brandi with obvious warmth.

"OF COURSE!" Brandi responds instantly, squeezing his hand. "I've heard so many stories about him, I feel like I know him already."

OWEN TURNS TO JETTA, eyebrows raised in question. "Jetta? It'll be fun, I promise. Much more relaxed than that party at Micah's where we first met. Just friends, good wine, maybe some embarrassing stories about Ethan that he'd prefer remained buried."

JETTA'S WINE glass hovers halfway to her lips as calculations run behind her eyes. Another social gathering. Another evening as the third wheel. Another night watching Brandi and Owen orbit each other while she stands on the periphery. The weight of these thoughts sits heavy in her chest, pressing against her ribs.

BUT BENEATH THIS familiar reluctance runs a current of something else—curiosity, perhaps, or an inexplicable pull toward a name that seems to resonate at a frequency just beyond her conscious recognition. Ethan Cole. The syllables echo in her mind, striking faint chimes of memory that she can't quite place.

BRANDI GIVES her an encouraging look across the table, her expression open and hopeful. The silent plea is clear: Come with me. Be part of this. Don't retreat again.

SILVERWARE CLINKS against plates around them. The candle between them gutters briefly as someone passes, casting shifting shadows across their faces. In this momentary darkness, Jetta makes her decision.

"SURE, WHY NOT?" The words emerge with a casualness she doesn't entirely feel. She takes another sip of wine, using the motion to cover the slight tremor in her hand. "I could use a night out."

"PERFECT!" Owen's smile is genuine, inclusive. "Ethan's a bit intense at first meeting, but I think you'll like him once you get past the resting intimidation face."

"RESTING INTIMIDATION FACE?" Brandi repeats with a laugh.

"IT'S A REAL CONDITION," Owen insists. "He doesn't mean to look like he's assessing whether you're a security threat—his face just does that automatically."

· · ·

JETTA FORCES A SMILE, though something cold has settled at the base of her spine—a physical reaction to a mental uncertainty she can't quite name. The restaurant continues its symphony around them: the soft clink of silverware against plates, the murmur of conversations rising and falling like a tide, the occasional burst of laughter from a nearby table. Shadows from the candle flicker across their faces, playing across features that reveal everything and nothing at once.

SHE RAISES her glass when Owen proposes a toast to friendship and new beginnings, the crystal catching amber light as it meets the others with a musical chime. The wine tastes richer now, notes of cherry and oak more pronounced on her tongue as she swallows, washing down the strange apprehension that has taken root in her chest. One more social obligation, she tells herself. One more evening of practised smiles and careful distance.

YET AS THEIR conversation turns to other topics, Jetta finds her thoughts returning to that name—Ethan Cole—and the odd certainty that agreeing to this party has set something in motion that she won't be able to stop.

CHAPTER 4

Ghosts of High School Past

STRING lights twist overhead like luminous snakes, casting a deceptively warm glow across Owen's apartment. Jetta steps through the doorway behind Brandi, her fingers tightening around the neck of the wine bottle she's brought—a peace offering to herself for agreeing to attend yet another social gathering where she'll stand on the periphery, watching others connect with an ease she's never mastered. The space pulses with conversations already in full swing, laughter rising and falling like unpredictable waves threatening to pull her under.

"You made it!" Owen materialises from the crowd, arms spread wide in welcome. His fitted button-down catches the amber light, the sleeves rolled precisely to mid-forearm—a casual elegance that seems effortless on him.

Brandi steps into his embrace with practised familiarity, her body fitting against his as if designed for the space. "We wouldn't miss it," she says, her voice bright with the anticipation that's been building since Owen first mentioned this party.

JETTA OFFERS a smile that feels thin across her face, a mask already slipping. The apartment surrounds her with unfamiliar stimuli—the mingled scents of appetisers warming in the oven and cologne that's been applied with too heavy a hand, the press of bodies that seem to shrink the already modest space, the constant percussion of ice against glass as drinks are refreshed and refilled.

A "WELCOME HOME" banner stretches across one wall, its block letters slightly askew as if hung in haste or excitement. Beneath it, a table holds an arrangement of photographs— Owen and another man in various settings, their poses growing more mature as the timeline progresses from what must be college to recent years. Jetta doesn't look closely at the other man's face. Something keeps her gaze skittering away from those images, a subconscious avoidance she doesn't examine.

"LET ME TAKE THAT," Owen says, reaching for the wine bottle Jetta clutches like a talisman. His smile is genuine, inclusive, making her momentarily regret her reluctance. "Come in, come in. Let me introduce you to everyone."

BRANDI LOOPS her arm through Jetta's, tugging her forward as Owen leads them deeper into the apartment. Jetta scans the room with the practised eye of someone mapping escape routes. The front door they've just entered. A hallway leading presumably to a bedroom and bath. French doors opening onto a small balcony where a few guests stand in the evening air, their cigarettes glowing like distant warning signals.

"ISN'T THIS WONDERFUL?" Brandi whispers, her breath warm against Jetta's ear. "Look how excited Owen is—he's been planning this for weeks."

JETTA NODS, not trusting her voice. Her palms have grown damp, a thin film of sweat making her skin feel like it doesn't quite belong to her. She wipes them surreptitiously against her jeans as Owen hands them each a glass of something amber that catches the light when she tilts it.

"THESE ARE MY WORK FRIENDS—ALICIA from marketing, Dev from IT," Owen is saying, gesturing to a small group who offer polite smiles and half-waves. Jetta returns their greetings mechanically, her attention fragmented. The conversations wash over her in broken phrases, punctuated by laughter that seems to come a beat too late or too loud. Her responses emerge from some automated part of her brain that knows how to perform sociability without engaging it.

"GRAPHIC DESIGN? HOW INTERESTING..."

"YES, I CO-OWN A BOOKSHOP DOWNTOWN..."

"NO, mostly new titles, though we have a rare books section..."

. . .

HER HEARTBEAT ACCELERATES with no clear trigger, a rabbit sensing danger before identifying its source. The ice in her glass shifts, clinking against the sides as her hand trembles slightly. She takes a sip to steady herself, the whiskey burning a path down her throat, settling like a small fire in her stomach.

"OH! THERE'S OWEN!" Brandi exclaims, seemingly forgetting they've already greeted their host. She points across the room where Owen has moved to answer the door. "Let's go say hi properly—he's been so busy playing host we barely got to talk."

BEFORE JETTA CAN RESPOND, Brandi pulls her through the crowd, navigating with the confident ease of someone who expects spaces to accommodate her passage. Jetta follows in her wake, murmuring apologies as they brush past conversations in progress.

THEY'RE HALFWAY across the room when the door opens again, and a deep laugh cuts through the ambient noise of the party. The sound strikes Jetta like a physical blow, stopping her mid-step. Her body recognises it before her conscious mind makes the connection—a visceral response that sends blood rushing to her extremities in a primal preparation for fight or flight.

SHE KNOWS THAT LAUGH. Knows it from hallways that stretched endlessly before her, from whispers that followed her between classes, from a particular afternoon that divides her life into before and after.

. . .

ETHAN COLE STEPS into the apartment, and the space seems to contract around his presence. He's tall—taller than she remembers—with the build of someone who views physical fitness as a non-negotiable aspect of existence. His dark hair is cut close at the sides, longer on top, the style of a man who pays for quality but isn't vain enough to fuss. He moves with the confident grace of someone accustomed to being watched, to having his presence noted and accommodated.

OWEN EMBRACES him with genuine affection, clapping him on the back before turning to present him to the gathered guests. "The man of the hour has arrived!"

A CHEER GOES UP, glasses raised in welcome. Ethan acknowledges the greeting with a nod that manages to be both modest and commanding. His smile transforms his face, softening the hard angles of his jaw, crinkling the corners of eyes that Jetta now remembers as an impossible blue—the kind of colour that seems enhanced, though she knows it isn't.

BRANDI TUGS AT HER ARM, oblivious to the way Jetta has frozen in place. "Come on, let's go meet him. Owen says he's fascinating—all that international security work sounds like something from a movie."

"I—" Jetta begins, but her voice falters as Ethan's gaze sweeps the room and locks onto her face.

TIME PERFORMS A CRUEL TRICK, stretching and compressing simultaneously. The party continues around them—glasses clinking, laughter bubbling, conversations flowing—but between them, a private moment expands into its own universe. Recognition dawns in his eyes, confusion followed by clarity, his expression shifting through micro-adjustments that she can read with unwanted precision.

MEMORY FLOODS her consciousness like ice water. The girls' locker room after gym class. The shower running. Her clothes disappearing. The desperate search, wrapped in a towel that felt too small, too precarious. Then the towel being tugged away, leaving her exposed, vulnerable. The laughter—his laughter, leading the chorus—as she tried to cover herself with hands that weren't enough, would never be enough to shield her from their stares, their pointing fingers, their phones raised to capture her humiliation.

HER LUNGS CONSTRICT, refusing to draw breath. The room tilts slightly, the string lights overhead blurring into streaks of gold against the ceiling. She forces air into her body in a shallow gasp that tastes of whiskey and panic.

ETHAN'S EXPRESSION SHIFTS AGAIN, settling into something unreadable—not quite recognition, not quite remorse, not quite anything she can name. His jaw tightens, a muscle flexing beneath the skin in a tell she remembers from before, when he was younger and less skilled at masking his reactions.

HER FINGERS CURL into fists at her sides, nails pressing half-moons into her palms—a physical pain to anchor her in the present when the past threatens to drag her under. She holds his gaze with defiance that costs her, each second a deliberate choice not to look away, not to concede, not to be sixteen again and stripped of more than clothing.

"JETTA?" Brandi's voice comes from somewhere distant, concern evident in the question. "Are you okay? You look like you've seen a ghost."

A GHOST. Yes. That's exactly what Ethan Cole is—a spectre from a past she'd thought safely buried, now risen and standing in Owen's apartment beneath string lights that suddenly seem less warm and more exposing, illuminating what should have remained in darkness.

"I'M FINE," she manages, the lie bitter on her tongue. "Just fine."

JETTA MUMBLES AN EXCUSE to Brandi about needing the bathroom, though the words barely register in her own ears. Her body moves on autopilot, navigating away from the centre of the party, away from Ethan's presence that seems to fill the room like smoke, seeping into every corner, inescapable. She finds refuge near a bookshelf lined with hard-covers that appear chosen for their matching spines rather than their content—decoration rather than literature. The observation would normally prompt internal commentary, but now her mind can only process one reality: Ethan Cole is here, and the past she's carefully walled off has come crashing through her defences.

. . .

SHE GRIPS her drink with white-knuckled intensity, the whiskey sloshing dangerously close to the rim. Her pulse thrums in her wrists, her throat, her temples—a percussion of panic keeping time with the music playing softly in the background. The string lights overhead cast strange patterns across the hardwood floor, shadows that shift and stretch like living things.

BREATHE, she commands herself. Just breathe.

BUT AIR COMES in shallow sips, barely reaching her lungs before escaping again. The party continues its orbit around her still point—laughter, conversation, the clink of glasses creating a soundscape that feels increasingly distant, as if she's underwater and everyone else remains on the surface.

SHE SENSES him before she sees him—a shift in the air currents, a presence that registers on some primal level of awareness. His cologne reaches her first, something with notes of cedar and bergamot, expensive but not ostentatious. The scent triggers another memory: her clothes in the school swimming pool, floating like pale ghosts beneath the surface while his cologne lingered in the air, a signature left at the scene of the crime.

ETHAN MATERIALISES at the edge of her sanctuary, maintaining a distance that acknowledges the force field of her hostility. He holds a tumbler of what looks like straight bourbon, the amber liquid catching light when he rotates the glass between his fingers. Neither speaks. The silence between them expands, charged with a decade of unaddressed history.

. . .

HIS EYES ARE EXACTLY as she remembers—that impossible blue, clear and penetrating. Age has only refined his features, chiselling away the softness of youth to reveal the architectural precision beneath. The boy who tormented her has grown into a man whose presence commands attention without demanding it—a quality she might admire in anyone else.

"JETTA KINSLEY," he finally says, her name emerging from his lips as if he's testing its weight. His voice is low, controlled, a deliberate modulation that reveals his awareness of their precarious situation. "Didn't expect to see you here."

SHE TAKES a slow sip of whiskey, using the glass as a barrier between them, buying seconds to compose herself. "Believe me," she replies, the words coated in frost, "if I'd known you were Owen's best friend, I wouldn't be."

SOMETHING FLICKERS ACROSS HIS EXPRESSION—TOO quick to read, gone before she can name it. "Small world," he offers, a peace offering so inadequate she almost laughs.

"MICROSCOPIC," she agrees, no warmth in the word.

ETHAN SHIFTS HIS WEIGHT, his body angling toward her despite the distance he maintains. "You look good," he says, then immediately grimaces as if regretting the words. "I mean —it's been a long time."

. . .

"NOT LONG ENOUGH." The whiskey burns pleasantly as she takes another sip, liquid courage flowing into her veins. "Though I'm touched you recognise me with my clothes on."

THE BARB FINDS ITS MARK. Ethan's jaw tightens, that same muscle flexing beneath the skin. "I see you haven't forgotten."

"FORGOTTEN?" The word escapes as a bitter laugh. "Should I have? Was it that forgettable for you?"

HIS EYES NARROW SLIGHTLY. "I remember plenty," he counters, voice dropping lower. "Like how you keyed my car afterwards. 'Asshole' scratched into the driver's door. Cost two thousand to repair."

"WORTH EVERY PENNY," she replies without hesitation, a vicious satisfaction curling through her at the memory—her keys dragging across the pristine paint of his precious Mustang, metal biting into metal, leaving a scar he couldn't simply wash away.'

"IT WAS a joke that went too far," he says, the words practised, as if he's rehearsed this justification many times. "We were kids. I didn't think—"

"NO, YOU DIDN'T THINK," she interrupts, her voice low but intense. "You didn't think about how I had to walk through those hallways afterward, with everyone who'd seen the photos whispering, laughing. You didn't think about how the principal called it a 'regrettable prank' and gave you detention while telling me to be more careful with my belongings. You didn't think about how I had to change schools because the rumours and pictures followed me everywhere."

THE MUSIC CHANGES to something with a heavier bass line, the vibrations travelling through the floorboards beneath their feet. Around them, the party continues unaware of their private battlefield.

"I DIDN'T POST THOSE PICTURES," Ethan says after a moment, his voice tight. "That was Harris. I told him to delete them."

"HOW NOBLE," she replies, sarcasm dripping from each syllable. "Your one moment of decency came after you'd already orchestrated the whole thing."

"I WAS AN ASSHOLE," he admits, the concession surprising her. "I was showing off, trying to impress my friends, and you were just... collateral damage." He takes a drink, his throat working as he swallows. "I was seventeen and stupid and cruel in the way only teenagers who've never faced consequences can be."

"AND THAT MAKES IT OKAY?" she demands, though her voice has lost some of its edge.

. . .

"No," he says simply. "It doesn't."

THEY FALL SILENT AGAIN, the acknowledgment hanging between them like smoke—visible but impossible to grasp. Jetta studies him over the rim of her glass, noting the way his shoulders remain tense beneath his well-cut shirt, the controlled way he holds himself, as if accustomed to monitoring his own physical presence in relation to others.

DESPITE HERSELF, she registers other details: the faint scar above his right eyebrow, the slight asymmetry of his features that saves him from conventional handsomeness and pushes him into something more interesting, the way his fingers wrap around his glass with precise pressure—not too tight, not too loose.

"I HEARD you went into the military," she says, the words emerging before she can examine her motivation for continuing this conversation.

"AFTER COLLEGE," he confirms. "Four years active duty, then private sector." His gaze lifts from his drink to meet hers directly. "You own a bookshop."

IT'S NOT A QUESTION, which means he's asked about her— Owen or Brandi providing information she hasn't authorised for his consumption. The thought irritates her anew.

"WITH BRANDI," she says, offering nothing more.

. . .

"It suits you." The comment seems genuine, which somehow makes it worse. "You always had your nose in a book. Even in gym class, if you could get away with it."

The fact that he remembers this detail about her—that he noticed her at all before deciding to target her—sends an unwelcome warmth spreading across her skin. She blames the whiskey, the proximity, the strange intimacy of shared history, however painful.

"Don't," she says, the single word carrying multiple warnings.

"Don't what?"

"Don't pretend you knew me. Don't act like we were anything to each other except perpetrator and victim."

His expression hardens, a fortress rising. "Is that how you've cast it in your mind all these years? Me the villain, you the innocent?"

"Are you suggesting another interpretation?" she challenges, her body unconsciously shifting closer to his, drawn by the magnetic pull of confrontation.

. . .

THEY STAND BARELY a foot apart now, their bodies angled toward each other despite their mutual antipathy. Something electric charges the narrow space between them—anger, resentment, and beneath it all, an awareness neither wants to acknowledge. His gaze drops briefly to her lips, so quickly she might have imagined it, before returning to her eyes.

"I'M SUGGESTING," he says carefully, "that people are rarely just one thing. Villains. Victims. We're usually both, in different measures, at different times."

"HOW CONVENIENT FOR the villain to philosophise about moral complexity," she retorts, though something in his words catches in her mind like a burr, refusing easy dismissal.

THE CORNER they occupy feels increasingly removed from the party, a pocket dimension where only they exist, trapped in the gravity of shared history. His cologne mingles with the scent of her perfume, creating something new in the air between them. The string lights cast shadows across his face, highlighting angles, obscuring others, making him both familiar and strange.

"WE'RE NOT those people anymore, Jetta," he says, her name soft on his lips despite the tension between them.

"AREN'T WE?" she asks, genuinely curious despite herself. "Or are we just better at hiding who we really are?"

. . .

HE DOESN'T ANSWER IMMEDIATELY, considering her question with unexpected seriousness. When he finally speaks, his voice carries a weight that suggests the words cost him something. "I've spent years trying to be better than who I was. I don't always succeed."

THE ADMISSION, in its unvarnished simplicity, disarms her momentarily. She searches his face for signs of manipulation, finding instead a complexity she's reluctant to acknowledge—the possibility that the boy who humiliated her has grown into a man capable of reflection, perhaps even remorse.

"ONE APOLOGY DOESN'T ERASE the past," she says, but the ice in her voice has begun to thaw, revealing uncertainty beneath.

"I WASN'T OFFERING ONE," he replies, a challenge in his eyes. "Not yet."

THE IMPLIED 'YET' hangs between them, a promise or a threat, she isn't sure which. What she is certain of is the strange, unwelcome awareness of him as a man rather than merely a symbol of past pain—his height, his scent, the controlled power in his frame, the intensity of his gaze when it meets hers.

SHE HATES that awareness almost as much as she hates him. Almost.

. . .

"THERE YOU ARE!" Owen's voice breaks through their private standoff like sunlight piercing storm clouds—unwelcome in its brightness, impossible to ignore. He approaches with two fresh drinks in hand, his smile betraying no awareness of the charged atmosphere he's walking into. "I see you two found each other. Been catching up on old times?" The innocent question lands between them with the impact of a grenade, its pin already pulled.

JETTA'S FINGERS tighten around her glass, the pressure threatening to crack the tumbler. She forces her features into something approximating a smile, though the expression feels foreign on her face, like a mask that doesn't quite fit.

"JUST GETTING REACQUAINTED," Ethan says, the smoothness of his response revealing years of practice in diplomatic evasion. His posture shifts subtly, opening their closed circle to include Owen—a tactical retreat from the intensity of their confrontation.

OWEN CLAPS a hand on Ethan's shoulder, the gesture speaking of years of comfortable friendship. "Ethan just got back from Munich," he tells Jetta. "Some hush-hush security thing for a tech billionaire. He's basically James Bond without the government pension."

"HARDLY," Ethan demurs, though Jetta catches the flash of pride that crosses his face before he suppresses it. "Risk assessment and personal security protocols. Less glamorous than it sounds."

. . .

"HE'S BEING MODEST," Owen continues, unaware of how each word about Ethan feels like sandpaper against Jetta's raw nerves. "Last year he extracted some CEO's daughter from a kidnapping situation in Eastern Europe. Wouldn't tell me details, but I saw the bruises when he got back."

JETTA'S GAZE flicks to Ethan's hands, noting for the first time the faint scars across his knuckles, the slight callus at the base of his right thumb. Hands that have inflicted damage, received it in return. She wonders suddenly how many times he's bled for his choices, then immediately resents the thought for its implied sympathy.

"FASCINATING," she manages, the word emerging more clipped than she intends.

ETHAN MEETS HER EYES, something passing between them —an acknowledgment of their shared performance, this pretence of normality for Owen's benefit. His jaw relaxes slightly, gratitude or relief softening the hard line of his mouth.

"JETTA CO-OWNS A WONDERFUL BOOKSHOP DOWNTOWN," Owen tells Ethan, continuing his unwitting role as social bridge. "You should check it out while you're home. They have an amazing rare books collection."

THE SUGGESTION of Ethan entering her space—her sanctuary—sends a jolt of alarm through Jetta's body. "We're actually quite busy this season," she says quickly. "Limited browsing hours for non-members."

Owen's brow furrows in confusion. "I didn't realise you had a membership program."

"New policy," she lies, the words bitter on her tongue. She rarely lies, especially not to those she cares about, but the thought of Ethan among her shelves, touching her books, breathing the air of the one place that feels entirely hers is intolerable.

Before Owen can question her further, Brandi appears at his side, her cheeks flushed from dancing or wine or both. Her eyes move between Jetta and Ethan, narrowing slightly as she registers the strange tension vibrating in the air.

"Everything okay over here?" she asks, the question casual, but her gaze sharp as it settles on Jetta's face.

"Just fine," Jetta answers too quickly. "Owen was telling us about Ethan's international adventures."

Brandi's intuition—always inconveniently accurate —picks up on the undercurrent Jetta is trying to conceal. She moves to Jetta's side, linking their arms in a gesture that manages to be both affectionate and protective. "Well, don't let Owen monopolise the conversation. He'd have you believe

Ethan single-handedly maintains world peace between security contracts."

Owen laughs, wrapping an arm around Brandi's waist and pulling her against his side. "I'm just proud of my friend. Is that a crime?"

"Only when you embellish to the point of fiction," Ethan says with a small smile that transforms his face, softening the hard angles and revealing a glimpse of the charming boy he must have been before cruelty calcified in him—or the man he's become since, Jetta can't be sure which.

The four of them stand in an awkward quartet, two couples that aren't—one bound by romance, the other by a history none would envy. Jetta feels the weight of Brandi's concern like a physical touch, knows her friend is picking up on signals she can't decipher. If she asks later, as she surely will, what will Jetta tell her? The truth would fracture this fragile social ecosystem, forcing Owen to choose between his best friend and his girlfriend's best friend.

Ethan seems to reach the same conclusion simultaneously. He clears his throat, drawing their attention. His expression shifts into something carefully neutral as he extends his hand toward Jetta in a calculated gesture.

"For Brandi and Owen's sake," he says, his voice pitched for their ears alone, "truce?"

· · ·

His blue eyes hold a challenge—or perhaps a plea—as they meet hers. The moment stretches between them, elastic with possibility. Brandi's arm tightens around hers, a silent question mark.

Jetta studies Ethan's outstretched hand—strong, capable, marked with the evidence of a life lived beyond the borders of their shared past. The boy who humiliated her has grown into a man offering not quite an apology, not quite forgiveness, but something adjacent to both: pragmatic coexistence.

For Brandi, she thinks. For the woman who's stood beside her through breakups and breakthroughs, who never questions Jetta's social limitations but celebrates her small victories. For the friend who deserves happiness with Owen without the complication of ancient grudges.

"Fine," she says, reaching out to take his hand. "Civil facades it is."

His palm meets hers, warm and dry and slightly rough with calluses. The contact sends an unwelcome current up her arm, a physical awareness she immediately resents. His fingers close around hers with precise pressure—not too firm, a restraint that acknowledges the fragility of their agreement.

The handshake lingers a moment too long, neither willing to be the first to break contact. When they finally separate, Jetta feels the ghost of his touch lingering on her skin like a memory that refuses to fade.

"GREAT!" Owen says, oblivious to the subtext crackling between them. "Now that's settled, you have to try these stuffed mushrooms. I've been hiding them from the other guests." He gestures toward the kitchen, already turning to lead the way.

BRANDI HESITATES, her gaze moving between Jetta and Ethan. "You coming?" she asks Jetta, the question carrying layers of meaning.

"IN A MINUTE," Jetta promises. "Save me one of those mushrooms."

BRANDI SQUEEZES her arm once more before following Owen, leaving Jetta and Ethan in their temporary ceasefire. The silence between them feels different now—still charged, but with a new frequency.

"I MEANT WHAT I SAID," Ethan offers after a moment. "A truce. I can be civil if you can."

"I'M ALWAYS CIVIL," Jetta replies, though the edge in her voice belies the claim. "It's one of the many differences between us."

. . .

His mouth quirks in what might almost be amusement. "I suppose I deserved that."

"You deserve a lot more than that," she says, but the words lack their earlier venom. "But for tonight—for them —I can pretend we're just two people with no history."

"Quite the acting challenge," he observes. "Should we practice our small talk? The weather's been unseasonably warm. The stock market continues to baffle economists. How about those local sports teams?"

Despite herself, Jetta feels the corner of her mouth lift in reluctant appreciation of his dry delivery. She suppresses the reaction immediately, unwilling to give him the satisfaction. "I think we can manage to avoid each other at a party this size," she says. "Just stay on your side of the room, I'll stay on mine."

"Diplomatic relations established through strategic avoidance," he says with a nod. "I've negoti- ated worse treaties."

They part without further words, each retreating to opposite sides of the apartment. Jetta rejoins Brandi and Owen in the kitchen, accepting a mushroom cap filled with something rich and savoury that she barely tastes. She laughs at appropriate moments, contributes to conversations when expected, maintains the illusion of presence while her aware- ness remains fixed on Ethan's location like a compass finding north.

. . .

He does the same, she notices. Though he engages with other guests, his body remains oriented toward her position, his gaze periodically sweeping the room until it finds her, then sliding away before the contact can be acknowledged. They orbit each other with careful precision, maintaining maximum distance while remaining acutely aware of the other's gravitational pull.

An hour passes in this strange dance. The party ebbs and flows around them, conversations forming and dissolving, music shifting from one playlist to another. Jetta finishes one drink, then another, the alcohol creating a pleasant buffer between her raw emotions and the social performance she maintains.

She's listening to Brandi describe a difficult customer from earlier that week when she feels it—the weight of a stare more intense than the casual glances they've exchanged throughout the evening. She turns to find Ethan watching her from across the room, his expression unreadable in the amber glow of the string lights. Their eyes lock for a prolonged moment, neither willing to look away first.

Then, with deliberate slowness, he raises his glass slightly in her direction—not a toast exactly, more an acknowledgment. Of their truce, their history, the strange tension that still vibrates between them. Something in the gesture feels like a punctuation mark—not a period ending their story, but a semicolon, suggesting that what follows is intimately connected to what came before.

. . .

JETTA DOESN'T RETURN the gesture. But she doesn't look away either, holding his gaze across the crowded room, across years of pain and resentment, across the uncertain territory that stretches before them. The string lights overhead cast everyone in a warm glow that softens edges and obscures flaws, but even in this flattering illumination, she sees Ethan clearly —not just the boy he was or the man he appears to be, but something more complex than either.

AND THOUGH SHE would never admit it, not even to herself, what frightens her most isn't that she still hates him.

IT'S that she might not hate him enough.

CHAPTER 5

Uneasy Alliances

LATE AFTERNOON SUNLIGHT slants through the bookshop windows, painting golden rectangles across the hardwood floor. Jetta lifts a stack of historical fiction novels from their cardboard shipping box, her hands trembling slightly as she arranges them on the display table. Three times she adjusts the same book, her movements jerky and distracted, her mind clearly elsewhere as the shop's closing time approaches. She knocks a paperback sideways with her elbow, then stares at it for a long moment before pushing it back into place with fingers that don't seem entirely under her control.

"THAT'S the fourth time you've rearranged those," Brandi says from behind the counter, her voice gentle but observant. She slides her reading glasses up onto her head, where they nestle in her blonde hair like they've found their natural habitat. "And you've been staring at the same invoice for twenty minutes without marking it."

. . .

JETTA FORCES a smile that doesn't reach her eyes. "Just tired. Tuesday rush wore me out."

"IT'S THURSDAY," Brandi points out, moving around the counter. Her steps are deliberate as she approaches, like someone approaching a skittish animal. "And we had exactly seven customers today, two of whom only bought bookmarks."

THE LAST CUSTOMER left fifteen minutes ago, the bell above the door signalling their departure with a cheerful jingle that had made Jetta flinch. Now the shop feels too quiet, too still, the silence pressing against her skin like something tangible.

"I THINK that's enough inventory for today," Brandi decides, gently removing a novel from Jetta's hands. She doesn't comment on how Jetta's knuckles have whitened around the spine, or how the cover now bears the damp imprint of anxious fingers. "Come on. Coffee time."

JETTA ALLOWS herself to be guided toward the back corner of the shop, where their reading nook creates a small sanctuary away from the front windows. Two armchairs face each other across a low table, beneath the stained-glass pendant lamp that casts pools of amber and blue across the floor. Brandi gestures toward the chair with the slight depression in the cushion— Jetta's favourite—while she busies herself with the small coffee maker they keep on a side table.

· · ·

"You don't have to—" Jetta begins, but Brandi waves away her protest.

"Sit. Before you knock over an entire display with whatever nervous energy is coursing through you right now."

The familiar routine of their closing ritual continues around them. The coffee maker gurgles and hisses. Outside, streetlights flicker on as dusk deepens. A siren wails in the distance, then fades. Jetta sits rigidly in her chair, spine not touching the backrest, as if prepared to flee at any moment.

Brandi places a steaming mug into Jetta's hands. The ceramic burns slightly against her palms, but she welcomes the sensation—something concrete to focus on besides the thoughts spinning like trapped birds inside her skull. She clutches the mug tightly, watching the surface of the liquid ripple with the subtle tremors she can't seem to control.

"So," Brandi says, settling into the chair opposite. "Are we going to talk about what's been eating you since Owen's party, or are we going to pretend everything's fine while you slowly have a nervous breakdown over the historical fiction display?"

Jetta's eyes remain fixed on her coffee. "It's nothing."

"You've been jumpy for days. You keep checking your phone like you're expecting terrible news. And yesterday you practically dove behind the romance section when a tall man walked past our window." Brandi leans forward, her voice softening. "This is about Ethan, isn't it?"

THE NAME alone sends a cold ripple down Jetta's spine. She takes a sip of coffee to hide her reaction, but the mug trembles against her lips, betraying her.

"I KNOW HIM," she finally admits, the words emerging barely above a whisper. "From before."

BRANDI WAITS, giving the silence room to breathe, to expand into the confession Jetta can feel building in her chest like pressure behind a dam.

"WE WENT TO HIGH SCHOOL TOGETHER." Another sip of coffee, another moment of delay. "Hillcrest Prep."

"I THOUGHT you went to Westlake for high school," Brandi says, confusion crossing her features.

"I TRANSFERRED THERE. For my junior and senior years." Jetta's fingers tighten around the mug. "After what happened with Ethan."

THE DAM BREAKS.

. . .

"IT WAS AFTER GYM CLASS. Swimming, actually. I was in the shower, and when I came out, my clothes were gone." Jetta's voice sounds distant to her own ears, as if someone else is telling the story. "Not just misplaced. Taken. I searched everywhere—lockers, benches, even the garbage cans. Nothing."

BRANDI'S EXPRESSION shifts from confusion to dawning comprehension, her eyes widening slightly.

"I WRAPPED myself in a towel from the shower room. It was small, barely covered me. I thought maybe someone had moved my stuff to another locker as a stupid prank." Jetta swallows hard. "I had to leave the locker room to find a teacher. The hall was empty at first, and then—"

SHE STOPS, her throat constricting around the memory.

"ETHAN WAS THERE. With his friends. They were waiting." The words come faster now, tumbling out like she needs to expel them before she loses her nerve. "One of them grabbed my towel, pulled it away. I tried to cover myself, but there were so many of them, laughing, pointing. Someone had a phone, was recording everything. I tried to run, but where could I go? Half-naked in the school hallway."

BRANDI'S HAND reaches across the space between them, covering Jetta's where it grips the mug. The touch is gentle, anchoring.

· · ·

"The videos spread through the school in hours. 'Naked Jetta' they called me." Her laugh is brittle, sharp enough to cut. "So creative, high school bullies. For weeks, people would make towel-dropping gestures when I walked by. Boys would ask if I wanted to 'go for a swim.' Someone printed screenshots and put them in my textbooks."

"Oh, Jetta," Brandi whispers, her voice thick with emotion.

"I went to the principal. He called it a 'regrettable prank.' Gave Ethan detention for a week. Told me to be more careful with my belongings, like I'd been careless instead of targeted." Jetta finally looks up, meeting Brandi's eyes. "My parents transferred me to Westlake after someone created a fake social media account in my name with those pictures. Started over. Never looked back."

"And now he's here," Brandi says, understanding blooming in her expression. "In our lives. Best friend of who your best friend is dating."

Jetta nods, a sharp, jerky movement. "The universe has a sick sense of humour."

The stained-glass lamp above them casts fractured light across their faces—Jetta's drawn with remembered pain, Brandi's flushed with protective anger. For a long moment, neither speaks. The coffee grows cool in Jetta's mug, forgotten.

. . .

"WE CAN CREATE SOME DISTANCE," Brandi finally says, her voice gentle but firm. "I'll talk to Owen. He'll understand. We don't have to do the double-date thing. You don't have to see Ethan at all."

"NO." Jetta shakes her head, setting her mug on the table with a decisive click. "I won't come between Owen and his best friend. I've seen how happy he makes you. How much you care about him. And he clearly adores Ethan, looks up to him."

"BUT AFTER WHAT HE DID—"

"IT WAS A DECADE AGO. We were teenagers." The words taste strange on Jetta's tongue, almost like she's defending him, though that's the last thing she wants to do. "I'm not saying I forgive him. I don't. But I won't be the reason your relationship gets complicated."

BRANDI STUDIES HER, concern evident in the furrow between her brows. "Are you sure? Because I'll absolutely create a buffer zone if you need it."

"I'LL FIND a way to coexist with him," Jetta says, her jaw set with determination despite the vulnerability still visible in her eyes. "I managed it at the party, didn't I? No one even noticed anything was wrong."

. . .

"I noticed," Brandi corrects softly. "I always notice when you're hurting."

The simple truth of this—the reminder that she is seen, known, cared for—nearly breaks Jetta's careful composure. She blinks rapidly, looking up at the stained-glass lamp to keep tears from falling.

"Thank you," she whispers. "For listening. For not making me feel stupid about still being affected by high school drama."

"There's nothing stupid about trauma," Brandi says fiercely. "And nothing has an expiration date on how long it gets to hurt."

Outside, the street has darkened completely, the bookshop windows now reflecting their own interior light back at them rather than showing the world beyond. Jetta feels lighter somehow, as if sharing the weight of her history has redistributed it, made it more bearable.

"So what now?" Brandi asks after a moment. "How do we handle this?"

"Now," Jetta says, straightening her shoulders, "we close up shop. Go home. And I figure out how to exist in the same social circle as Ethan Cole without clawing his eyes out. Or showing how much he still gets to me."

. . .

"And if that doesn't work?"

Jetta manages a smile, small but genuine. "Then I'll borrow your reading glasses as a disguise and avoid him forever."

Brandi laughs, the sound breaking the last of the tension between them. "They're basically a Clark Kent-level disguise. No one ever recognises me without them, even though they're on top of my head half the time."

They stand together, the moment of vulnerability gently closing as they return to their closing routine. Jetta feels Brandi's gaze on her as they move through the familiar motions—emptying the register, turning off the coffee maker, checking the back door lock. The concern is still there, but it's tempered now with understanding, with respect for Jetta's choice to handle this her way.

As they prepare to leave, Jetta pauses at the historical fiction display, adjusting one final book that still sits slightly askew. Her hands are steady now, her movements deliberate. Whatever comes next, she won't face it alone.

The sports bar thrums with the collective energy of a dozen televisions broadcasting the same game from different angles. Ethan watches the action without really seeing it, the players moving across the screen in meaningless patterns while he nurses his second beer of the evening. The amber liquid in his glass has grown warm, neglected during the twenty minutes he's spent listening to Owen's enthusiastic plans for future outings. Every time Jetta's name enters the conversation, Ethan feels a tightening between his shoulder blades, a physical response he can't entirely control.

"AND THEN THE client actually asked if we could 'make the logo more blue, but also less blue at the same time,'" Owen finishes, his face contorting with mock seriousness before dissolving into laughter.

ETHAN FORCES his attention back to his friend, manufacturing a laugh that sounds convincing even to his own ears. Years of security work have made him adept at feigning appropriate responses while his mind works on other problems. Right now, the problem is Jetta Kinsley and the uncomfortable reality of their shared past inserting itself into his present.

"CLIENTS," he says, shaking his head with practised commiseration. "Almost makes international security work seem simple."

OWEN CLAPS him on the shoulder, his easy physicality a reminder of their years of friendship. "At least no one's shooting at you over a PowerPoint presentation."

"WEEK'S STILL YOUNG," Ethan replies dryly, taking a sip of his neglected beer.

. . .

Owen's phone buzzes against the bar top. He glances at the screen, a small smile instantly softening his features. "Brandi," he explains unnecessarily, the name emerging with an unmistakable warmth. He types something quickly, then sets the phone aside. "She's with Jetta at the bookshop. Closing up."

The name lands between them like a stone dropped in still water, sending ripples of tension through Ethan's body that he immediately works to suppress. He takes another drink, longer this time, using the motion to hide whatever might show on his face.

"Speaking of," Owen continues, oblivious to the sudden tightness in Ethan's jaw, "I was thinking we should all go to that new restaurant that opened downtown. The one with the rooftop garden? Brandi mentioned it last week, and it seems perfect for a double date situation."

"Double date," Ethan repeats, the words feeling awkward in his mouth. "You're getting ahead of yourself. I haven't even met anyone here yet."

Owen waves this objection away with a dismissive hand. "Not a romantic double date. Just the four of us. You, me, Brandi, and Jetta. Friends hanging out. Getting to know each other better."

On screen, a player makes an impressive play. The bar erupts in cheers and groans depending on team allegiance. Ethan focuses on the moment, grateful for the distraction.

. . .

"DID YOU SEE THAT?" he asks, gesturing toward the nearest television. "Completely unnecessary risk. Should've passed to the open man on his left."

"CLASSIC WILLIAMS," Owen agrees easily, turning to watch the replay. "All flash, no fundamentals." He signals the bartender for another round, then swivels back to Ethan. "So, dinner next week? I already know you don't have plans— unless you're holding out on me about some secret European girlfriend."

ETHAN'S FINGERS tense around his glass, pressing hard enough that he half-expects the material to crack beneath his grip. He forces himself to relax, to breathe evenly, to maintain the casual demeanour that has become second nature in tense situations.

"NOT SURE IF dinner works with my schedule," he says, aiming for casual disinterest. "Still getting settled back in. A lot of loose ends to tie up."

"WHAT LOOSE ENDS? You live in my spare room with a duffel bag and a laptop." Owen laughs, completely missing the subtle deflection. "Come on, it'll be fun. Brandi's been wanting us all to hang out since the welcome home party. Says Jetta's been asking about you."

. . .

ETHAN NEARLY CHOKES on his beer. "Asking what, exactly?"

"JUST THE USUAL STUFF. Where you've been, what you've been doing. She doesn't know many people in international security." Owen shrugs, his attention already drifting back to the game. "I think she's curious about your work. Brandi says she reads a lot of spy novels."

THE IRONY of Jetta Kinsley expressing curiosity about him—rather than just thinly veiled contempt—is almost enough to make Ethan laugh. Almost.

"MY WORK ISN'T EXACTLY like the novels," he says instead, voice carefully neutral. "Less car chases, more sitting in hotel lobbies watching for suspicious behaviour."

"STILL COOLER THAN MY JOB," Owen insists. "Yesterday I spent four hours choosing between three nearly identical fonts for a client who ended up picking the one we started with." He clinks his fresh beer against Ethan's. "So, dinner? Tuesday maybe? Or Thursday if that's better?"

THE PERSISTENCE IS PURE OWEN—GOOD-NATURED, optimistic, and completely blind to any undercurrents of discomfort. It's what makes him excellent at navigating office politics and terrible at recognising when someone wants to change the subject. His conflict-avoidant nature means he simply doesn't register tension unless it explodes in his face.

· · ·

"Let's just watch the game," Ethan suggests, deliberately turning toward the screen. "We can figure out schedules later."

"Fine, fine." Owen holds up his hands in mock surrender. "But I'm texting Brandi that you're tentatively in for Thursday."

"I didn't say—"

"Tentatively," Owen repeats, already typing on his phone. "With an asterisk. And a question mark. The universal symbols for 'Ethan is being difficult but will eventually agree because I'm very persuasive.'"

A cheer goes up from the bar patrons as someone scores. Ethan doesn't register which team; his attention caught on Owen's casual certainty that this dinner will happen, that the four of them will sit around a table making pleasant conversation while he and Jetta pretend they don't share a history that includes one of his greatest shames.

"You know," Owen says, setting his phone down again, "Jetta's pretty great once you get to know her. She comes off a bit reserved at first, but she's got this dry sense of humour that sneaks up on you." He takes a swig of beer, oblivious to how each word lands like a physical weight on Ethan's chest. "I think you two would actually get along if you gave it a chance."

. . .

"Maybe," Ethan manages, voice carefully noncommittal.

"Definitely," Owen corrects with the confidence of someone who has never had his optimism seriously challenged. "She's smart, reads like a hundred books a year. And she doesn't put up with bullshit, which I know you appreciate in people."

The irony of this assessment—that Jetta Kinsley doesn't put up with bullshit, specifically his bullshit from a decade ago—twists in Ethan's gut like a knife. He takes another drink, longer this time, using the action to compose his features.

"You really like her," he observes, steering the conversation slightly away from himself.

"She's Brandi's best friend," Owen says, as if this alone is recommendation enough. "And yeah, she's great. A little guarded sometimes, I think something may have happened to her in the past, but it's not my place to ask, but who isn't these days?" He glances at the television as the crowd groans at a missed opportunity. "Besides, it's important to me that my best friend and my girlfriend's best friend get along. Makes everything easier, you know?"

Ethan nods, not trusting himself to speak. The weight of Owen's innocent hopes presses against him—the desire for his social circle to mesh seamlessly, for the people he cares about to care about each other. It's so quintessentially Owen to want harmony, to be completely oblivious to the fault lines running beneath the surface.

"So Thursday?" Owen presses, circling back with the tenacity of someone who has never learned to read reluctance in others. "I'll make reservations. Seven o'clock? Or is eight better?"

Ethan's fingers tighten once more around his glass, his knuckles whitening briefly before he consciously relaxes them. "Let me check my schedule," he says, knowing it's just delaying the inevitable. "I'll let you know tomorrow."

"Perfect!" Owen grins, already considering the matter settled. "It's going to be great. The four of us, good food, maybe some drinks after. The beginning of a tradition."

As Owen launches into descriptions of other restaurants they should try, other activities the four of them might enjoy together, Ethan returns his attention to the game, nodding at appropriate intervals without really listening. On screen, players move in practised formations, each knowing exactly where the others will be, a choreography built on shared understanding and clear rules.

If only real life were so straightforward.

Jetta slides the key into the lock of the front door, its familiar resistance requiring the practised twist of her wrist—

slightly up, then right, then the final turn that secures the bookshop for the night. The glass reflects her face back at her, features drawn with exhaustion after the emotional conversation with Brandi. Street lamps flicker to full brightness outside, their glow transforming the quiet street into a stage set for evening commerce—restaurants filling with dinner crowds, the cocktail bar across the way already humming with early patrons. She pockets the keys and turns to find Brandi waiting, purse slung over her shoulder, phone in hand as she checks the time.

"OWEN WANTS to know if we're up for dinner next Thursday," Brandi says, looking up from her screen. "Some new place downtown with a rooftop garden." Her voice carries a careful neutrality that tells Jetta she's trying not to pressure her either way.

"YOU SHOULD GO," Jetta replies, tugging her jacket closer against the evening chill. "Don't let my issues dictate your social calendar."

"HE'S SUGGESTING all four of us," Brandi clarifies, watching Jetta's face closely. "You, me, him, and Ethan."

THE NAME SENDS a small electric current down Jetta's spine, despite her best efforts to appear unmoved. She turns away, pretending to check that the door is properly locked, using the moment to compose her features before facing Brandi again.

. . .

"I'LL THINK ABOUT IT," she says, the noncommittal response buying her time she doesn't really need. She already knows she'll go, will sit across from Ethan and make polite conversation, will maintain the facade of normalcy that seems suddenly to be her responsibility. The alternative—explaining to Owen why his best friend and his girlfriend's best friend can't be in the same room—feels impossibly complex, a nuclear option she's not willing to deploy.

THEY STEP AWAY from the storefront, the bookshop's warm interior lights dimming automatically behind them on their timer. The street is alive with Thursday evening energy—people leaving offices, meeting friends, beginning the slow slide toward weekend freedom. Jetta moves to start walking toward their apartment six blocks north, but something catches her eye across the street—a tall figure moving with familiar purpose through the gathering crowd.

HER BODY REACTS before her mind fully processes what she's seeing. Her fingers clench around the keys in her pocket, metal edges biting into her palm with painful clarity. Her spine straightens, shoulders tensing as if preparing to absorb a physical blow. The breath she was taking halts midway, trapped in her lungs as her focus narrows to that distant silhouette.

IS IT HIM? The height is right, the breadth of shoulders, the confident stride. The figure passes under a street lamp, and for a moment, she thinks she catches the flash of blue eyes looking in her direction. Her heart hammers against her ribs like a trapped bird.

· · ·

"JETTA?" Brandi's voice seems to come from far away. "What is it?"

JETTA BLINKS, forcing herself to exhale the breath she's been holding. "Nothing," she says automatically, though her eyes remain fixed on the figure now moving away, disappearing into the evening crowd. "Thought I saw someone I knew."

BRANDI FOLLOWS HER GAZE, scanning the pedestrians across the street with a small frown of concentration. "Who? I don't see anyone familiar."

"IT WASN'T—" Jetta shakes her head, forcing her fingers to relax their death grip on the keys. "I was mistaken."

BUT BRANDI ISN'T EASILY DEFLECTED. Her eyes narrow as understanding dawns. "You thought you saw Ethan," she says, not a question but a statement of fact. She touches Jetta's arm gently. "Are you sure you can handle being around him? Really sure? Because we can find a way to create some distance without making it weird for Owen."

JETTA STRAIGHTENS her shoulders and turns away from the window, deliberately breaking her gaze from the spot where the figure disappeared. "I survived it once," she says with forced lightness that doesn't reach her eyes. "I can do it again." She echoes from earlier

· · ·

THEY BEGIN WALKING toward their apartment, falling into step beside each other with the ease of longtime roommates. The evening air carries the scent of approaching autumn— crisp leaves, woodsmoke from somewhere distant, the faint sweetness of late-blooming flowers making their final stand before frost. Jetta breathes it in, using the sensory input to ground herself in the present moment, to push away the past that keeps threatening to overtake her.

"IT'S NOT JUST ABOUT SURVIVING," Brandi says after they've walked a block in companionable silence. "You deserve more than that. You shouldn't have to constantly brace your-self every time we make plans."

"IT WON'T BE CONSTANT," Jetta counters, stepping around a couple stopped to look at a restaurant menu. "How often will the four of us really hang out? Once a month, maybe? I can handle that."

THEY PAUSE AT A CROSSWALK, waiting for the signal. In the red glow of the traffic light, Brandi's concern is painted in stark relief across her features. "You shouldn't have to handle it at all. What he did was cruel, Jetta. Deliberately cruel."

"WE WERE TEENAGERS," Jetta says, the words still strange in her mouth, still feeling like a defence she doesn't want to offer. "Teenagers do stupid, cruel things without thinking about the consequences."

. . .

THE LIGHT CHANGES. They cross, their pace unconsciously quickening as they approach their building. Jetta's mind races with contradictions—the memory of adolescent humiliation vivid in her mind, the image of Ethan's adult face at the welcome home party superimposed over it like a double exposure. The boy who orchestrated her worst high school memory and the man who offered a tentative truce at Owen's party seem simultaneously the same and entirely different people, a paradox she can't quite resolve.

"PROMISE ME SOMETHING," she says as they reach their building, pausing before entering. "Don't tell Owen about what happened. About Ethan and me. About any of it."

BRANDI'S EXPRESSION TURNS TROUBLED. "Jetta, he should know—"

"No," Jetta says firmly. "This happened a decade ago. Owen and Ethan have been friends for years. I won't be the reason Owen has to reconsider that friendship or feel caught in the middle." She takes Brandi's hands in hers, squeezing gently. "Promise me. This stays between us."

THE STREET LAMP above them flickers, casting momentary shadows across their faces. Brandi studies Jetta, clearly torn between respecting her wishes and her own protective instincts.

"I PROMISE," she finally says, reluctance evident in her voice. "But if he does anything—anything at all—to make you uncomfortable, or if this gets to be too much, you have to tell me. No suffering in silence. Deal?"

"Deal," Jetta agrees, releasing Brandi's hands to dig for her apartment keys.

As they climb the stairs to their third-floor unit, Jetta maintains her composure, her steps steady, her expression carefully neutral. But inside, her mind continues its relentless cycling between past and present—between the boy who stood laughing while she tried to cover herself with inadequate hands, and the man whose eyes held something like regret when they met hers across Owen's apartment.

She unlocks their apartment door, goes through the motions of hanging up her coat, checking the mail, filling the kettle for evening tea. Normal actions, ordinary moments strung together to create the illusion of stability. And beneath it all runs a current of quiet determination—to maintain this fragile peace for everyone's sake, to coexist with the architect of her worst memory, to move forward rather than remain trapped in a past she can't change.

"I'm making chamomile," she calls to Brandi, who has disappeared into her bedroom to change. "Want some?"

"Please," comes the muffled reply.

. . .

JETTA REACHES FOR TWO MUGS, arranges tea bags, waits for the kettle to boil. Her movements are precise, controlled, a physical manifestation of the composure she's determined to maintain. The apartment windows frame the city lights beyond, a constellation of lives unfolding in parallel to her own, each with their own complications, their own unresolved histories.

SHE WILL GO to dinner next Thursday. She will sit across from Ethan Cole and make pleasant conversation. She will smile at the right moments and laugh at the appropriate jokes. And no one—not Owen, not the other restaurant patrons, perhaps not even Ethan himself—will know what it costs her to do so.

THE KETTLE WHISTLES, a high, thin sound that cuts through her thoughts. Jetta lifts it from the stove, steam rising around her face like a veil as she pours hot water over waiting tea bags. The scent of chamomile rises, soothing and familiar. She breathes it in deeply, centering herself in this small, ordinary moment.

ONE STEP AT A TIME, she tells herself. One dinner, one evening, one interaction. She can do this. She has to.

CHAPTER 6

Sabotage at the Club

BASS REVERBERATES through Jetta's body like a second heartbeat as they enter Pulse, the club's name flickering in electric blue above the entrance. She feels the music before hearing it—a physical pressure against her skin, her organs, her bones. The door closes behind them with a finality that makes her stomach clench, trapping them in this pressurised container of sound and bodies and shifting light. Brandi's hand clutches her elbow, guiding her deeper into the throbbing mass of humanity, while Owen follows close behind, his fingers linked with Brandi's free hand. The connection between them is palpable, a tether that Jetta isn't part of.

"ISN'T THIS AMAZING?" Brandi shouts, her mouth close to Jetta's ear. Her reading glasses are absent tonight, replaced by contacts that make her eyes seem larger, more vulnerable somehow. "The DJ is supposed to be incredible!"

JETTA NODS, not bothering with words that would be swallowed by the sonic assault. The club stretches before them

—a cavernous space dissected by lasers and strobe lights that transform the crowd into a collection of freeze-frames, faces caught in expressions of ecstasy or concentration or predatory interest. Sweat already beads along her hairline despite the aggressive air conditioning fighting against hundreds of heated bodies.

"LET'S DANCE!" Brandi tugs at Owen's hand, already moving toward the centre of the floor where the press of people is densest. She glances back at Jetta with an inviting tilt of her head. "Coming?"

"I'LL GET A DRINK FIRST," Jetta replies, gesturing toward the illuminated bar that runs along one wall. "Save me some space!"

BUT BRANDI and Owen are already turning away, their bodies gravitating toward each other with magnetic inevitability. Within seconds, they're absorbed into the pulsing crowd, visible only in flashes when the lights sweep across their location. Jetta watches them for a moment—the easy way they move together, the casual intimacy of Owen's hand at Brandi's waist, the unconscious synchronisation of their movements. A familiar ache settles beneath her ribs, not quite jealousy but adjacent to it—recognition of something she's chosen to live without.

SHE TURNS TOWARD THE BAR, shoulders set with determination. This is a night for enjoyment, not for standing on the periphery watching others connect. She'd agreed to this outing despite knowing Ethan would be present, had convinced herself she could handle his proximity for Brandi's sake. And handle it she will—by having an excellent time completely independent of his existence.

THE BARTENDER NOTICES HER IMMEDIATELY—A small victory she attributes to her carefully chosen outfit, a deep green top that makes her eyes look almost feline in certain light. She orders something with vodka and cranberry, something that won't slow her down or dull her edges. While waiting, she surveys the crowd with practised nonchalance, cataloguing faces and bodies with the detached interest of a naturalist observing a new species.

THAT'S when she sees him.

ETHAN STANDS at the opposite end of the bar, his height making him visible despite the crowd. The club lights catch on his profile in rhythmic pulses—illuminating, then shadowing, then illuminating again the clean line of his jaw, the confident set of his shoulders beneath a dark blue shirt that fits him with suspicious perfection. Women near him glance over with poorly disguised interest, their bodies angling toward him even in casual conversation with others. Jetta watches him order drinks with the easy authority of someone accustomed to being attended to immediately—not demanding, but expecting, which is somehow worse.

SHE TURNS away before he can catch her staring, accepting her cocktail from the bartender with a smile that feels tight across her face. The first sip burns pleasantly down her throat, liquid courage settling into her stomach as she turns her attention deliberately away from Ethan's corner of the bar.

A MAN CATCHES HER EYE—TALL but not imposingly so, with kind eyes and a mouth that looks accustomed to smiling. He stands slightly apart from a group near the edge of the dance floor, his attention drifting occasionally as if he, too, is surveying options. When their gazes meet, he doesn't look away, instead offering a small, questioning smile that Jetta finds herself returning before she's consciously decided to.

DECISION MADE, she moves toward him with a confidence she doesn't entirely feel but can certainly fake. The path requires navigating through clusters of people engaged in shouted conversations, bodies pressing against hers briefly before yielding space. She's hyperaware of her movements— the sway of her hips, the deliberate grace she employs to avoid spilling her drink, the practised smile that feels more natural with each step.

"HI," she says when she reaches him, the word almost lost beneath a particularly aggressive bass drop. She leans closer, her mouth near his ear. "I'm Jetta."

"MARCUS," he replies, his voice warm against her skin. "Nice to meet someone who still uses actual names instead of just Instagram handles."

THE JOKE IS CORNY, but delivered with enough self-awareness that she finds herself genuinely smiling. "I'm old-fashioned that way," she says. "I also occasionally make phone calls and write emails with complete sentences."

"A DYING BREED," he agrees, his eyes crinkling at the corners. "Can I buy you another drink when you're done with that one?"

THE CONVERSATION FLOWS with surprising ease, lubricated by the alcohol and the tacit understanding that they're both here seeking connection, however temporary. Marcus works in graphic design, loves obscure documentaries, and has a dog named after a character from a science fiction novel she's actually read. Jetta finds herself leaning closer than strictly necessary, her hand occasionally touching his arm to emphasise a point. It feels good—this simple exchange, this uncomplicated interest without the weight of history or expectation.

SHE'S LAUGHING at something Marcus has said when she feels it—a presence at her back, a subtle shift in the air currents that her body recognises before her mind processes the reason. Then liquid splashes against her arm, cool and sticky, and she turns to find Ethan standing too close, a half-empty glass in his hand and an expression of exaggerated surprise on his face.

"SORRY ABOUT THAT," he says, though his tone carries no actual remorse. "Someone bumped into me." His eyes flick to Marcus, assessing him with a thoroughness that feels invasive even to Jetta, who is merely witnessing it. "I don't think we've met. Friend of Owen's?"

· · ·

MARCUS SHAKES HIS HEAD, clearly caught off guard by the interruption and Ethan's intensity. "Just met Jetta, actually."

"INTERESTING." Ethan's smile doesn't reach his eyes as he extends his hand. "Ethan Cole. An old friend of Jetta's. Very old friend. We go way back, don't we?"

THE EMPHASIS MAKES Jetta's stomach clench. She wipes at the spilled drink on her arm with more force than necessary. "Not that far back," she corrects, voice tight. "And not that close."

ETHAN IGNORES THIS, focusing instead on Marcus with an expression of friendly concern that Jetta immediately distrusts. "So what do you do, Marcus? Just here for fun, or are you meeting someone specific?"

"I'M A GRAPHIC DESIGNER," Marcus answers, glancing between them with growing discomfort. "Just out with some work friends, nothing special."

"GRAPHIC DESIGN?" Ethan repeats, his tone suggesting he's never heard anything more fascinating. "That must be... creative. What kind of clients do you work with? Any major brands, or more local stuff?"

THE RAPID-FIRE QUESTIONS come with an intensity that makes Marcus shift his weight, clearly sensing something off about the interaction but unable to identify exactly what. "Mostly corporate branding, some startup work. Nothing you'd recognise probably."

"Huh." Ethan takes a deliberate sip of his remaining drink. "Jetta here co-owns a bookshop. Very successful. Independent businesses are so vulnerable these days, don't you think? Takes real commitment to make them work."

The implication—that Marcus lacks such commitment —hangs in the air between them. Jetta opens her mouth to intervene, but Ethan continues seamlessly.

"She's incredibly dedicated. Works constantly. Barely has time for social engagements, which makes tonight quite special." He places subtle emphasis on the word 'special' that transforms it into something weighted with significance.

Marcus glances at his watch, then over Ethan's shoulder as if suddenly spotting someone urgent. "I should probably check on my friends," he says, gesturing vaguely toward a cluster of people by the DJ booth. "Nice meeting you, Jetta. Maybe I'll see you around later?"

But his tone makes it clear he has no intention of seeking her out again. He slides away into the crowd with the relieved expression of someone escaping an uncomfortable situation.

. . .

Jetta turns to Ethan, fury building in her chest like pressure behind a dam. "What the hell was that?"

He blinks at her with practised innocence, though something like satisfaction flickers in his eyes. "What? Just being friendly."

"You deliberately scared him off," she accuses, voice low but intense.

"If he scares that easily, I did you a favour." Ethan shrugs, draining the last of his drink. "Anyway, enjoy your evening. I see someone I need to talk to."

Before she can respond, he melts into the crowd with surprising grace for someone of his size, leaving Jetta standing alone, her cocktail warming in her hand and her carefully constructed enjoyment of the evening already crumbling around her.

Jetta drains her cocktail in one defiant swallow, the alcohol burning a path to her stomach where it settles like liquid armour. The dance floor pulses before her, a shifting sea of bodies moving in approximate rhythm to the relentless beat. She won't allow Ethan Cole to dictate the course of her evening—not after she's spent years reclaiming her life from the shadow he cast over it. The night is young, the club filled with possibilities that have nothing to do with him. She deposits her empty glass on a nearby table and steps onto the dance floor with renewed determination, her body finding the rhythm almost despite itself.

THE MUSIC SHIFTS to something with a slower, more insistent bass line that she feels in her chest cavity, her heartbeat adjusting to match its tempo. Sweat gathers at her temples, at the nape of her neck, between her shoulder blades—physical evidence of her presence in this space, her refusal to retreat to the margins. She scans the crowd as she moves, her eyes skipping deliberately past any section where Ethan might be lurking.

A MAN CATCHES HER ATTENTION—DARK hair styled in careful waves, white button-down with sleeves rolled to expose forearms traced with subtle tattoos. He dances alone but with the confidence of someone who knows he's being watched. When their eyes meet across the shifting bodies between them, his interest is immediate and unconcealed. He smiles—a genuine expression that transforms his face from merely handsome to something more compelling.

JETTA RETURNS THE SMILE, allowing her movements to become more deliberate, more inviting. The space between them seems to contract without either making an obvious approach, other dancers unconsciously shifting to create a path. He moves toward her with the unhurried confidence of someone accustomed to positive responses, his eyes never leaving hers.

"I'M ALEX," he says when they're finally close enough to speak, his mouth near her ear to be heard over the music. His cologne smells expensive but not overwhelming—sandalwood and something citrus, applied with restraint.

"JETTA," she replies, not stepping back after the introduction, maintaining the proximity that the loud music justifies. "Nice to meet you."

"LIKEWISE." His hand finds her waist, the touch light enough to be easily rejected if unwelcome. When she doesn't move away, his fingers settle more firmly against the thin material of her top. "You move like you hear something different in the music than everyone else."

THE OBSERVATION SURPRISES HER—SPECIFIC, perceptive, not the generic compliment she expected. "Maybe I do," she says, allowing herself to be drawn slightly closer as the crowd around them densifies. "Or maybe I'm just following my own rhythm."

"I LIKE THAT," he tells her, his smile warming further. "Independence is rare in places like this where everyone's trying so hard to sync up."

THE CONVERSATION CONTINUES in this vein—shouted fragments that somehow manage to reveal actual personality despite the environment working against meaningful exchange. Alex is a physical therapist who plays bass in a band on weekends. He asks questions and listens to her answers with flattering attention. Their bodies move together with increasing synchronicity, finding a shared language in motion that complements their verbal exchange.

JETTA FEELS HERSELF RELAXING, the tension from Ethan's earlier interference melting under Alex's obvious interest and engaging presence. When his hand slides from her waist to the small of her back, the contact sends a pleasant shiver up her spine. She leans closer, allowing her fingers to rest lightly on his shoulder, testing the firm muscle beneath the fabric of his shirt.

"CAN I GET YOU A DRINK?" he asks after several songs have blended together, the prolonged dancing having left them both slightly breathless.

"I'D LIKE THAT," she agrees, already planning their path to the bar, calculating the probability of Ethan's presence there and how to avoid it.

BUT BEFORE THEY can step off the dance floor, a familiar figure materialises beside them, his height making him impossible to mistake even in the chaotic lighting. Ethan's sudden appearance feels like a conjuring, as if her mere thoughts of avoiding him had somehow summoned him instead.

"THERE YOU ARE," he says to Jetta, his tone suggesting they'd made plans to reconnect. Before she can contradict him, he turns to Alex with a smile that doesn't reach his eyes. "Ethan Cole. Friend of Jetta's."

· · ·

ALEX RETURNS the handshake with a slightly confused expression. "Alex Chen. Nice to meet you."

"ALEX, HUH?" Ethan glances between them, his expression shifting to one of exaggerated concern. "Listen, man, I probably shouldn't say anything, but as one guy to another..." He lowers his voice, though still loud enough for Jetta to hear clearly. "She's still getting over her ex. Messy breakup, like, two weeks ago. I think she might be using this—" he gestures vaguely between them, "—as a rebound situation."

JETTA'S MOUTH drops open in stunned outrage. "That's completely—"

"IT'S OKAY," Ethan interrupts, placing a hand on her shoulder that she immediately shrugs off. "It's totally normal. But I figured Alex here would want to know what he's getting into." He turns back to Alex with a conspiratorial expression. "She was talking about the ex earlier tonight. Three drinks in, waterworks. It was rough."

ALEX TAKES A SMALL STEP BACK, his hand dropping from Jetta's waist. "I, uh—that sounds complicated."

"IT'S NOT," Jetta insists, fury making her voice sharper than intended. "He's lying. There is no ex."

BUT THE DAMAGE IS DONE. Alex's expression has already shifted from interest to wariness, his body language telegraphing retreat. "Look, you seem great, but I'm not really looking to be someone's therapy session. Maybe another time?" He doesn't wait for a response before backing away, disappearing into the crowd with the practised ease of someone who's made similar escapes before.

JETTA ROUNDS ON ETHAN, her hands curling into fists at her sides. "What is wrong with you?" she demands, the question emerging as a hiss rather than the shout it would be if not for the public setting.

"JUST LOOKING OUT FOR YOU," Ethan replies with infuriating calm. "That guy seemed shady. The tattoos, the too-smooth approach."

"YOU DON'T GET to decide who I talk to," she says, stepping closer to ensure he hears every word despite the music. "You lost that right—no, you never had that right—when you decided to humiliate me in front of the entire school."

SOMETHING FLICKERS ACROSS HIS FACE— DISCOMFORT, perhaps, or something adjacent to remorse— but it's gone before she can properly identify it. "Ancient history," he says with a dismissive shrug. "Thought we had a truce."

"A TRUCE DOESN'T MEAN you get to sabotage my evening," she retorts. "It means we coexist without making each other miserable. Clearly, you've forgotten that part."

· · ·

SHE TURNS away before he can respond, needing distance before she says something that can't be taken back, something that would ripple outward to affect Brandi and Owen. As she navigates through the crowd, her anger crystallises into determination. If Ethan wants to play games, she can play too—and she has no intention of losing.

SCANNING THE CLUB, her attention catches on a woman near the VIP section—blonde hair styled in deliberate waves, outfit precisely calibrated to draw attention without seeming to try too hard. She laughs with her entire body, head thrown back, one hand touching the arm of the person she's speaking with. Even without an introduction, Jetta recognises the type immediately—the marketing coordinator, the social butterfly, the collector of connections and dispenser of insider information.

AS IF CONFIRMING HER ASSESSMENT, the woman's voice carries across the space between them despite the music—distinctive, slightly too loud, designed to be heard. "Oh my god, you HAVE to come to this underground thing next weekend—it's invite only, but I can totally get you in."

JETTA WATCHES as Ethan spots the woman, his body language shifting subtly as he assesses and approaches. His movements become more deliberate, shoulders straightening, stride lengthening. He's hunting, and this woman is clearly his preferred quarry—bright, social, uncomplicated.

HE INTRODUCES himself with that same confident smile that had no doubt opened countless doors throughout his life.

The woman—Claire, Jetta remembers from Brandi's descriptions of the local party scene—responds immediately, her posture opening to him, her smile widening to reveal perfect teeth. Ethan leans closer, says something that makes Claire laugh again, her hand coming to rest on his forearm in a gesture that manages to be both casual and possessive.

JETTA MOVES BEFORE FULLY FORMING a plan, her feet carrying her across the club with determined strides. She approaches from Claire's side, carefully positioning herself to enter the conversation at precisely the right angle.

"CLAIRE?" she exclaims with perfectly calibrated surprise and delight. "Oh my god, I thought that was you!"

CLAIRE TURNS, confusion flashing briefly across her features before social training kicks in. "Hi! Oh, wow, it's been forever!"

JETTA EMBRACES her like an old friend, ignoring Ethan's narrowed eyes over Claire's shoulder. "You look amazing," she gushes, channelling the exact tone of female bonding that men find impenetrable. "That top is incredible on you."

"THANK YOU!" Claire preens slightly, her attention successfully diverted from Ethan. "I just got it last week. The boutique on Maple, you know the one with the snooty salesgirl?"

. . .

"WITH THE BANGS?" Jetta asks, committing fully to the fabricated shared history. "God, she's the worst. But their clothes are worth it." She loops her arm through Claire's, turning her slightly away from Ethan. "How have you been? Are you still at that marketing firm?"

CLAIRE LAUNCHES into an enthusiastic update about her job, complete with animated hand gestures that further create a barrier between her and Ethan. Jetta nods and responds with appropriate interest, all while maintaining an awareness of Ethan's growing frustration visible in her peripheral vision.

"OH!" Jetta exclaims suddenly, pointing across the club. "Isn't that the guy from the gallery opening? The one who does those incredible light installations? He was asking about you the other night."

CLAIRE'S HEAD SWIVELS IMMEDIATELY, her eyes widening with interest. "Really? Where?"

"OVER BY THE DJ BOOTH. Come on, I'll introduce you." Jetta guides her away from Ethan with gentle but insistent pressure, not looking back as they weave through the crowd.

SHE FEELS RATHER than sees Ethan's stare following them —a prickling awareness between her shoulder blades that should be uncomfortable but instead feels like victory. As she introduces Claire to a random group of people who play along with confused politeness, Jetta finally glances back to find

Ethan still standing where they left him, his jaw tight with barely concealed frustration.

She raises her glass in a mock toast, mirroring his earlier gesture from Owen's party. His eyes meet hers across the distance, acknowledgment and challenge passing between them in silent communication.

Game on.

Sweet victory courses through Jetta's veins as she watches Claire disappear into the crowd, absorbed by a group of strangers who welcomed her with confused but polite smiles. From across the club, she feels Ethan's glare like heat against her skin—a physical sensation that should be uncomfortable but instead feels satisfying, proof that she's disrupted his plans as thoroughly as he disrupted hers. She turns away deliberately, chin lifted in defiance, determined to enjoy what remains of the night despite his attempts to ruin it. The club continues its assault on her senses—music pounding through the floorboards, lights slicing through darkness to reveal fragments of faces, bodies pressed close in the primal communion of movement and sound. Somewhere in that chaos, Brandi and Owen dance in oblivious happiness, unaware of the cold war escalating around them.

The alcohol in Jetta's system has reached that perfect equilibrium—enough to dull her social anxiety but not enough to impair her judgment. She moves through the club with renewed confidence, stopping at the bar for another drink that she nurses slowly, her eyes constantly scanning for both opportunity and threat. The threat, she knows, is six-foot-something with impossible blue eyes and a jaw that tightens when he's angry. The opportunity arrives in the form of a man with kind eyes and a gentle smile, who offers her a compliment about her earrings that seems genuine rather than calculated.

THEIR CONVERSATION FLOWS EASILY, an exchange about favourite local restaurants that reveals compatible tastes and a shared appreciation for authentic Thai food. He stands at a respectful distance despite the crowded space, attentive without being overbearing. Jetta feels herself relaxing into the interaction, cautiously optimistic that Ethan might have found another target for his interference.

THIS HOPE EVAPORATES when she spots him approaching, weaving through the crowd with purpose, his eyes fixed on them with predatory focus. She tenses, fingers tightening around her glass as she prepares for whatever sabotage he's planned this time.

"HEY, MAN," Ethan says, clapping a hand on the shoulder of Jetta's companion with forced camaraderie. "Just wanted to give you a heads-up—her boyfriend just walked in, and he's the jealous type. Like, seriously jealous. Had a little incident last month with a guy who was talking to her. Cops were called."

THE MAN'S EYES WIDEN, darting around the club as if expecting imminent violence. "Boyfriend? She didn't mention—"

. . .

"THEY'RE ON A BREAK," Ethan explains with exaggerated sympathy. "But he doesn't really accept that. Big guy, works in construction, anger management issues." He gestures vaguely toward the entrance. "Looks like he's spotted you already."

JETTA OPENS her mouth to protest, but the man is already backing away, hands raised in a gesture of surrender. "Sorry, I'm not looking for trouble," he says, not meeting her eyes. "Have a good night."

HE DISAPPEARS into the crowd with remarkable speed, leaving Jetta facing Ethan across the small space he's vacated. "Are you serious right now?" she demands, fury making her voice vibrate with intensity despite her attempt to control it.

ETHAN SHRUGS, a small smile playing at the corner of his mouth. "Just looking out for public safety."

"YOU'RE UNBELIEVABLE," she seethes, stepping closer to ensure he hears her over the music. "What exactly are you trying to accomplish?"

"COULD ASK YOU THE SAME QUESTION," he counters, his smile fading into something more challenging. "Seems like you're determined to cycle through every man in this club tonight. Setting a personal record?"

. . .

THE INSULT LANDS WITH PRECISION, sending a flush of anger up her neck and into her cheeks. "Better than attaching myself to anyone with a pulse and an empty head," she retorts, the words emerging sharper than intended.

HIS EYES NARROW, a muscle in his jaw flexing before he manages a cold smile. "Careful, Jetta. Your bitterness is showing."

"AND YOUR ENTITLEMENT IS SHOWING," she fires back. "Still think you can control everyone around you, don't you? Still think you have the right to decide what happens and who gets hurt."

SOMETHING FLICKERS IN HIS EXPRESSION—A brief crack in his composure that reveals something more complex than simple antagonism. But it's gone before she can identify it, replaced by the mask of casual indifference he wears so effectively.

"ENJOY YOUR EVENING," he says with deliberate politeness. "What's left of it."

HE TURNS AWAY, leaving her standing alone, vibrating with frustration and something adjacent to regret—not for what she's said, but for allowing him to affect her so thoroughly. She watches him move through the crowd toward a woman standing near one of the support columns, her dress catching light when she shifts position.

· · ·

WITHOUT CONSCIOUS DECISION, Jetta finds herself moving in their direction, driven by an impulse she doesn't examine too closely. She approaches from behind Ethan, tapping the woman on the shoulder as if recognising her.

"HI THERE," she says with manufactured warmth. "Aren't you Marissa's friend? From spin class?"

THE WOMAN SHAKES HER HEAD, confusion evident. "No, sorry, I don't know any Marissa."

"OH, MY MISTAKE." Jetta laughs lightly, then lowers her voice to a conspiratorial level. "I should warn you, though— this guy? Still lives with his mother. Like, in her basement. Has a whole system of rules about when he can have the car." She gestures subtly toward Ethan, whose back is turned as he orders drinks. "Just thought you should know before you waste your time."

THE WOMAN'S expression shifts from confusion to vague distaste. By the time Ethan returns with drinks, she's checking her phone with exaggerated interest, making an excuse about needing to find her friends before slipping away into the crowd.

ETHAN'S GAZE FOLLOWS HER, then snaps to Jetta with dangerous intensity. "What did you say to her?"

. . .

"JUST GIRL TALK," Jetta replies with mock innocence. "You know how it is. Sharing information, looking out for each other."

HIS EYES narrow to blue slits, jaw clenching visibly. "This is childish, even for you."

"SAYS the man who invented a fictional jealous boyfriend to scare someone away from me," she counters, standing her ground despite the tension vibrating between them. "What's your excuse for that level of maturity?"

THE MUSIC SHIFTS to something with a harder edge, the bass so deep it seems to rearrange her internal organs. Around them, the crowd pulses in rhythm, unaware of the private battle being waged in their midst. Somewhere on the dance floor, Brandi and Owen move together in their own world, sealed off from the escalating hostility between their best friends.

FOR THE NEXT HOUR, Jetta and Ethan circle each other like wary predators, their eyes meeting across the club in silent acknowledgment of their ongoing game. When she approaches a bartender with a friendly smile, Ethan appears nearby to mention her "complicated relationship history." When he strikes up a conversation with a woman by the restrooms, Jetta materialises to share fictional details about his "recent restraining order situation." Their sabotage grows increasingly pointed, increasingly personal, the pretence of casualness abandoned in favour of open warfare.

. . .

THEIR EYES MEET across the dance floor—hers flashing with defiance, his dark with frustration—a moment of connection more honest than anything they've shared since his return. The air between them feels charged, electric with antagonism and something else neither is willing to name.

JETTA TURNS AWAY FIRST, needing distance, needing air that isn't thick with the scent of his cologne when he passes too close. She finds a relatively quiet alcove near an emergency exit, where the music recedes enough to allow actual conversation and the crowd thins to occasional passersby. The wall feels cool against her back as she leans against it, closing her eyes briefly, gathering herself.

"WHAT THE HELL IS YOUR PROBLEM?"

ETHAN'S VOICE cuts through her moment of respite. She opens her eyes to find him standing before her, close enough that she can smell the woodsy notes of his cologne, see the slight sheen of perspiration at his temples from the heat of the club. His height forces her to tilt her head back to meet his gaze, a position that makes her feel cornered despite the open space beside them.

"MY PROBLEM?" she repeats, indignation rising in her chest. "You're the one who's been following me around all night, scaring off anyone who talks to me."

"AND YOU'VE BEEN DOING EXACTLY the same thing," he counters, stepping closer, his voice dropping to an intense murmur that somehow carries over the distant thrum of music. "Making up lies, interfering in conversations that have nothing to do with you."

"POT, KETTLE," she fires back, refusing to be intimidated by his proximity. "You started this."

"DID I?" His eyes search hers with uncomfortable intensity. "Or did it start ten years ago in that high school hallway?"

THE DIRECT REFERENCE to their shared past hits her like a physical blow. "Don't you dare bring that up," she hisses, hands curling into fists at her sides. "You don't get to use that like it's just some anecdote from our past."

"I'M NOT," he says, his voice surprisingly soft despite the tension vibrating between them. "I'm asking if that's what this is really about. If that's why you can't stand the idea of me having a good time, of me being happy in any way."

"YOU HAVEN'T CHANGED at all since high school, have you?" The words escape her in a rush, laden with years of accumulated resentment. "Still the same entitled jerk who thinks he can control everyone around him. Still the same bully who enjoyed seeing someone humiliated."

HIS EXPRESSION HARDENS, a fortress rising behind his eyes. "And you're still the same judgmental girl who thinks she knows everything about everyone," he retorts, each word precisely targeted. "So quick to assign motives, to decide who deserves what. Did it ever occur to you that I might have reasons for what I do? That I might have changed in the decade since I was a stupid kid making terrible choices?"

"YOUR ACTIONS TONIGHT SUGGEST OTHERWISE," she says, gesturing toward the club where they've spent hours undermining each other. "What possible reason could you have for making sure I don't connect with anyone? What gives you the right to interfere in my life?"

"MAYBE I'M TRYING to protect you," he says, the words emerging with an intensity that surprises them both.

"PROTECT ME?" She laughs, the sound sharp with disbelief. "From what? Having a conversation with someone? Making a connection? Having fun for once in my life?"

"FROM PEOPLE who don't deserve you," he snaps, stepping even closer. "From guys who see a beautiful woman alone at a club and think they've found an easy target."

THE COMPLIMENT EMBEDDED in his accusation catches her off guard, momentarily stalling her next retort. They stand in charged silence, close enough that she can see the flecks of darker blue in his irises, can feel the heat radiating from his body.

· · ·

"I DON'T NEED YOUR PROTECTION," she finally says, each word carefully measured. "I don't need anything from you except distance. The same distance I've maintained for ten years while rebuilding what you destroyed."

"I DIDN'T DESTROY ANYTHING," he argues, though something like uncertainty flickers across his features. "It was a stupid prank that went too far. A mistake. One I've regretted more than you know."

"REGRETTED?" She steps toward him now, anger making her bold. "Was that before or after you became best friends with my best friend's boyfriend? Before or after you inserted yourself back into my life like you have any right to be there?"

THEIR VOICES HAVE RISEN with each exchange, the alcove no longer providing enough separation from the main club. Nearby, people glance over with curious expressions, sensing the tension, hungry for potential drama.

"I DIDN'T KNOW you were Brandi's friend when I came back," Ethan insists, his frustration evident in the tightness around his mouth. "I didn't plan this, Jetta. But I'm not going to apologise for being in Owen's life, or for trying to find some way to coexist with you for their sake."

"COEXIST?" she echoes, gesturing between them. "Is this your idea of coexistence? Following me around, ruining my night, making me relive the worst period of my life every time I see your face?"

. . .

THE RAW HONESTY of this last statement hangs between them, impossible to take back or soften. Ethan's expression shifts, something that might be genuine remorse crossing his features before hardening into defensive anger.

"MAYBE IF YOU weren't so determined to hate me, to see only the worst in me, we could actually move past what happened," he says, his voice lower but no less intense. "Maybe if you could accept that people change, that I'm not the same person I was—"

"JETTA? ETHAN?" Brandi's concerned voice cuts through their argument like a blade. She stands at the entrance to the alcove, Owen beside her, both wearing expressions of confused concern. "What's going on? We could hear you shouting from the dance floor."

THE INTRUSION BREAKS the charged bubble that had formed around Jetta and Ethan. They step apart, both suddenly aware of how close they'd been standing, how intense their exchange had become. The air between them still feels electric, charged with words spoken and unspoken, with resentments old and new.

"NOTHING," Jetta says automatically, though the flush on her cheeks and the tension in her posture tell a different story. "Just a disagreement."

. . .

"DIDN'T SOUND LIKE NOTHING," Owen observes, his usually easy-going expression replaced by something more serious. "Sounded pretty heated from where we were standing."

ETHAN RUNS a hand through his hair, a gesture that speaks of frustration and something adjacent to embarrassment. "Just clearing the air," he says, not meeting Owen's questioning gaze. "Ancient history."

BRANDI MOVES to Jetta's side, her hand finding her friend's arm in a gesture of support and inquiry. "Are you okay?" she asks quietly, eyes searching Jetta's face.

JETTA NODS, though the motion feels mechanical, disconnected from the turmoil still churning inside her. "Fine," she manages. "Just ready to go home, I think."

THE FOUR OF them stand in awkward tableau—Brandi and Owen confused and concerned, Jetta and Ethan avoiding each other's eyes while remaining acutely aware of each other's presence. The music continues its relentless pulse from the main club area, but in their alcove, the silence stretches, filled with questions no one seems ready to ask or answer.

"MAYBE THAT'S A GOOD IDEA," Owen finally says, breaking the stalemate. "It's getting late anyway."

AS THEY GATHER themselves to leave, Jetta risks one final glance at Ethan. He's already looking at her, his expression unreadable in the dim light, but something in his eyes speaks of unfinished business, of conversations yet to be had. She looks away quickly, focusing instead on Brandi's concerned face, on the exit sign glowing red above the nearby door, on anything but the complicated man whose presence has shattered the careful peace she's built around her memories.

THE NIGHT, with all its promised enjoyment, lies in ruins around them—another casualty in a war neither seems able to end.

CHAPTER 7

Unexpected Hero

JETTA JERKS her arm away from Brandi's concerned touch, the fury inside her still burning too hot for comfort. "I need another drink before we go," she says, the words clipped and brittle. "You two get our coats. I'll meet you at the entrance in five." Before anyone can protest, she turns and cuts through the crowd toward the bar, her shoulders rigid with tension, each step putting necessary distance between herself and Ethan's insufferable presence. The strobe lights slice across her vision in seizure-inducing flashes, transforming the dance floor into a stuttering film reel of disconnected images.

BRANDI CALLS AFTER HER, voice laced with worry, but Jetta pretends not to hear. She can't bear another moment of concerned glances and unasked questions, of Owen's confused expression and Ethan's—whatever was in Ethan's eyes. Anger? Regret? Something else entirely? She doesn't care. She won't care.

. . .

THE CLUB PULSES around her like a living organism with a fever. Artificial fog crawls along the floor in ghostly tendrils, catching the colored lights before dissipating into nothing. The bass vibrates through the floorboards and up through her boots, a second heartbeat that threatens to override her own. Bodies press against her as she navigates the narrow passages between dance clusters—shoulders brushing hers, someone's drink sloshing dangerously close to her sleeve, perfume and sweat and alcohol combining into a potent miasma that clogs her nostrils.

WHEN SHE FINALLY REACHES THE bar, she feels like she's been swimming upstream. She wedges herself into a small opening between two groups, lifting her hand to signal the bartender. Her fingers tremble slightly, adrenaline from her confrontation with Ethan still coursing through her system.

"LET ME GET THAT FOR YOU."

THE VOICE COMES from her right, smooth as aged whiskey and just as practised. She turns to find a man watching her with a smile that reveals perfect teeth—too perfect, almost artificial in their uniformity. His navy button-down looks expensive, the fabric so fine it appears to absorb rather than reflect the chaotic light show around them. A watch glints on his wrist as he raises his hand to the bartender—platinum, she thinks, or white gold, catching blue light when he moves.

"I CAN BUY MY OWN DRINK," Jetta says, the words emerging sharper than intended.

· · ·

"OF COURSE YOU CAN." His smile doesn't falter. "Consider it an apology for taking the last spot at the bar." He extends his hand. "I'm Robert."

SHE NOTICES HIS MANICURED NAILS, buffed to a subtle shine that suggests regular maintenance rather than a one-time treatment. His palm looks soft when she reluctantly shakes it, but his grip is firm, holding hers a beat longer than necessary.

"JETTA," she offers, withdrawing her hand.

"BEAUTIFUL NAME." His eyes assess her with careful precision, moving from her face to her shoulders to her waist and back again. There's nothing overtly lewd in the evaluation, just a methodical cataloguing that makes her skin prickle with unease. "What are you drinking, Jetta?"

SHE HESITATES, watching as he shifts his position slightly, angling his body to block the most direct path back to the dance floor. A coincidence, perhaps. Or perhaps not.

"VODKA CRANBERRY," she says finally, deciding that one drink might help take the edge off her anger. One drink to flush Ethan Cole from her system before she meets Brandi and Owen to leave. One drink to help her forget the way his eyes burned into hers during their argument, the intensity that made her feel simultaneously furious and something else she refuses to name.

· · ·

ROBERT FLAGS down the bartender with practised efficiency, ordering her vodka cranberry and a whiskey neat for himself. As they wait, he asks her standard questions—how long has she lived in the city, what does she do for work, does she come to Pulse often? She gives vague answers, volunteering nothing beyond the minimum politeness requires. When he mentions his work in tech sales, something about his delivery feels rehearsed, as if he's giving a pitch rather than sharing information.

THE DRINKS ARRIVE. Robert pays with a black credit card that he handles with casual ostentation, making sure she notices it before it disappears back into his wallet. She takes her glass, nodding thanks but maintaining the distance between them as much as the crowded bar allows.

"CHEERS," he says, raising his glass. "To unexpected encounters."

JETTA FORCES a smile and takes a sip, the tart sweetness of cranberry barely masking the bite of alcohol beneath. When a group near them erupts in laughter, she glances over instinctively. In that brief moment, Robert's hand moves with swift precision over her glass—a slight of hand so practised she wouldn't have even caught it if she hadn't turned back at exactly the right moment. His pinky finger taps against the rim as his hand withdraws, and something in his expression shifts for a heartbeat before the practised smile returns.

ICE SLIDES DOWN HER SPINE. Did he just—? No, she must be imagining things. The confrontation with Ethan has left her paranoid, seeing threats where none exist. Still, the unease lingers as she stares at her drink, now suspicious of its contents.

"Everything okay?" Robert asks, his concern so perfectly calibrated it wraps back around to insincerity.

"Fine," she says, bringing the glass to her lips but not drinking. "Just tired. It's been a long night."

His eyes, she notices now, never quite warm with his smile. They remain coolly observant, constantly scanning—her face, her body, the space around them—assessing and calculating with machine-like efficiency.

"Let me guess," he says, leaning slightly closer. "Boy trouble? I saw you arguing with that tall guy earlier. Ex-boyfriend?"

The mention of Ethan sends a fresh surge of irritation through her. "Definitely not," she says, and takes a larger sip than intended, needing to wash away the very suggestion.

"Good," Robert says, his smile widening. "He seemed like bad news."

Jetta almost laughs at the irony—this stranger labelling Ethan as "bad news" when every instinct in her body is now screaming caution about Robert himself. She takes another sip, rebellion against her own wariness fueling the action. She won't let Ethan ruin her night, and she won't let paranoia about this man do it either.

THREE SIPS IN, and something shifts. The club lights begin to blur at their edges, streaking across her vision when she turns her head. The bass seems to deepen, vibrating not just through the floor but through her bones, her organs, making her feel hollow and overfull simultaneously. Robert's voice comes to her as if through water, words distinguishable but strangely distant.

"...FEELING ALRIGHT? YOU LOOK A LITTLE FLUSHED."

HIS FACE SEEMS to float before her, features shifting in and out of focus. The room tilts slightly, forcing her to grip the bar for stability. Her tongue feels too large for her mouth, clumsy and uncooperative when she tries to speak.

"I'M FINE," she manages, though the words sound slurred to her own ears. "Just hot."

"LET'S GET SOME AIR," Robert suggests, his hand closing firmly around her elbow. His fingers press into her flesh with purpose, no longer maintaining the pretence of casual interest. "You look like you need it."

. . .

JETTA TRIES TO PULL AWAY, but her limbs respond sluggishly, as if she's moving through honey. The room spins slowly around her, faces blurring into featureless smears of colour, voices merging into an incomprehensible drone. Through this haze, one clear thought emerges: something is very, very wrong.

"MY FRIENDS," she tries to say, but Robert is already guiding her away from the bar, his grip unyielding.

"THEY'LL UNDERSTAND," he says, his voice now coming from somewhere above her as her head droops forward. "You're not feeling well. I'm helping you outside for some fresh air."

SHE WANTS TO SCREAM, to pull away, to find Brandi or Owen or even Ethan, but her body refuses to cooperate. The exit sign swims in her vision, a blurred red beacon growing larger as Robert steers her toward it with practised ease. His voice comes to her in fragments now, meaningless pleasantries that sound hollow and far away, as artificial as his smile.

THE LAST COHERENT thought she manages is a bitter irony: after everything that happened tonight, it's not Ethan Cole she should have been afraid of.

THE HEAVY METAL door swings shut behind them with a dull thud, sealing off the music and leaving them in the relative quiet of the alley. Cold air slaps against Jetta's face like an open palm, momentarily shocking her system but doing nothing to clear the thickening fog in her mind. Her feet catch on uneven pavement, and she would fall if not for Robert's grip on her elbow—a touch that no longer pretends to be supportive but has become nakedly controlling, his fingers digging into the soft flesh above her elbow with bruising force.

"CAREFUL NOW," Robert says, his voice no longer carrying the warm timbre he cultivated inside. It sounds stripped, functional, like equipment being tested for efficiency rather than pleasure. "Just a little further."

JETTA TRIES to turn her head to look back at the club door, but the movement sends the world tilting on its axis. Brick walls swim in her vision, stretching and contracting like something breathing. Distant street lamps cast pools of sickly yellow that don't reach the depths of the alley where shadows gather in patient clumps. Her tongue feels swollen, too large for her mouth, and when she tries to speak, the words emerge as shapeless sounds.

"N-NO," she manages, the single syllable requiring tremendous effort. "Back... inside."

"YOU NEED SOME AIR," Robert counters, his grip tightening as he pulls her deeper into the alley. "You're not feeling well."

HER LEGS MOVE AS if belonging to someone else—heavy, uncoordinated appendages she can command but not control.

Each step feels like wading through cement that's slowly hardening around her knees, her ankles, her feet. The ground seems to rise and fall beneath her, a malevolent sea intent on unbalancing her. She stumbles again, and this time Robert's impatience shows as he jerks her upright, his façade of concern evaporating.

"WALK," he hisses, no longer bothering with the pretence of helping.

THROUGH THE CHEMICAL haze clouding her vision, Jetta sees it—a car idling at the alley's end, its headlights extinguished, nothing but the faint red glow of taillights revealing its presence. Two silhouettes stand beside it, their features indistinct in the gloom, but their postures alertly waiting. Fear cuts through the fog in her mind, a cold blade of clarity that makes her heart race even as her limbs refuse to respond properly.

SHE TRIES to plant her feet, to become dead weight against Robert's pulling, but her body betrays her. Her resistance is feeble, easily overcome by his determined grip. Her free hand lifts to claw at his fingers, but the movement is sluggish, uncoordinated, her nails barely grazing his skin.

"STOP FIGHTING," Robert says, his voice flat with annoyance. "You'll only make it worse for yourself."

AS THEY DRAW CLOSER to the car, the figures beside it become clearer. One is massive—a mountain of a man with a shaved head that gleams dully under the distant street lamp. Tribal tattoos curl up his thick neck and around bulging fore-arms exposed by a tight black t-shirt despite the evening chill. He watches their approach with the impassive patience of a predator who knows its prey can't escape.

THE SECOND MAN remains partially obscured by shadows, leaning against the car's hood with studied casualness, only the cherry glow of a cigarette occasionally illuminating a portion of his face.

"ABOUT TIME," the tattooed man calls, his voice a gravelly rumble that seems to vibrate in the narrow space between buildings. "Thought maybe you got lost in there, Reid."

"SHUT UP, JIM," Robert snaps, his refined accent slipping to reveal something harder beneath. "She's heavier than she looks."

JETTA'S MIND latches onto the name—Jim—a concrete detail to anchor herself as reality continues to warp around her. She tries again to call for help, to make any sound that might attract attention, but her voice emerges as nothing more than a slurred whisper that doesn't even reach the end of the alley.

JIM STEPS FORWARD, moonlight catching on a heavy silver ring as he cracks his knuckles with deliberate showmanship. Up close, Jetta can see his face—the broken nose that healed crooked, the scar bisecting one eyebrow, the small eyes set too close together. His gaze travels over her body with crude appreciation, lingering on her chest, her hips, her legs.

"NICE MERCHANDISE," he says, reaching out to touch her face.

JETTA JERKS HER HEAD AWAY, the sudden movement sending waves of nausea rolling through her stomach. Jim laughs, the sound utterly devoid of humour.

"FEISTY," he observes. "Those are always more fun."

"JUST HELP me get her in the car," Robert says, his voice tense with impatience. "We're too exposed here."

THE THIRD MAN pushes himself away from the car, dropping his cigarette and crushing it under his boot. "How much did you give her?" he asks, his face still partially hidden. "She's barely standing."

"ENOUGH," Robert replies tersely. "She won't remember anything tomorrow. Not that it matters."

THE CASUAL CERTAINTY in his voice sends ice sliding down Jetta's spine. This isn't their first time. The realisation crashes through her drugged haze—they've done this before, will do it again, have a system for it. The thought galvanises her remaining strength. She twists suddenly in Robert's grip, nearly breaking free as her desperation lends her muscles momentary coordination.

"HELP!" she tries to shout, but the word comes out garbled and weak. "Please... help..."

ROBERT CURSES, grabbing her by both arms now, his fingers digging into her flesh hard enough to leave marks. "Shut her up," he hisses to Jim.

THE BIG MAN moves with surprising speed for his size, one meaty hand clamping over Jetta's mouth while the other grips her jaw with bruising force. His palm smells of cigarettes and something metallic, the pressure of his fingers making it difficult to breathe through her nose.

"NOBODY CAN HEAR YOU, SWEETHEART," Jim says, his breath hot against her ear, reeking of tobacco and beer. "Just be a good girl now."

JETTA'S PHONE slips from her pocket during the struggle, clattering to the ground with a sound that seems impossibly loud in the confined space of the alley. All four of them freeze for a moment, eyes dropping to the device now lying screen-up on the dirty pavement, its display illuminating with an incoming text message—Brandi's name briefly visible before the screen darkens again.

. . .

"GET THAT," Robert snaps at the third man, who bends to retrieve the phone.

JETTA TRIES TO KICK OUT, to stomp on the man's hand as he reaches for her phone, but her coordination fails her again. Her leg moves in slow motion, missing its target entirely and throwing her further off-balance. Jim's grip tightens painfully as she sways.

"STOP THRASHING," he growls, giving her a shake that makes her teeth click together. "Unless you want me to make you stop."

THE THIRD MAN pockets her phone, then moves to open the car's rear door. The interior light briefly illuminates an empty backseat with dark upholstery, the floor covered with what looks like plastic sheeting. The sight sends a fresh wave of terror through Jetta's system, momentarily burning through the drug's effects.

"NO," she manages with sudden clarity, the word muffled against Jim's palm but distinctly recognisable.

THE MEN LAUGH—THREE different versions of the same cruel sound. Robert's is controlled and quiet, Jim's a barking explosion, the third man's a nasal snicker.

"SHE SAID NO," Jim mocks, his voice falsetto in crude imitation. "Guess we should just let her go then, huh?" He returns to his normal register, voice dropping to a threatening rumble. "Doesn't work that way, sweetheart."

"GET HER IN THE CAR," Robert orders, glancing toward the mouth of the alley with increasing nervousness. "We've been here too long."

THEY BEGIN MOVING her toward the open door, her feet dragging against the pavement in weak resistance. The world tilts and spins around her, buildings leaning in at impossible angles, shadows stretching into grotesque shapes that seem to reach for her with grasping fingers. Through the chemical haze, one thought burns with terrible clarity: if they get her into that car, she won't be coming back out.

"THINK we'll have time to have some fun before delivery?" Jim asks, his voice thick with anticipation as they maneuver her toward the waiting vehicle.

"THAT WASN'T THE ARRANGEMENT," Robert replies sharply. "She's merchandise, not a party favour."

"MIGHT AS WELL SAMPLE THE GOODS," the third man chimes in, his features coming into view as he leans forward— thin lips stretched in a smile that doesn't reach his flat eyes. "Not like she'll remember anyway."

THEY DISCUSS her fate as if she isn't present, as if she's already been reduced to an object rather than a person. Jetta feels darkness pressing in at the edges of her vision, her consciousness threatening to slip away entirely. She fights to stay awake, knowing that surrendering to the drug now means surrendering everything.

As they reach the car, Robert's grip shifts to her wrist, twisting her arm behind her back to force her compliance. The pain cuts through the fog momentarily, bringing a gasp that Jim's hand quickly smothers. The car door yawns open before her like a mouth, waiting to swallow her whole.

"Let her go." The command cuts through the night air like a blade, precise and uncompromising. Jetta's drugged mind struggles to process the familiar voice, to connect it to a name, a face, a memory. She manages to turn her head just enough to see Ethan standing at the mouth of the alley, his silhouette backlit by distant street lamps. Even through her fractured perception, she registers the change in his posture—gone is the casual confidence of the social setting, replaced by something coiled and deadly, a predator recognising other predators in his territory.

The three men freeze, their grips on Jetta momentarily slackening in surprise. Robert recovers first, his features rearranging into a mask of concerned innocence so quickly that if Jetta weren't feeling his bruising grip on her wrist, she might question her own understanding of the situation.

"Just helping a friend who had too much to drink," Robert calls, his voice smooth with practised sincerity. "She's pretty wasted. We're giving her a ride home."

．．．

ETHAN TAKES three measured steps forward, each placement of his feet deliberate, eating up distance without appearing rushed. His breathing remains even, controlled, his gaze moving between the three men with quick assessment before returning to Jetta's face.

"THAT'S NOT what it looks like," he says, voice deceptively conversational despite the tension vibrating beneath its surface. "It looks like three men forcing a drugged woman into a car with plastic sheeting on the floor."

JIM SHIFTS HIS WEIGHT, his massive frame angling to present a more intimidating profile. His hand drops from Jetta's mouth, moving to his side where it hovers near his waistband. "Mind your own business, man," he growls. "Walk away while you still can."

JETTA TRIES to form Ethan's name, to call out to him, but her tongue refuses to cooperate. What emerges is a slurred approximation that bears little resemblance to any word at all. Even this small effort depletes her remaining energy, leaving her sagging between Robert and Jim, her legs barely supporting her weight.

"SHE DOESN'T SEEM able to consent to anything right now," Ethan observes, continuing his slow advance. His eyes never leave the three men, but his words are directed to Jetta. "How much did they give you? Can you walk?"

．．．

ROBERT'S SMILE hardens at the edges. "Look, this is a misunderstanding. Our friend just needs to sleep it off. We've got this handled."

"I DON'T THINK she's your friend," Ethan replies, now close enough that Jetta can make out his expression even through her blurred vision. His face seems carved from stone, all trace of the earlier argument erased, replaced by cold focus. "Last chance. Let her go."

THE THIRD MAN, who has remained partially in shadow until now, reaches into his jacket. The movement is subtle but not subtle enough. Ethan notices immediately, his attention sharpening.

"I WOULDN'T," he advises, his tone making it clear this isn't a suggestion.

"FUCK THIS," Jim spits, releasing Jetta entirely and lunging toward Ethan with surprising speed for his size, meaty fists raised.

WHAT HAPPENS NEXT UNFOLDS with such precision that Jetta's drugged mind struggles to process the sequence. Ethan sidesteps Jim's charge with minimal movement, pivoting on one foot while his hand strikes out—not a wild punch but a targeted jab to Jim's throat. The big man stumbles, choking, his momentum carrying him forward as Ethan's elbow connects with the back of his head in a sharp, controlled strike.

· · ·

JIM CRASHES TO ONE KNEE, gasping for air. Before he can recover, Ethan has already turned his attention to the third man, who has produced a small switchblade that gleams dully in the low light.

"STAY BACK!" the man warns, slashing the knife through the air between them in wild arcs that betray his inexperience.

ETHAN DOESN'T RESPOND VERBALLY. His breathing remains measured, almost meditative, as he watches the knife's movement with clinical detachment. When the man lunges forward, Ethan moves with economical grace—a slight shift of weight, a deflection with his forearm that redirects the blade harmlessly past his ribs, followed by a devastating kick to the man's knee. Bone cracks with audible finality. The man screams, the knife clattering to the ground as he collapses.

ROBERT RELEASES JETTA'S WRIST, shoving her roughly against the car as he reaches into his jacket. Before his hand can emerge with whatever weapon he's concealed there, Ethan closes the distance between them in two fluid strides. His fist connects with Robert's solar plexus—not a wild haymaker but a precision strike that forces all air from Robert's lungs in a pained whoosh. As Robert doubles over, Ethan's knee rises to meet his descending face. The crack of cartilage signals a broken nose, blood immediately streaming down Robert's once-perfect features.

THROUGHOUT THE VIOLENCE, Ethan's expression barely changes. There is no rage, no enjoyment, just focused intention behind each movement. His breathing remains controlled, his actions neither hurried nor delayed but executed with perfect timing. This isn't the frenzied fighting of someone fueled by adrenaline; it's the calculated violence of professional training.

JETTA SLIDES down the side of the car as her legs finally give out, her body surrendering to gravity now that Robert's grip no longer holds her upright. Through increasingly fractured perception, she watches as Jim recovers enough to pull a knife from his boot—larger than the previous blade, with a serrated edge that catches what little light penetrates the alley.

"GONNA CUT YOU," Jim rasps, his voice hoarse from the earlier strike to his throat. He circles Ethan warily now, knife extended, more respect in his posture than before.

ETHAN'S FOCUS narrows to the blade, his body adjusting subtly to maintain optimal distance. When Jim slashes forward, Ethan doesn't retreat. Instead, he steps into the attack, his left hand capturing Jim's wrist while his right delivers a short, savage strike to the elbow joint. The crack is audible even over Jim's howl of pain. The knife drops from suddenly nerveless fingers as Jim's wrist bends at an angle nature never intended.

THE THIRD MAN has already begun crawling toward the mouth of the alley, dragging his injured leg behind him, whimpering with each movement. Robert, blood streaming from his nose and staining his expensive shirt, scrambles backward toward the car door, fumbling with the handle.

. . .

"Keys!" he shouts to Jim, who has collapsed to his knees, cradling his broken wrist against his chest.

Jim manages to extract the car keys from his pocket with his uninjured hand, tossing them to Robert with a pained grunt. Ethan makes no move to stop the exchange, his attention divided between ensuring the men's retreat and checking on Jetta's condition with quick glances.

Robert flings himself into the driver's seat, starting the engine with trembling hands. Jim limps around to the passenger side, casting one hate-filled glance back at Ethan before wrenching the door open and falling inside. The car lurches forward before Jim's door is fully closed, tires squealing against the pavement as Robert accelerates toward the alley's exit, narrowly missing the crawling third man.

Ethan steps out of the vehicle's path, his body still poised for further conflict even as the immediate threat recedes. He watches the car's taillights disappear around the corner, memorising the license plate with practised efficiency. Only when the sound of the engine has faded does he fully turn his attention to Jetta, crouching beside her slumped form against the wall.

His breathing, which remained measured even during the height of combat, finally quickens slightly as concern replaces tactical focus. Blood from the confrontation spatters his knuckles and the sleeve of his shirt, but his movements are gentle as he reaches toward her face.

. . .

"JETTA," he says, her name emerging softer than any word she's heard from him since his return. "Can you hear me?"

THE WORLD FRACTURES and reforms around Jetta in jagged pieces that refuse to fit together properly. Ethan's face hovers above her, his features sharpening briefly into focus before dissolving again like sugar in hot water. His hand cups her cheek, turning her face gently toward the dim light filtering into the alley. She feels the rough texture of his palm against her skin, calluses scraping softly as his thumb brushes her cheekbone with unexpected tenderness. "Jetta, focus on me," he says, his voice anchoring her temporarily in the swirling chaos of her consciousness. "Can you hear me? Nod if you can understand what I'm saying."

SHE MANAGES a slight movement of her head, the effort monumental against the heaviness that seems to press down on her from all sides. His fingers move to her wrist, pressing against the pulse point with practised precision. The touch is so different from Robert's bruising grip that tears spring to her eyes, though she can't articulate why even to herself.

"YOUR HEART'S RACING," Ethan murmurs, his brow furrowed with concern. He shifts to check her pupils, gently lifting one eyelid and then the other. "Pupils dilated. Skin clammy." His assessment continues with clinical efficiency despite the worry evident in his expression. "Jetta, I think they gave you GHB or Rohypnol. Maybe ketamine. I need to get you to a hospital."

. . .

She tries to respond, but her tongue still feels three sizes too large, her mouth dry as desert sand. What emerges is a slurred sound that resembles no word in any language. Frustration burns through the chemical haze—she wants to thank him, to ask why he followed her, to understand how they went from screaming at each other to this moment of unexpected care.

Ethan seems to read some of this in her expression. "I saw you at the bar with that guy," he explains, his fingers now pressed against the side of her neck, monitoring her pulse with the focus of someone who has done this before. "Something felt wrong. The way he watched you, not your face but everything else. The way he positioned himself between you and the exit." His jaw tightens briefly. "I've seen that predatory assessment before, in places much worse than nightclubs."

His phone appears in his hand, the screen illuminating his face from below as he dials. "This is Ethan Cole," he says when the call connects, his voice shifting into a tone of calm authority that cuts through the background noise of the city. "I'm in the alley behind Pulse nightclub with a woman who's been drugged. Likely GHB. She's conscious but severely impaired. Three male assailants fled the scene in a dark sedan, license plate Sierra-Victor-Romeo-eight-four-two." He provides additional details with crisp precision—cross streets, Jetta's approximate weight, the time that has passed since she was drugged.

While speaking, he shrugs out of his jacket with a smooth one-armed movement, wrapping it around her shoulders without interrupting his flow of information. The fabric carries his warmth and scent—clean laundry, faint cologne, and now the metallic hint of blood from the fight. It settles around her like armour, unexpectedly comforting despite its owner.

"THEY'RE SENDING AN AMBULANCE," he tells her after ending the call, his focus returning fully to her face. "Should be here in less than five minutes." His hand returns to her cheek, the gesture seemingly unconscious as he checks her responsiveness. "I need you to stay awake, okay? No sleeping until the doctors clear you."

JETTA FEELS the pull of unconsciousness tugging at the edges of her awareness, a seductive darkness promising relief from the confusion and fear. It would be so easy to surrender to it, to slip away from this fractured reality where nothing makes sense—especially not Ethan Cole kneeling beside her with concern etched into the lines of his face.

"HEY, NO," Ethan says sharply, noticing her eyelids drooping. He shifts to sit beside her against the wall, his arm around her shoulders to keep her upright. "Stay with me. Talk to me. What's the name of your bookshop?"

THE QUESTION PENETRATES THE FOG, connecting to something concrete she can grasp. "B-bound... Together," she manages, the words slurred but recognisable.

. . .

"Good," he encourages, his voice warming with approval. "Who's your business partner?"

"Brandi," she whispers, the name emerging more clearly than anything else she's said since being drugged.

Ethan nods, reaching for his phone again with his free hand. "I should let her know what's happening," he says, composing a text message one-handed while maintaining his supportive hold on her. "She and Owen are probably wondering where you are."

The distant wail of sirens penetrates the alley, growing steadily louder. Ethan's attention remains fixed on Jetta, his eyes constantly assessing her condition. She notices for the first time the state of his hands—knuckles raw and bloodied from the fight, yet so gentle as they check her pulse again, adjust his jacket around her shoulders, brush hair from her face with careful fingers.

"Why did you... follow me?" she asks, the question requiring immense effort to formulate.

Something complex crosses his expression— regret, perhaps, or something adjacent to it. "We were arguing about me interfering with your night," he says with a mirthless laugh. "Seemed wrong to stop just when it actually mattered."

. . .

THIS ISN'T the whole truth—she can see it in the way his eyes shift slightly away from hers—but whatever remains unsaid will have to wait. The effort of focusing depletes her limited reserves, sending her head lolling against his shoulder.

"STAY AWAKE," he reminds her, the command firm but not harsh. His fingers brush her cheek again, leaving trails of warmth against her clammy skin. "Tell me about the last book you read. Just one sentence. You can do that."

SHE STRUGGLES TO COMPLY, grasping for coherent thought among the fragments of her drugged mind. "Woman... lighthouse... disappears," she manages, each word a victory against the chemical trying to shut down her consciousness.

"GOOD ENOUGH," Ethan says, his approval evident in the slight squeeze of his arm around her shoulders. "Sounds intriguing. You'll have to tell me more when you're feeling better."

THE ASSUMPTION of future conversation hangs between them—a bridge extending from this moment of crisis toward something neither could have imagined hours earlier. Jetta's head rests against the solid warmth of his shoulder, his heartbeat steady beneath her ear while hers continues its erratic fluttering. Despite everything—their history, their antagonism, the violence she just witnessed—she feels safe within the circle of his arm.

. . .

FLASHING lights paint the alley entrance in strobes of red and blue. The ambulance has arrived, its siren cutting off abruptly and leaving a ringing silence in its wake. Footsteps approach at a run, voices calling out with professional urgency. Ethan raises his free hand to signal their location without disturbing Jetta's position against him.

TWO PARAMEDICS APPEAR, equipment bags in hand, their movements quick but controlled as they crouch beside Jetta. Questions fly—what drug, how long ago, any allergies, any other injuries. Ethan answers each with precision, his voice rumbling through his chest against her ear.

"I FOUND her being forced into a car by three men," he explains, shifting slightly to give the paramedics better access while maintaining his supporting arm around her. "Based on her symptoms and the situation, I suspect GHB, possibly mixed with something else. Administered approximately thirty to forty minutes ago in a drink."

THE FEMALE PARAMEDIC NODS, checking Jetta's pupils with a penlight while her partner prepares an IV. "You did the right thing keeping her conscious," she says to Ethan. "We'll take it from here."

"I'M COMING WITH HER," Ethan states, not a question but a decision already made. His blood-spattered knuckles tighten slightly against Jetta's shoulder, an unconscious gesture of protectiveness.

. . .

THE PARAMEDICS EXCHANGE A GLANCE, noting his determined expression and the state of his hands. "Are you family?" the male paramedic asks, though his tone suggests he already knows the answer.

"No," Ethan admits, then adds with surprising conviction, "but I'm all she has right now."

THEY HELP JETTA ONTO A STRETCHER, her limbs still uncooperative, her consciousness fading in and out like a radio signal caught between stations. Ethan's jacket remains around her shoulders, its weight a tangible reminder of his protection. As they secure her to the stretcher, Ethan steps back only as far as necessary, his eyes never leaving her face.

"SIR, YOUR HANDS NEED ATTENTION TOO," the female paramedic points out, nodding toward his bloodied knuckles.

"LATER," he dismisses, already moving to follow as they lift the stretcher. "They can look at them at the hospital after she's taken care of."

As THEY WHEEL her toward the ambulance, Jetta manages to turn her head enough to keep Ethan in her narrowing field of vision. Their eyes meet, and something passes between them—not forgiveness exactly, not yet, but recognition. Recognition that the person who once caused her greatest pain has now prevented something far worse. Recognition that people can be, as he said during their argument, both villain and victim in different measures, at different times.

. . .

HER LAST COHERENT thought before the drug pulls her under completely is the realisation that her history with Ethan Cole isn't finished after all. It's merely entering a chapter neither of them could have anticipated.

CHAPTER 8

Hospital Vigil

FLUORESCENT LIGHTS ASSAULT Jetta's eyes as consciousness returns in stuttering fragments. The ceiling above her moves—no, she's moving, the gurney rolling beneath her as masked figures guide it through double doors into a space that smells sharply of antiseptic and something metallic. Each sound arrives with painful clarity—wheels squeaking against linoleum, monitors beeping, voices calling out medical terms she can't quite grasp. Her limbs feel weighted, disconnected from her commands, and her thoughts scatter like marbles dropped on a hard floor whenever she tries to collect them.

"FEMALE, MID-TWENTIES, SUSPECTED GHB INTOXICATION." A male voice recites above her. "Found in the alley behind Pulse. Altered mental status, tachycardic on scene."

"BAY THREE IS PREPPED." A woman's voice, brisk and

authoritative, cuts through the haze. "Get a tox screen and basic metabolic panel. Start an IV, normal saline, wide open."

Jetta tries to turn her head toward the voice, but the movement sends the room spinning. Her eyelids flutter against the harsh overhead lights that seem to drill directly into her brain. Shadows move around her—people in scrubs and white coats, their faces blurring whenever she tries to focus.

"I'm Dr. Sirindi," the authoritative voice materialises beside her as a woman in a white coat leans into Jetta's field of vision. Her face is lined with efficiency, dark eyes sharp behind slim reading glasses that have slipped halfway down her nose. "You're at Mercy Hospital. Do you know your name?"

Jetta tries to answer, but her tongue feels swollen, uncooperative. "J-Jetta," she finally manages, the word slurred and barely recognisable to her own ears.

"Good, Jetta. You've been drugged," Dr. Sirindi says, her directness somehow comforting in its lack of sugar-coating. She shines a penlight into Jetta's eyes, examining the pupillary response with clinical precision. "Your friend brought you in. We're going to take care of you."

Friend? The word registers dimly as Jetta tries to place who might have—

. . .

"How is she?" A deep voice cuts through the medical chatter, and despite her disorientation, she recognises it immediately. Ethan.

Memories surface like air bubbles rising through murky water—the club, the drink, Robert's hand on her elbow, the alley, and then Ethan appearing like some avenging figure, his movements precise and devastating as he confronted her attackers.

"Sir, you need to step back and let us work," Dr. Sirindi responds without looking up from where she's examining Jetta's arms for injection sites or injuries.

"I'm staying." The words aren't a request. Through the forest of medical personnel around her bed, Jetta glimpses Ethan pacing at the periphery of the treatment bay. His knuckles are raw and bloodied, his shirt spattered with dark stains. He flexes his hands repeatedly, wincing slightly at the movement, his eyes never leaving her for more than a few seconds.

A nurse with gentle hands attaches sticky pads to Jetta's chest beneath her shirt, connecting them to wires that lead to a monitor. Its rhythmic beeping fills the space—too fast, she realises dimly, matching the fluttering panic in her chest as fragments of the night rearrange themselves in her mind.

"Need access." Another nurse appears at her side, tying a rubber tourniquet around Jetta's upper arm. The pinch of a needle follows, then the strange pressure of an IV catheter sliding into her vein. "Got it. Drawing labs now."

DR. SIRINDI MOVES with practised efficiency, her hands never hesitating as she conducts her examination. "Respiratory rate normal. Pulse elevated but regular. Skin clammy. Moderate mydriasis." She directs her commands to the surrounding staff while maintaining an even, professional tone. "Let's get that blood to the lab stat. Full tox screen, comprehensive metabolic panel, and add a CBC with diff."

JETTA'S LIMBS begin to tremble—a fine, uncontrollable shaking that starts in her fingers and spreads through her body. The sensation is distant, as if happening to someone else, but the tremors intensify until her teeth chatter. A nurse notices immediately, pulling a warmed blanket from a nearby cabinet and laying it over her.

"IS SHE GOING TO BE OKAY?" Ethan's voice again, closer now, tension evident in every syllable.

DR. SIRINDI finally acknowledges him directly, turning to where he hovers at the foot of the bed. "Are you family?"

"No, I—" He hesitates, then straightens his shoulders. "I found her. Stopped the men who drugged her."

THE DOCTOR'S eyes flick to his bloodied knuckles, then back

to his face, her expression revealing nothing. "Your hands need attention."

"LATER." He dismisses this with a sharp gesture. "What about Jetta?"

JETTA WATCHES this exchange through half-lidded eyes, strangely moved by the concern etched into Ethan's features. His face, usually composed into careful neutrality or deliberate charm, now displays raw worry that he makes no effort to conceal. It's an expression she's never seen on him before—one she would never have believed possible from the man who once orchestrated her worst humiliation.

"BASED on her symptoms and the situation you described, this is consistent with GHB or possibly Rohypnol," Dr. Sirindi explains, her tone clipped and professional. "We're running tests to confirm exactly what's in her system. She'll need monitoring overnight to ensure her respiratory function remains stable as the drug metabolises."

ETHAN NODS, absorbing this information with the focus of someone accustomed to assessing threats and calculating responses. "What can I do?"

"NOTHING RIGHT NOW," Dr. Sirindi replies, but something in Ethan's expression—perhaps the same intensity that Jetta finds herself unable to look away from—causes her to add, "But it's good she's not alone. These cases are..." She doesn't finish the sentence, doesn't need to.

THE IMPLICATIONS of what might have happened without Ethan's intervention hover in the air, unspoken but understood by everyone in the room. Jetta feels a wave of nausea rise through her chest, and she turns her head to the side with a small sound of distress. A nurse is there immediately with a basin, supporting her as she dry heaves painfully.

"THAT'S THE DRUG," Dr. Sirindi explains, making a note on her tablet. "Nausea is common as it begins to wear off." She turns to a nurse. "Let's get 4 mg of ondansetron IV."

AS THE MEDICAL team continues their work, Jetta becomes aware of Ethan moving closer to the head of her bed. When she manages to focus on him again, she notices something unexpected—beneath the concern, beneath the tension in his jaw and the blood on his knuckles, there's a vulnerability in his eyes that seems completely at odds with the controlled violence she witnessed in the alley.

HER ATTEMPT TO speak results in a dry, cracked sound. Immediately, a nurse offers her small ice chips in a plastic spoon. The cold melting against her tongue provides momentary relief from the terrible dryness in her mouth.

"BETTER?" Ethan asks, his voice dropping to a gentleness that seems to surprise even him. He clears his throat, as if embarrassed by the softness, but doesn't retreat or correct himself.

. . .

JETTA MANAGES A SLIGHT NOD, overwhelmed by the strangeness of finding comfort in his presence. The man she's hated for a decade stands guard beside her bed, his bloodied hands testament to the protection he provided without hesitation. The contradiction is too much for her drug-addled mind to process, so she simply accepts it as part of the surreal quality of the night.

"THE MEDICATION SHOULD HELP with the nausea," Dr. Sirindi says, returning to check the monitor readings. "Your vitals are stabilising. That's a good sign." She turns to Ethan. "The police will want a statement. They're on their way."

"I'LL BE HERE," he replies, the simple statement carrying weight beyond its three syllables. His eyes meet Jetta's again, and something passes between them—not quite understanding, not forgiveness, but a recognition of changed circumstances, of shifted ground beneath the foundation of their mutual antagonism.

THE TREMBLING in Jetta's limbs gradually lessens as whatever the nurse added to her IV takes effect. The nausea recedes, leaving exhaustion in its wake. Her eyelids grow heavy, but each time they drift closed, the memory of being pulled toward that waiting car jerks her back to wakefulness.

ETHAN NOTICES, his brow furrowing. "You're safe," he says quietly, for her ears alone. "I'm not going anywhere."

. . .

THE PROMISE SETTLES over her like another blanket, unexpected in its comfort. As the medical team continues their efficient work around her, Jetta finds herself watching Ethan through increasingly heavy eyelids. The harsh fluorescent lights illuminate angles of his face she's never properly noticed before—not the arrogant boy who humiliated her, not the antagonistic man from the club, but someone altogether different. Someone who, when it mattered most, became exactly what she needed.

THIS REALISATION FOLLOWS her as she drifts into an uneasy sleep, the steady beeping of monitors and the solid presence of her unlikely protector keeping the worst of the fear at bay.

JETTA SURFACES from a fitful sleep to the sound of Brandi's voice, high and taut with worry. "Oh my god, Jetta!" The familiar tone cuts through the medical haze that's kept her drifting between consciousness and something adjacent to sleep since arriving at the hospital. Her eyelids feel weighted as she forces them open, the treatment bay now dimmer than before—someone has mercifully adjusted the overhead lights. Brandi's face swims into focus, mascara smudged beneath red-rimmed eyes, blonde hair escaping its usual neat ponytail.

"YOU'RE HERE," Jetta manages, her voice still raspy but more recognisable than before. The words no longer feel trapped behind an uncooperative tongue, though her mouth remains desert-dry.

. . .

"OF COURSE I'M HERE." Brandi's hand finds hers, warm fingers wrapping around Jetta's cold ones with gentle pressure. The contact feels grounding, a tether to normalcy amid the clinical strangeness of the ER. "Ethan texted us. We came as soon as we could."

JETTA'S GAZE shifts beyond Brandi to where Owen stands near the foot of the bed, his normally relaxed posture replaced by something stiff and uncomfortable. His easy smile is nowhere to be seen, his features drawn with an unfamiliar solemnity that makes him look older, less boyish. He shifts his weight from one foot to the other, hands shoved deep in his pockets as if he doesn't trust what they might do if left unoccupied.

"HEY," he says when he notices her looking at him. The single syllable carries a weight of discomfort. "How are you feeling?"

BEFORE SHE CAN ANSWER, Brandi interjects, "The doctor said you were drugged. GHB. That they were trying to—" Her voice catches, unable to complete the sentence.

THE ANTISEPTIC SMELL of the hospital seems to intensify as the reality of what nearly happened settles more firmly in Jetta's consciousness. The trembling returns to her hands, and Brandi tightens her grip in response.

"WHERE'S ETHAN?" Jetta asks, surprised by her own question. She scans the treatment bay, momentarily alarmed by his absence until she spots him standing just outside the curtained area, speaking with a uniformed police officer. Even from this distance, she can see the rigid set of his shoulders, the controlled precision of his gestures as he describes something to the officer who nods and takes notes.

"HE HASN'T LEFT since they brought you in," Brandi says, following her gaze. Something in her tone—a careful neutrality that doesn't quite mask her curiosity—makes Jetta wonder what Ethan told them, how much they know about the complicated history that makes his protective presence here so unexpected.

OWEN APPROACHES THE BED, finally extracting his hands from his pockets to rest one hesitantly on the metal railing. "Ethan said—" he begins, then stops, swallowing hard. "He said if he hadn't followed you, these guys would have—" Like Brandi, he can't seem to finish the thought.

THE MONITOR beside Jetta's bed registers her increased heart rate with faster beeping. A nurse appears almost immediately, checking the readout before adjusting something in her IV line. "Try to stay calm," she advises before slipping away again, the curtain swishing closed behind her.

ETHAN RETURNS, the police officer visible through the gap in the curtain as he continues down the corridor. The contrast between the bustling activity in the hallway and the tense quiet of the treatment bay creates a strange sense of isolation, as if they exist in a bubble separate from the ordinary emergencies unfolding around them.

.   .   .

"THEY'VE GOT THE LICENSE PLATE," Ethan reports, his voice steady though the tightness around his eyes betrays his tension. "And descriptions. They're putting out an alert."

"TELL THEM WHAT HAPPENED," Brandi says, turning to Ethan with an expression Jetta can't quite read. "Everything."

ETHAN'S EYES meet Jetta's briefly, seeking permission. When she gives a small nod, he addresses all of them, his tone shifting into something more formal, more measured—the voice of someone giving an official report rather than recounting a personal experience.

"THREE MEN TARGETED Jetta at the club. The primary one approached her at the bar after we—" he hesitates, glancing at Jetta again, "—after our disagreement. I saw him slip something into her drink when she looked away. Classic predator tactics—isolated her, drugged her, then guided her toward the exit once the effects began."

THE CLINICAL PRECISION of his description should make it easier to hear, but somehow does the opposite. Jetta closes her eyes briefly, fragments of memory aligning with his words —Robert's manicured hand near her glass, the strange warmth spreading through her limbs, the world tilting as he steered her toward the door.

"I FOLLOWED THEM OUTSIDE," Ethan continues. "They had a car waiting in the alley. Three men total. The one from the bar, plus two accomplices. They were trying to force her into the vehicle when I intervened." The passive voice doesn't quite conceal what that intervention entailed, especially with his still-raw knuckles on display.

"THEY RAN THE TESTS," Jetta adds, her voice stronger now. "Dr. Sirindi says it was definitely GHB. They've seen an increase in cases recently."

BRANDI'S FINGERS tighten around hers again, a tremor passing between them. "If Ethan hadn't been there..."

"BUT HE WAS," Jetta says quickly, unable to face the alternative even hypothetically.

BRANDI RISES SUDDENLY, crossing to where Ethan stands. Before he can react, she wraps her arms around him in a fierce hug that visibly startles him. His hands hover awkwardly for a moment before settling lightly on her back, his expression a complex mixture of discomfort and something more vulnerable.

"THANK YOU," Brandi says, her voice muffled against his chest. "Thank you for saving her. I don't know what would have happened if you hadn't been there."

ETHAN'S EYES find Jetta's over Brandi's shoulder, something unreadable passing through them. "I was just in the right place," he says, the modesty at odds with the intensity of his gaze.

OWEN STEPS forward as Brandi releases Ethan, extending his hand. "I should have noticed something was wrong," he says, voice rough with emotion. "I'm sorry I wasn't paying attention."

ETHAN ACCEPTS THE HANDSHAKE, his bloodied knuckles stark against Owen's unmarked skin. "You couldn't have known," he replies, though the tightness around his mouth suggests he might not entirely believe this absolution.

THE TWO MEN move toward the corner of the room, their conversation dropping to murmurs as Owen asks more detailed questions about the attackers. Jetta catches fragments —descriptions of the men, the car, what the police said about the chances of apprehending them.

BRANDI RETURNS TO HER SIDE, brushing hair from Jetta's forehead with gentle fingers. "How are you really?" she asks quietly. "And don't say 'fine' because I know that's not true."

JETTA CONSIDERS THE QUESTION, taking inventory of her physical and emotional state. The nausea has mostly subsided, replaced by a bone-deep exhaustion. Her thoughts are clearer than before but still fragmented at the edges, like a puzzle with missing pieces. The fear remains, a cold knot in her stomach that tightens whenever she remembers the car waiting in the alley, the plastic sheeting on its floor.

. . .

"I'M HERE," she finally says, choosing the simplest truth. "I'm still here."

BRANDI NODS, understanding the weight behind those words. "The doctor says they want to keep you overnight for observation, but you should be able to go home tomorrow if everything stays stable."

"WILL YOU STAY?" Jetta asks, hating the vulnerability in the question but unable to suppress it.

"OF COURSE. Wild horses couldn't drag me away." Brandi squeezes her hand again. "And I don't think Ethan's planning to leave either. He was like a sentinel when we got here—practically interrogated us before letting us near you."

THIS IMAGE—ETHAN standing guard, protecting her even from her friends until he was certain of their intentions—sends an unexpected warmth through Jetta's chest. She glances toward the corner where he stands with Owen, his back to the wall, positioned to see both the bed and the entrance to the treatment bay. Even in conversation, his attention periodically shifts to check her status; his awareness of his surroundings never entirely disappearing.

"IT'S STRANGE," Brandi says, following Jetta's gaze. "I've never seen him like this. Owen says he gets intense sometimes, but this is different."

. . .

JETTA NODS, understanding exactly what Brandi means. This Ethan—protective, vigilant, quietly concerned—bears little resemblance to either the cruel teenager from her past or the antagonistic man from recent weeks. It's as if crisis has stripped away those versions, revealing something more essential beneath.

"HE SAVED ME," Jetta whispers, the simple statement containing complexities she's not yet ready to examine. "He could have walked away after our fight, but he didn't."

BRANDI'S EXPRESSION softens with something adjacent to hope. "Maybe some good can come from this awful night," she says carefully, watching Jetta's face for a reaction. "Not that I'd ever wish this on you, but maybe it's a chance to—"

"LET'S not get ahead of ourselves," Jetta interrupts, though without the sharpness such a suggestion might have provoked days ago. "One trauma at a time."

THE CORNERS of Brandi's mouth lift slightly at this hint of Jetta's usual dry humour returning. In the periphery of the treatment bay, beyond the bubble of their quiet conversation, the hospital continues its relentless rhythm—monitors beeping, staff calling to each other, gurneys wheeling past the curtained entrance. The contrast between this ordinary medical chaos and the extraordinary night they've experienced creates a sense of unreality that Jetta suspects will linger long after the drugs have left her system.

. . .

As she drifts back toward sleep, the voices of her friends merging into a comforting murmur around her, one thought remains clear: nothing between her and Ethan will ever be the same again. Whether that's healing or simply a different kind of wound remains to be seen.

~

The hospital night stretches into unfamiliar hours— that strange liminal time when corridors empty of all but the most essential personnel and sounds become muted echoes of daytime urgency. Jetta wakes to this hushed world, her mind clearer now as the drug continues its slow exodus from her system. The treatment bay is dimly lit, Brandi asleep in a chair pulled close to the bed, her hand still loosely holding Jetta's even in slumber. Owen is nowhere to be seen—bathroom, perhaps, or seeking coffee from some vending machine in the depths of the building. It's Ethan who commands her attention, standing just outside the curtained entrance, his profile visible as he speaks with a uniformed police officer in the corridor.

The harsh overhead lighting of the hallway casts half his face in sharp relief, the other half in shadow—a visual metaphor so on-the-nose that Jetta might find it amusing under different circumstances. He stands with his back straight, shoulders squared, feet planted slightly apart in a stance that suggests military training rather than civilian habit. His hands, still unbandaged despite several offers from nurses to treat his raw knuckles, gesture with precise economy as he describes something to the officer, who nods and makes notes on a small pad.

. . .

THERE'S nothing of the antagonistic man from the club in his demeanour now, no trace of the cruel teenager from her memories. This version of Ethan moves with controlled purpose, speaks with measured authority, watches the corridor with the hypervigilance of someone accustomed to identifying threats before they materialise. His eyes periodically scan the hallway, returning to check on her between sentences, maintaining awareness of all potential approaches to her bed.

THE OFFICER ASKS something that makes Ethan's jaw tighten, a muscle flexing beneath the skin in that tell she'd noticed years ago. His response is too quiet to hear, but his body language shifts subtly—shoulders tensing, stance widening slightly, as if physically bracing against an unpleasant memory or thought. The officer writes something down, nods, and extends a hand, which Ethan shakes briefly before turning back toward the treatment bay.

JETTA DOESN'T PRETEND to be asleep. Their eyes meet as he parts the curtain, and something passes between them—a current of understanding that transcends their complicated history. He pauses, momentarily caught in that silent exchange, before approaching her bed with quiet steps that suggest consideration for Brandi's sleeping form.

"YOU'RE AWAKE," he says, his voice pitched low. It's not a question but an acknowledgment, his eyes searching her face with an intensity that might be uncomfortable if she weren't looking at him with equal focus.

. . .

"MORE OR LESS," she replies, her voice steadier than earlier but still rough around the edges. "The room has stopped spinning, at least."

HE NODS, accepting this as the improvement it is. "Doctor says the worst is over. The drug should be mostly metabolised by morning."

THEY FALL SILENT, the beeping monitors and Brandi's soft breathing the only sounds in their small enclosure. The quiet stretches between them, not uncomfortable but weighted with unspoken thoughts. Jetta studies his face in the dim light—the shadows beneath his eyes suggesting exhaustion, the lingering tension in his jaw, the careful neutrality of his expression that doesn't quite mask his concern.

"YOU SAVED ME," she finally whispers, the words emerging with an honesty that surprises even her.

ETHAN SHIFTS HIS WEIGHT, discomfort flashing across his features at the naked gratitude in her voice. "Anyone would have done the same," he replies, gaze dropping momentarily to his raw knuckles.

JETTA SHAKES HER HEAD, the movement no longer sending the room into a tailspin. "Not anyone," she counters with quiet certainty. "You." She hesitates, then adds, "Even after everything between us. Even after our fight at the club. You still followed me. Still protected me."

· · ·

HE LOOKS up sharply at this, something fierce and unexpectedly vulnerable crossing his expression. "I would never—" he begins, then stops, recalibrating. "Whatever our history, Jetta, I would never let someone hurt you like that. Never."

THE VEHEMENCE in his voice sends a shiver through her that has nothing to do with the hospital's aggressive air conditioning. She believes him—not just about tonight, but in some larger sense she's not yet ready to fully examine.

WITHOUT CONSCIOUS DECISION, she reaches for his hand, surprising them both. His fingers are warm against hers, rough with calluses that speak of a life very different from the privileged boy she once knew. He freezes at the contact, his eyes widening slightly before his hand turns to hold hers with careful pressure, mindful of the IV line taped to her skin.

"THANK YOU," she says simply, the words insufficient but necessary.

HE NODS ONCE, accepting what she offers without pushing for more—a restraint that seems characteristic of this new Ethan she's discovering. His thumb brushes lightly over her knuckles, the gesture so gentle compared to the controlled violence she witnessed in the alley that it creates a cognitive dissonance she can't quite reconcile.

THE CURTAIN PARTS AGAIN, revealing Dr. Sirindi, her white coat slightly rumpled after hours on shift, but her movements no less precise for the late hour. She takes in the tableau before her—Jetta and Ethan's clasped hands, Brandi sleeping in the chair—with a flicker of understanding in her tired eyes before her professional mask returns.

"GOOD TO SEE YOU MORE ALERT," she says to Jetta, approaching the bed. "How's the nausea?"

"BETTER," Jetta reports, reluctantly withdrawing her hand from Ethan's as the doctor begins checking vital signs. "Head's clearer too."

DR. SIRINDI NODS, making notes on her tablet. "The tox screen confirmed GHB, as we suspected. We'll keep you overnight for observation, but barring any complications, you should be able to go home in the morning." She glances at Ethan, then back to Jetta. "You'll need someone to stay with you for the next 24 hours. The after-effects can sometimes include mood swings, disorientation, or anxiety."

"I'LL STAY WITH HER," Brandi says, suddenly awake in her chair, her voice thick with sleep but her eyes alert. "Our apartment has a guest room if you want to keep an eye on her too," she adds to Ethan, the offer extended with careful neutrality that doesn't quite disguise her dawning awareness of the shifted dynamic between them.

ETHAN HESITATES, glancing at Jetta as if seeking her permission before responding. The deference surprises her— another adjustment to her understanding of who he is now.

. . .

"IF JETTA WANTS THAT," he says finally, leaving the decision entirely in her hands.

THE RESPONSIBILITY of choice feels momentarily overwhelming after hours of having no control, of being at the mercy of chemicals invading her system and men intent on harm. She takes a breath, considering what she actually wants rather than what she thinks she should want.

"I'D FEEL SAFER," she admits, the honesty costing her but also feeling like a small reclamation of agency. "If you were nearby."

SOMETHING SOFTENS IN HIS EXPRESSION—NOT quite a smile, but an easing of the vigilant tension he's maintained since the alley. "Then I'll be there."

DR. SIRINDI FINISHES HER EXAMINATION, seemingly satisfied with Jetta's progress. "Try to get some rest," she advises, her professional demeanour warming slightly. "The body needs sleep to recover from trauma, both physical and psychological." Her gaze moves between Jetta and Ethan, something adjacent to approval flickering in her expression before she slips away through the curtain.

OWEN RETURNS MOMENTS LATER, balancing four paper cups of vending machine coffee that steam weakly in the cool air of the treatment bay. He distributes them with careful movements, his usual easy charm subdued by the gravity of the night's events.

"POLICE STILL OUT THERE?" he asks Ethan quietly as he hands him a cup.

ETHAN NODS, accepting the coffee with a murmured thanks. "They're taking it seriously. Description's out to all patrol units. The fact that there were three of them operating so smoothly suggests this wasn't their first attempt."

THE IMPLICATION—THAT other women might not have been as fortunate as Jetta—hangs in the air, adding another layer of sobriety to the already subdued atmosphere. Jetta closes her eyes briefly, the weight of what could have happened pressing against her chest until it's difficult to breathe.

A WARM HAND COVERS HERS, and she opens her eyes to find Ethan watching her with quiet understanding. "They didn't get you," he says simply, the words a reminder and a reassurance in one.

AS EXHAUSTION RECLAIMS HER, Jetta feels herself drifting toward sleep, the trauma of the night temporarily held at bay by the protective circle formed around her bed. Ethan remains beside her, his bruised hand gently adjusting the blanket when it slips from her shoulder. The gesture is small but laden with care that contradicts every assumption she's held about him for a decade.

. . .

THROUGH HALF-CLOSED EYES, she sees Brandi and Owen exchange a look—a silent communication full of meaning as they observe this unexpected tenderness between former enemies. Owen's eyebrows lift in question; Brandi responds with a small shrug that somehow conveys both surprise and cautious hope.

THE NIGHT'S trauma has carved a new path between them all, reshaping the landscape of their relationships in ways none could have anticipated. As sleep claims her, Jetta's last conscious thought is that perhaps there's truth in what Ethan once told her—that people are rarely just one thing, villains or victims, but both in different measures, at different times. The bridge forming between them may be built of terrible circumstances, but it offers a crossing nonetheless, a way forward neither could have imagined mere hours ago.

CHAPTER 9

Thawing Ice

CANDLELIGHT FLICKERS across the white tablecloth, casting soft shadows that dance between the four wine glasses. Jetta shifts in her seat, the leather cushion sighing beneath her as she glances up from her menu to find Ethan studying the pasta selections with unnecessary concentration. His hands rest on the table's edge, and she can't help but notice the healing scars across his knuckles—faint red lines that tell a story no one in this intimate Italian restaurant would ever guess. Two weeks ago, those hands had protected her, had struck with precise violence to keep her safe. Now they simply turn a menu page, and something in her chest tightens at the ordinary grace of the movement.

"PLEASE TELL me you're not ordering the plain spaghetti," she says, breaking the comfortable silence that has settled around their corner table. "That would be tragically predictable."

· · ·

ETHAN LOOKS UP, one eyebrow arching in that way that once irritated her but now sends a strange flutter through her stomach. "As opposed to your adventurous choice of... let me guess, margherita pizza?" His lips curve into a smile that transforms his face, softening the sharp angles she once found intimidating.

"WRONG. I'M THINKING THE RISOTTO." She taps the menu with her fingernail, the sound barely audible above the gentle murmur of surrounding conversations and the soft Italian music flowing from hidden speakers.

"THE RISOTTO you'll pick at for twenty minutes before declaring you're full after eating exactly six bites?" His eyes meet hers across the table, a challenge wrapped in teasing familiarity.

BRANDI LEANS FORWARD, elbows on the table, her wine glass cradled between her palms. "He's got you there, Jetta. You've never finished a restaurant risotto in your life."

"THAT'S because they always make the portions too large," Jetta protests, but she's smiling despite herself, unable to summon the indignation she might have felt at such an observation weeks ago. "Some of us don't have hollow legs like this one." She tilts her head toward Ethan, who's now examining the wine list with exaggerated interest.

"I HAVE A HEALTHY APPETITE," he counters without

looking up. "Unlike someone who considers coffee a food group."

OWEN LAUGHS, the sound warm and inclusive, his arm draped casually across the back of Brandi's chair. "I think I've witnessed Jetta subsist on nothing but espresso and spite for entire weekends."

"THAT WAS FINALS WEEK," Jetta protests, though she's laughing too. "Extraordinary circumstances."

THE WAITER APPROACHES, a bottle of red wine cradled in his arm like a newborn. "Have we decided on our selections this evening?" His voice carries the faint lilt of an accent that might be authentic or affected for atmosphere.

AS THEY PLACE THEIR ORDERS—ETHAN choosing the lamb ragu that Jetta had privately predicted, herself going with the risotto despite his teasing—she notices how he leans slightly forward when speaking, how his fingers absently trace one of the scars on his knuckle when he hands the menu back. The gesture pulls her back to the hospital, to the moment she woke to find him still there, keeping watch despite his own exhaustion.

"EARTH TO JETTA," Brandi's voice cuts through her memories. "Red or white?"

. . .

"OH—RED, PLEASE." She pushes her wine glass forward, watching as the waiter pours with practised precision. The ruby liquid catches the candlelight, sending fractured reflections across the white tablecloth.

ETHAN'S GLASS IS NEXT, and as the waiter fills it, his fingers brush against Jetta's where her hand rests on the table. The contact is brief—perhaps accidental—but neither pulls away immediately. His skin is warm against hers, the fleeting touch sending an electric current up her arm that she refuses to acknowledge.

WHEN THE WAITER DEPARTS, promising their appetisers shortly, a momentary pause settles over the table. Jetta lifts her wine glass, using the action to disguise how her heart has inexplicably accelerated.

"TO GOOD COMPANY," Owen offers, raising his glass in a toast that seems innocent enough on the surface, though his eyes flick between Jetta and Ethan with barely concealed curiosity.

"AND TO NO MORE HOSPITAL FOOD," Ethan adds, his voice dropping slightly as he meets Jetta's gaze over the rim of his glass. It's an inside joke, a reference to the awful gelatin cups and soggy sandwiches they'd shared during her overnight stay, when he'd refused to leave despite her insistence that she was fine.

· · ·

JETTA FEELS her lips curve into a smile she doesn't try to suppress. "God, yes. To real food that doesn't come in sealed plastic containers."

THEIR GLASSES MEET with a delicate chime that seems to hang in the air between them. When Jetta takes a sip, she notices Brandi watching her with the particular intensity she reserves for customers she suspects might be shoplifting— careful observation masked as casual interest.

"SO," Brandi says, setting her glass down with deliberate precision, "I'm thinking we should make this a regular thing. The four of us, dinner, maybe once a week?"

OWEN NODS ENTHUSIASTICALLY, his easy charm smoothing any potential awkwardness. "Absolutely. There's that new Thai place over on Maple that's supposed to be amazing."

"THAI FOOD? With Miss Six-Bites-of-Risotto over here?" Ethan gestures toward Jetta with his wine glass, but there's no edge to the teasing now, just a warm familiarity that makes her stomach do something complicated.

"I EAT THAI FOOD," Jetta protests, leaning forward to swat at his arm. Her fingers connect with the solid warmth of his forearm, lingering a heartbeat too long before she pulls back. "I just avoid anything that might be attempting to poison me through excessive spice."

. . .

"So you eat... what? Plain rice and those spring rolls with nothing in them?" Ethan leans toward her, closing the distance she's just created, his voice dropping to a conspiratorial whisper that somehow feels more intimate than their brief touch. "Living dangerously."

She finds herself leaning in as well, drawn by some invisible gravity she's not ready to name. "At least I try new things. When was the last time you ordered something you couldn't pronounce?"

His laugh is soft, meant only for her despite their friends' presence across the table. "Last week, actually. That French place Owen dragged me to. I'm still not entirely sure what I ate, but it had tentacles."

"Impressive," she concedes, suddenly aware of how close they're sitting, how his knee occasionally brushes against hers beneath the table when he shifts position. "I take back at least ten per cent of my criticism."

Across the table, Brandi clears her throat, a sound laden with meaning that draws Jetta's attention reluctantly away from Ethan's amused expression. She finds her friend watching them with raised eyebrows and a poorly concealed smile, while Owen studies the ceiling with exaggerated interest.

The waiter's return with bread and antipasti creates a momentary reprieve from whatever Brandi was about to say.

As plates are arranged and wine is topped up, Jetta catches Ethan watching her with an expression she can't quite decipher—something softer than she's accustomed to seeing on his face, something that makes her chest feel too small for her lungs.

WHEN THEIR FINGERS brush again as they both reach for the same piece of bruschetta, neither pretends it's an accident.

THE MAIN COURSES arrive in a procession of steaming plates and fragrant aromas that momentarily silence the table. Jetta's risotto gleams with butter and herbs, while Ethan's lamb ragu sits in a rustic ceramic bowl, rich sauce clinging to wide ribbons of pappardelle. She watches him take his first bite, his eyes closing briefly in appreciation, and finds herself oddly satisfied by his enjoyment. Their shared hospital vigil seems both distant and immediate—a strange crucible that transformed years of antagonism into something she still can't properly name. When he catches her watching, she doesn't look away as she might have before.

"BETTER THAN THE HOSPITAL PUDDING?" she asks, voice light with teasing.

HIS GRIMACE IS immediate and exaggerated. "God, that pudding. I'm still not convinced it wasn't actually industrial adhesive."

"THE WORST PART was how they served it with such pride," Jetta continues, leaning forward as the memory takes shape between them. "Like, 'Here's your gelatinous beige substance, madam, paired with a plastic spoon that will definitely snap halfway through your struggle.'"

Ethan's laugh bursts forth unexpectedly—a full, rich sound that draws curious glances from nearby tables. "And you ate it anyway! I watched you methodically consume the entire cup while making increasingly creative comparisons to actual food."

"I was drugged," she protests, laughter bubbling beneath her words. "My judgment was severely impaired. I think at one point I compared it to 'sad, melancholy vanilla.'"

"'The ghost of desserts past,'" Ethan quotes, his eyes crinkling at the corners in a way that transforms his entire face. "That was my personal favourite."

Their shared laughter continues, building on itself until Jetta has to press her napkin to her mouth to contain it. Something warm and unfamiliar expands in her chest—the simple pleasure of an inside joke, of shared history that isn't weighted with pain or resentment.

Owen leans back in his chair, watching them with open curiosity as he reaches for the wine bottle. "I feel like I'm missing an epic story here."

. . .

"Hospital food critique became our midnight entertainment," Ethan explains, still smiling as he pushes his glass toward Owen for a refill. "Limited options when you're stuck in an ER treatment bay at three in the morning."

"It was either that or stare at the ceiling tiles," Jetta adds, nodding thanks as Owen tops up her glass as well. "I counted forty-seven of them, by the way. In case anyone was wondering."

Brandi sits back, wine glass cradled in her palm, her eyes moving between Jetta and Ethan with subtle assessment that Jetta recognises from years of friendship. It's the look Brandi gets when she's solving a puzzle, pieces clicking into place one by one. Jetta feels transparent beneath that gaze, as if her confused emotions are projected in neon above her head.

"You two have certainly come a long way from that club night," Brandi observes, her tone carefully neutral despite the weight of the observation.

Ethan shifts in his seat, his fork pausing halfway to his mouth. "Amazing what nearly being kidnapped will do for interpersonal relationships," he says, the dry humour masking something more complex.

"I feel like there should be a greeting card for that," Jetta adds, grateful for his deflection. "'Sorry, we hated each other until life-threatening circumstances intervened.'"

· · ·

OWEN LAUGHS, diffusing the momentary tension. "Hallmark's really missing a market segment there."

JETTA RETURNS TO HER RISOTTO, taking a deliberate bite to avoid further examination of how completely her feelings toward Ethan have transformed. The rice is creamy, perfectly al dente, but she barely registers the flavour. Her awareness has narrowed to the man beside her—the rhythm of his movements, the occasional brush of his arm against hers when he reaches for his wine, the subtle scent of his cologne that she's come to recognise even with her eyes closed.

WHEN SHE SHIFTS POSITION, her napkin slips from her lap, landing in the narrow space between her chair and Ethan's. She bends to retrieve it just as he notices and reaches down as well. Their hands collide in the small space, his fingers wrapping around both the napkin and her hand in a single warm grasp.

TIME SEEMS TO SUSPEND ITSELF. Their faces are suddenly close, eyes meeting at this unexpected proximity. She can see the varied blues in his irises—darker at the edges, lighter around the pupils—and the slight roughness of stubble along his jaw. His breath touches her cheek, warm and scented faintly with wine. Neither moves to pull away immediately, caught in a moment that stretches beyond its physical boundaries.

HIS FINGERS TIGHTEN BRIEFLY around hers before they both seem to remember themselves, straightening up too quickly. The napkin remains in Ethan's hand, which he extends to her with formal politeness that contradicts the flush rising from beneath his collar. Jetta takes it, her own cheeks burning as she carefully arranges it back across her lap, smoothing nonexistent wrinkles with trembling fingers.

"THANK YOU," she murmurs, reaching for her wine glass with a hand that isn't quite steady. The cool stem grounds her, giving her something to focus on besides the lingering sensation of his fingers against hers.

ETHAN CLEARS HIS THROAT, suddenly fascinated by the remaining pasta in his bowl. "No problem."

A CHARGED SILENCE DESCENDS, broken only by the clink of silverware against plates. Jetta becomes intensely aware of how she's angled toward him in her seat, how her body has unconsciously oriented itself in his direction throughout the meal. She forces herself to sit straighter, to create distance that might cool the heat still flooding her face.

OWEN, watching this exchange with increasing amusement, sets down his wine glass with deliberate precision. His easy smile spreads across his face as he looks between them, eyes twinkling with mischief that makes Jetta instantly wary.

"So," he says, the single syllable hanging in the air with dangerous potential, "do you two need your own table next time?"

. . .

THE QUESTION LANDS like a stone in still water, sending ripples of panic through Jetta's body. She sits up even straighter, her spine rigid as her fingers tighten around her wine glass. Beside her, Ethan's posture changes with similar abruptness—shoulders squaring, jaw setting in a line that would look like annoyance if not for the deepening colour at the base of his throat.

"WHAT?" The word escapes Jetta as more of a squeak than a question. She coughs to cover it, eyes suddenly finding intense interest in the ornate ceiling moulding above their table. The intricate plasterwork has never seemed so fascinating—swirls and flourishes that demand complete attention.

ETHAN BECOMES EQUALLY ABSORBED in the restaurant decor, his gaze fixed on a framed landscape painting on the nearest wall. "This is a nice place," he comments, the non sequitur hanging awkwardly in the air. "Good... art."

BRANDI'S EYEBROWS CLIMB HIGHER, a smile playing at the corners of her mouth as she watches this mutual panic unfold. She takes a deliberate sip of wine, saying nothing but communicating volumes with her knowing expression.

JETTA'S WINE glass remains suspended halfway to her lips, forgotten in the moment of crisis. Owen's question exposes something she's been carefully avoiding examining—the subtle shift from grudging civility to whatever this new awareness is, electric and unsettling. She catches Ethan stealing a glance at her from the corner of his eye, then quickly returning his attention to the suddenly captivating salt and pepper shakers.

"The tiramisu here is excellent," Brandi finally offers, her tone innocent despite the amusement dancing in her eyes. "Should we order dessert?"

Jetta has never been more grateful for a change of subject in her life.

"We're just being civil," Jetta blurts, the words tumbling out before she can temper them. At the exact same moment, Ethan declares with equal vehemence, "We barely tolerate each other." Their responses collide in the air between them, too loud against the restaurant's gentle murmur of conversation. Heat floods Jetta's face as she realises they've both protested far too strongly, creating exactly the impression they're trying to dispel.

A middle-aged couple at the adjacent table turns to look, the woman's eyebrows lifting with undisguised interest before her companion murmurs something that draws her attention reluctantly back to their own meal. Jetta wishes desperately for the polished wooden floor to open beneath her chair and swallow her whole.

"I just meant," she continues, her voice now carefully modulated to avoid further attention, "that we've reached a point of mature coexistence. For everyone's sake." She gestures vaguely between Brandi and Owen, as if their happiness depends entirely on this newfound civility.

"EXACTLY," Ethan agrees, nodding with excessive conviction. His fingers drum a nervous pattern against the tablecloth, betraying the composure his voice strains to project. "It's called being adults."

BRANDI TAKES a deliberate sip of wine, her eyes visible over the rim of her glass, alight with an awareness that makes Jetta want to slide under the table. When she sets the glass down, her expression is carefully neutral, though the slight twitch at the corner of her mouth suggests barely contained amusement.

"OF COURSE," Brandi says, drawing out the words with delicate precision. "Just two adults being completely normal and not at all defensive about a simple joke."

OWEN LOOKS between them with genuine surprise, his easy smile faltering slightly as he registers the intensity of their reaction. "I was just teasing," he says, raising his hands in a gesture of surrender. "Didn't mean to hit a nerve."

"YOU DIDN'T," Jetta and Ethan say simultaneously, then glance at each other with matching expressions of horror at their continued synchronicity.

. . .

SILENCE DESCENDS OVER THE TABLE, broken only by the clink of silverware against plates from nearby diners and the soft Italian music that now seems impossibly loud in the absence of conversation. Jetta stares fixedly at her risotto, pushing a single grain of rice with her fork as if it holds the secret to escaping this moment of acute discomfort.

"So," Brandi says finally, her voice bright with forced casualness, "I wanted to tell you all about the author event we're hosting next month at the bookshop. We finally confirmed Eliza Monteith for a reading from her new mystery series."

THE CHANGE of subject acts like a release valve, tension visibly draining from Ethan's shoulders as he leans forward with apparent interest. "The one with the lighthouse keeper detective? Owen was reading that last week."

"IT WAS FANTASTIC," Owen confirms, gratitude for the new conversation direction evident in his enthusiastic response. "The twist at the end with the harbormaster's secret identity? Never saw it coming."

AS THE DISCUSSION flows around her, Jetta allows herself to breathe again, though her heart continues its accelerated rhythm. She's acutely aware of Ethan beside her—how carefully he's positioned himself now, maintaining a precise distance between them that wasn't there earlier in the evening. The space feels deliberate, constructed, and somehow more revealing than their previous unconscious proximity.

. . .

"JETTA'S the one who convinced her to come," Brandi continues, drawing her back into the conversation. "She wrote this incredibly persuasive email about the store's commitment to supporting female mystery writers."

"IT WASN'T THAT BIG A DEAL," Jetta demurs, grateful to focus on something familiar and safe. "Her publisher was looking for stops on the East Coast anyway."

"YOU'RE TOO MODEST," Brandi insists. "The woman specifically mentioned your analysis of her narrative structure as the reason she chose our shop over that big chain store downtown."

AS THE CONVERSATION CONTINUES, revolving around books and upcoming events at Bound Together, Jetta feels herself relaxing incrementally. The familiar topic grounds her, returning her to a version of herself she recognises—the businesswoman, the bookseller, the person who existed before Ethan Cole re-entered her life and complicated everything.

YET EVEN AS she discusses order quantities and promotional strategies, a part of her attention remains fixed on Ethan—the way he listens with genuine interest, asks thoughtful questions about authors she's mentioned, offers suggestions about security considerations for a high-profile event. This version of him still surprises her, though it shouldn't anymore. The careful, protective intelligence she witnessed in the hospital continues to manifest in unexpected ways.

. . .

WHEN THE DESSERT MENUS ARRIVE, Owen and Brandi immediately begin debating the merits of tiramisu versus cannoli, their heads bent together in comfortable intimacy. In their momentary distraction, Jetta glances at Ethan, only to find him already looking at her, his expression unguarded in a way that makes her breath catch. Something passes between them—a recognition, a question, an acknowledgment of whatever this is that neither seems ready to name.

THEY BOTH LOOK AWAY QUICKLY, but not before Brandi glances up, catching the tail end of the exchange. Her eyes narrow slightly, cataloguing and analysing in that quiet way she has, though she says nothing as she returns her attention to the dessert options.

THE REMAINDER of the dinner passes without further incident—desserts are shared, coffee is poured, the bill is settled with minimal argument over who pays what. As they gather their coats and prepare to leave, Jetta feels oddly reluctant for the evening to end, despite the moments of discomfort. Something has shifted, not just between her and Ethan, but within the dynamics of their foursome.

IN THE RESTAURANT PARKING LOT, the night air carries the crisp edge of approaching autumn. Their breath forms faint clouds that dissipate into the darkness as they stand in a loose circle beside their cars, exchanging goodbyes that somehow feel more significant than the occasion warrants.

"WE SHOULD DO this again next week," Owen suggests, his

arm draped casually around Brandi's shoulders. "That new Thai place, maybe?"

"WITH APPROPRIATE SPICE levels for those with delicate palates," Ethan adds, the teasing directed at Jetta lacking any of the edge it might have held weeks ago.

"SOME OF US prefer to taste our food, not just survive it," she retorts, but she's smiling despite herself, unable to summon even pretend annoyance.

OWEN AND ETHAN move toward Owen's car, their conversation shifting to some work matter that requires their attention. Jetta watches them go, aware of Brandi's presence beside her, patient and observant in a way that has always made hiding anything from her nearly impossible.

"SO," Brandi says, her voice soft in the quiet parking lot, "are we going to talk about what's happening between you two, or are we pretending there's nothing to discuss?"

JETTA CONTINUES WATCHING the men as they reach Owen's car, noticing how Ethan glances back toward her before opening the passenger door. Even across the distance, something in his gaze makes her stomach flutter traitorously.

"THERE'S NOTHING TO DISCUSS," she says automatically, the denial sounding hollow even to her own ears.

· · ·

BRANDI MAKES A SMALL, noncommittal sound that manages to convey volumes of disbelief without a single word. She follows Jetta's gaze to where Ethan now leans against Owen's car, his tall figure illuminated in the glow of a nearby streetlamp.

"FOR WHAT IT'S WORTH," Brandi says after a moment, her voice gentle with understanding, "I think it would be okay if there were."

THE SIMPLE PERMISSION—TO feel whatever this is, to explore the possibility of something beyond their complicated history—settles around Jetta's shoulders like a warm shawl against the cool night air. She doesn't respond, but as she and Brandi walk toward their own car, she allows herself one last glance at Ethan, finding him already looking back at her, his expression thoughtful in the soft golden light.

CHAPTER 10

Movie Night Mayhem

JETTA STANDS in the hallway outside Ethan and Owen's apartment, her knuckles hovering inches from the door as she questions, for the third time, why she agreed to this transparently orchestrated movie night. The paper bag of specialty popcorn clutched in her other hand crinkles as her grip tightens. Behind this door waits Ethan, and the strange new reality where his presence sends her heart into uncomfortable acrobatics rather than inspiring the familiar burn of resentment. She takes a steadying breath before knocking, already anticipating Brandi's poorly disguised satisfaction when she arrives alone instead of conveniently "running into" Ethan somewhere along the way as her friend had repeatedly suggested.

THE DOOR SWINGS open before her knuckles make contact. Brandi stands there, flushed with excitement that borders on manic energy, her blonde hair twisted into a casual knot atop her head.

. . .

"YOU'RE HERE!" she exclaims, as if Jetta's arrival is somehow surprising rather than the result of three days of persistent texts. "Come in, come in. We're just getting everything set up."

THE APARTMENT REVEALS itself as Jetta steps inside—an open-concept space with exposed brick walls and tall windows that offer glimpses of city lights beginning to twinkle against the darkening sky. Bookshelves line one wall, filled with an eclectic mix of titles that speak to both residents' tastes. She spots a worn copy of "The Great Gatsby" beside technical manuals on security systems, a visual representation of the contradiction that is Ethan Cole.

"YOU BROUGHT THE TRUFFLE POPCORN!" Brandi takes the bag from Jetta's hands. "Perfect. I'll add it to our spread."

JETTA FOLLOWS her friend to the living area where Owen arranges cushions on a sectional sofa that faces a large flatscreen television. Ethan stands near the kitchen island, uncorking a bottle of red wine. His eyes find hers immediately, a silent acknowledgment passing between them that makes her pulse quicken despite her efforts to remain composed.

"HEY," he says, the single syllable somehow carrying more weight than it should.

"HEY YOURSELF," she replies, shrugging off her jacket to hide the slight tremor in her hands.

. . .

Brandi bustles around them, arranging an elaborate display of snacks on the coffee table with the precision of a museum curator. Chocolate-covered pretzels are artfully piled beside strawberries and a cheese plate that seems excessive for what was supposedly a casual movie night. She straightens a row of wine glasses, rearranges a stack of napkins, and fluffs cushions that Owen has already positioned to her specifications.

"Sit, sit," she urges, gesturing toward the couch while exchanging a look with Owen that contains an entire conversation in a single glance.

Jetta notices the deliberate arrangement immediately—the side chairs have been moved away, leaving only the deep sectional with its inviting cushions and, most tellingly, a single oversized throw blanket folded neatly across its center. The setup couldn't be more obvious if Brandi had installed a neon sign reading "ROMANTIC OPPORTUNITY" above the couch.

"What are we watching?" Jetta asks, perching on the far end of the sectional, as far from where she assumes Ethan will sit as possible.

"'When Harry Met Sally,'" Owen answers, remote in hand, his casual tone betrayed by the slight twitching at the corner of his mouth. "Brandi's choice."

· · ·

"A CLASSIC," Brandi declares, dimming the overhead lights until the room is bathed only in the soft glow from a single lamp and the television screen. "Who doesn't love a story about friends who realize they're meant to be more?"

THE LOOK she gives Jetta is about as subtle as a brick through a window.

ETHAN APPROACHES with two glasses of wine, offering one to Jetta. Their fingers brush during the exchange, a momentary point of contact that feels electric in its simplicity. He settles onto the couch, leaving a careful foot of space between them.

"BLANKET?" Brandi holds up the throw with exaggerated innocence. "It gets chilly in here with the air conditioning."

BEFORE EITHER CAN RESPOND, she unfurls it over both their laps, creating a shared space that immediately heightens Jetta's awareness of every inch between them. The soft fabric settles across her legs, bridging the gap she so carefully established. Beneath the blanket, her skin prickles with heightened sensitivity, as if expecting contact.

OWEN DIMS THE FINAL LAMP, plunging the room into darkness relieved only by the blue glow of the television as the movie's opening credits begin. Brandi settles beside him on the opposite end of the sectional, their bodies automatically finding comfortable alignment with practiced ease.

. . .

THE FILM STARTS, but Jetta finds herself unable to focus on the dialogue. Her attention fragments between the screen and the man beside her, whose presence seems to generate its own gravitational field. She maintains her position, spine straight, hands folded primly in her lap, though every cell in her body hums with awareness of his proximity.

WHEN ETHAN REACHES for the popcorn, his arm brushes against hers—a fleeting touch that feels deliberate in its gentleness. She stiffens momentarily before forcing herself to relax, to pretend this casual contact doesn't send warmth spreading up her arm and across her chest.

"SORRY," he murmurs, voice low enough that only she can hear.

"IT'S FINE," she whispers back, though nothing about this feels fine—it feels dangerous, exhilarating, inevitable.

ON SCREEN, Harry and Sally debate whether men and women can ever truly be friends without attraction complicating things. The irony isn't lost on Jetta, who finds herself stealing glances at Ethan's profile illuminated by the shifting light. The strong line of his jaw, the slight curve of his lips when he smiles at a joke in the film—these details shouldn't fascinate her, yet she catalogs them with helpless precision.

HALFWAY THROUGH THE MOVIE, she realizes the space between them has decreased. Neither has moved deliberately, yet some magnetic pull has drawn them closer, their bodies shifting incrementally until only inches separate them. When she reaches for her wine glass, her knee bumps against his—a contact that lingers rather than breaking, as if neither wants to be the first to withdraw.

"MORE WINE?" Brandi's voice cuts through the darkened room, though her eyes remain fixed on the screen with studied casualness.

"I'LL GET IT," Owen offers immediately, rising with the enthusiasm of someone who's been waiting for his cue.

THEY MOVE TOGETHER toward the kitchen, their synchronized choreography revealing the rehearsed nature of this moment. Jetta watches them with narrowed eyes, recognizing the setup but unable to summon proper indignation. Part of her—a growing, insistent part—is grateful for their transparent machinations.

"OH!" Brandi exclaims suddenly, pausing the film at a completely arbitrary moment. "We need more of those chocolate things. And maybe those special crackers from the pantry."

"THE ONES on the top shelf that will take several minutes to locate?" Owen asks, his attempt at innocence undermined by the grin he can't quite suppress.

. . .

"Exactly those," Brandi confirms, already moving toward the kitchen. "You two keep watching if you want. This might take a while."

They disappear into the kitchen, their footsteps followed by the distinct sound of a door opening and closing —not the pantry, Jetta realizes, but the door to the hallway. The apartment falls silent except for the gentle hum of the refrigerator and the suddenly deafening sound of her own heartbeat.

"Did they just..." Ethan begins.

"Leave? Yes, I think they did," Jetta confirms, trying for dry amusement but achieving something closer to breathless anticipation.

The click of the door closing behind Owen and Brandi echoes with finality, leaving them alone in the dimly lit room, side by side beneath the shared blanket, the paused image on the television screen the only witness to whatever might happen next.

The silence expands between them, thick with possibilities neither has allowed themselves to acknowledge until now. Jetta stares at the frozen image on the screen— Harry mid-sentence, his finger pointed in emphatic disagreement about something that suddenly seems completely irrelevant. She's acutely aware of Ethan beside her, the blanket across their laps now feeling less like Brandi's transparent matchmaking prop and more like a shared secret space where their hands rest inches apart. His breathing has changed, becoming deeper, more measured, as if he's consciously controlling each inhale and exhale. She wonders if he can hear her heart hammering against her ribs.

"THEY WEREN'T EXACTLY SUBTLE," Ethan finally says, his voice breaking the tension with unexpected gentleness.

JETTA MANAGES a small laugh that comes out shakier than intended. "Brandi's about as subtle as a flashing neon sign. I'm surprised she didn't scatter rose petals on the couch."

"OWEN SUGGESTED IT. I vetoed the idea." His admission brings her eyes to his face, where she finds a smile playing at the corners of his mouth—not the practised charm he once wielded like a weapon, but something softer, more genuine.

"YOU'RE JOKING." She shifts slightly toward him, the movement closing an inch of the remaining space between them.

"I WISH I WERE." He reaches for the remote, his arm brushing against hers in a touch that feels deliberate this time. "Should we continue watching? See if Harry and Sally figure things out before our friends decide they've given us enough time alone?"

. . .

SHE NODS, not trusting her voice as he presses play. The movie resumes, dialogue flowing around them without truly penetrating the bubble of awareness that has formed in their shared space. When a particularly ridiculous scene unfolds—Sally faking an orgasm in a crowded diner—Ethan's quiet laugh vibrates through the cushion between them.

"YOU HAVE TO ADMIRE HER COMMITMENT," he comments, and something about his dry delivery breaks through Jetta's nervous tension.

SHE LAUGHS—GENUINELY, unreservedly—the sound surprising in its authenticity. "Not exactly a subtle approach to making a point."

"SUBTLETY SEEMS OVERRATED TONIGHT." His eyes meet hers, holding the connection longer than casual conversation warrants. Something shifts in his expression—a vulnerability she's only glimpsed in rare, unguarded moments.

HER FINGERS FIND the edge of the blanket, nervously pleating the soft fabric between her thumb and forefinger. The repetitive motion grounds her as her mind races ahead, calculating risks, remembering history, acknowledging the inexorable pull she's been fighting since that night at the hospital.

"WHEN DID THIS HAPPEN?" she asks quietly, her question hanging in the space between them. "This... whatever this is."

. . .

"I DON'T KNOW," he admits, his voice dropping to match her hushed tone. "Maybe it was always there, underneath everything else."

THE THOUGHT SHOULD FRIGHTEN HER—THAT years of carefully cultivated resentment might have been masking something else entirely—but instead, it creates a strange sense of inevitability. As if they've been moving toward this moment through all their antagonism, all their carefully maintained distance.

WITHOUT CONSCIOUS DECISION, they shift toward each other, the last few inches dissolving until their thighs press together, warm and solid through the layers of clothing. The contact sends electricity racing up her spine, pooling low in her stomach with an intensity that makes her breath catch.

"THIS FEELS DIFFERENT," Ethan says, the words barely above a whisper. His eyes search hers, seeking confirmation or permission—perhaps both.

"EVERYTHING FEELS DIFFERENT NOW." Her usual sharp wit has abandoned her, leaving only raw honesty in its place. "I don't know how to make sense of any of it."

"MAYBE WE DON'T NEED to make sense of it yet." His hand moves with deliberate slowness, giving her time to pull away if she wants. She remains still, heart pounding, as his fingers brush against her cheek, tucking a strand of hair behind her ear. The touch lingers, his palm warm against her skin.

. . .

TIME SEEMS SUSPENDED BETWEEN THEM, the moment stretching as their eyes hold a conversation more honest than any they've had with words. On screen, the movie reaches its romantic climax—confessions of love at a New Year's Eve party—providing a soundtrack to their own suspended moment of truth.

SHE ISN'T sure who moves first. Perhaps they both do, drawn by the same magnetic pull that's been drawing them closer since the moment she woke in that hospital bed to find him keeping watch. Their lips meet with gentle hesitation, testing, questioning—a kiss that asks rather than demands.

THE SOFTNESS LASTS only seconds before something breaks open between them. Years of repressed feeling surge to the surface, transforming the tentative touch into something hungry and urgent. His hands frame her face, fingers threading into her hair with a reverence that contradicts the growing desperation of his mouth against hers. She grips the front of his shirt, bunching the fabric in her fists, pulling him closer as if to eliminate any remaining space between them.

ETHAN TASTES like wine and something distinctly his own —a flavour she realises with startling clarity that she's been curious about for longer than she's willing to admit. His tongue traces the seam of her lips, seeking entrance that she grants without hesitation, the kiss deepening into something that makes her head spin more effectively than any alcohol could.

. . .

A SMALL SOUND escapes her throat—half sigh, half moan—and she feels him respond, his grip tightening in her hair. Emboldened, she shifts, moving instinctively until she's straddling his lap, her knees sinking into the cushions on either side of his thighs. The new position brings their bodies flush against each other, creating friction that draws a groan from deep in his chest.

"JETTA," he murmurs against her mouth, her name transformed into a question and answer all at once.

SHE RESPONDS by kissing him harder, her hands now exploring the broad expanse of his shoulders, the firm muscles of his chest beneath his shirt. His own hands slide down her back, fingers splaying across her waist before slipping beneath the hem of her sweater. The first touch of his skin against hers —warm palms against the sensitive small of her back—sends a shudder through her entire body.

THEY BREAK APART JUST LONG ENOUGH to breathe, foreheads pressed together, sharing air in the minimal space between them. His eyes are darker now, pupils dilated with desire that mirrors her own racing pulse. When he speaks, his voice has roughened to a texture that scrapes pleasantly across her nerves.

"TELL me this isn't just me," he whispers, vulnerability bleeding through the desire in his expression.

. . .

INSTEAD OF ANSWERING WITH WORDS, she recaptures his mouth, pouring ten years of complicated emotions into a kiss that leaves no room for doubt. His hands grow bolder beneath her sweater, tracing the curve of her spine, the edges of her ribs, thumbs brushing the undersides of her breasts through the thin fabric of her bra. Each touch ignites new sparks beneath her skin, heat coiling tighter in her core.

THE FORGOTTEN MOVIE PLAYS ON, its happy ending unfolding in cheerful oblivion to the much more compelling drama occurring on the couch. Dialogue and music flow around them unheeded as they lose themselves in exploration, in the heady discovery of each other's bodies after years of carefully maintained distance.

JETTA FEELS herself sinking deeper into sensation, rational thought dissolving under the onslaught of Ethan's hands and mouth. Nothing exists beyond this moment—not their complicated history, not her carefully constructed defences, not even the awareness that their friends could return at any moment. There is only Ethan, solid and warm beneath her, his heartbeat thundering against her palm as she slides her hand between them.

THE WORLD NARROWS to points of contact—his mouth on her neck, her fingers in his hair, the press of his body against hers through increasingly frustrating layers of clothing. Years of tension unravel with each kiss, each touch, transforming into something new and unexpectedly beautiful.

. . .

A SHARP KNOCK shatters their private world—three decisive raps against wood that slice through the haze of desire like a blade. They freeze, lips still connected, hands stilled in mid-exploration. For a suspended moment, neither moves, as if immobility might somehow make the interruption disappear. The knock comes again, more insistent this time. Jetta pulls back, her lips swollen from kissing, hair mussed where Ethan's fingers have tangled through it. Their eyes meet in shared panic, a wordless conversation passing between them: Who? and Not now and perhaps most urgently, Don't answer.

"ETHAN?" A female voice calls from the hallway, unfamiliar to Jetta but clearly known to Ethan, whose face transforms with recognition that borders on alarm. "I know you're in there. I can hear the TV."

BEFORE EITHER CAN RESPOND, the door swings open without invitation or preamble. The woman who strides into the apartment moves with the confidence of someone who believes all spaces rightfully belong to her. Her flame-red hair catches the television's glow, creating an eerie halo effect that makes her look otherworldly and dangerous. She's striking rather than conventionally beautiful—angular features arranged with precision, green eyes that assess the room with calculating efficiency.

THOSE EYES LAND on the couch and narrow fractionally as she processes what she's interrupted. For a heartbeat, naked rage flashes across her features before dissolving into a brilliant smile that doesn't reach her eyes.

. . .

"ETHAN, DARLING!" she exclaims, crossing the room with deliberate steps that remind Jetta of a predator approaching cornered prey.

JETTA SCRAMBLES off Ethan's lap, face burning with embarrassment and confusion. She tugs her sweater down where it had ridden up, painfully aware of her dishevelled appearance. Ethan stands too, movements jerky with surprise, his expression a complex mix of emotions Jetta can't fully decode.

"ALICE," he says, the name emerging strangled and hoarse. "What are you doing here? How did you—"

BEFORE HE CAN FINISH, Alice reaches them. Without hesitation, she slides between them, creating physical separation where moments ago there had been none. Her hand finds Ethan's chest in a possessive gesture that speaks of established intimacy, and Jetta's stomach plummets as if the floor has disappeared beneath her feet.

"THE DOORMAN REMEMBERED ME, OF COURSE," Alice says, her voice melodic and confident. "I told him I was surprised you. He was so sweet, letting me right up."

THEN, with a fluid movement that speaks of practice, she pulls Ethan toward her and kisses him. Not a greeting between casual acquaintances, but a claiming—deep and possessive and unmistakably intimate. Her body arches into his, one hand sliding behind his neck to hold him in place.

. . .

"I'VE BEEN WAITING for you to come back to me, just like you promised," she announces when she finally releases him, her voice pitched loud enough to ensure Jetta catches every word. "These little breaks of yours always make the reunion so much sweeter, don't they?"

THE WORLD TILTS beneath Jetta's feet. She watches Ethan's face, searching desperately for denial, for outrage, for any sign that this woman's claims are false. But what she sees destroys her—his stunned expression, his failure to immediately push Alice away or contradict her statement. The hesitation lasts perhaps only seconds, but to Jetta, it stretches into an eternity of confirmation.

THE HEAT that had suffused her body moments ago drains away, leaving her cold and hollow. Blood rushes in her ears, muffling sounds as if she's suddenly underwater. Her vision tunnels, focusing with painful clarity on Ethan's hands—the same hands that had touched her with such reverence now hanging limply at his sides, neither embracing Alice nor pushing her away.

PROMISED. The word echoes in her mind, a terrible confirmation of her worst fears—that she's been played, that their moment of connection was nothing but a diversion for him, a way to pass time until he returned to this flame-haired woman who clearly knows him in ways Jetta has only just begun to discover.

. . .

216

SHE MOVES MECHANICALLY, fingers trembling as she gathers her phone from the coffee table, shoves her feet into the shoes she'd kicked off hours earlier. Tears blur her vision, hot and humiliating, but she refuses to let them fall. Not here. Not with Alice's triumphant gaze tracking her movements like a cat watching a wounded bird.

"JETTA," Ethan finally speaks, her name emerging as if dragged from somewhere deep. He takes a step toward her, Alice's hand sliding from his chest without breaking contact, maintaining connection along his arm. "This isn't—she's not—"

"DON'T." The single word emerges sharper than she intends, slicing through his attempted explanation. She can't bear to hear whatever lie or half-truth he might offer. "I need to go."

"PLEASE, JUST LET ME EXPLAIN." He moves again, attempting to step around Alice, who shifts subtly to maintain her position between them.

"I THINK she's made her feelings quite clear, darling," Alice says, her smile sharpening into something predatory. "We should respect that, give her some space. We have so much catching up to do, after all."

JETTA STUMBLES BACKWARD, unable to watch this performance for another second. Her back hits the door frame, providing momentary orientation in a world that's spinning out of control. She turns, vision blurred with unshed tears, and pushes through the doorway into the hallway beyond.

"JETTA, WAIT!" Ethan calls after her, his voice holding an urgency that might have stopped her minutes ago, before Alice's arrival changed everything. Now it merely hastens her retreat.

SHE'S HALFWAY to the elevator when it opens, revealing Brandi and Owen, arms laden with bags that clearly contain the snacks they supposedly left to find. Their faces shift from conspiratorial excitement to confusion as they take in her tear-streaked face and desperate expression.

"JETTA?" Brandi's voice fills with immediate concern. "What happened? What's wrong?"

"ASK HIM," Jetta manages, the words catching on a sob she can no longer suppress. "Ask him about Alice."

SHE PUSHES past them into the waiting elevator, jabbing at the close door button with frantic energy. Through the narrowing gap, she catches a final glimpse of the apartment doorway where Ethan now stands, his face a mask of distress. Alice appears beside him, her hand sliding possessively around his waist, her expression a perfect blend of concern and triumph that makes Jetta's stomach twist with fresh nausea.

· · ·

THE DOORS FINALLY CLOSE, sealing her off from the tableau. Only then does she allow herself to truly break, tears flowing freely as she leans against the elevator wall for support. Her lips still burn from Ethan's kisses, her body still hums with the ghost of desire, making the betrayal all the more visceral and devastating.

SHE WRAPS her arms around herself as the elevator descends, trying to hold together the pieces that feel like they're shattering inside her chest. Of course, this would happen. Of course, the moment she finally lowered her guard, finally began to believe in the possibility of something genuine with Ethan, reality would crash in to remind her why she'd built those walls in the first place.

THE ELEVATOR REACHES the ground floor with a gentle chime that feels mockingly cheerful. As the doors slide open, Jetta straightens her shoulders, wipes furiously at her tears, and steps out into the lobby. The doorman—the same one who so helpfully allowed Alice upstairs—gives her a concerned look that she ignores, pushing through the building's front doors into the cool night air.

ONLY ONCE SHE'S OUTSIDE, away from watchful eyes, does she allow herself to stop, leaning against the building's façade as fresh tears threaten. Her phone buzzes in her pocket —Brandi already, or perhaps Ethan himself. She ignores it, focusing instead on the simple mechanics of breathing, of placing one foot in front of the other.

. . .

BEHIND HER, the building holds the wreckage of what might have been. Ahead lies the long walk home, where she can finally fall apart in private, away from triumphant green eyes and the devastating memory of Ethan's hesitation when it mattered most.

CHAPTER 11

Confrontations and Clarity

THE APARTMENT DOOR flies open with a crack that seems to split the air. Brandi stands in the doorway, shopping bags dangling forgotten from her fingers, her face a mask of confusion that hardens into something sharper as she takes in the scene before her. Beside her, Owen's easy smile evaporates, replaced by the wary alertness of someone who's just walked into an ambush. The living room, so carefully arranged for intimacy minutes ago, has transformed into a battlefield— Ethan standing rigid by the coffee table, his face drained of colour, while a red-haired woman prowls the perimeter of the room like a caged animal, her green eyes glittering with malicious triumph.

"WHAT IS GOING ON HERE?!" Brandi's voice cuts through the charged atmosphere, her shopping bags dropping to the floor with a thud. "We just saw Jetta in the elevator. She was crying."

· · ·

THE RED-HAIRED WOMAN—ALICE, Brandi realises with sudden clarity—turns toward them, her lips curving into a smile that doesn't touch her eyes. Her movements are fluid, precise, like a dancer performing for an audience only she can see. The light catches on her hair, turning it to burning copper as she tosses it over one shoulder with practised nonchalance.

"OH, was that her name? The little mouse who scurried away?" Her voice drips with honeyed venom. "How appropriate. She certainly didn't stick around to fight for what she wants."

ETHAN'S HANDS clench at his sides, the tendons in his wrists standing out like cords. "Stop it, Alice. This isn't what you're making it out to be."

"NO?" Alice arches one perfectly shaped eyebrow. "It looked exactly like what it was—you passing time with some bookish nobody until I came back." She moves closer to Ethan, her fingers reaching to trail along his arm. He flinches away, the movement small but unmistakable.

OWEN STEPS further into the apartment, closing the door behind him with deliberate care that belies the tension in his shoulders. His eyes meet Ethan's across the room—a silent exchange that asks questions neither can voice aloud.

"SHE'S a little nobody who wouldn't know a decent man if he tripped over her," Alice continues, her voice rising as she paces beside the low leather sofa. Her heels click against the hardwood floor, each step a percussive punctuation to her cruelty. "Playing at sophistication in that pathetic little bookshop. Did she think she was somehow special? That she could keep your interest beyond a momentary distraction?"

THE WINE GLASSES on the coffee table catch the light, half-empty and abandoned. In one, a lipstick mark stains the rim— Jetta's—the faint pink imprint now a ghostly reminder of moments ago.

"I NEVER WANTED to be with you," Ethan says, his voice low but firm. He crosses his arms, creating a physical barrier between himself and Alice. "Not then, not now. I've never made you any promises."

ALICE LAUGHS, the sound sharp enough to cut glass. "That's not what you said the night before you left. Not what your body told mine." She moves again, restless energy making her pace tighter circles. "You always come back to me, Ethan. It's what you do."

BRANDI'S PATIENCE SHATTERS. She drops her tote bag onto the nearby ottoman with enough force to make the wine glasses rattle, then strides forward, her small frame suddenly occupying more space than should be physically possible.

"YOU NEED TO LEAVE," she says, each word carefully measured and precisely delivered. "Now."

. . .

ALICE TURNS TOWARD HER, green eyes widening in mock surprise. "Excuse me? This is between Ethan and me. You're just—"

"HE'S BEEN HOME FOR WEEKS," Brandi cuts her off, her voice firm and unwavering. "If he wanted you in his life, he would've called you himself." She steps closer, unintimidated by Alice's height advantage. "This desperation is pathetic. Read the room and fuck off."

THE BLUNT WORDS land with physical force. Alice recoils, her carefully constructed façade cracking to reveal genuine shock beneath. For a moment, the apartment holds its breath, suspended in the aftermath of Brandi's verbal strike.

"YOU HAVE no idea what exists between us," Alice finally says, but her voice has lost its melodic confidence, the words emerging strangled and thin. "You don't know our history."

"I KNOW ENOUGH," Brandi replies, unrelenting. "I know my best friend just ran out of here in tears because of whatever manipulative game you're playing. I know Ethan looks like he'd rather be anywhere than standing here with you."

OWEN MOVES to stand beside Brandi, his presence a silent reinforcement. "I think you should go," he says, his usually friendly tone replaced by something harder. "This isn't going to work out how you planned."

. . .

ALICE'S GAZE darts between the three of them, searching for an ally and finding none. Her composure fractures further, mouth twisting into something ugly before she manages to smooth it back into a brittle smile.

"FINE," she spits, snatching her purse from where it lies on the sofa. "Have your little nobody. When you're bored with playing house in this pathetic city, you know where to find me." She storms toward the door, her movements no longer graceful but jagged with fury.

AS SHE PASSES ETHAN, she pauses, leaning close to whisper something that makes his jaw tighten, the muscle there jumping beneath his skin. Then she's past them all, wrenching open the door with enough force to make the hinges protest.

THE SLAM of the door behind her reverberates through the apartment, leaving a ringing silence in its wake. Ethan exhales, a long, shuddering breath that seems to deflate him. His shoulders slump as he runs a hand through his hair, dishevelled from where Jetta's fingers had been tangled in it not long ago.

"I'M SORRY," he says, the words inadequate but seemingly all he can manage. "I had no idea she would—"

"ARE YOU OKAY?" Owen interrupts, crossing to his friend with quick strides. "What the hell was that?"

. . .

"SOMEONE WHO DIDN'T GET the message that we were over," Ethan replies, his voice hollow. His eyes fix on the doorway, as if seeing beyond it to Jetta's retreating form. "But that doesn't matter now. I need to find Jetta, to explain—"

"SHE'S PROBABLY HOME BY NOW," Brandi says, her anger redirecting into concern. "And honestly, Ethan, what are you going to explain? That woman made it sound like you've been stringing both of them along."

"IT'S NOT TRUE." The vehemence in his voice startles them both. "Alice and I—it was brief, meaningless. Before I came back here. I never promised her anything." His hands drop to his sides, palms open in a gesture of helpless honesty. "But Jetta... she matters. She's all that matters."

THE SIMPLE DECLARATION hangs in the air between them. Brandi studies his face, searching for any hint of deception, but finds only raw desperation.

"THEN you better find a way to tell her that," she says finally. "Because right now, she thinks she's just been played by the same guy who humiliated her in high school."

ETHAN'S EYES flash with something like pain. "I need to go to her."

"YES," Brandi agrees, already reaching for her phone. "But

give me a few minutes first. Let me make sure she's okay with seeing you tonight."

OWEN PICKS up the abandoned wine glasses, carrying them to the kitchen with careful movements that fill the painful silence. The apartment feels hollowed out, the intimate atmosphere of earlier evaporated into something colder and more uncertain.

"I CAN'T LOSE HER," Ethan says quietly, more to himself than to anyone else in the room. "Not when I've just found her."

ETHAN'S KNUCKLES hover before Jetta's door, his heart hammering against his ribs with enough force that he wonders if she can hear it through the wood. The hallway stretches empty in both directions, silent except for the persistent hum of the building's heating system and the harsh sound of his own breathing. Twice he's raised his hand to knock, twice he's lowered it, paralysed by the possibility that she might refuse to see him—that the hurt in her eyes as she fled his apartment might have hardened into something permanent and impenetrable. But the alternative—losing her without fighting for what they've found—is unthinkable. He knocks, three rapid taps that seem to echo in the quiet corridor.

THE WAIT STRETCHES, each second a small eternity. He knocks again, more urgently, leaning closer to listen for movement inside. "Jetta, please. I know you're in there."

. . .

THE LOCK CLICKS, and the door opens just enough to reveal her standing in the shadowed entryway. His breath catches. Her eyes are red-rimmed, swollen with tears he caused, and she's wrapped herself in an oversized sweater that swallows her frame, making her look smaller and more vulnerable than he's ever seen her. The sight hits him with physical force, a visceral ache spreading through his chest.

"WHAT DO YOU WANT?" Her voice is rough-edged, scraped raw from crying.

"FIVE MINUTES," he says, the words rushing out before she can close the door. "Just give me five minutes to explain."

HER FINGERS TIGHTEN on the door's edge. "There's nothing to explain. I get it. She's gorgeous, you have history, and I was just—"

"NO," he interrupts, desperation making him step forward. "That's not what happened. Not what's happening."

SHE TRIES to push the door closed, but he blocks it with his foot, the pressure uncomfortable but insignificant compared to the pain of losing her. "Please, Jetta. Five minutes."

SOMETHING IN HIS VOICE—PERHAPS the naked fear trembling beneath his words—makes her hesitate. She steps back, allowing the door to open wider, though her arms remain crossed tightly over her chest, a physical barrier between them.

ETHAN FOLLOWS her into the apartment, keeping a careful distance as she retreats to the living room. The space is dim, lit only by a single lamp that casts long shadows across the walls. Books line the shelves, their spines a muted rainbow in the low light. A half-empty mug of tea sits abandoned on the coffee table, steam no longer rising from its surface.

"FIVE MINUTES," she says, turning to face him, her back to the window where city lights spill in like distant stars. "That's all."

HE STANDS in the centre of the room, hands opening and closing at his sides, suddenly unsure where to begin. The speech he rehearsed on the way over evaporates, leaving only raw truth.

"ALICE MEANS NOTHING TO ME," he starts, the words emerging with quiet intensity. "She's someone I dated briefly before I came home. It was casual, physical—a distraction from everything I was running from." He takes a breath, steadying himself. "I never promised her anything. Never told her I'd come back to her. That was a fiction she created."

JETTA'S EXPRESSION REMAINS GUARDED, but something shifts in her eyes—a flicker of uncertainty where before there was only pain. "She seemed very sure of her welcome."

· · ·

"ALICE HAS ALWAYS BEEN sure of herself, even when she's wrong." Ethan risks a small step closer. "I ended things before I left. She didn't want to hear it then, and apparently, she still doesn't."

"WHY SHOULD I BELIEVE YOU?" The question hangs between them, simple and devastating in its honesty.

"BECAUSE THE ONLY person I want is you, Jetta." His voice cracks on her name. "It's always been you."

SHE BLINKS, confusion crossing her features. "What are you talking about? You hated me in high school. You helped them humiliate me."

ANOTHER STEP CLOSER. The distance between them measured now in feet rather than yards, in breaths rather than words. "I never hated you. I was a coward."

THE CONFESSION COSTS HIM, each word pulled from some deep, protected place he's never allowed anyone to see. "I helped humiliate you because my friends pressured me. But the real reason—" He stops, throat working as he struggles to continue. "The real reason was that I liked you too much, and I was too much of a coward to admit it."

HER LIPS PART IN SURPRISE, eyes widening as she processes his words. "That doesn't make any sense."

. . .

"IT DOES when you're seventeen and terrified of your own feelings." He takes another step, close enough now to see the flutter of her pulse at the base of her throat. "I had this perfect life mapped out—the popular crowd, the right college, the future my family expected. And then there was you, with your sharp mind and sharper tongue, who saw through everything and everyone, including me. I was terrified of how much I wanted to be near you."

THE TRUTH POURS out of him now, unstoppable. "So when friends suggested the prank, I went along with it. Told myself it was just a joke. That it would help me get over this... fascination. But afterwards, seeing what we'd done to you—" His voice roughens with remembered shame. "I've never forgiven myself for that day."

JETTA'S ARMS loosen their protective hold around her body, one hand rising to press against her mouth as if to physically contain her reaction. When she speaks, her voice trembles with emotions too complex to name.

"I KEYED your car because I had feelings for you, too." The admission seems to surprise her as much as him. "You broke my heart before I even knew what that meant."

THE REVELATION HANGS BETWEEN THEM, rewriting a decade of history in six simple words. Ethan sways slightly, absorbing the impact of what might have been if he'd been braver then, if he'd chosen differently.

· · ·

"I'm not that boy anymore," he says softly. "I haven't been for a long time."

"And I'm not that girl." Her gaze meets his, direct and unflinching despite the tears still shimmering in her eyes. "The one who let people hurt her without fighting back."

The remaining distance between them seems to evaporate with each breath, neither quite aware of moving until they stand close enough that the heat of their bodies mingles in the cool air of the apartment. His hand lifts, hesitates, then gently —so gently—touches hers. Their fingers connect, tentative at first, then interlacing with desperate certainty.

"I'm sorry," he whispers, the words insufficient but necessary. "For everything."

Her free hand rises to his face, fingertips tracing the sharp line of his jaw as if memorising its contours. "I'm sorry too. For not seeing you clearly until now."

The kiss, when it comes, feels inevitable—like the closing of a circle begun years ago in a high school hallway. His lips find hers with reverent hunger, different from their earlier embrace on his couch. That had been discovery, exploration. This is recognition, homecoming. Her mouth opens beneath his, a soft sound escaping her throat as her body arches into him.

. . .

Suddenly, their hands are everywhere, tearing at each other's clothes with a desperate urgency. His arms wrap around her waist, lifting her slightly as he presses her back against the wall. Her hands slide into his hair, fingers tangling in the short strands at the nape of his neck. The contact is electric, sending currents of heat through her body that pool low in her stomach, igniting a hunger that demands immediate satisfaction.

He breaks the kiss, his breath ragged, and looks into her eyes. "Jetta," he breathes, her name a prayer and a plea. She responds by dropping to her knees, her hands working at his belt, then the button and zipper of his jeans. He groans as she takes him into her mouth, her tongue swirling around his shaft, her head bobbing as she takes him deeper.

He pulls her up before he can reach the edge, his hands eagerly removing her sweater. He lays her down on the couch, his body covering hers as he kisses his way down her stomach. He hooks his fingers into the waistband of her jeans, tugging them off along with her underwear. His mouth finds her centre, his tongue lapping at her folds, his fingers slipping inside her. She arches off the couch, her hands gripping his hair as waves of pleasure crash over her. Her legs now over his shoulders while he continues his relentless assault on her most sensitive areas.

He pulls back and stands, deliberately sucking on his fingers that he just withdrew from her, his cock hard and ready. He lifts her and turns her around, bending her over the armrest of the couch. "Fuck me," she breathes. He positions himself at her wet entrance and slams into her with a hard thrust, his hips moving with a primal rhythm. She meets each thrust, her body pressing back against his, their skin slapping together. The punishing force is what they both want and need; they both cry out in pleasure at the sensation.

SUDDENLY, he turns her around again, lifting her up while gripping her ass. Her legs wrap around his waist, her arms around his neck. He carries her to the bedroom, his cock still buried deep inside her. He lays her down on the bed, his body covering hers. His hips move with a needy urgency, his cock sliding in and out of her with a desperate pace.

SHE MATCHES HIS RHYTHM, her hips lifting to meet his thrusts. Their bodies are slick with sweat, their breaths coming in ragged gasps. The room fills with the sound of their love-making, the scent of their desire.

HE LEANS DOWN, his mouth capturing hers in a fierce kiss. She moans into his mouth, her body tensing as she reaches the peak. He swallows her cries, his own body stiffening as he finds his release.

THEY COLLAPSE ONTO THE BED, their bodies entwined, their hearts pounding against each other. The past with all its pain and misunderstanding finally recedes, giving way to the present moment—to the heat of skin against skin, to whispered confessions between kisses, to the discovery that sometimes the longest journey leads exactly where you need to be.

CHAPTER 12

Alice's Revenge

THE BLUE GLOW of the laptop screen casts Ethan's face in harsh relief as he squints at the spreadsheet before him, numbers swimming together after three hours of continuous work. His office—a converted spare bedroom in the apartment —feels smaller at night, the walls pressing in with each passing hour as the city beyond his window transitions from evening bustle to midnight stillness. A half-empty mug of cold coffee sits forgotten amid scattered papers, file folders, and a framed photo of him and Owen from their college graduation that he's angled to face him—a reminder of simpler times.

HE ROLLS HIS SHOULDERS, wincing at the tight knots that have formed along his spine. The security proposal needs finishing by morning, but his concentration has frayed along with his patience. Thoughts of Jetta keep intruding—her smile this morning as she left his apartment, the way her hair spilled across his pillow last night, how easily they've fallen into a rhythm that feels both novel and somehow inevitable. For the first time in years, maybe ever, he feels settled, grounded in something real.

• • •

His phone buzzes against the desk, screen illuminating with a notification. Then another. And another. A rapid succession that suggests urgency or persistence—neither boding well at this hour. Ethan's hand hovers over the device, instinct telling him not to look, not to break the fragile peace he's found. The phone buzzes again, more insistent than seems possible for an inanimate object.

When he finally flips it over, the name on the screen makes his stomach clench. Alice. Not saved in his contacts— he deleted her number weeks ago—but he recognises it instantly. Some numbers burn themselves into memory.

Ten messages in twenty minutes. All from her.

He swipes open the first, breath catching as the image loads—Alice in black lingerie, posed on what he recognises as his old bedspread that he gave her when he was getting rid of things before his travels. Her flame-red hair spills over pale shoulders, green eyes staring directly into the camera with an expression that once would have excited him but now only creates a cold knot of dread in his stomach.

Miss me yet? reads the caption.

The second message is another photo, more explicit, her body contorted to display what she considers her best assets. The third continues the pattern, each image progressively more revealing, more desperate in its attempt to provoke a response.

THE FOURTH BREAKS THE PATTERN. No image, just text: *You can't just erase me, Ethan. Not after everything.*

HIS JAW TIGHTENS as he scrolls through the remaining messages, each one darker than the last, evolving from seduction to something that borders on threat.

DOES your little bookstore mouse know about us? About what you're really like?

REMEMBER THAT NIGHT IN CHICAGO? How wild you got? Bet she'd love to hear about that.

I STILL HAVE THE VIDEO, you know. The one where you told me what you really wanted to do to me. So graphic. So unlike your public persona.

MAYBE I SHOULD FORWARD it to her. Or post it somewhere she'll see it.

YOU KNOW I don't give up easily. On anything.

WE'RE NOT DONE until I say we're done.

. . .

THE FINAL MESSAGE arrived seconds ago: *Check your email.*

ETHAN'S HAND is shaking as he opens his inbox. There it is, from an address he doesn't recognise but knows instantly is hers—one of many she cycles through to bypass filters. The subject line reads: "For your bookworm's eyes only."

HE OPENS it to find a video attachment. His throat constricts. He doesn't need to watch it to know what it contains—him, drunk on scotch after a particularly difficult job, saying things he barely remembers to a camera he hadn't realised was recording. The thumbnail image shows his face, flushed with alcohol and what he thought then was desire.

THE MUSCLES in his shoulders bunch like steel cables. His fingers grip the phone so tightly that the case creaks in protest. A familiar sensation crawls up his spine—the hyperawareness that preceded violence in another life, one he's tried to leave behind. He forces himself to breathe, to release the tension in increments, counting silently as he was taught.

FOUR IN. Hold. Four out.

HE TYPES A REPLY, fingers stabbing at the screen with precise fury.

STOP. Now. Whatever you think we had, it's over. These messages are harassment. The photos and video were taken without my consent. If you contact me again, or if you attempt to contact Jetta, I will take legal action.

His thumb hovers over the send button. Will this make it worse? Alice has never responded well to direct confrontation. She feeds on reaction, any reaction. The last time he tried to establish boundaries, she showed up at his door at three in the morning, causing a scene that resulted in police involvement.

But silence isn't an option either. Not with threats directed at Jetta. Not with whatever game Alice is playing.

The cursor blinks, waiting. He adds another line:

I'm blocking this number after this message. Any further contact will be documented and provided to authorities.

Still not satisfied, he adds:

I'm sorry if I hurt you. That was never my intention. But this needs to end.

He reads it over, questioning the apology. Is he truly sorry, or just saying what he thinks might defuse her rage? The complexity of his feelings toward Alice—a mix of regret, pity, and growing fear—doesn't fit into text messages. Nothing about their brief, intense relationship had been healthy. He'd been running from his past, from his feelings for Jetta that he hadn't been ready to confront. Alice had been convenient, available, uncomplicated in the moment until she wasn't.

HE HITS SEND BEFORE he can overthink further.

THE MESSAGE SHOWS AS DELIVERED, then read almost instantly. Three dots appear, indicating she's typing. He watches, heart pounding in his chest, as the dots appear and disappear several times. Minutes pass in suspended animation.

FINALLY, a single line arrives:

YOU'LL REGRET THIS.

ETHAN SETS the phone down on his desk with deliberate care, as if it might detonate if handled roughly. He leans back in his chair, dragging both hands through his hair, leaving it standing in dishevelled spikes. The overhead light feels suddenly too bright, too exposing. He reaches up and switches it off, leaving only the glow of his laptop screen.

IN THE NEW SEMI-DARKNESS, his reflection stares back from the window—a ghost superimposed over the city lights, eyes hollow with worry. Beyond his transparent image, night envelops buildings and streets like a velvet cloak, punctuated by the steady rhythm of traffic signals changing from red to green to yellow and back again. Life continuing its ordered patterns while his has suddenly veered into chaos.

· · ·

HE NEEDS TO TELL JETTA. About Alice, about the threats, about everything. No more secrets, no more past errors haunting their present. But not tonight. Not via text or phone call. Tomorrow, face to face, he'll find the words to explain the complicated mess he's brought to her doorstep. For now, he blocks Alice's number, closes his laptop, and surrenders to the knowledge that sleep will be elusive, replaced by vigilance against what might come next.

◈

MORNING LIGHT FILTERS through the tall windows of Bound Together, transforming ordinary dust motes into drifting constellations that dance above the polished oak shelves. Jetta inhales the comforting scent of paper and binding glue as she arranges a display of new releases, each cover a promise of worlds waiting to be discovered. The shop feels particularly welcoming today, a sanctuary of stories and possibilities that mirrors the hopeful feeling that's taken root in her chest since things with Ethan have settled into something real and sustaining.

SHE STEPS BACK to assess the display, tilting her head as she considers moving the mystery novels to a more prominent position. The morning has been pleasantly busy—a steady stream of regulars mixed with curious tourists who wander in from the nearby cafés. Across the shop, Brandi arranges a selection of local authors' works, her blonde hair caught in a messy bun that bobs as she hums along to the soft indie music playing through hidden speakers.

"EXCUSE ME," a soft voice interrupts Jetta's thoughts. An older woman with wire-rimmed glasses and a well-worn canvas tote approaches. "My book club is reading 'The Lighthouse Keeper's Daughter' this month. Would you happen to have it in stock?"

"We do," Jetta smiles, leading the woman toward the fiction section. "It's one of my favourites from last year's releases. The author does such a beautiful job with the coastal setting—you can almost taste the salt air."

As she pulls the book from the shelf, the small bell above the door chimes. Jetta glances up automatically, the welcoming smile freezing on her face as flame-red hair catches the sunlight streaming through the windows. Alice stands in the doorway, her sharp gaze sweeping the shop with predatory assessment. She's dressed impeccably—a green silk blouse that matches her eyes, fitted black pants that emphasise her slender frame, heels that add unnecessary inches to her already considerable height.

Something cold slides down Jetta's spine, settling in her stomach like a swallowed ice cube. She forces herself to continue her conversation with the customer, explaining the book club discount while her peripheral vision tracks Alice's deliberate progress through the store. Each click of Alice's heels against the hardwood floor sends a small jolt through Jetta's nervous system.

"Thank you, dear," the woman says, accepting the book. "Would you mind ringing me up? I'm meeting friends for lunch soon."

. . .

"OF COURSE." Jetta leads her to the counter, hyperaware of Alice now examining a display of poetry collections, her manicured fingers trailing over spines with possessive intimacy. Brandi has noticed her too; Jetta catches the sharp narrowing of her friend's eyes, the way she straightens to her full height, shoulders squaring with protective instinct.

JETTA FOCUSES ON THE TRANSACTION, swiping the customer's credit card with hands that aren't quite steady. The machine whirs, printing a receipt that she tears off with a practised motion.

"WOULD YOU LIKE A BOOKMARK? We just got these lovely new ones with local landmarks—" she begins, but falls silent as a waft of expensive perfume announces Alice's arrival at the counter. The customer takes her purchase with a curious glance between them before departing, the bell chiming her exit.

"JETTA, RIGHT?" Alice's voice drips with manufactured sweetness. "I thought that was you. Funny running into you here."

HEAT FLOODS JETTA'S CHEEKS. She's acutely aware of the three customers browsing nearby, their attention drawn by Alice's slightly-too-loud greeting. One woman glances up from a cookbook, her expression openly curious.

"THIS IS MY SHOP," Jetta manages, proud that her voice

remains level despite the adrenaline flooding her system. "What can I help you with?"

ALICE'S SMILE WIDENS, revealing perfect teeth. There's something shark-like in the expression, a predator's display rather than genuine pleasure. "Your shop? How charming. Ethan mentioned you worked with books, but I had no idea it was such a... quaint little place."

THE DELIBERATE PAUSE, the subtle emphasis on "little"— it's calculated to diminish, to establish hierarchy. Jetta's fingers press against the counter's edge, seeking stability as her knees threaten to liquefy beneath her.

"DID YOU NEED A BOOK RECOMMENDATION?" Jetta asks, clinging to professionalism like a life raft. "Or were you just browsing?"

"OH, I'm not much of a reader." Alice picks up a small crystal paperweight from the counter display, turning it in her hands as if assessing its value. "I prefer more... physical activities. As Ethan knows quite well."

THE IMPLICATION HANGS in the air, impossible to miss. The cookbook woman is openly staring now, a teenage boy pretending to examine graphic novels while clearly eavesdropping. Jetta's throat constricts, words evaporating before they can form.

. . .

"Is there something you need, Alice?" Brandi's voice cuts through the tension as she approaches, positioning herself slightly in front of Jetta. Her tone is professional but carries an undercurrent of steel that Jetta recognises from rare confrontations with difficult customers.

Alice's gaze shifts to Brandi, assessing and dismissing her in a single sweep. "Just catching up with an old friend. Well, perhaps 'friend' isn't quite the right word." She turns back to Jetta, green eyes glittering with malice. "What would you call someone who's sleeping with your man? Is there a specific term for that?"

The words land like individual blows. Jetta's breath catches, her vision narrowing momentarily as blood rushes to her face. The teenage boy has abandoned all pretence of browsing, openly watching the drama unfold. The cookbook woman whispers something to another customer, both their eyes fixed on the scene at the counter.

"I think it's time for you to leave." Brandi steps fully between them now, her small frame somehow expanding to create a barrier. Her voice remains even but has dropped to a register Jetta rarely hears—the tone that emerges when Brandi's protective instincts override her usual sunny disposition.

"Am I making you uncomfortable?" Alice's question is directed past Brandi, her eyes fixed on Jetta with artificial concern. "I just thought we should get to know each other, given our... shared interests. Ethan and I have such history together. So many intimate moments. It seems only fair you should know what you're getting into."

JETTA'S HANDS tremble as she sorts bookmarks that don't need sorting, desperate for something to do, some way to appear unaffected by this calculated attack. Her sanctuary feels violated, the shop's peaceful atmosphere corrupted by this intrusion. Worst of all is the doubt that seeps in around the edges of her mind—what history? What moments? How much doesn't she know?

"THAT'S ENOUGH." Brandi's voice has lost all pretence of politeness. "This is private property, and you're harassing my business partner. Leave now, or I'll call security."

ALICE SIGHS DRAMATICALLY, replacing the paperweight with exaggerated care. "Another time, then." She turns, addressing the shop at large as if concluding a performance. "Such a lovely little store. So... provincial. It really suits you, Jetta."

WITH THAT PARTING SHOT, she strides toward the door, heels striking the floor with percussive finality. The bell chimes her departure, the sound hanging in the sudden silence that envelops the shop. The remaining customers exchange glances, their discomfort palpable as they pretend to resume browsing.

JETTA EXHALES SHAKILY, her legs suddenly unsteady. Brandi's arm wraps around her waist, providing silent support as they retreat to the small office behind the register area. Once the door closes behind them, Jetta collapses into the desk chair, hands covering her face.

"WHAT WAS THAT?" she whispers, voice trembling. "Who does that?"

"SOMEONE UNHINGED," Brandi replies, kneeling beside her. "And desperate. That was not the behaviour of someone who feels secure in their relationship."

JETTA LOWERS HER HANDS, meeting her friend's concerned gaze. "You think she's lying? About her and Ethan?"

"I THINK SHE'S MANIPULATING," Brandi says carefully. "Using fragments of truth to create maximum damage. Have you talked to Ethan about her? Really talked, beyond what happened that night at his apartment?"

"NOT IN DETAIL," Jetta admits. "It's been so good between us, I didn't want to drag that back into it."

BRANDI SQUEEZES HER HAND. "Call him. Now. Before your imagination runs wild with whatever poison she just tried to plant."

JETTA NODS, reaching for her phone with unsteady fingers. Whatever game Alice is playing, she won't let it succeed without a fight.

SLANTED AMBER light filters through the kitchen windows as Owen dices tomatoes with the practised efficiency of someone who finds peace in culinary ritual. The knife moves in steady rhythm against the cutting board, transforming firm red flesh into perfect cubes that he sweeps into a waiting bowl. Through the open archway to the living room, he can hear Ethan's voice—low and measured as he discusses something work-related over the phone—the familiar background sound-track to their shared domestic space. The pasta water bubbles on the stove, steam rising in translucent curls that catch the late afternoon sunlight, transforming ordinary kitchen steam into something almost magical.

OWEN REACHES for the bunch of basil waiting on the counter, inhaling its sharp, sweet fragrance before beginning to tear the leaves. Tonight feels important somehow—Jetta is coming over for dinner, the first time she's visited since she and Ethan have become officially a couple. The domesticity of preparing a meal for them fills Owen with quiet satisfaction. After years of watching his best friend hold everyone at arm's length, seeing Ethan genuinely happy brings a particular kind of joy.

HE'S JUST REACHING for the garlic when the front door swings open without warning—no knock, no call, just the sudden draft of outside air disturbing the kitchen's warmth. Owen turns, expecting Brandi, who sometimes arrives early to help with cooking, or perhaps Jetta herself.

. . .

THE KNIFE CLATTERS from his hand, bouncing once on the cutting board before settling against the tomatoes.

ALICE STANDS IN THE DOORWAY, her flame-red hair loose around her shoulders, wearing what can only generously be called clothing—black lace lingerie barely covered by a sheer robe that does nothing to conceal the pale expanse of her skin. Her lips are painted a deep crimson that matches her hair, her eyes outlined in dramatic black that makes the green of her irises seem to glow with unnatural intensity.

"ETHAN, I knew you'd be expecting me," she purrs, stepping inside with the confidence of someone entering their own home. Her gaze lands on Owen, surprise flickering briefly across her features before her mouth curves into a predatory smile. "Oh. You're not Ethan."

"ALICE, WHAT ARE YOU DOING HERE?" Owen manages, his voice emerging as a strangled near-whisper. His brain struggles to process the scene—Alice essentially naked in his kitchen, the door she shouldn't have a key to standing open behind her, the calculating gleam in her eyes as she assesses his shock.

"I'M HERE FOR ETHAN, OBVIOUSLY." She gestures down at her body with theatrical emphasis. "Special delivery."

BEFORE OWEN CAN RESPOND, Ethan appears in the archway, phone still in hand, his expression transforming from confusion to cold fury as he takes in the scene. He ends his call with a sharp tap, sliding the device into his pocket as he moves forward, positioning himself between Owen and Alice.

"ALICE, GET OUT," he growls, his voice carrying a dangerous edge that Owen rarely hears—the voice from Ethan's military days, the tone that brooks no argument.

ALICE'S SMILE falters momentarily before she recovers, batting her eyelashes with exaggerated innocence. "Don't be like that, baby. I thought we could pick up where we left off." She runs one hand down her exposed torso in a gesture clearly meant to be seductive. "Remember how much you loved this set? You said I looked like sin incarnate."

OWEN SHIFTS UNCOMFORTABLY, suddenly feeling like an intruder in his own kitchen. He should leave, give them privacy, but something in Ethan's rigid posture keeps him rooted to the spot—a silent witness to whatever is unfolding.

"HOW DID YOU GET IN HERE?" Ethan demands, ignoring her attempt at seduction. "This isn't my apartment. This is Owen's house."

ALICE SHRUGS, the movement causing her robe to slip further down one shoulder. "The door was unlocked. I was looking for your place the other day, but this address came up when I searched. Thought I'd surprise you." Her voice drops to a theatrical whisper. "I think the universe wanted us to be alone. Your roommate can leave."

. . .

"I'M NOT LEAVING ANYWHERE. This is my house," Owen says, finding his voice as indignation overcomes his initial shock. "And the door was definitely locked."

ETHAN'S EYES narrow as he studies Alice's face. "Did you pick the lock? Or did you tell the security guard some story about being expected?"

HER LAUGHTER—HIGH and brittle—confirms the latter. "He was very understanding when I explained I was your girl-friend coming to surprise you. Men are so helpful when you smile at them the right way."

"YOU'RE NOT MY GIRLFRIEND. You never were." Ethan's voice remains controlled, but Owen recognises the tension in his jaw, the slight tremor in his hands that signals barely contained anger. "We had a brief thing years ago. It meant nothing, and it's over. I've made that abundantly clear."

ALICE'S EXPRESSION SHIFTS, playfulness giving way to something harder, more desperate. "You promised we'd recon-nect. You can't just ignore me after everything we shared."

"I NEVER PROMISED YOU ANYTHING," Ethan says, each word precise and final. "Whatever you think happened between us was entirely in your head. Now leave, before I call the police."

. . .

"YOU WOULDN'T DARE." Her voice drops to a hiss. "Not with everything I know about you. The things you told me. The things we did." She steps closer, her perfume—too sweet, too heavy—filling the space between them. "Does your little bookshop mouse know about Chicago? About what you asked me to do to you?"

OWEN WATCHES his friend's face, sees the moment calculation replaces anger—Ethan weighing options, considering consequences with the strategic mind that served him well in crisis zones.

"OWEN," Ethan says without turning, "could you call the police, please? Report an intruder who picked the lock."

THE REQUEST BREAKS THE SPELL. Alice steps back, her confidence visibly crumbling. "You're bluffing."

"TRY ME." Ethan's voice is ice. "You're trespassing in my friend's home. You've been harassing me with texts and emails containing explicit material I never consented to. You showed up at Jetta's workplace today to intimidate her. That's at least three criminal charges."

OWEN REACHES FOR HIS PHONE, making the motion deliberately visible. Alice's eyes widen, tracking the movement.

"YOU'RE MAKING A MISTAKE," she says, but the threat

sounds hollow now. "We're good together. We make sense in a way you and that mousy little nobody never will."

"LEAVE," Ethan says, the single word carrying the weight of absolute finality. "Now. And don't come back. Don't contact me, don't contact Jetta, don't contact Owen. If you do, there will be legal consequences."

FOR A MOMENT, Owen thinks she might refuse, might escalate the confrontation further. Something dark and unhinged flashes in her eyes—a glimpse of whatever obsessive fixation drives her behaviour. Then, with a fluid movement that somehow manages to combine grace with fury, she turns and stalks toward the door.

"THIS ISN'T OVER," she calls over her shoulder, the words almost lost as she slams the door behind her with enough force to rattle the windows.

THE SILENCE that follows feels oppressive, heavy with unspoken questions. Ethan remains frozen in place, staring at the closed door as if expecting it to burst open again at any moment. Owen sets his phone down, the motion seeming to break whatever spell has held them both immobile.

"I'M SORRY, OWEN," Ethan says finally, turning to face him. The controlled anger has drained from his expression, leaving something raw and apologetic in its place. "I had no idea she'd show up here. No idea she'd go this far."

· · ·

OWEN SHAKES HIS HEAD, bending to retrieve the knife that still lies forgotten among the tomatoes. "It's not your fault, Ethan." He places the knife in the sink, a deliberate action that helps ground him in normalcy after the surreal intrusion. "But we need to do something about her. This isn't normal behaviour."

"I KNOW." Ethan runs a hand through his hair, the gesture betraying his agitation more clearly than words could. "I'll handle it. She won't bother us again."

"Us? Ethan, I'm worried about you. And Jetta." Owen moves to the stove, turning down the now-boiling pasta water with methodical calm that belies his concern. "Alice doesn't seem like someone who gives up easily."

"SHE ISN'T," Ethan agrees, his expression hardening with resolve. "But neither am I. And I won't let her hurt the people I care about. Not again."

THE SIMPLE STATEMENT carries layers of meaning that Owen doesn't miss—the acknowledgment of past mistakes, the determination to protect what matters now. As Ethan turns toward the living room, shoulders set with renewed purpose, Owen can't help but wonder what comes next in this unexpected battle—and whether his friend is truly prepared for whatever Alice might do when she realises she can't have what she wants.

CHAPTER 13

Safe Haven

STEAM RISES from the two mugs on the counter, curling into the cool morning air of the bookshop. Jetta wraps her fingers around the ceramic warmth, inhaling the rich scent of fresh coffee as sunlight spills through the front windows, painting golden rectangles across the wooden floor. Bound Together always feels different before opening—peaceful, expectant, like a theatre before the curtain rises. She savours these quiet moments with Brandi, their morning ritual of coffee and conversation before customers arrive.

"You look exhausted," Brandi observes, leaning against the counter. Her blonde hair is twisted into a messy bun, tendrils escaping around her face. "Nightmares again?"

Jetta nods, taking a long sip of coffee. The bitterness coats her tongue, momentarily drowning the lingering taste of fear that's become her constant companion. "I keep hearing noises, thinking she's outside my door."

· · ·

BRANDI'S EXPRESSION SHIFTS, determination replacing concern. "That's what I wanted to talk to you about. This has gone on long enough." She sets her mug down with a decisive clink. "Alice showed up at Owen's place last night. In lingerie."

"WHAT?" The word escapes as a horrified whisper. Jetta's fingers tighten around her mug until her knuckles blanch white.

"SHE PICKED the lock or talked her way past security—Owen wasn't clear on which." Brandi shudders, wrapping her cardigan tighter around her shoulders despite the growing warmth in the shop. "She was practically naked, Jetta. Standing in their kitchen like she belonged there."

THE COFFEE TURNS sour in Jetta's stomach. "What did Ethan do?"

"THREATENED TO CALL THE POLICE. She left, but not before making more threats." Brandi leans forward, her voice dropping though they're alone in the shop. "This is escalating. Fast. You two need to stick together—safety in numbers."

JETTA'S BREATH catches as she realises what Brandi is suggesting. "You mean...?"

"ETHAN SHOULD MOVE IN WITH YOU," Brandi states it plainly, as if suggesting nothing more complicated than a new book display. "Your apartment isn't connected to either of you in any paperwork. Alice doesn't know about it."

"Move in together?" The words feel strange on Jetta's tongue, too big, too consequential. "We've only been dating for—"

"This isn't about dating milestones," Brandi interrupts. "It's about safety. Alice is unhinged, and she's fixated on both of you." Her expression softens, hand reaching across the counter to cover Jetta's. "Besides, I'm practically living at Owen's anyway. The apartment feels empty without me, doesn't it?"

It does. The silence has grown heavier each night, expanding to fill every corner with shadows and imagined sounds. Still, the thought of sharing her space, her sanctuary, with Ethan—

The bell above the door chimes, interrupting her thoughts. They both turn to find Ethan standing in the doorway, a cardboard box balanced in his arms. Sunlight catches in his dark hair, gilding the edges with amber. His expression is guarded, uncertain, so different from his usual confidence.

"Brandi called me," he explains, his eyes finding Jetta's across the shop. "I hope this is okay."

. . .

TIME SEEMS SUSPENDED between one heartbeat and the next. The reality of what they're considering—what they're about to do—settles over Jetta with sudden weight. Sharing breakfast, bathroom schedules, the mundane intimacies that couples normally ease into over months, not weeks. And all because a flame-haired woman can't accept rejection.

"LET'S CLOSE EARLY," Brandi announces, already moving toward the door to flip the sign. "Get you settled in before the afternoon rush."

THE DRIVE to Jetta's apartment passes in relative silence, Ethan following in his own car loaded with essentials. Brandi fills the quiet in Jetta's vehicle with chatter about practical arrangements, but Jetta barely hears her, mind racing ahead to what awaits.

THEY REACH HER BUILDING—A converted warehouse with exposed pipes and industrial charm—and take the freight elevator to the fourth floor. Ethan joins them in the hallway, box still in his arms, his face a careful mask that doesn't quite hide his apprehension.

"THIS IS IT," Jetta says unnecessarily as they reach her door. She fumbles with the keys, suddenly hyperaware of every movement, every breath. The lock clicks, the door swings open, and they stand at the threshold—Ethan outside, Jetta inside, the doorway a boundary between separate lives and what comes next.

· · ·

"YOU DON'T HAVE to do this," he says quietly, for her ears alone. "We can find another solution."

HER HEART SWELLS at the offer, at his willingness to prioritise her comfort over his plans. But the memory of Alice in their shop, of her venomous words and predatory smile, strengthens her resolve.

"COME IN," she says, stepping aside. "It's not much, but it's home."

HE CROSSES the threshold with careful steps, as if entering sacred ground. When she reaches to take some of his burden, their fingers brush across the cardboard surface. They both freeze, electricity arcing between them at this simple contact. His eyes meet hers, dark and unreadable in the apartment's dim light.

"WHERE SHOULD I...?" he asks, breaking the spell.

"ANYWHERE FOR NOW," she manages, stepping back to create distance between them. "We can sort it all out later."

THE APARTMENT REVEALS itself around them—open-concept living space with weathered brick walls painted white, tall windows framed in black metal that flood the room with natural light. Bookshelves line one wall, crammed beyond capacity with volumes arranged by colour rather than author, creating a gradient from deepest blue to vibrant red. Throw blankets drape over every available surface—the grey sofa, the reading chair in the corner, the bench beneath the window. Small touches of Jetta everywhere—candles on the coffee table, a collection of crystals catching light on the windowsill, plants flourishing in mismatched pots.

"THIS IS GORGEOUS," Ethan says, setting his box down carefully beside the sofa. He turns slowly, taking in every detail with appreciative eyes. "It suits you."

"LET me give you the grand tour, I mean, I know you have been here before, but what the hell, right?" Brandi announces with exaggerated enthusiasm, linking her arm through Ethan's. "Kitchen through here—temperamental oven, but great counter space. Bathroom down the hall—the hot water takes forever, but pressure's amazing once it gets going."

JETTA WATCHES them move through her space, Brandi's cheerful commentary washing over her as she catalogues Ethan's reactions. The careful way he listens, the respectful distance he maintains from her personal items, the slight smile that touches his lips when he spots her collection of first editions behind glass. His presence should feel intrusive, but instead, it fits—like a piece of furniture she hadn't realised was missing until now.

"AND THIS," Brandi announces with theatrical flair as they reach the final door, "is the bedroom. Where all the magic happens. Or will happen. Or whatever." She winks at Jetta, whose cheeks flood with heat.

"Brandi," she hisses, mortification rising like a tide.

"What? Just completing the tour." Brandi's innocence is entirely feigned, her eyes dancing with mischief. She glances at her watch with exaggerated surprise. "Oh! Would you look at the time? I promised Owen I'd meet him for lunch." She grabs her purse from where she dropped it by the door, already halfway out. "You two get settled. Call if you need anything. Use protection!"

The door closes behind her with decisive finality, leaving them alone in sudden silence. Jetta stands frozen, acutely aware of Ethan's presence, of the space between them that seems both too vast and not nearly enough.

"So," he says, his voice gentle in the quiet apartment. "Where do we start?"

∾

Twilight softens the apartment's edges, shadows lengthening across the hardwood floors as Jetta lights the candle on her kitchen counter. The flame catches, sending a warm glow across the small space where Ethan stands, examining the contents of her refrigerator. Six hours into their new living arrangement, they've unpacked his essentials—clothes in the spare dresser, toiletries arranged beside hers in the bathroom, laptop set up on the small desk in the corner of the living room. Now comes the first test of their domestic compatibility: dinner.

. . .

"I THINK we can work with this," Ethan says, pulling out a half-full box of pasta, some cherry tomatoes, and a slightly wilted bunch of basil. "Simple pasta? Unless you'd rather order in."

"PASTA WORKS." Jetta reaches past him for the garlic hanging in a braid by the window, their arms brushing. She steps back quickly, surprised by how such a casual touch sends electricity racing up her spine. "I, um, have wine too. If you want."

THE KITCHEN FEELS IMPOSSIBLY small with both of them in it. Every movement becomes a choreographed dance of near-misses and accidental contacts—his elbow grazing her shoulder as he fills a pot with water, her hip bumping his when she reaches for the cutting board. Each touch leaves a trail of heat that lingers on her skin.

"YOU CAN HANDLE THE SAUCE," she suggests, desperate for breathing room. "I'll set the table."

ETHAN NODS, rolling up his sleeves with methodical precision that draws her attention to the defined muscles of his forearms, the scars on his knuckles that have almost healed. She forces herself to turn away, focusing on the simple task of placing plates and silverware on her small dining table. The wine glasses catch the candlelight as she sets them down, sending fractured patterns dancing across the white tablecloth.

. . .

STEAM RISES from the pot as water begins to boil, filling the kitchen with humid warmth. Ethan moves with unexpected grace in the small space, dicing garlic with practiced efficiency, the sharp scent releasing as his knife works through the cloves. The domestic intimacy of the moment—a man cooking in her kitchen, the quiet sounds of chopping and simmering—feels both foreign and strangely right.

"I DIDN'T KNOW you could cook," she says, breaking the silence that has stretched between them.

HE GLANCES UP, a half-smile lifting the corner of his mouth. "There's a lot we don't know about each other."

THE SIMPLE TRUTH of his statement hangs in the air. Despite their history—both distant past and recent present—they remain largely mysteries to one another. Their relationship has been built on extremes: teenage animosity, adult hostility, the crisis that brought them together, and now the intensity of their physical connection. The quiet middle ground of everyday preferences and habits remains largely unexplored territory.

"WHAT'S YOUR FAVOURITE BOOK?" she asks suddenly, reaching for the bottle opener. The question feels both trivial and enormous—the kind of basic information friends exchange early, but they've skipped all the normal steps.

ETHAN PAUSES, considering as he adds tomatoes to the pan. They sizzle against the hot oil, filling the kitchen with their sweet-sharp scent. "'The Great Gatsby,'" he finally answers. "I know it's cliché, but there's something about Fitzgerald's writing that gets to me. The yearning in it."

THE ANSWER SURPRISES HER—NOT the choice itself, but the thoughtfulness behind it. "I saw it on your shelf," she admits, pouring deep red wine into both glasses. "Underlined passages and everything."

"WHAT ABOUT YOU?" He stirs the sauce, adding a pinch of salt without measuring. "Let me guess—something classic but underappreciated. Woolf? Hardy?"

"CLOSE." She smiles despite herself. "I love 'Jane Eyre.' The quiet defiance of her, the way she refuses to compromise herself even when it would be easier."

HE NODS, as if this makes perfect sense. "That fits you."

THE CONVERSATION FLOWS MORE EASILY after that, moving from books to music (she prefers acoustic indie, he has an unexpected passion for jazz), to travel destinations (she dreams of the narrow streets of Prague, he misses the stark beauty of New Mexico, where he once trained). With each revealed preference, each shared opinion, the awkwardness between them dissipates like morning fog beneath a strengthening sun.

. . .

THE PASTA IS PERFECT—SIMPLE but flavorful, the sauce bright with garlic and basil. Their knees occasionally brush beneath the small table; these contacts no longer causing them to startle but instead lingering, deliberate. The wine loosens something in both of them, allows laughter to come more freely, stories to flow without careful editing.

"I NEVER WOULD HAVE GUESSED you'd have such strong opinions about poetry," Jetta says, refilling their glasses. "You seemed more like—"

"A MUSCLEBOUND SECURITY consultant with no appreciation for the arts?" He raises an eyebrow, challenge in his tone, though his eyes remain warm with amusement.

"I WAS GOING to say 'more like a thriller reader,' but your version works too." She smiles, enjoying the easy rhythm they've found.

ETHAN'S PHONE buzzes against the table, screen lighting up with a notification. His expression transforms instantly, jaw tightening as he glances down. The name visible on the screen sends a chill through the warm atmosphere: Alice.

HE TURNS the phone face down without opening the message, but the damage is done. The spectre of flame-red hair and venomous green eyes has invaded their sanctuary, poisoning the comfortable space they've created. Ethan's shoulders tense, his posture shifting subtly into something more guarded, more alert.

· · ·

JETTA SETS DOWN HER FORK, her hand trembling slightly against the white tablecloth. The wine turns sour on her tongue as fear crawls back up her throat, familiar and unwelcome. She thinks of Alice standing in their bookshop, of her calculated cruelty, of her willingness to break into Owen's apartment. What boundaries wouldn't she cross?

"SHE WON'T FIND US HERE," Ethan says, reaching across the table to cover her hand with his. His palm is warm, solid, anchoring her to the present moment. "The apartment's not in either of our names. The shop's mail goes to a P.O. box. There's no connection she can trace."

THEIR EYES LOCK across the flickering candlelight. Something passes between them—not just reassurance, but a deeper current of understanding, of shared vulnerability transformed into strength. His thumb traces small circles against her wrist, the touch both comforting and charged with something more intense.

A SHARP KNOCK at the door shatters the moment. They both jump, wine sloshing in glasses, Ethan's hand instinctively tightening around hers. Jetta's heart pounds against her ribs, breath coming in short, shallow gasps. Alice's text, now this— the timing too perfect to be coincidence.

ETHAN RISES from the table in one fluid motion, his body language transforming as he moves toward the door. His shoulders square, stance widening slightly, every line of him radiating protective readiness. Jetta follows, keeping behind him, her fingers curling around the back of his shirt without conscious thought.

"WHO IS IT?" Ethan calls, voice neutral but carrying a subtle edge of warning.

"IT'S MRS. HENDERSON FROM 4C," comes the muffled reply, an elderly voice that couldn't be further from Alice's smooth purr. "Just wondering if I could borrow some sugar. Making cookies for my grandson's visit tomorrow."

THE TENSION DRAINS from Ethan's body so suddenly it's almost comical. He glances back at Jetta, relief replacing vigilance in his expression. When he opens the door, they find a tiny white-haired woman in a floral housecoat, empty measuring cup in hand.

"SO SORRY TO BOTHER YOU, DEARS," she says, peering up at them with birdlike curiosity. "Oh! You must be Jetta's young man. I don't believe we've met."

THE ABSURDITY OF THE MOMENT—THEIR terror transformed into this mundane interaction, the contrast between the threat they imagined and the reality of this harmless neighbor—bubbles up inside Jetta's chest. A small laugh escapes her, quickly covered by her hand. Ethan's shoulders shake with suppressed mirth as he solemnly introduces himself to Mrs. Henderson.

. . .

By the time they've measured sugar into the cup and exchanged pleasantries about the weather, they're both struggling to maintain composure. The door closes behind their neighbor, and the laughter they've been containing erupts—deep, cleansing peals that bend them double, hands braced on knees, tears gathering at the corners of their eyes.

"Her face," Jetta gasps between bursts of laughter. "When she saw you—like she'd found a movie star in the hallway."

"I thought you were going to lose it when she asked if I was your 'young man,'" Ethan replies, wiping his eyes. "Like we're in a Jane Austen novel."

Their laughter gradually subsides, leaving them facing each other in the entrance hall, cheeks flushed, eyes bright. The shared absurdity has washed away the fear that Alice's intrusion brought, replacing it with something lighter, more intimate—the private joke of new lovers, the conspiratorial closeness of shared relief.

Ethan reaches out, tucking a strand of hair behind her ear with gentle fingers. "Your young man," he repeats softly, testing the phrase. "I like how that sounds."

The simple declaration hangs between them, transforming the air into something charged and expectant. Jetta's breath catches as his hand lingers against her cheek, his eyes asking a question she's suddenly ready to answer.

· · ·

MIDNIGHT STRETCHES the shadows across Jetta's apartment, transforming familiar shapes into looming silhouettes. She moves through the darkness with practised steps, fingers trailing along walls until she reaches the front door. For the third time since they retired to bed—separate beds, Ethan's offer to take the couch accepted with a mixture of relief and regret—she tests the deadbolt, the chain lock, the doorknob. Each mechanism responds with satisfying resistance, yet the ritual brings her no peace. Sleep remains elusive, her mind conjuring scenarios where flame-red hair and green eyes materialise despite every precaution.

"STILL LOCKED?" Ethan's voice comes soft from the hallway behind her.

SHE TURNS to find him watching, a tall shadow against the deeper darkness. The borrowed t-shirt he wears for sleep stretches across his shoulders, the thin fabric doing little to disguise the defined muscles beneath. His hair stands in rumpled spikes, evidence of his own restless attempts at sleep.

"I KNOW IT'S RIDICULOUS," she admits, hand still resting on the cold metal of the deadbolt. "Checking over and over won't make it more locked."

HE STEPS CLOSER, moonlight from the living room windows catching his profile in silver outline. "It's not ridiculous. It's how our brains process threat."

. . .

THE UNDERSTANDING in his voice wraps around her like a blanket, warm and unexpectedly comforting. No judgment, no impatience—just acceptance of her fear and its manifestations.

"I CAN SLEEP ON THE COUCH," he offers again, the words soft in the darkness between them. "If having me here is making this harder."

JETTA SHAKES HER HEAD, suddenly certain of what she wants despite the knot of anxiety that's lodged beneath her ribs since Alice's text. "That's not necessary." The words come out steadier than she feels. "Actually, I think I'd sleep better if you were... closer."

THE ADMISSION HANGS in the air, its implications expanding to fill the space between them. Ethan remains perfectly still, as if afraid any movement might shatter this fragile moment of honesty.

"CLOSER," he repeats, the single word a question and answer all at once.

THEY GRAVITATE toward each other in the dim hallway, movement so gradual it feels inevitable rather than chosen. The distance between them diminishes breath by breath until she can feel the warmth radiating from his skin, smell the faint trace of her soap on him. Her pulse accelerates, a fluttering beneath her skin that has nothing to do with fear and everything to do with anticipation.

. . .

ETHAN'S FINGERS trace the curve of her cheek with a reverence that makes her breath catch. His touch is feather-light, exploring the contours of her face as if committing them to memory through fingertips alone. When his thumb brushes the corner of her mouth, she can't contain the small sound that escapes her throat—part sigh, part invitation.

"I WON'T LET anything happen to you," he whispers, the promise fierce despite its softness. "Not ever again."

SHE KNOWS HE MEANS ALICE, the immediate threat that's driven them into this shared space. But something in his tone suggests more—a broader vow that encompasses all potential harm, all future pain. The intensity of it should frighten her, this absolute protectiveness from a man she's only recently stopped hating. Instead, it unlocks something within her chest, some final resistance giving way to trust.

HER LIPS FIND his in the darkness, the kiss tentative at first —a question asked with the gentle press of mouth against mouth. His response is immediate but restrained, returning the pressure with careful control. For three heartbeats, they remain in this suspended state of gentle exploration. Then something shifts, ignites, transforms.

THE KISS DEEPENS with sudden urgency, control fracturing beneath the weight of desire too long denied. His hands cradle her face, fingers threading through her hair to hold her closer as their mouths move together with increasing hunger. Her back presses against the wall, the solid surface a necessary anchor as her knees threaten to buckle beneath the onslaught of sensation.

ETHAN'S BODY presses against hers, hard planes meeting soft curves, the heat between them building with each ragged breath. His lips leave hers to trail fire down her neck, teeth grazing the sensitive skin where her pulse throbs visibly. She gasps, hands clutching at his shoulders, fingers digging into muscle that tenses beneath her touch.

"JETTA," he breathes against her collarbone, her name transformed into both question and prayer. "Tell me this is okay."

"MORE THAN OKAY," she manages, voice thick with need. "Please, Ethan."

THEY STUMBLE TOWARD HER BEDROOM, unwilling to break contact long enough for coordinated movement. Clothing falls away in their wake—his t-shirt discarded by the bathroom door, her sleep shorts abandoned in the hallway. By the time they reach her bed, they're more undressed than not, skin heated and sensitized by anticipation.

THE SHEETS ARE cool against her back as he lowers her to the mattress, his body following to cover hers with careful weight. Moonlight spills across the bed, illuminating his face as he looks down at her with an expression that makes her heart stutter—desire mixed with something deeper, more vulnerable than simple want.

THEIR EXPLORATION IS both urgent and deliberate—hands mapping territories both new and somehow familiar, mouths learning the geography of pleasure that makes each gasp and shudder. When he slides into her at last, they both freeze at the perfect completion of it, at the rightness that defies their complicated history. Then he begins to move, and thought dissolves into pure sensation.

THEIR LOVEMAKING CARRIES the intensity of their shared fear, transformed into desperate affirmation of life and connection. His hands tangle in her hair, her nails score paths down his back, their bodies finding a rhythm that builds toward something transcendent. The headboard knocks softly against the wall, the sound keeping time with their accelerating heartbeats.

WHEN RELEASE FINDS HER, it's with his name on her lips, her body arching beneath his as pleasure crests and breaks in waves that leave her trembling. He follows moments later, face buried against her neck, a groan torn from deep in his chest as his body tenses, then relaxes into the cradle of hers.

THEY LIE TANGLED TOGETHER AFTERWARD, skin cooling in the night air, breath gradually slowing to normal rhythm. His weight shifts to her side, one arm remaining draped across her waist in possessive comfort. The silence between them feels rich rather than empty, filled with unspoken revelations too new and raw for words.

. . .

A SOUND BREAKS THE QUIET—AN engine idling, too close to be street traffic. Ethan tenses instantly, his body transforming from languid satisfaction to alert readiness in a heartbeat. He rises from the bed in a fluid movement, crossing to the window with predatory grace that reminds her of his military past.

JETTA CLUTCHES the sheet to her chest, cold fear replacing the warmth of moments before. "Is it—"

"CAR," he confirms, voice flat as he peers through the narrow gap in the curtains. "Black sedan. Can't see the driver."

HER HEART POUNDS against her ribs, fight-or-flight response flooding her system with useless adrenaline. They're four stories up, doors locked, windows secured. Yet the knowledge that someone watches from below—that it might be Alice with her venomous smile and dangerous obsession—makes her feel exposed despite the walls around them.

LONG MINUTES PASS, marked only by their shallow breathing and the distant tick of the kitchen clock. Then the sound changes—engine revving, tires moving against pavement. Ethan's shoulders relax incrementally as the noise recedes into the distance.

"THEY'RE GONE," he says, turning back to her. The moonlight catches the planes of his face, revealing the tension still evident in his jaw despite his reassuring words. "Probably nothing. Just someone waiting for a friend, or taking a phone call."

THEY BOTH KNOW it might be a lie, but neither challenges the comforting fiction. When he returns to bed, Jetta moves into his arms without hesitation, seeking the security of his solid presence against the chill of fear that lingers in her veins.

"I WAS AFRAID OF THIS," she confesses into the darkness, her words muffled against his chest. "Not just Alice. Us. Letting myself trust anyone after what happened in high school."

HIS HAND STROKES slow patterns along her spine, soothing without dismissing. "I know."

"EVERY TIME I start to feel safe with you, I remember who you were then, what you did." The admission costs her, each word pulled from some deep, protected place. "Then I remember who you are now, what you've done since, and it's like my brain can't reconcile the two versions."

ETHAN'S ARMS tighten around her, his heartbeat steady beneath her ear. "I wanted you even then," he whispers, the confession equally raw. "Since that first day in English class when you argued with Mrs. Peterson about 'The Scarlet Letter.' You were so passionate, so absolutely certain of your interpretation. I'd never met anyone like you."

. . .

THE REVELATION SETTLES into her chest, rearranging pieces of their shared past into a new configuration. "Then why did you—"

"BECAUSE I WAS A COWARD." His voice remains soft but carries the weight of years of regret. "Because wanting you terrified me. Because hurting you was easier than admitting how I felt."

SILENCE FOLLOWS HIS ADMISSION, not empty but filled with processing, with acceptance of a truth too complex for immediate response. When she finally speaks, her voice carries the drowsiness of emotional exhaustion.

"I WANTED YOU TOO," she murmurs, the words slipping out as sleep begins to claim her. "Even through the hate. Maybe that's why it hurt so much."

HIS LIPS PRESS against her forehead, a benediction rather than a demand. "Sleep," he whispers against her skin. "I've got you."

AS CONSCIOUSNESS FADES, Jetta surrenders to the protective circle of his arms, to the rhythm of his breathing against her hair. The threat of Alice temporarily recedes, pushed beyond the boundaries of their joined bodies, their shared warmth. Tomorrow will bring new fears, new challenges. But for now, in this moment, they've found peace in the eye of the storm.

~

MORNING LIGHT SPILLS across the kitchen counter where Jetta measures coffee grounds with practised precision. One week into their unexpected cohabitation, and routines have already formed around each other's presence—the careful dance of shared space no longer awkward but comfortably choreographed. She adds an extra scoop to the filter, knowing Ethan prefers his coffee stronger than she does, a small accommodation that feels significant in its simplicity. Behind her, the bathroom door opens, releasing a cloud of steam that carries the mingled scents of her shampoo on his hair, her soap on his skin.

"COFFEE'S ALMOST READY," she calls, not turning as she presses the brew button. The machine gurgles to life, its familiar sounds punctuated by Ethan's approaching footsteps.

"BLACK WITH ONE SUGAR," he says, reaching past her for the canister on the shelf. His body curves around hers momentarily, water droplets from his damp hair falling cool against her shoulder. "Still can't believe you memorised that after one morning."

SHE SHRUGS, pleased by his notice of this small gesture. "Bookshop owner. Details stick."

HIS LAUGH VIBRATES through the small space between them as he drops a kiss on her shoulder, casual affection that still sends ripples of warmth through her body. Seven days of waking to his presence, of learning the terrain of shared domesticity, and still each touch carries a charge that catches her by surprise.

"Found something interesting about you this morning," she says, turning to face him. His hair is still wet from the shower, curling slightly at the nape where it's growing too long. "You read in the shower."

Ethan's expression shifts to mock outrage, hand pressing against his chest in theatrical offence. "Invasion of privacy. I demand a lawyer."

"The soggy paperback on the sink counter speaks for itself, counsellor." She hands him the sugar bowl, enjoying the easy rhythm they've found. "Though I'm impressed by your dedication to multitasking."

"It's a security consultant thing," he says with exaggerated seriousness. "Maximum efficiency in all environments."

"Efficiency. Right." She smirks, pouring coffee into the waiting mugs. "Nothing to do with being so engrossed in the story you can't put it down for ten minutes."

He accepts the coffee with a grateful nod, lips quirking with pleasure at her accurate preparation. "Says the woman I found reading at three a.m. because, and I quote, 'I just needed to know if the detective survived the warehouse explosion.'"

THE TEASING PASSES between them as naturally as breathing, the bitter edge that once characterised their interactions transformed into something warm and sustaining. Jetta marvels at the shift, at how quickly they've adapted to each other's presence, how easily their separate lives have merged into shared space. Ethan's running shoes beside her boots at the door, his coffee mug—a ridiculous souvenir from New Mexico featuring a UFO—next to her plain ceramic one, his laptop open beside her stack of inventory spreadsheets on the dining table.

THE APARTMENT HAS CHANGED with his presence, becoming somehow more vibrant, more alive. Even the plants seem to respond to the altered energy, stretching toward sunlight with renewed vigour. Or perhaps it's just her perception that's shifted, colored by the contentment that's settled into her bones despite the circumstances that brought them together.

HER LAPTOP CHIMES from the coffee table, the familiar sound of an incoming video call. Brandi's name flashes on the screen, accompanied by the ridiculous photo Jetta set as her contact image—Brandi mid-sneeze at last year's Christmas party, eyes crossed and mouth contorted.

"READY FOR THE INTERROGATION?" Ethan asks, settling beside her on the couch as she accepts the call.

. . .

Brandi and Owen appear on screen, crowded together to fit in the frame. Owen's kitchen forms the background, morning light catching on copper pots hanging behind them. Brandi waves with excessive enthusiasm, her smile wide enough to suggest she's already had at least two cups of coffee.

"There they are!" she exclaims, leaning closer to the camera. "Our favourite cohabitators! How's domestic bliss treating you?"

"We're fine, Brandi," Jetta replies, feeling heat rise in her cheeks at her friend's knowing expression. "Just having coffee."

"Is that what they're calling it these days?" Owen interjects, wiggling his eyebrows suggestively. "Coffee?"

Ethan chokes slightly on his drink, coughing into his fist to cover his reaction. "Good to see you too, man."

"The apartment still standing?" Brandi asks, her teasing tone barely masking genuine concern. "No murders yet? No passive-aggressive notes about toilet paper orientation?"

"We've negotiated a ceasefire on bathroom territories," Jetta says dryly. "Though someone keeps leaving wet towels on the bed."

. . .

"ONE TIME," Ethan protests, arm settling comfortably around her shoulders. "I did that one time."

THE EASY BANTER CONTINUES, conversation flowing between them with the comfort of established friendship. Jetta watches the screen, noting how Brandi and Owen move together with unconscious coordination—his hand resting on her shoulder, her body leaning slightly into his side. Their relationship has a settled quality that makes her both envious and hopeful. Could she and Ethan find that same ease, that same certainty, if given enough time?

OWEN'S EXPRESSION SHIFTS, something serious replacing his earlier playfulness. "Look, not to bring down the mood, but there's something you should know." He glances at Brandi, who nods encouragement. "Alice has been asking questions around town. At the coffee shop near your bookstore, at the gym I go to."

THE WARMTH that's filled the apartment all morning dissipates instantly, replaced by a chill that settles beneath Jetta's skin. Beside her, Ethan's body tenses, his arm tightening imperceptibly around her shoulders.

"WHAT KIND OF QUESTIONS?" he asks, voice flat with controlled emotion.

"ABOUT YOUR SCHEDULE, about where Jetta might be staying." Owen's expression darkens further. "She told the barista she was your fiancée, trying to plan a surprise."

. . .

BILE RISES in Jetta's throat, bitter and burning. The image of Alice's calculating green eyes, her predatory smile, superimposes itself over the apartment's peaceful morning atmosphere, corrupting everything it touches.

"SHE'S GETTING DESPERATE," Brandi adds, concern evident in her furrowed brow. "That's dangerous, but it also means she's running out of options. She can't find you."

THE VIDEO CALL ends shortly after, promises to stay vigilant exchanged along with reassurances of support. But the damage is done—Alice's shadow has fallen across their sanctuary, across the careful peace they've built this past week.

"I SHOULD CONFRONT HER," Ethan says as soon as the screen goes dark. He sets his mug down with controlled precision, jaw tight with restrained anger. "End this directly. Make it absolutely clear that her behaviour has consequences."

"No." The word emerges sharper than Jetta intends, fear making her voice brittle. "Confronting her will only escalate things. She's unhinged, Ethan. Who knows what she might do if challenged directly?"

HE STANDS, restless energy propelling him toward the window where he scans the street below with habitual vigilance. "We can't just hide forever. This is our lives she's disrupting, our peace she's threatening."

. . .

"AND WHAT HAPPENS when your confrontation makes things worse?" Jetta follows him, arms wrapped around herself as if warding off a physical chill. "What happens when she decides that if she can't have you, no one can? People like her don't respond to reason."

"SO WE JUST WAIT?" He turns to face her, frustration evident in the hard line of his mouth. "Wait for her to find us? To show up here like she did at Owen's? To keep poisoning every moment with the threat of her appearance?"

"I DON'T KNOW!" The admission costs her, fear and uncertainty bleeding into her voice. "I just know I can't lose you now that I've found you." Her voice breaks on the final words, emotion overwhelming her carefully maintained control. "Not to her. Not after everything we've been through to get here."

THE ANGER DRAINS from his expression, replaced by something tender and fiercely protective. In two strides, he crosses the distance between them, pulling her against his chest with gentle urgency. His heartbeat thunders beneath her ear, rapid but strong.

"YOU WON'T," he promises, the words vibrating through his chest into hers. "Not ever."

. . .

SHE TILTS HER FACE UP, seeking reassurance in his eyes, finding instead a heat that matches the sudden flare of need within her own body. Fear transforms into desperate desire— the primal urge to affirm life in the face of threat, to claim connection when everything feels precarious.

THEIR MOUTHS COLLIDE with bruising intensity, the earlier argument dissolving into urgent touches. His hands grip her waist, lifting her effortlessly until her legs wrap around his hips, her back pressed against the nearest wall. Books tumble from a shelf as they move against it, pages fluttering to the floor unheeded.

THEY DON'T MAKE it to the bedroom. The couch becomes their destination, clothes discarded in hasty desperation. Jetta straddles him, taking control with an intensity born of fear and need combined. His hands grasp her hips, guiding her movements as they chase release with single-minded focus. The passion between them carries an edge of desperation this time—each touch, each kiss a defiance against the shadow hanging over them.

WHEN PLEASURE CRESTS, it's with his name on her lips, her fingers digging into the solid muscle of his shoulders. He follows moments later, face buried against her neck, arms wrapped around her waist with protective possession.

THEY REMAIN ENTWINED AFTERWARD, breathing gradually slowing, neither willing to break the connection that anchors them against uncertainty. The morning sun continues its path across the apartment floor, bathing their tangled limbs in golden light that belies the darkness gathering beyond their walls.

ETHAN'S PHONE buzzes from somewhere in the discarded clothing heap beside the couch. Once, twice, three times in rapid succession. Text messages, not a call. Something about the persistence sends a chill down Jetta's spine even before Ethan reaches for the device, his movements reluctant.

THE SCREEN ILLUMINATES WITH NOTIFICATIONS. All from Alice. The most recent contains an image that makes Ethan's body go rigid beneath her, his breath catching in a sharp inhale.

JETTA SHIFTS to see the screen, heart freezing in her chest as recognition dawns. There on the display, perfectly framed and unmistakable, is a photo of their apartment building. Not a generic shot from real estate listings or online maps, but a picture taken from across the street, clearly captured today—the morning light angle identical to what currently streams through their windows.

THE ACCOMPANYING message contains just three words: "Found you, lovebirds."

ETHAN'S ARMS tighten around her reflexively, his eyes meeting hers over the phone's glowing screen. In his gaze, she sees her own dread reflected—the realisation that their sanctuary has been compromised, that the walls they thought would protect them are nothing but an illusion of safety.

ALICE IS COMING. And there's nowhere left to hide.

CHAPTER 14

Shadows of the Past

MORNING LIGHT BLEEDS RELUCTANTLY

through the narrow gaps in the blinds, casting thin stripes across the hardwood floor. Jetta steps out of the bedroom, her body heavy with exhaustion after a night of fitful sleep punctuated by Ethan's periodic checks of the windows and doors. The silence of the apartment feels brittle, as if the walls themselves hold their breath in anticipation. She's halfway to the kitchen when she sees it—a small white rectangle on the floor near the front door, the edge peeking beneath like a secret demanding attention. Her heart stops, then races, blood rushing in her ears as she approaches the innocent-looking paper that couldn't possibly have good intentions.

HER FINGERS TREMBLE as she reaches down, the floor suddenly miles away. The paper—a photograph, she realises— feels unnaturally heavy in her hand as she turns it over. The image strikes her like a physical blow: her fifteen-year-old self staring back with uncertain eyes and a hesitant smile, caught in that awkward transition between childhood and adulthood. What makes her stomach clench isn't the photo itself—it's the perfect red circle drawn around her face, the colour so bright it seems to pulse with malice.

SHE DOESN'T HEAR Ethan approach, doesn't register his presence until his voice breaks through the roaring in her ears.

"JETTA? WHAT IS IT?" His words feel distant, underwater.

SHE CAN'T SPEAK, can only hold the photograph toward him with fingers that won't stop shaking. The hallway narrows around her, air thinning until each breath scrapes her lungs.

"JESUS," he whispers, taking the photo. His free arm wraps around her waist, solid and warm, anchoring her to the present as the past threatens to pull her under. "Let's sit down."

HE GUIDES her to the kitchen, where their investigation materials spread across the table—yearbooks, old diaries, school records they'd started combing through after Alice's text last night. Evidence of a shared history they're only now truly understanding. The wooden chair feels cool against her legs as she sinks into it, her hand still tingling where it touched the photograph.

"SHE WAS IN OUR BUILDING," Jetta manages, her voice sounding strange to her own ears. "She stood right outside our door."

. . .

ETHAN PLACES the photograph face down in the centre of the table, as if hiding the image might diminish its power. "The building has security cameras. I'll call the management office as soon as they open."

JETTA LOOKS AROUND THE APARTMENT—THEIR sanctuary transformed overnight into something more complicated. The drawn blinds that once felt protective now seem to trap the morning light, creating shadows where there should be none. Extra locks gleam on the door, new additions Ethan installed after Alice's message. The space feels simultaneously like a fortress and a prison, protection and confinement intertwined until she can't separate which is which.

"HOW DID SHE FIND US?" The question emerges as barely more than breath.

"I DON'T KNOW." Ethan drags his hand through his hair, leaving it standing in dishevelled spikes. "But I'm starting to think this goes deeper than we realised."

HE PULLS the nearest yearbook toward him, flipping pages with purpose until he finds what he's looking for. Their junior year, the same year as the photograph Alice left. The same year, everything fell apart.

"I'VE BEEN THINKING about it all night," he continues, voice tight with realisation. "The timing of everything back then—how perfectly orchestrated it all was. The way I ended up involved in hurting you when I'd never..." He pauses, knuckles white against the yearbook's edge. "I think she planned everything from the beginning."

"THAT'S IMPOSSIBLE," Jetta says, but uncertainty threads through her denial. "We were teenagers. No one's that calculated at fifteen."

"ALICE WAS." His certainty sends a chill down her spine.

THEY LEAN over the yearbook together, shoulders touching as they examine the pages. The contact grounds her, his body heat seeping through the thin fabric of her sleep shirt. His finger traces across a group photo—debate team, standing in neat rows with awkward adolescent smiles. Alice stands near the centre, flame-red hair already her signature feature, green eyes bright with confidence beyond her years.

"SHE ALWAYS HAD to be in control," Ethan says, his voice dropping lower. "Even then. Especially then."

THEIR INVESTIGATION CONTINUES, minutes stretching as they turn pages marked with Post-it notes from last night's session. Jetta becomes increasingly aware of each point of contact between them—his shoulder pressed against hers, their knees occasionally brushing beneath the table, fingers accidentally touching as they reach for the same document. Each connection sends small sparks along her skin, the physical reminder of his presence a counterpoint to the growing dread in her chest.

. . .

"Look at this." He slides a yearbook toward her, opened to the senior tributes section, where students left messages for their friends.

Jetta scans the page, breath catching when she sees her own photo in the corner. Around it, messages written in different handwriting—cruel comments about her appearance, her intelligence weaponised against her, suggestions that she thought herself better than everyone else. Words that had cut deep at seventeen, that still hold power to wound a decade later.

"I never understood who started this," she says, fingers hovering above the page without touching, as if the cruelty might be contagious. "It appeared right before graduation. People I thought were friends..."

"Look here." Ethan points to the corner of the page, to a small, elegant signature nearly hidden in the yearbook's binding crease.

A.S. Alice Stilman. The flowing script unmistakable even in miniature.

"She signed her work," he says, voice hardening. "Like it was something to be proud of."

Jetta's body goes rigid, a cold wave washing over her as memories cascade through her mind—the whispers that followed her through hallways, the gradual isolation as friends withdrew, the culminating humiliation that drove her to change schools. All orchestrated by one person.

HER FINGERS CURL into fists against the table, nails biting into her palms. The pain is grounding, real, pulling her back from the edge of panic. "Why?" The single word contains multitudes—why me, why then, why now.

ETHAN'S HAND COVERS HERS, gently uncurling her fingers before she can break skin. "I'm starting to think I know." His touch is warm, solid, present. "And if I'm right, this isn't going to stop until we make it stop."

THE PHOTO on the table between them—her circled face like a target—seems to pulse with quiet menace in the striped morning light. Outside their locked door, beyond their drawn blinds, Alice waits. Planning. Watching. A shadow from their past that refuses to fade.

"SHE WAS ALWAYS THREE STEPS AHEAD," Ethan says, pushing the yearbook aside to reach for a leather-bound journal—his own from senior year, its cover worn smooth at the corners from handling. The morning has stretched into afternoon, their investigation intensifying with each passing hour. He flips to a dog-eared page, handwriting less polished than his current script. "I started noticing patterns too late. Things that didn't add up."

. . .

JETTA LEANS CLOSER, her chair scraping against the hardwood as she shifts. Their shoulders press together, the contact both comforting and electric. The table before them has transformed into an archaeological dig of their shared past —artifacts carefully excavated and examined for hidden truths.

"LIKE WHAT?" she asks, voice hushed as if they might be overheard despite being alone.

"MESSAGES, FOR ONE." His finger traces down a page of notes. "Alice volunteered to be the go-between for our friend groups sophomore year. She'd deliver notes, relay conversations." He shakes his head, jaw tightening. "I found out later she was changing things—little alterations that created misunderstandings, made people defensive. By the time I figured it out, the damage was done."

THE REVELATION SETTLES into Jetta's chest like a stone. She remembers the subtle shift in those days—friendly waves that stopped, conversations that grew strained. The gradual isolation had seemed random then, the cruel lottery of teenage social hierarchies. Now it takes on a more sinister shape.

"THERE WAS MORE," Ethan continues, flipping to another marked page. "The gym clothes incident."

JETTA'S BREATH CATCHES, her body tensing involuntarily. "The bleach prank."

. . .

His eyes find hers, regret etched in the lines around them. "It wasn't supposed to be bleach. Alice told us she had access to the theater department's fake blood. Said it would wash out easily." He runs his hands through his hair, frustration evident in the gesture. "But when she handed me the container to pour on your clothes, it was chemical bleach. I didn't know until it was too late. And then I panicked, and so did the guys so they took the clothes away."

The memory rises unbidden—her gym uniform ruined, white splotches blooming across the fabric like disease. She'd had to wear it anyway, had no choice with the strict gym teacher who accepted no excuses. The laughter that followed her through the basketball drills, the whispers, the stares.

"She said it was an accident," Ethan continues, voice dropping lower. "That someone must have switched containers. I believed her because I wanted to." His hand finds hers on the table, fingers wrapping around hers with gentle pressure. "I'm sorry, Jetta. I should have seen through it."

Her throat tightens, the apology both too late and exactly what she needs to hear. "We were kids," she manages, though the excuse feels hollow even to her own ears.

"Kids don't orchestrate systematic destruction." His thumb traces circles on her wrist, the gentle motion at odds with the harshness of his words. "She convinced my friends that you were spreading rumors about them. Horrible things that would turn anyone against you."

· · ·

JETTA'S free hand curls into a fist against her thigh, nails biting into her palm. The therapy sessions after her transfer to a new school flash through her mind—hours spent unpacking the trauma, learning to trust again, rebuilding her sense of self-worth piece by painful piece.

"SHE WAS ALWAYS THERE," Ethan says, his voice taking on a hollow quality. "Always whispering something in someone's ear, always making suggestions that seemed innocent until you looked back at the pattern." His gaze drifts to the window where afternoon light has begun to fade. "Always watching for weaknesses she could exploit."

OUTSIDE, the sun slips lower, casting longer shadows across the room. Neither of them moves to turn on additional lights, as if the gathering darkness provides necessary cover for these painful revelations. The kitchen feels smaller in the dimming light, more intimate, their bodies naturally drifting closer in response.

"WHY ME?" Jetta asks, the question that's haunted her for years finally given voice. "Why target me specifically?"

"BECAUSE SHE SAW what I couldn't admit to myself." His eyes find hers in the fading light, something vulnerable and honest in his gaze. "That I was drawn to you from the first day. That you challenged me in ways no one else did." His fingers tighten around hers. "Alice couldn't stand competition. Not even potential competition."

. . .

THE REALISATION LANDS with crushing weight—years of pain caused by one person's obsessive need for control, for possession. Jetta's body trembles slightly as memories resurface, each more painful than the last. The isolation. The whispers. The culminating humiliation that drove her from the school. The years of therapy afterward, learning to trust again, to rebuild what had been systematically destroyed.

AS EVENING SETTLES FULLY around them, the apartment grows darker until they sit in near darkness, only the faint glow from street lamps outside illuminating their faces. Their voices have dropped to whispers, as if afraid that speaking these truths too loudly might conjure Alice from the shadows.

"SHE WAS CALCULATED EVEN THEN," Ethan says, his face half-hidden in shadow. "Every move deliberate. Every 'accident' planned." He shifts closer, chair legs scraping softly against the floor. "She's doing the same thing now—isolating us, creating fear, trying to control the narrative."

JETTA REALISES they've moved closer still, their chairs now pressed together, his arm against hers from shoulder to elbow. The physical contact anchors her as the past and present collide within her mind—teenage trauma meeting adult fear in a volatile mixture.

"IF SHE ORCHESTRATED ALL that in high school," she whispers, "what is she capable of now?"

. . .

ETHAN'S ARM slides around her shoulders, drawing her against his side. The warmth of him seeps through her thin shirt, combating the chill that's settled in her bones. "We won't wait to find out. This time, we're ahead of her."

HIS CONVICTION SHOULD BE COMFORTING, but Jetta can't shake the feeling that they're still playing catch-up to a game whose rules Alice wrote long ago. Their apartment— their sanctuary—feels suddenly vulnerable, its walls too thin, its locks insufficient against someone who's spent years perfecting the art of intrusion.

"SHE KNEW where I lived in high school, too," Jetta murmurs, the memory surfacing unbidden. "She sent anonymous notes. Left things in my mailbox."

ETHAN'S BODY tenses against hers. "You never mentioned that."

"I THOUGHT IT WAS EVERYONE. Part of the general harassment." She leans her head against his shoulder, seeking stability as the room seems to tilt with revelation. "But it was just her, wasn't it? Always her."

HIS HAND FINDS HER CHIN, tilting her face up until their eyes meet in the dim light. "We'll stop her," he promises, voice low and fierce. "Together this time."

. . .

THE KISS that follows is gentle, a contrast to the harsh truths they've uncovered. His lips press against hers with a tenderness that brings tears to her eyes—not passion but comfort, a physical reminder that the past cannot reach them unless they allow it.

WHEN THEY PART, something has shifted between them—a deeper connection forged in shared understanding of what they're truly facing. Not just a jealous ex-girlfriend, but someone who has spent years perfecting the art of manipulation, someone who views people as pieces to be moved on a board of her own design.

"WE SHOULD EAT SOMETHING," Ethan says, though neither makes a move to break contact. "It's been hours."

JETTA NODS, but her attention remains fixed on the photograph still lying face-down on the table—tangible proof that their past has found them, that the walls they've built aren't enough to keep Alice at bay. In the growing darkness of their apartment, that single piece of paper radiates threat more effectively than any weapon could.

THE BACK OFFICE of Bound Together feels smaller after hours, the desk lamp casting a warm pool of light that doesn't quite reach the corners. Brandi adjusts her reading glasses, the day's receipts blurring before her eyes as her attention drifts for the third time in as many minutes. The shop hums with familiar night sounds—the refrigerator's gentle rumble from the small kitchenette, the occasional car passing on the street outside, the building's old pipes ticking as they cool. Normally, these sounds comfort her, but tonight they feel insufficient against the worry gnawing at her edges.

"I CAN'T FOCUS ON THIS," she admits, pushing aside the stack of invoices she's been pretending to review. The chair creaks as she leans back, removing her glasses to rub the bridge of her nose.

OWEN PAUSES his pacing between the mystery and romance sections, the floorboards sighing beneath his weight. His usual easy charm has evaporated, replaced by a tight-shouldered vigilance that looks foreign on his normally relaxed frame.

"WE COULD FINISH TOMORROW," he suggests, though they both know that paperwork isn't the real issue.

"I NEVER SHOULD HAVE PUSHED them together," Brandi says, the confession bursting out with sudden force. Her fingers nervously adjust her reading glasses, folding and unfolding the arms with repetitive precision. "The double dates, the movie night setup—it's all my fault."

"THAT'S NOT FAIR." Owen abandons his pacing to perch on the edge of the desk, his proximity offering comfort she doesn't feel she deserves. "We couldn't have known about Alice."

. . .

"COULDN'T WE, THOUGH?" She looks up at him, guilt sharpening her tone. "I knew something traumatic happened to Jetta in high school. I knew Ethan was part of it. I just thought..." She trails off, shaking her head. "I just thought they needed to get past old grudges. I had no idea I was reintroducing her to someone connected to actual trauma."

THE INVENTORY SHEETS spread across the desk—normally so important, each number representing the shop's lifeblood —now seem trivial compared to her friend's safety. The day's receipts curl slightly at the edges in the office's warmth, forgotten beside a half-empty mug of tea gone cold hours ago.

"YOU WERE TRYING TO HELP," Owen says, his voice gentle but lacking its usual conviction. His gaze drifts to the window where streetlights cast elongated shadows across the empty shop floor. "We both were."

"AND NOW ALICE IS STALKING THEM." Brandi stands, too restless to remain seated. "Photographing their building. Sending threats. Breaking into your apartment."

THE REMINDER of Alice's intrusion causes Owen's expression to darken further. "That's what worries me most. The escalation." He runs a hand through his hair, the gesture betraying his agitation. "This isn't normal ex-girlfriend behaviour. There's something... calculated about it."

BRANDI MOVES from behind the desk, seeking the comfort of the bookshop's familiar spaces. The shelves rise around them like protective walls, filled with stories of people over-coming obstacles far greater than their own. The smell of paper and binding glue mingles with the lingering scent of the day's last coffee, creating the distinctive aroma that usually brings her peace. Tonight, even these sensory touchstones fail to calm her racing thoughts.

"I KEEP THINKING about her face when I told her to leave that day," Brandi says, trailing her fingers along the spines of new releases they'd arranged just yesterday—a lifetime ago, it seems now. "There was something in her eyes that wasn't... right. Like she was calculating rather than feeling."

"ETHAN SAID SHE WAS ALWAYS POSSESSIVE," Owen replies, following her into the main shop area. "But this goes beyond possessiveness. The breaking in, the surveillance, tracking them down after they moved..."

A CAR PASSES OUTSIDE, its headlights sweeping across the shop's interior, briefly illuminating the cozy reading nooks and carefully curated displays that Brandi and Jetta have built together over years. The light catches on the copper coffee machine behind the counter, the leather armchairs in the corner, the handwritten staff recommendation cards—all the familiar elements that define their shared dream. The warm, intimate space they've created stands in stark contrast to the cold threat lurking outside.

"WHAT IF SHE HURTS JETTA?" Brandi's voice drops to a whisper, the fear she's been avoiding finally given voice. "I encouraged them. I pushed them together. If something happens—"

"Nothing's going to happen," Owen interrupts, though his tone lacks the certainty his words attempt to convey. He places his hands on her shoulders, grounding her with the contact. "Ethan knows how to handle himself. He's taking precautions."

"Precautions aren't enough against someone unhinged." She looks up at him, seeing her own worry reflected in his eyes. "You didn't see Jetta after high school. Whatever happened broke something in her. It took years of therapy for her to trust people again."

Owen's expression shifts, something harder emerging beneath his usual warmth. "Then we make sure history doesn't repeat itself." His voice takes on an edge she rarely hears from him. "We protect them both."

The refrigerator in the kitchenette clicks on suddenly, the sound startling in the quiet shop. Brandi jumps slightly, her nerves raw with worry. Owen's arm slides around her shoulders, pulling her against his side in a gesture both protective and seeking comfort.

"I've been thinking," he says after a moment. "What if we install some extra security here at the shop? Alice has already shown up here once. She might try again."

. . .

BRANDI NODS, leaning into his embrace. "I was thinking the same thing. Maybe cameras? And we should change the locks." Her mind races ahead, planning defences against an enemy whose capabilities they're only beginning to understand. "And we should take shifts—make sure Jetta's never alone in the shop."

"GOOD IDEA." Owen's chin rests atop her head, his voice rumbling through his chest against her ear. "I'll call my security contacts tomorrow. Get something installed right away."

THEY STAND TOGETHER in the soft lamplight, surrounded by books and familiar comforts that suddenly seem insufficient protection against the threat they face. The shop—usually a sanctuary—now feels vulnerable, its large windows and multiple entrances potential weaknesses rather than welcoming features.

"I THINK we need to be honest with ourselves," Brandi says finally, pulling back to look up at him. "Alice isn't just some jealous ex. This level of fixation, the stalking, the breaking in—it's not normal."

"NO," Owen agrees, his expression solemn. "It's not. And I'm starting to think there's more to the story than Ethan has told us." He glances toward the window, as if expecting to see flame-red hair and watchful green eyes peering in from the darkness. "We need to watch out for them both. Alice isn't just calculated—she's dangerous."

. . .

303

THE WORD HANGS in the air between them, giving shape to the fear they've both been circling. Dangerous. Not merely jealous or unstable, but actively threatening. The recognition shifts something in Brandi's chest—guilt giving way to protective determination.

"TOMORROW," she says, decision crystallising into action, "we start making this place a fortress. And we don't let Jetta out of our sight."

OWEN NODS, something in his posture changing as well—the worried friend becoming the security consultant, already assessing vulnerabilities, planning defences. "I'll call in some favours. Get people I trust."

OUTSIDE, the wind picks up, rattling the shop's sign against its chains. The sound—usually quaint and charming—now carries an ominous note, like distant warning bells. Within the warm confines of Bound Together, surrounded by stories with guaranteed happy endings, Brandi and Owen face the unsettling reality that their own story has veered into uncertain territory—and the next chapter might be darker than any of them anticipated.

LAMPLIGHT CASTS soft shadows across the bedroom walls as night settles fully over the city. They've migrated from the kitchen to here, investigation materials spread across the rumpled bedspread—yearbooks open to marked pages, printed screenshots of Alice's messages, timeline notes scrawled in Ethan's precise handwriting. Jetta sits cross-legged in the centre of the bed, Ethan beside her with his back against the headboard, their bodies angled toward each other like flowers seeking shared light. The intimate setting—soft sheets beneath them, the gentle glow of the bedside lamp, the vulnerability of night—transforms their investigation into something that feels almost sacred, a ritual of truth-seeking.

"THERE'S SOMETHING ELSE," Ethan says, his voice low and hesitant. He reaches toward the duffel bag beside the bed, the one he hasn't fully unpacked since moving in. "Something I've kept for years. As evidence, initially. Then as a reminder to be more careful about who I trust."

JETTA WATCHES as he pulls out a small book bound in faded green fabric, its edges worn soft with handling. Even before he passes it to her, she knows what it is—the distinctive shape of a teenage girl's diary, the kind sold in mall shops with promises of secrecy and self-discovery.

"ALICE'S DIARY?" Her voice catches on the name, fingers hovering above the book without touching, as if it might burn her. "How did you get this?"

"FOUND it in my locker senior year, after everything happened with you." He runs a hand through his hair, the gesture now familiar to her as his response to discomfort. "She left it deliberately—wanted me to read about her feelings, her 'devotion.' I started to, then realised there was more in there than just teenage crush entries."

. . .

THE DIARY FEELS UNNATURALLY heavy as Jetta finally takes it, the fabric cover cool against her palm. A small brass lock hangs broken from its clasp, the mechanism forced open long ago. The pages fall open naturally to a well-read section, the handwriting inside precise and controlled—nothing like the chaotic scrawl most teenagers produce.

"SHE DOCUMENTED EVERYTHING," Ethan continues, shifting closer until his thigh presses warm against her knee. "Plans, outcomes, next steps. Like some twisted project management for destroying lives."

JETTA'S EYES scan the first visible page, stomach tightening at what she finds. Dates, names, detailed observations of social dynamics—who was friends with whom, which relationships had tensions that could be exploited, which teachers could be manipulated with the right approach. Her own name appears repeatedly, always accompanied by assessments that feel clinical in their detachment: "J.K. values integrity—use this against her" and "J.K. sensitive about academic performance—potential vulnerability."

"THIS IS..." She struggles to find words adequate to the violation she feels, reading this calculated analysis of her teenage self.

"KEEP GOING," Ethan says gently, his hand coming to rest at the small of her back, a warm anchor as she turns the page.

.   .   .

WHAT SHE FINDS next steals her breath—detailed diagrams of the school gym, complete with notations about blind spots in teacher supervision, schedules marking when certain staff would be absent, lists of which students could be counted on to spread information quickly. An entire plan laid out with military precision, all focused on a single goal explicitly stated at the top of the page: "Separate E.C. from J.K. permanently."

"SHE PLANNED IT ALL," Jetta whispers, fingers trembling as they trace the neat lines of the diagram. "The gym incident wasn't just a cruel prank. It was surgical. Calculated."

"SHE WANTED me for herself even back then," Ethan says, voice hollow with disbelief despite having clearly read these pages before. "Every interaction, every 'coincidence' that pushed us further apart—it was all by design."

THE DIARY CONTINUES FOR PAGES, each entry more disturbing than the last. Alice had mapped social connections like battle plans, identified weaknesses like military targets, deployed rumours and manipulations like precision weapons. All to isolate Jetta. All to claim Ethan for herself.

"LOOK AT THE DATES," he says, pointing to the corner of a particularly detailed entry. "She started planning this the first week of sophomore year. Two years before it all came to a head."

JETTA'S HANDS shake so violently that the diary slips from her grasp, falling onto the bedspread between them. Past trauma collides with present danger in a wave that leaves her breathless, the room tilting slightly as her mind struggles to process the scope of what they've uncovered. This wasn't teenage jealousy or impulsive cruelty—this was calculated destruction executed with patience and precision by someone who never stopped watching, waiting, planning.

"I'm sorry I didn't see it then," Ethan whispers, reaching for her hand. His touch grounds her, warm fingers wrapping around her cold ones with gentle pressure. "I was blind to so much. Wrapped up in my own world, my own image."

She looks up, finding his eyes in the soft lamplight. The regret there is palpable, a living thing that has clearly grown and evolved over years of reflection. "You were seventeen," she says, though the words feel insufficient against the weight of what they've discovered.

"So was she," he counters, nodding toward the diary. "Age doesn't excuse what any of us did. Or failed to do."

The simple acknowledgment—that he bears responsibility for his role, even as they uncover Alice's greater culpability—loosens something tight in Jetta's chest. This is what she needed all those years ago. Not excuses or deflections, but honest recognition of harm caused, intended or not.

"She's not fifteen anymore," Jetta says, the diary between them now a bridge rather than a barrier. "And neither are we. Whatever she's planning now—"

"Will be worse," Ethan finishes, the words gentle despite their harsh truth. "More sophisticated. More dangerous."

"Why did you date her before you left for overseas?" Jetta asks, then adds, "I mean if you knew all of this."

"It was so many years after that, I had forgotten about the diary until she started up again, I wouldn't call it dating really, we seemed to run into each other, I was lonely, things happened, but almost immediately she became possessive on a weird level, so when I was offerred work abroad I jumped at the chance, every effort I had made to end it didn't work."

THE BEDROOM suddenly feels both safer and more vulnerable—their most private space, where they sleep unguarded, now invaded by these revelations. The soft lamp-light that moments ago seemed comforting now creates too many shadows, too many dark corners where threats might hide. Outside their window, the city continues its nighttime rhythm, oblivious to the small universe of fear and discovery contained within these walls.

ETHAN REACHES FOR HER, the movement deliberate and questioning. When she doesn't pull away, he draws her against his chest, arms wrapping around her with protective intensity. Her body melts into his embrace, seeking the security of phys-ical connection as her mind reels from the diary's contents.

"WE'LL FIGURE THIS OUT," he murmurs against her hair, voice vibrating through his chest beneath her ear. "Together. No more blindness. No more manipulation."

. . .

THEIR EMBRACE TIGHTENS, bodies pressed together as if physical proximity might shield them from the threat they now understand more clearly. His heartbeat thunders against her cheek, steady and strong despite the fear she knows he shares. Her fingers curl into the fabric of his shirt, anchoring herself to this moment, to him.

"I WON'T LET her hurt you again," he promises, the words fierce with conviction. "Not through me. Not in any way."

THE DIARY LIES FORGOTTEN beside them on the bed, its pages open to diagrams and plans that no longer have power over their past but cast long shadows over their future. Around them, evidence of their investigation litters the bedspread—photographs, notes, yearbooks—physical manifestations of a history they're only now truly understanding.

AS THE NIGHT deepens outside their window, exhaustion finally overcomes vigilance. They shift together without discussion, bodies arranging themselves instinctively—his arm beneath her head, her leg thrown over his, faces close enough to share breath. The lamp remains lit, neither willing to surrender completely to darkness.

"STAY AWAKE," Jetta murmurs, even as her eyelids grow heavy with the emotional toll of the day's discoveries. "Just a little longer."

"I'M HERE," Ethan whispers back, his hand stroking slow circles on her back. "Not going anywhere."

THEY DRIFT toward sleep in tandem, bodies intertwined so completely it's difficult to tell where one ends and the other begins. The evidence of Alice's obsession surrounds them like fallen leaves, but in this moment of shared vulnerability, they've found something she can never touch—a connection forged in truth rather than manipulation, in shared understanding of both past wounds and present dangers.

THE DIARY'S pages flutter slightly in the gentle current from the heating vent, the movement almost like breathing. As consciousness fades, Jetta's last coherent thought is that knowledge is its own kind of protection—that seeing the pattern means they're no longer blindly following Alice's script. The fear remains, wrapped around them like the shadows at the edges of the lamplight, but alongside it grows something stronger: the determination to write their own ending to this story, one Alice can no longer control.

CHAPTER 15

Breaking Point

THE LAMP on the nightstand still burns, casting amber shadows across the bedroom. Ethan sleeps with one arm draped protectively over Jetta's waist, her body curled against his chest, their breathing synchronised in the quiet rhythm of deep slumber. Around them, the detritus of their investigation remains scattered across the bedspread—Alice's diary splayed open near their feet, yearbook pages marked with sticky notes, the photograph with Jetta's face circled in malevolent red now face-down on the floor where Ethan discarded it. Their bodies form a small island of warmth and connection in a sea of disturbing revelations.

OUTSIDE THE WINDOW, occasional headlights sweep across the bedroom ceiling, briefly illuminating their sleeping forms before continuing on into the night. The digital clock on the dresser reads 3:17, its red numbers glowing steadily in the half-darkness. Ethan shifts in his sleep, pulling Jetta closer, his subconscious mind still engaged in the protective instinct that kept them from turning off the lamp before exhaustion claimed them both.

THE FIRST SOUND is barely audible—a subtle click that might be mistaken for the building settling, for pipes expanding or contracting with temperature changes. It slips beneath the threshold of consciousness, not yet enough to disturb their hard-won rest. The second sound comes minutes later—metal against metal, the whisper of a tool working against the deadbolt's mechanism. This too fails to penetrate their sleep, though Ethan's brow furrows slightly, some part of his brain registering the intrusion on a level below waking.

THE THIRD SOUND IS SHARPER—THE security chain snapping with a controlled force that speaks of calculation rather than brute strength. The front door opens with a nearly imperceptible creak, followed by the soft thud of it closing again. In the bedroom, Ethan's body tenses, though his eyes remain closed. Years of security training have rewired his nervous system; danger registers in his muscles before his conscious mind can name it.

ALICE STANDS motionless in the entryway, allowing her eyes to adjust to the apartment's darkness. Her flame-red hair is pulled back in a severe ponytail, practical for the night's work. She wears all black—leggings, turtleneck, soft-soled boots that make no sound as she moves across the hardwood floor. Gone are the designer clothes and perfect makeup that normally armoured her against the world. This is Alice stripped to essential purpose, her beauty rendered dangerous rather than enticing.

. . .

HER MOVEMENTS through the apartment reveal an unsettling familiarity with its layout. She navigates around the coffee table without bumping it, avoids the creaky floorboard near the kitchen that she couldn't possibly know about—unless she's been here before, watching, waiting, learning the terrain of her enemies' sanctuary. In her right hand, a gun hangs at her side, its metal surface absorbing rather than reflecting the minimal light. Her fingers curl around it with practised ease, the weapon an extension of her arm rather than a foreign object.

SHE PAUSES at the partially open bedroom door, her breathing controlled despite the adrenaline coursing through her system. Through the gap, she can see them on the bed, tangled together in sleep, surrounded by the evidence of their investigation into her past. A smile flickers across her face—not the brilliant, calculated charm she deploys in public, but something smaller, more genuine, and infinitely more disturbing. They think they understand her now. They think knowledge will protect them. The presumption of it feeds the fire burning behind her eyes.

THE BEDROOM DOOR yields to the gentle pressure of her fingertips, hinges releasing a small creak that hangs in the air like a warning. She steps across the threshold, gun now raised to shoulder height, aimed with steady precision at the sleeping forms on the bed.

THE SOUND finally penetrates Ethan's consciousness. His eyes snap open, mind instantly alert in the way only those who have lived in danger zones can achieve—no gradual surfacing from sleep, no moment of confusion. His body remains perfectly still except for the subtle tightening of the arm around Jetta's waist. Years of training have taught him that movement draws attention, that the first seconds of threat assessment are crucial to survival.

THE BEDROOM APPEARS unchanged at first glance—lamp still burning, investigation materials still scattered across the bed and floor. But a new shadow stretches across the foot of the bed, too solid, too deliberate to be cast by inanimate objects. His eyes adjust quickly to the contrast between light and darkness, focusing on the figure standing in the doorway.

RECOGNITION HITS him with the force of a physical blow. Alice. In their bedroom. The gun in her hand glints dully in the lamplight, its barrel aimed directly at them with unwavering steadiness. His mind races through options with cold efficiency—the distance between them, the likelihood of reaching her before she can fire, the probability of Jetta being hit if he moves too slowly or too quickly.

HE SHIFTS his body with microscopic precision, angling himself to cover more of Jetta's sleeping form without alerting Alice to his wakefulness. His hand slides beneath the pillow where his phone lies charging, fingers seeking the emergency button he can activate without looking. The movement is imperceptible, a hunter's patience governing each muscle.

ALICE STEPS further into the room, her silhouette backlit by the faint glow of streetlights filtering through the living room windows. Her face emerges from shadow into the lamp's amber sphere, revealing an expression Ethan has never seen before—a strange calm that suggests she's finally arrived at a destination long sought. The gun in her hand doesn't waver, its aim shifting slightly to centre on Jetta's sleeping form.

THE THREAT to Jetta crystallises Ethan's options into a single imperative. His body tenses, preparing for the lunge that will either save them both or doom them. Every sense heightens to painful clarity—he can hear the soft whistle of air through Alice's slightly parted lips, smell the cold metal of the gun mixed with the unfamiliar chemical scent clinging to her clothes, feel Jetta's heartbeat accelerating against his arm as she begins to stir.

"HELLO, ETHAN," Alice whispers, her voice carrying the intimate tone of a lover rather than an intruder. "Aren't you going to introduce me to your bedroom properly?"

JETTA STIRS AGAINST HIM, awareness seeping into her body as tension replaces the relaxation of sleep. Her breathing changes, the subtle shift telling him she's awake now, though her eyes remain closed. He tightens his arm around her in silent warning, praying she'll understand the danger before she fully surfaces into consciousness.

"ALICE," he acknowledges, his voice controlled, betraying none of the calculations running behind his eyes. He shifts again, incremental movements bringing his body more fully between the gun and Jetta. "Put the gun down. This isn't what you want."

. . .

HER SMILE WIDENS, revealing teeth that seem too sharp in the half-light. "But it is exactly what I want, darling. It's time we had a proper conversation. All three of us." The gun remains steady, a black hole pulling all light and hope from the room. "No one leaves until we settle things once and for all."

JETTA'S EYES snap open to a nightmare made flesh. Alice stands at the foot of their bed, gun aimed directly at her face, flame-red hair pulled back from features twisted with a smile that sends ice coursing through Jetta's veins. The lamp's glow catches on the metal barrel, transforming it into the sole focus of the room. Jetta's gasp feels like it's been torn from deep inside her chest, her body instinctively pressing back against the headboard as if she could somehow melt through the wood and escape.

"GOOD MORNING, SLEEPING BEAUTY," Alice purrs, the gun never wavering despite the theatrical tilt of her head. "So nice of you to join our little reunion."

ETHAN'S BODY SHIFTS SUBTLY, angling more completely between Jetta and the weapon. His movements are controlled, deliberate, each micro-adjustment positioning him as a human shield while appearing almost casual. Jetta feels the tension radiating from him, the coiled readiness that contradicts his outwardly calm demeanour.

"ALICE," he says, voice measured and low, "let's talk about this. Whatever you're feeling, whatever you want—there are better ways to address it than this."

· · ·

ALICE'S APPEARANCE strikes Jetta as profoundly wrong—the immaculate woman who invaded the bookshop is gone, replaced by someone coming apart at the seams. Her black clothing hangs slightly askew, as if hastily donned. No makeup covers the dark hollows beneath her eyes or the raw chafing at the corners of her mouth where she's been worrying at her own skin. Only her hand remains steady, the gun an extension of her arm pointing with unwavering certainty at its target.

"SURPRISE," Alice says, the word accompanied by a smile that stops miles short of her eyes. "Did you really think those extra locks would keep me out?" She gestures vaguely toward the apartment's entrance with her free hand. "Amateur security for amateur lovers. I've been watching this building for weeks. Did you know your landlord keeps spare keys poorly hidden in his office? That your building's security camera on the east entrance has been broken for months?"

EACH REVELATION LANDS like a physical blow—their sanctuary was never secure, their precautions meaningless against Alice's obsessive surveillance. Jetta's fingers find Ethan's beneath the sheets, gripping with desperate strength as her mind races to process the immediate danger.

"YOU DON'T NEED the gun, Alice," Ethan says, his thumb brushing reassuringly against Jetta's knuckles despite the tension vibrating through his frame. "Put it down, and we can discuss whatever's troubling you like rational adults."

A SHARP LAUGH erupts from Alice's throat, the sound too bright, too brittle for the predawn darkness. "Rational? Is that what you think this is about?" She begins pacing at the foot of the bed, her movements caged and frenetic while the gun remains steadily aimed. "We're well beyond rational, Ethan. We crossed that line the moment you chose her over me. Again."

THE EMPHASIS ON "AGAIN" sends a chill down Jetta's spine, the word connecting their present danger to the past trauma they've been excavating. Alice's gaze shifts between them, catching on the open diary near their feet. Her expression flickers—surprise, then something darker.

"BEEN READING MY OLD JOURNALS, have we?" she asks, her voice dropping to a dangerous whisper. "A bit of light bedtime reading about how I orchestrated your pathetic little high school drama? Did you enjoy my work?"

ETHAN SHIFTS AGAIN, creating more space between himself and Jetta, a subtle repositioning that she understands instinctively—he's preparing to move, calculating angles and distances. "Alice, whatever happened in high school is in the past. We were all different people then."

"WERE WE?" Alice stops pacing, her body going unnaturally still. "Or were we exactly who we are now, just with fewer resources at our disposal?" The gun wavers slightly, the first break in her perfect control. "I knew what I wanted then. I know what I want now. It's everyone else who can't seem to follow the script."

. . .

"WHAT SCRIPT?" Jetta asks, finding her voice at last, though it emerges thinner than intended. "What are you talking about?"

THE QUESTION IGNITES something in Alice's eyes—a terrible eagerness, as if she's been waiting for precisely this opening. "You want the truth, little bookshop mouse? Here it is." She resumes pacing, her movements more agitated now. "I was the one who told the football team about your pathetic crush on Ethan. I suggested the prank with your clothes. I switched the fake blood for bleach myself."

THE CONFESSION POURS out of her like poison from a lanced wound, each revelation confirming what they've pieced together while adding new, horrifying details. Jetta's breath catches, the old pain of that public humiliation freshly reopened.

"I KNEW Ethan would feel guilty enough to pull away from you," Alice continues, her voice taking on a singsong quality that raises goosebumps along Jetta's arms. "Guilt is such a powerful motivator for people with consciences. And once you were gone, once you'd transferred schools like the coward you are, he was supposed to turn to me for comfort." Her expression hardens, gun hand tensing. "He was supposed to be mine."

"JESUS, ALICE," Ethan breathes, genuine shock breaking through his composed facade. "We were fifteen. How could you have calculated all that?"

· · ·

"Because I saw what you refused to admit," she snaps, eyes flashing with sudden fury. "The way you looked at her in English class. How you always volunteered to be her lab partner. How you defended her ideas in debate club. You wanted her even then, and it was wrong. You were meant for me."

The pieces click into place for Jetta—the systematic isolation, the calculated cruelty, the years of therapy required to rebuild what Alice had methodically destroyed. Not random teenage cruelty but targeted destruction fueled by obsessive jealousy. Her stomach churns with the realisation that her teenage trauma wasn't just collateral damage in high school politics—she was the specific target of a campaign designed to eliminate her from Ethan's life.

"Alice," she says carefully, the name feeling like broken glass in her mouth, "that was ten years ago. We've all moved on."

"Have we?" Alice's laugh holds no humour, only jagged edges that could cut flesh. "Because here we are, the same three players, the same basic problem." Her gaze fixes on Ethan with burning intensity. "You still haven't learned your lesson. Still making the wrong choice."

The diary lies open between them on the bed, its pages covered in the meticulous planning of a teenage girl with a terrifying capacity for manipulation. Jetta stares at it, then at the woman before them—the logical evolution of that calculating mind, now armed not just with social weapons but with actual, physical ones.

. . .

"IT DOESN'T HAVE to be this way," Ethan says, his voice gentler now, almost hypnotic in its calm. "Put the gun down, Alice. Let's talk about what you really want."

"WHAT I WANT?" Alice's voice rises, cracking slightly at the edges. "I want what should have been mine from the beginning. I want you to make the right choice this time." The gun steadies again, pointing directly at Jetta's heart. "I want her gone, permanently this time. No second chances, no redemptive arc, no happily ever after with what belongs to me."

THE NAKED HATRED in Alice's eyes strips away any doubt about her intentions. This isn't a threat or a negotiation—it's the culmination of years of obsession, the final act in a play Alice has been directing since they were teenagers. Jetta feels the blood drain from her face as she realises that the woman before them hasn't just come to frighten or intimidate—she's come to finish what she started a decade ago.

"YOU SHOULD HAVE STAYED GONE after high school," Alice snarls, her voice dropping to a hiss that seems to fill the entire bedroom. "Or after the club. I gave you so many chances to disappear from his life." The gun trembles slightly in her hand, the first visible crack in her control. Jetta's heart hammers against her ribs with such force she's certain everyone can hear it, the sound filling her ears as she watches Alice's finger caress the trigger with terrifying intimacy.

"THE CLUB?" Ethan's voice remains carefully measured, though Jetta feels his muscles tensing beside her. "What are you talking about, Alice?"

A CRUEL SMILE twists Alice's lips, her eyes never leaving Jetta's face. " I saw you when you returned, and when I went to approach you, there she was again! Her and her friend, talking to you like you were all family, I arranged for her to be dealt with, a small trauma that would have rebroken her enough to be untouchable, and then you step in like a hero, The brake lines on her car? How convenient they failed in the parking lot of that restaurant where you were meeting, right as a delivery truck was backing up?" Her laugh holds no humour, only a hollow satisfaction. "It should have worked the first time in high school. And it would have worked at the club if Ethan hadn't played hero, and then with the car he had to be a hero again, pulling you out of the way."

THE REVELATION LANDS like a physical blow. Jetta remembers the incident three weeks ago—her car's brakes failing as she arrived to meet Ethan, the truck that nearly crushed her, Ethan's quick reflexes yanking her to safety. They'd attributed it to bad luck, to mechanical failure. The mechanic had mentioned something about damaged brake lines, but hadn't suggested sabotage.

"THAT WAS YOU?" Jetta whispers, horror crawling up her throat like bile. "You tried to kill me before?"

"I TRIED TO SOLVE A PROBLEM," Alice corrects, as if explaining something simple to a child. "I've been watching you both for weeks. Learning your routines, your habits, the way you move together." Her eyes glitter in the lamp's glow, feverish with obsession. "I know when you shower, when you sleep, what side of the bed you prefer. I know you check the locks three times before bed, Jetta. Fat lot of good that did you."

JETTA FEELS VIOLATED in ways that transcend the immediate threat. The image of Alice watching them, studying them like specimens, transforms their intimate moments into something tainted. Beside her, Ethan shifts again, creating another inch of space between them—preparation disguised as nervous movement.

"I'VE BEEN PATIENT," Alice continues, her voice rising as she paces more frantically at the foot of the bed. "So patient. Waiting for the perfect moment to eliminate you from the equation permanently." The gun sweeps in a small arc that makes Jetta flinch. "Do you have any idea how many opportunities I've had? How many times I could have ended this? But I wanted it to be perfect. I wanted him to understand why it had to happen."

ALICE'S MOVEMENTS grow more erratic, her carefully controlled facade crumbling with each passing second. She knocks against the dresser, sending a framed photo crashing to the floor. The glass shatters, the sound startlingly loud in the tense bedroom.

"YOU'VE MANIPULATED us since high school," Ethan says, voice steady despite the escalating danger. "Orchestrated situations to drive us apart. Stalked us. Broken into our home. And now you're threatening murder. This isn't love, Alice. This is insanity."

. . .

"Don't call it that!" Alice shrieks, her composure shattering completely. "You don't get to label my feelings! You don't get to decide what's real!" Her voice rises to a pitch that must be audible through the apartment walls. "I am the only one who truly understands you, Ethan. The only one who sees your potential, what you could become without her dragging you down!"

In the adjacent apartment, a light flicks on. Jetta hears movement—the neighbour awakened by Alice's shouting. A thin hope threads through her terror; someone might hear, might call for help.

"Alice, please," Jetta tries, searching for any human connection in those wild green eyes. "This isn't going to end how you want it to. There's still time to walk away."

"Walk away?" Alice's laugh verges on hysterical. "There's no walking away. There's only forward, to the inevitable conclusion." She takes two steps closer, gun aimed directly at Jetta's chest. "You are the obstacle. The problem. The thing standing between me and what should have been mine all along."

Ethan moves with deliberate caution, sliding to the edge of the bed, bare feet finding the floor. "Alice, look at me. Not her. Me." His voice drops lower, a technique Jetta recognises from his security work—commanding attention, drawing focus. "Whatever happens next is between us. Let's talk about this, just you and me."

FOR A HEARTBEAT, Alice's focus wavers, her gaze flicking to Ethan. In that moment, Jetta lunges in the opposite direction, rolling across the bed toward the far side of the room. The sudden movement startles Alice, whose gun swings wildly between the two targets now moving in different directions.

"STOP IT!" she screams, backing up as her control of the situation disintegrates. "Stay where I can see you both!"

HER BACKWARD STEP collides with the bedside table. The lamp wobbles, then crashes to the floor, plunging the room into darkness broken only by the faint glow of streetlights through the curtains. In the sudden shadow, Jetta scrambles off the bed, crouching behind its protective bulk.

"ETHAN?" she calls, heart in her throat as she loses sight of him in the darkness.

"YOU THINK THIS CHANGES ANYTHING?" Alice's voice comes from near the doorway, edged with desperation. "I can still see enough to end this!" Something large—the dresser, perhaps—scrapes across the floor as someone collides with it.

THROUGH THE WALL, Jetta hears their neighbour's voice, muffled but distinct: "Hello? Police? I need to report a disturbance. There's shouting, things breaking. I think someone might be in danger."

THE KNOWLEDGE that help might be coming provides a surge of desperate hope. Jetta moves carefully around the perimeter of the room, using the darkness as cover while Alice continues to shout threats into the shadowed space. Her fingers brush against something solid—Ethan's leg, tense with readiness as he crouches behind the overturned bedside table.

IN THE DISTANCE, barely audible at first, comes the wail of sirens. The sound seems to penetrate Alice's frenzied state, her head turning toward the window as the implications register.

"NO," she whispers, then louder: "No! We're not finished!" The gun waves erratically in the darkness, seeking targets now hidden from her sight. "Come out, or I start shooting blindly. How confident are you in your hiding spots?"

THE SIRENS GROW LOUDER, drawing closer to their building. Alice's breathing becomes ragged, panic overtaking calculation as her carefully constructed plan unravels.

"ALICE," Ethan's voice comes from beside Jetta, low and steady. "It's over. Put the gun down before someone gets hurt."

"IT'S NOT over until I say it's over!" The hysteria in her voice is complete now, all pretence of control abandoned. "I decide when things end! Me!"

THE SIRENS STOP ABRUPTLY, replaced by the sound of car doors slamming, voices in the street below. Alice's attention diverts to the window for a crucial second—the opening Ethan has been waiting for.

HE LAUNCHES from his crouched position with explosive force, crossing the distance between them in a single bound. His body collides with Alice's, driving her backward as his hands grapple for the gun. They slam into the wall with enough force to shake the entire room, picture frames raining down around them.

THE GUN DISCHARGES with a deafening crack, the muzzle flash momentarily illuminating the struggle in stark relief. Plaster dust rains from the ceiling where the bullet embeds itself, inches from where Jetta stands frozen in horror. The acrid smell of gunpowder fills the room, mingling with the copper scent of blood—someone's bleeding, though in the darkness Jetta can't tell who.

HEAVY FOOTSTEPS POUND up the building's stairs, voices calling out commands. Ethan and Alice remain locked in their desperate struggle, grunting with effort as they wrestle for control of the weapon. Another crash as they collide with the bookshelf, volumes tumbling around them like literary hail.

"POLICE! OPEN UP!" Fists hammer against the apartment's front door, the authoritative demand cutting through the chaos of the bedroom.

"IT'S OVER, ALICE," he pants, voice ragged with exertion. "It's finally over."

THE FRONT DOOR splinters as police force their way in, flashlight beams cutting through the apartment's darkness. Their shouts—"Police! Hands where we can see them!"—blend with Alice's screams, her rage dissolving into broken sobs as officers flood into the bedroom.

"SHE HAS A GUN," Jetta calls out, finding her voice at last. "My boyfriend disarmed her. She broke in, tried to kill us."

CHAPTER 16

Justice Served

FLASHLIGHT BEAMS SLICE through the darkness like searchlights, catching dust particles and plaster fragments still hanging in the air from the discharged bullet. Jetta presses her back against the wall, heart hammering against her ribs as uniformed officers flood into the bedroom, their commands overlapping in a wave of authoritative voices. Blue and red lights from patrol cars outside pulse through the gaps in the curtains, painting Alice's contorted face in alternating cold hues as she stands with the gun still clutched in her white-knuckled grip, eyes wild and unfocused.

"DROP THE WEAPON! NOW!" The command cuts through the chaos, a single voice rising above the others with practised authority. "Drop it and get on the ground!"

ALICE'S BODY GOES RIGID, her flame-red hair dishevelled around her face like a demonic halo. The gun wavers in her hand, barrel shifting between Jetta and the advancing officers.

Her lips pull back in a feral grimace, revealing teeth that catch the strobing lights from outside.

"She's mine to eliminate," Alice hisses, the words barely audible beneath the shouting. "My problem to solve."

Ethan shifts his weight, his body still positioned between Jetta and the gun. His breathing comes in controlled bursts, muscles tensed for movement. Jetta feels rather than sees his preparation—the subtle coiling of energy, the microscopic adjustments of balance that telegraph his intent to anyone who knows how to read him.

"Last warning!" An officer advances, weapon raised, flashlight beam fixed directly on Alice's face, forcing her to squint against the harsh light. "Drop the weapon or we will take you down!"

Time stretches like heated glass, seconds expanding into what feels like minutes. Alice's finger twitches against the trigger, her eyes darting between the officers and Jetta with frantic calculation. There's a moment—brief but unmistakable—when decision crystallises in her expression, a terrible resolve forming behind those green eyes.

Before she can act on it, three officers move in perfect coordination. The first knocks her gun arm upward, the second tackles her midsection, and the third secures her legs. They hit the floor with a thunderous impact that shakes picture frames from the walls. The gun flies from Alice's grasp, spinning across the hardwood with a metallic clatter before coming to rest beneath the overturned dresser.

"No!" Alice's scream pierces the air, primal and raw. "Get off me! You don't understand!"

HER BODY BUCKS and twists beneath the officers' weight, surprising strength fueled by manic desperation. Nails claw at faces, teeth snap at exposed wrists. An officer curses as Alice's teeth find flesh, but they maintain their hold, wrestling her arms behind her back with practised efficiency. Metal handcuffs gleam in the strobing light, then click shut around her wrists with mechanical finality.

JETTA'S LEGS threaten to fold beneath her, adrenaline giving way to trembling exhaustion. Ethan's arm snakes around her waist, supporting her weight as they watch the struggle unfold. His body radiates heat against her side, his heartbeat rapid but steady beneath her palm. She notices with detached fascination that her fingers have curled into the fabric of his T-shirt, knuckles white with tension.

"SECURE!" calls one of the officers as they finally subdue Alice, her body now pinned face-down on the floor.

TWO OFFICERS HAUL Alice to her feet, her hair hanging in her face, obscuring her expression until she tosses her head back. The hatred that blazes from her eyes as they lock onto Jetta's face carries physical weight, a tangible force that makes Jetta's breath catch in her throat.

. . .

"THIS ISN'T OVER," Alice spits, voice dropping to a venomous hiss. "This will never be over."

THE OFFICERS BEGIN MOVING her toward the door, but she plants her feet, resisting their forward momentum with surprising strength. Her body twists toward Ethan, face transforming with pleading desperation.

"YOU WERE SUPPOSED to be mine, Ethan!" The words tear from her throat, raw and bleeding with conviction. "We were perfect together! She ruined everything—just like in high school!" A sob breaks through her rage, genuine pain flashing across her features. "Why couldn't you see that? Why couldn't you just choose right?"

"MOVE," commands an officer, physically lifting Alice's resisting form.

AS THEY DRAG her through the doorway, her mask of control shatters completely. She thrashes against the officers' grip, neck craning to maintain eye contact with Ethan until the last possible moment.

"I WOULD HAVE GIVEN YOU EVERYTHING!" she screams, voice cracking with strain. "Everything she can't! Everything you really need!" Her laughter spills out, high and broken as they force her down the hallway. "She'll never understand you like I do! Never!"

. . .

HER VOICE RECEDES down the corridor, trailing threats and declarations that grow fainter but no less disturbing as the distance increases. Officers remain in the bedroom, one securing the weapon, others photographing the scene, but Jetta barely registers their presence. The world has narrowed to the circle of Ethan's arms, to the solid warmth of him against her trembling form.

"SHE WAS GOING TO KILL ME," Jetta whispers, the reality of it finally landing with full weight. "She actually came here to murder me."

ETHAN'S ARMS tighten around her, his face buried in her hair. "But she didn't. She couldn't."

THEY STAND LOCKED TOGETHER as officers move around them, documenting evidence, speaking into radios, restoring order to chaos. The blue-red lights continue to strobe through the curtains, casting their intertwined shadows against the wall in pulsing, distorted shapes.

"I CAN FEEL YOUR HEART," Ethan murmurs against her temple. "It's still beating. We're still here."

SOMETHING BREAKS loose inside Jetta's chest—a dam rupturing under pressure too great to contain. Her body shakes with delayed shock, with the comprehension of how close they came to death. Ethan holds her through it, his hands steady despite the scratches on his face still seeping blood, despite the tremor she can feel running beneath his skin.

"SIR, MA'AM," a gentle voice interrupts them. An officer stands respectfully at a distance, notebook in hand. "When you're ready, we'll need your statements."

ETHAN NODS but doesn't release his hold on Jetta. They remain anchored to each other, witnesses to the storm that has passed through their lives—battered but unbroken, still standing in its wake.

"WE'RE STILL HERE," Jetta repeats, finding unexpected strength in the simple declaration. She presses her palm against Ethan's chest, feeling the steady thump beneath her fingers. Proof of life. Proof of survival. "We're still here."

DAWN BLEEDS RELUCTANTLY through the apartment windows, revealing the full extent of destruction their bedroom has become. Jetta sits on the edge of the couch, a blanket someone draped around her shoulders hanging limply as her gaze tracks the methodical movements of police officers throughout the space. Evidence markers in bright yellow plastic stand like alien flowers among the wreckage—beside the gun on the floor, next to shattered picture frames, on the wall where the bullet embedded itself inches from where she had stood. Ethan's weight beside her is the only anchor in a room that no longer feels like the sanctuary they had created.

. . .

AN OFFICER with a camera circles the perimeter, the mechanical click and flash creating a rhythm that pulses against Jetta's temples. Each burst of light illuminates another fragment of their violated home—the overturned bedside table, books splayed open on the floor like wounded birds, Alice's diary still lying among the tangled sheets. Their private lives catalogued as evidence, intimate moments transformed into criminal documentation.

"YOU OKAY?" Ethan's voice comes low near her ear, his hand finding hers beneath the blanket. His knuckles are scraped raw from the struggle, tiny beads of blood still rising from the abraded skin.

BEFORE SHE CAN ANSWER, a new figure appears in the doorway—an older man in a standard police uniform rather than tactical gear, his salt-and-pepper hair neatly combed, wire-rimmed glasses perched on a nose that's been broken at least once. Unlike the other officers with their weapons and evidence kits, he carries only a worn leather folder and a gentle demeanour that seems out of place amid the chaos.

"MS. KINSLEY, MR. COLE." He approaches with unhurried steps, stopping at a respectful distance. "I'm Officer Toby Chance. I'd like to speak with you both, if you're up to it." His voice carries a naturally soothing quality, like warm honey over the room's jagged edges.

JETTA NODS, not trusting her voice yet. Ethan's hand tightens around hers.

. . .

"Do we need to do this now?" Ethan asks, protective edge in his tone. "We haven't even had a chance to—"

"I UNDERSTAND," Toby interrupts gently, pulling a nearby chair to sit across from them. "And we can keep it brief for now. But the sooner we get your statements, the better we can build our case." He settles into the chair with the ease of someone accustomed to difficult conversations. "I specialise in cases like this. Before joining the force, I was a social worker for fifteen years."

SOMETHING IN HIS MANNER—THE absence of the adrenaline-fueled intensity that fills the other officers, perhaps —allows Jetta's shoulders to drop a fraction. Toby notices, his eyes crinkling slightly at the corners.

"YOU'RE SAFE NOW," he says, the simple statement somehow more reassuring coming from him than from the tactical team that secured Alice. "Let's start very basic. Can you tell me how long Ms. Stilman has been fixated on you both?"

"HIGH SCHOOL," Jetta says, her voice emerging rougher than expected. "It started in high school, but we didn't realise the extent until recently."

TOBY NODS, making a note in his folder. "And the escalation to physical threats?"

. . .

JETTA'S BREATH CATCHES, her mind flashing to Alice standing at the foot of their bed, gun aimed directly at her heart. Her fingers begin to tremble. Ethan's hand slides to her back, settling between her shoulder blades, warm and steady.

"IT STARTED WITH MESSAGES," Ethan takes over, his voice controlled but tight. "Then she showed up at Jetta's bookstore, making veiled threats. She broke into my friend Owen's apartment while I was staying there." His fingers press slightly harder against Jetta's back as he continues. "Tonight, she admitted she'd tampered with Jetta's car brakes a few weeks ago—an incident we thought was just mechanical failure. And to having her drugged, unsure of what the plan was after that."

TOBY'S EXPRESSION REMAINS PROFESSIONAL, but his eyes sharpen with interest. "She admitted to the brake tampering? Those exact words?"

"YES," Jetta manages, the memory of Alice's cruel smile as she described the sabotage still fresh. "She said it 'should have worked' and seemed... proud of it."

TOBY MAKES ANOTHER NOTE, his pen moving smoothly across the page. He looks up, studying Jetta's face briefly before asking his next question. "And how did she get into your apartment tonight?"

JETTA FLINCHES INVOLUNTARILY, the violation of their sanctuary still raw. Toby immediately shifts his approach, his voice softening further.

. . .

"ACTUALLY, let's back up a bit. Are either of you injured? We have paramedics outside."

ETHAN SHAKES HIS HEAD. "Just scratches. Nothing serious."

"AND YOU, MS. KINSLEY?"

"JETTA," she corrects automatically. "No, I'm not hurt. Just..." She gestures vaguely at the destruction around them, words failing to encompass the emotional damage.

"I UNDERSTAND," Toby says, and somehow she believes he does. He continues with his questions, each one delivered with careful timing that allows them space to breathe between responses.

AS THE INTERVIEW PROGRESSES, Jetta finds herself leaning more heavily against Ethan, her body seeking his warmth as exhaustion seeps into her bones. His hand remains a constant presence on her back, fingers occasionally tensing when recounting particularly difficult details—Alice's stalking, her threats, the moment they realised she had been watching them for weeks.

"SHE HAD DETAILED knowledge of our routines," Ethan explains, jaw tightening. "Knew when we showered, slept, even that Jetta checks the locks three times before bed." His voice drops lower. "She's been watching us for longer than we realised."

TOBY NODS, his pen pausing above the page. "And the diary we found on the bed—you mentioned it contained plans from your high school days?"

"YES," Jetta says, finding her voice stronger now. "It documented everything—how she manipulated social situations, orchestrated incidents to isolate me, all with the goal of separating me from Ethan. She had diagrams, timelines, lists of vulnerabilities she could exploit." The clinical description helps, creating distance between her and the raw emotions those discoveries had triggered.

"AND YOU KEPT this diary all these years?" Toby asks Ethan, his tone curious rather than accusatory.

"SHE LEFT it for me to find after everything happened with Jetta," Ethan explains. "I held onto it as evidence of what she'd done, though I never thought..." He trails off, shaking his head slightly. "I never imagined we'd need it like this."

AS THE INTERVIEW CONTINUES, other officers move through the apartment, collecting evidence, taking photographs, securing the crime scene. Jetta watches them with detached fascination, as if observing actors on a stage rather than people in her home. The surreal quality of the situation—sitting on her couch providing a statement about attempted murder while dawn creeps across her living room floor—feels like something happening to someone else, viewed through thick glass.

"I THINK that's enough for now," Toby says finally, closing his folder. "We'll need you both to come to the station later today for formal statements, but this gives us a good start." He stands, adjusting his glasses with a practised gesture. "Officer Martinez will take you somewhere safe for the rest of the night, if you'd like. A hotel, perhaps, or a friend's place."

JETTA LOOKS around at the apartment—their home transformed into a crime scene, yellow evidence markers dotting the landscape of their private life. The thought of staying here, of trying to sleep where Alice stood with her gun and her hatred, sends a chill through her that has nothing to do with the early morning air.

"WE CAN'T STAY HERE," she whispers, the realisation settling heavily in her chest. Another thing Alice has taken from them—the safety of their own space.

"No," Ethan agrees, his arm tightening around her shoulders. "Not tonight."

TOBY NODS UNDERSTANDING, his kind eyes carrying the weight of many similar scenes he's witnessed throughout his career. "We'll arrange transportation when you're ready. Take your time."

. . .

THE POLICE STATION hums with fluorescent efficiency, a world of hard surfaces and muted colours that feels both alien and appropriate after the chaos of their apartment. Jetta's fingers trace the edge of the plastic chair as Toby leads them through a maze of desks and uniformed officers, past the holding cells where Alice presumably waits, though Jetta deliberately avoids looking in that direction. The borrowed NYPD sweatshirt hangs loosely from her shoulders, a replacement for her sleep shirt that became evidence along with most of their bedroom. Beside her, Ethan moves with the same protective closeness he's maintained since the officers first burst through their door, his body angled slightly toward hers as if still preparing to shield her from unseen threats.

"IN HERE," Toby says, holding open a door to a small interview room with institutional green walls that might once have been cheerful before years of harsh lighting leached the life from them. A metal table bolted to the floor dominates the space, flanked by four plastic chairs identical to the ones in the waiting area. "I know it's not comfortable, but it's private."

THE FLUORESCENT LIGHTS BUZZ OVERHEAD, a persistent electronic drone that sets Jetta's teeth on edge as they settle into the chairs. A camera blinks red in the corner of the ceiling, its unblinking eye recording every movement. The room smells faintly of coffee and disinfectant, underlaid with the ghost of too many anxious bodies that have occupied this space before them.

"I'M GOING to record this interview," Toby explains, setting a digital recorder on the table between them. "Standard procedure. We'll go through everything in more detail than earlier."

He places a folder beside the recorder, this one thicker than the one he carried at the apartment. "But first, let me explain what happens next."

JETTA NODS, her hands finding each other in her lap, fingers lacing together to stop their trembling. Ethan's chair scrapes closer to hers, his knee pressing against her thigh beneath the table, a silent reminder of his presence.

"ALICE STILMAN IS CURRENTLY BEING PROCESSED," Toby begins, his voice maintaining that same calm, measured tone that somehow cuts through the institutional sterility around them. "She'll be arraigned later today on multiple serious charges—breaking and entering, stalking, attempted murder. The DA will likely add more charges as we continue investigating."

THE WORDS HANG in the air between them, concrete and substantial in a way that makes Alice's actions suddenly real in a new dimension. Not just a personal nightmare but a series of criminal acts with names and consequences.

"BASED on what you've told us and the evidence we've collected, I don't anticipate any issues with holding her without bail," Toby continues, opening the folder to reveal a stack of forms and pamphlets. "But I want you both to be prepared for what comes next."

HE SLIDES several resources across the table—brochures about stalking victims' rights, contact information for victim advocates, a sheet explaining protective orders. Each glossy pamphlet feels like a confirmation that they aren't alone, that others have walked this path before them.

"THE LEGAL PROCESS can be almost as traumatic as the original events," Toby says, removing his glasses to clean them with a cloth from his pocket. The gesture is unexpectedly humanising in the sterile environment. "You'll have to tell your story multiple times. There may be a trial, though, with the evidence we have, a plea deal is more likely."

JETTA REACHES for one of the brochures, fingers tracing the bold lettering on its cover: "Rebuilding Safety After Stalking." The fact that such a resource exists—that there are enough victims to warrant its creation—brings a strange comfort. Their experience, while horrific, isn't unique or incomprehensible.

"BEFORE WE START THE FORMAL STATEMENT," Toby says, replacing his glasses, "there's something else you should know." He pulls a notepad from the folder, sliding it across the table. "We've been receiving calls since Alice's arrest was entered into the system."

JETTA LEANS FORWARD, Ethan doing the same beside her. The notepad contains a list of names, some familiar, others not. Next to each name is a brief notation: "Harassment, 2018." "Stalking, 2020." "Threats, 2016."

"WHAT IS THIS?" Ethan asks, his voice tight with confusion.

. . .

"OTHER VICTIMS," Toby says simply. "People who recognised Alice's name from our database entries. People who've had similar experiences with her but never filed formal charges."

JETTA'S FINGER stops on a familiar name—a girl from their high school debate team, someone who had suddenly transferred schools junior year. Next to her name: "Harassment, manipulation, 2013."

"THERE ARE SO MANY," she whispers, the realisation hitting her with physical force. "This goes back years."

"WE'RE JUST BEGINNING to piece together the pattern," Toby confirms, his expression grave behind his glasses. "But it appears Ms. Stilman has been engaging in similar behaviour with multiple targets. Usually, people she perceived as rivals or obstacles."

ETHAN'S HAND finds Jetta's beneath the table, his fingers wrapping around hers with gentle pressure. "She's been doing this to others all along," he says, voice hollow with realisation. "All these years, while we thought she'd moved on..."

"PREDATORS RARELY STOP," Toby says, the professional assessment delivered with quiet certainty. "They just find new hunting grounds when one becomes inhospitable."

. . .

JETTA AND ETHAN EXCHANGE GLANCES, a wordless communication passing between them—the dawning understanding that what happened wasn't just about them, wasn't just Alice's obsession with Ethan or hatred of Jetta. It was part of a larger pattern, a pathology that extended far beyond their history together.

"SOME OF THESE people are willing to provide statements," Toby continues, tapping the notepad. "Their experiences may not be admissible in court for your case, but they help establish a pattern of behaviour that strengthens the prosecution's position."

THE KNOWLEDGE SETTLES over Jetta like a blanket—not warm or comforting, but substantial, grounding. Alice's actions weren't unique to them. Her obsession, her manipulation, her violence—these were part of who she was, not reactions they had somehow provoked or deserved.

"WE'RE NOT ALONE," she says aloud, the realisation bringing unexpected tears to her eyes. "All this time, I thought it was just us. Just me."

"No," Toby says gently. "You were never alone in this. And that's important to remember as we move forward."

THE FORMAL INTERVIEW process takes over an hour, their stories recorded in methodical detail—from the high school manipulation through the recent stalking to the final confrontation in their bedroom. Toby's questioning remains gentle but thorough, each detail captured with professional precision. Throughout, Ethan's hand remains wrapped around Jetta's, his thumb occasionally stroking across her knuckles when particularly difficult memories surface.

BY THE TIME THEY FINISH, the fluorescent lights seem less harsh somehow, the green walls less institutional. The process of speaking their trauma aloud, of transforming it from nightmare into documented evidence, has begun the slow work of defanging it.

"THAT'S ALL FOR NOW," Toby says finally, stopping the recorder. "You've both been incredibly helpful. The officers who drove you here can take you wherever you need to go—a hotel, a friend's place."

"BRANDI AND OWEN'S," Jetta says immediately, the thought of her best friend's fierce protectiveness suddenly the only comfort she can imagine. "They'll be worried sick."

THEY STAND, bodies stiff from hours in the uncomfortable chairs, exhaustion pulling at their limbs like gravity turned heavy. Toby walks them through the station, past desks where officers now look up with recognition and something like respect in their eyes—no longer just victims but survivors whose testimony will help build a case.

OUTSIDE, the night has fully surrendered to morning, sunlight streaming between buildings to touch their faces as they step onto the station steps. The air tastes sweeter somehow, despite the city's usual blend of exhaust and humanity. Jetta fills her lungs with it, face turned upward to catch the warmth on her skin.

"I CAN'T BELIEVE it's only been a few hours," Ethan says beside her, his voice carrying the weight of their ordeal. "Feels like days."

"I KNOW." Jetta's hand finds his between them, fingers interlacing with the ease of habit now rather than desperate clinging. "But we made it through."

THEY STAND TOGETHER on the steps, physically exhausted but emotionally lighter than they've been in weeks. The shadow of Alice's obsession still stretches behind them, but no longer reaches to envelop them completely. The legal process ahead will be long and difficult, but for the first time since finding that circled photograph beneath their door, Jetta feels the tentative stirring of hope.

"READY?" Ethan asks, squeezing her hand gently.

SHE NODS, stepping down to the sidewalk beside him. They move together into the morning light, shoulders touching, pace synchronised without conscious effort. Behind them, the police station continues its efficient hum of justice being processed. Before them stretches a day of recovery, of friends' support, of beginning to rebuild what Alice tried to destroy.

. . .

"WE'RE STILL HERE," Jetta says, echoing her words from hours earlier, finding new strength in their simple truth. "We're still us."

ETHAN'S SMILE touches his eyes for the first time since the officers burst through their door, a small but genuine expression that warms something cold inside her chest. "Always," he promises, his voice low but certain. "Always us."

CHAPTER 17

Healing Together

THE CLOCK on Dr. Chen's desk ticks with quiet precision, each second measured and accounted for in the otherwise silent room. Jetta sits on the edge of the beige sofa, fingers working the sleeve of her sweater into a series of small pleats, then smoothing them out, only to begin again. Beside her, Ethan maintains a careful distance—close enough to reach her if needed, far enough to honour the boundary exercise from their last session. His posture remains alert, shoulders squared against invisible threats that no longer lurk in the corners of the softly lit office.

DR. MARISSA CHEN watches them both, her fountain pen poised above her notepad. Her office is a carefully constructed neutral territory—walls painted in soft taupe, abstract art in muted blues and greens, plants that require minimal attention thriving in corners. Nothing sharp, nothing sudden. A space designed for wounds to breathe.

. . .

"It's been four weeks since Alice's arrest," Dr. Chen says, her voice pitched in that perfect therapeutic timbre—not too soft to be patronising, not too clinical to feel impersonal. "How have you both been sleeping?"

Ethan glances at Jetta, the slight furrow between his brows betraying his concern before she even speaks. This is their pattern—his wordless check-in, her measured response.

"Better," Jetta says, though the shadows beneath her eyes suggest otherwise. "I'm down to waking up only twice a night instead of hourly."

Dr. Chen nods, pen making a small notation. "And the nightmares?"

"Less frequent." Jetta's fingers abandon her sleeve to twist a strand of hair instead. "But when they come, they're... vivid."

"She still calls out sometimes," Ethan adds, then catches himself. "Sorry. I should let Jetta speak for herself."

Dr. Chen's smile acknowledges his self-correction. "That's good awareness, Ethan. And Jetta, how do you feel when Ethan notices these things that you might not mention?"

The question hangs between them, heavier than it should be. Jetta's shoulders tense slightly.

. . .

"SOMETIMES IT FEELS like he's watching for cracks," she admits, her voice dropping. "Other times, it's... comforting. To know someone is paying attention."

"I'D LIKE to talk about hypervigilance today," Dr. Chen says, setting her notepad aside and leaning forward slightly. "It's a common response to trauma—our body's way of trying to prevent future harm by staying on high alert."

"I KNOW WHAT HYPERVIGILANCE IS," Jetta responds, a defensive edge creeping into her voice. "We both do."

"KNOWING the concept and recognising it in ourselves are different skills," Dr. Chen replies, unruffled. "Jetta, are there rituals or checks you find yourself performing regularly since the incident?"

JETTA'S GAZE fixes on the potted fern beside Dr. Chen's bookshelf, counting the fronds rather than meeting the therapist's eyes. Ethan shifts beside her, clearly wrestling with the urge to answer for her.

"I CHECK THE LOCKS," she finally admits, the words escaping like reluctant prisoners. "Before bed. Three times, sometimes four."

. . .

"AND DOORS, WINDOWS," Ethan adds gently. "The shower curtain, too."

"DO you want to add anything else to that list, Jetta?" Dr. Chen prompts.

JETTA'S FINGERS return to pleating her sleeve. "I keep my phone in my hand when I'm alone at the shop. Even in the bathroom. And I... I look for red hair everywhere I go." The admission costs her, her cheeks flushing with something between shame and anger. "I know she's in prison. I know she can't hurt us. But I still look."

"THAT'S your brain trying to protect you," Dr. Chen says. "It's not weakness or failure—it's a normal response to what you experienced." She turns slightly toward Ethan. "And you? What forms does your hypervigilance take?"

ETHAN STRAIGHTENS, as if being called to account. "I check my phone constantly when we're apart. I position myself between Jetta and the door in public places." His jaw works for a moment before he continues. "I wake up if she gets out of bed, even just to use the bathroom. I can't... I can't fall back asleep until she returns."

JETTA TURNS TO HIM, surprised. "I didn't know that."

"I DIDN'T WANT to worry you," he says, their eyes meeting briefly before he looks away. "And I know I hover too much.

I'm trying to give you space, but sometimes it feels impossible. Like if I look away for one second..."

"YOU'RE both carrying the weight of trauma," Dr. Chen observes. "But also carrying the weight of protecting each other from your own struggles. That's a heavy load for any relationship, especially one still finding its foundation."

THE OBSERVATION SETTLES BETWEEN THEM, undeniable in its accuracy. Jetta feels the truth of it in her chest —how carefully they've been stepping around each other's broken places, how exhausting the constant vigilance has become.

"I'D LIKE TO TRY SOMETHING," Dr. Chen continues. "I want each of you to identify one fear you're ready to release. Not eliminate completely—that's not realistic yet—but one fear you can begin to set down."

SILENCE FILLS THE ROOM, dense as fog. The clock continues its methodical counting, seconds stretching into a full minute as neither speaks. Jetta's throat tightens around words she isn't sure she's ready to voice.

"I'M AFRAID TO BE ALONE," she finally whispers, the admission barely audible. "Not just physically—though that too—but... I'm afraid that without the crisis binding us together, without the shared enemy, we might discover we don't..." She can't finish, the fear too raw once exposed to air.

. . .

ETHAN REACHES FOR HER HAND, his movement careful but deliberate. Their fingers intertwine, familiar landscapes finding each other in the dark.

"AND I'M afraid of not being there when you need me," he admits, his voice rough with emotion. "I'm afraid that if I relax my guard for even a moment, something will happen and I'll have failed you. Again."

THE "AGAIN" lands between them—his lingering guilt about high school, about not seeing through Alice's manipulations sooner, about all the harm that might have been prevented.

"THESE ARE POWERFUL ADMISSIONS," Dr. Chen says after giving their words space to breathe. "And interconnected in ways that can either strengthen your bond or strain it." She leans forward slightly. "Jetta needs room to rediscover her independence, to know she can stand alone. Ethan needs to honour his protective instincts without allowing them to become suffocating. The question becomes: how do we create boundaries that serve you both?"

THEY SPEND the remainder of the session establishing parameters—small steps toward balance. Ethan agrees to limit his check-in texts when they're apart. Jetta commits to expressing her needs directly rather than silently resenting his protectiveness. They create a code word for moments when the hypervigilance becomes overwhelming, a private signal that can communicate volumes without explanation.

. . .

As they prepare to leave, Dr. Chen offers one final observation: "Healing isn't linear. There will be setbacks. The goal isn't to never feel afraid again—it's to keep fear from making your decisions for you."

In the hallway outside the office, Ethan's hand finds the small of Jetta's back—not directing her movement, not controlling her path, just present. The contact is lighter than before, a request rather than an assumption. Jetta leans into it slightly, accepting the connection without surrendering to it.

"That wasn't so bad," she says as they walk toward the elevator, their reflections wavering in the polished doors ahead.

"Speak for yourself," Ethan replies, but there's a warmth in his voice that's been absent for weeks. "I feel like she dismantled me and put me back together with half the pieces facing backward."

Jetta surprises herself with a small laugh. "That's how healing works, I think. Nothing fits the same way twice."

The elevator arrives with a gentle chime, doors sliding open to reveal the empty car. Four weeks ago, Ethan would have entered first, checking for threats. Today, they step in together, side by side—a small victory neither mentions but both recognise. As the doors close, Jetta watches their reflection merge with the brushed metal, two figures standing not in each other's shadows, but in shared light.

. . .

THE APARTMENT GLOWS amber in the late afternoon light that streams through partially opened blinds. Jetta pauses in the entryway, keys still warm in her palm, taking in the subtle changes they've made since returning to this space after Alice's arrest. The bookshelves no longer form barricades around the perimeter; instead, they've rearranged them to create cozy nooks that invite rather than defend. Even the air feels different—lighter somehow, as if the weight of constant vigilance has begun to lift from the rooms they share.

"I'LL PUT THE KETTLE ON," she says, hanging her keys on the hook by the door—a deliberate act of permanence that would have seemed impossible six weeks ago, when everything felt temporary, precarious.

ETHAN NODS, already kneeling beside a cardboard box of books, sorting through new arrivals for Bound Together. "Earl Grey or that herbal thing Brandi brought over?"

"CHAMOMILE," Jetta answers, moving toward the kitchen. "Dr. Chen says it might help with sleep."

THEIR POST-THERAPY ROUTINE has become its own form of comfort—this gentle reentry into shared space, the mundane questions that anchor them to normalcy. Jetta fills the copper kettle, the weight of water steady in her hands. Through the kitchen doorway, she watches Ethan methodically creating stacks—fiction, non-fiction, rare editions—his broad shoulders relaxed in a way they rarely were before.

. . .

THE KETTLE BEGINS to warm on the stove, and Jetta leans against the counter, allowing herself the luxury of stillness. The apartment had been uninhabitable for days after Alice's intrusion—evidence markers tagging their intimate spaces, fingerprint dust coating surfaces like volcanic ash. When they finally returned, they'd rearranged everything, an exorcism of sorts. New sheets. New paint. New configuration of furniture that erased the memory map of that night.

"THE DISTRIBUTOR CALLED about that first edition Austen we ordered," Ethan says, his voice carrying easily between the rooms. "Shipping delay. They're saying next week now."

"MRS. HARGROVE WILL BE DISAPPOINTED," Jetta replies, reaching for the canister of loose tea. "She's been asking about it every time she comes in."

"WE COULD OFFER her first peek at the Victorian poetry collection that came in yesterday. Might soften the blow."

JETTA SMILES AT THE SUGGESTION—HIS understanding of their customers has deepened as he's spent more time at the shop. What began as a temporary safety measure—keeping close during working hours—has evolved into a genuine partnership. Ethan's security background translates surprisingly well to retail; his observant nature perfect for anticipating customer needs.

. . .

THE WATER BEGINS TO SIMMER, small bubbles forming at the kettle's edge. Jetta stretches toward the highest cabinet shelf for mugs—the mismatched pair they've claimed as their own. Her fingertips brush ceramic just as a car backfires on the street below, the sound sharp and sudden.

HER BODY RESPONDS before her mind can intervene—muscles tensing, breath catching, pulse accelerating. The mug teeters at the edge of the shelf as her hand jerks reflexively.

FROM THE LIVING ROOM, she feels rather than sees Ethan go still, his attention shifting entirely to her. Before, he would have been at her side in an instant, hands steady where hers faltered, body inserting itself between her and the perceived threat. Today, he remains where he is, though she notes the slight shift in his posture—ready but restraining himself.

"I'VE GOT IT," she says, voice steadier than the flutter in her chest. She reaches again, stretching until her fingers close around the mug handles, bringing them down with deliberate care. A small victory, claimed in inches.

"NEVER LIKED THAT CAR," Ethan comments casually, though they both recognise the neutralisation technique from therapy—acknowledge the trigger, then contextualise it. "Engine sounds like it's running on spite and WD-40."

JETTA LAUGHS, the sound surprising her with its ease. The kettle begins to whistle, and she pours steaming water over the tea leaves, releasing the earthy scent of chamomile into the kitchen. She brings both mugs to the coffee table, settling on the couch as Ethan finishes organising the last stack of books.

"SUCCESSFUL SESSION TODAY?" he asks, the question carefully phrased to respect her privacy while still expressing interest.

"I THINK SO," she answers, tucking her feet beneath her. "Though I'm not sure I'm ready to give up my lock-checking ritual just yet."

ETHAN MOVES TO JOIN HER, maintaining the respectful distance they're still learning to navigate. "No rush. Small steps, like Dr. Chen said."

THEY SIP their tea in companionable silence, the golden light shifting through the apartment as afternoon edges toward evening. Outside, the city continues its perpetual motion—cars passing, people calling to each other, delivery trucks rumbling past—but these sounds no longer feel like potential threats. They're just the background music of urban life, resuming after a long, discordant pause.

"I WAS THINKING ABOUT DINNER," Jetta says finally, setting her empty mug aside. "We have that chicken I marinated this morning."

"AND THOSE VEGETABLES FROM THE FARMERS' market," Ethan adds, already rising. "I'll chop if you'll cook."

. . .

THEIR KITCHEN DANCE has become fluid over these weeks of cohabitation—the awkward bumping of those first days replaced by intuitive coordination. Jetta preheats the oven while Ethan retrieves cutting boards and knives. He stays to her left as she moves right, their bodies flowing around each other with practised awareness.

"PASS THE OLIVE OIL?" she asks, and it appears beside her before she finishes the sentence, his anticipation of her needs no longer smothering but supportive.

JETTA SEASONS the chicken with rosemary and thyme while Ethan's knife makes quick work of bell peppers and zucchini. The steady rhythm of blade against board forms a percussion track beneath their occasional comments about the day—a difficult customer at the shop, a promising review of Jetta's upcoming author event, plans for the weekend.

"BRANDI WANTS us to try that new restaurant on Maple," Jetta says, reaching for the pepper grinder. "The one with the rooftop garden."

"OUTDOORS," Ethan observes, his knife pausing momentarily. "That's new for us."

THE OBSERVATION HANGS BETWEEN THEM, significant in its simplicity. Their social reemergence has been cautious—private homes, quiet cafés, places with limited exposure and multiple exits. A rooftop restaurant represents a boundary crossing.

"I THINK I'M READY," Jetta says, the words carrying weight beyond their surface meaning.

ETHAN NODS, resuming his chopping with a small smile. "Me too."

SHE TURNS to place the seasoned chicken in the oven, but the metal spoon balanced on the edge of the baking dish clatters to the floor, striking the tile with a sharp ping that echoes through the kitchen. Two months ago, such a sound would have sent Jetta into momentary paralysis, her body bracing for danger. Even two weeks ago, Ethan would have been instantly alert, positioned between her and the doorway.

TODAY, she simply bends to retrieve it, her breath catching only briefly before resuming its normal rhythm. When she straightens, she finds Ethan watching her, his eyes warm with understanding. No words are needed for this shared recognition—another small victory in their campaign to reclaim ordinary life.

"WE'RE GETTING BETTER AT THIS," she says, rinsing the spoon under the tap.

"BETTER AT DROPPING THINGS?" Ethan teases, sliding the chopped vegetables into a bowl.

"Better at picking them up again," she corrects, bumping her hip gently against his as she passes.

The chicken sizzles as it begins to cook, filling the apartment with savoury warmth that displaces the last lingering fragments of fear. Outside, streetlights flicker on as dusk descends, but inside, they move in a sphere of light they've created together—not perfect, not completely without shadows, but growing stronger by degrees.

Jetta arranges plates on the counter, no longer startling when Ethan's hand brushes hers as he places silverware beside them. Their fingers tangle briefly, a casual intimacy that feels earned rather than automatic. When she meets his eyes, she finds in them not the hyper-vigilant protector of weeks past, but a partner moving forward at her pace, learning alongside her how to balance caution with living.

"Almost ready," she says, and means more than just dinner.

The scent of garlic and herbs permeates Brandi and Owen's apartment, a welcome change from the antiseptic smell of the police station that still lingers in Jetta's nostrils. Warmth envelops her as she steps through the doorway, the soft amber lighting and familiar furnishings offering a sanctuary she hadn't realised she desperately needed. Brandi's collection of mismatched throw pillows scattered across the couch, Owen's vintage record player softly spinning jazz in the corner, the photographs of the four of them adorning the walls—everything here speaks of safety, of friendship, of normalcy that feels almost foreign after the past twenty-four hours.

"JUST IN TIME!" Brandi calls from the kitchen, her blonde hair twisted into a messy bun, flour dusting her cheek. "Owen, they're here!"

OWEN APPEARS FROM THE HALLWAY, his easy smile a balm to Jetta's frayed nerves. He embraces Ethan with a firm clap on the back, then turns to Jetta, his expression softening with concern, he quickly masks.

"WELCOME TO CASA COOPER-NIELSON," he says, gesturing grandly around the apartment. "Where the wine flows freely and judgment is strictly prohibited."

JETTA FEELS Ethan's hand settle at the small of her back, the gentle pressure grounding her in the present moment. His fingers trace small circles against her spine, a private communication of support.

"IT SMELLS AMAZING," she manages, her voice stronger than she expected. "What did you make?"

"EVERYTHING," Ethan murmurs near her ear, and the warmth of his breath against her skin sends a pleasant shiver down her neck.

. . .

"HE'S NOT EXAGGERATING," Brandi says, emerging from the kitchen with a wooden spoon in hand. "I've been stress-cooking since 6 AM. There's lasagna with the handmade pasta, roasted vegetables with that balsamic glaze you love, garlic bread that would make an Italian grandmother weep, and tiramisu for dessert." She pauses, studying Jetta's face. "I made extra of the butternut squash risotto. I know it's your favourite."

THE SIMPLE GESTURE—BRANDI remembering her food preferences amid the chaos—brings unexpected tears to Jetta's eyes. She blinks them away quickly, but Brandi notices and pulls her into a fierce hug that smells of rosemary and loyalty.

"COME ON," Owen says, guiding them toward the dining table already set with Brandi's mismatched vintage china. "Food first, feelings later. That's the rule tonight."

THE TABLE GLEAMS under soft lighting, wine glasses catching and fracturing the glow into tiny constellations. Ethan pulls out Jetta's chair, his fingers brushing against her shoulder as she sits—another small touch that anchors her to this moment of normalcy.

OWEN KEEPS the conversation flowing as they pass dishes around the table, regaling them with stories from his consulting firm—the client who insisted on conducting meetings while jogging, the office rivalry over the last bagel each morning, the disastrous team-building exercise involving kayaks and a sudden thunderstorm.

"I swear, Linda from accounting still twitches when she hears thunder," he concludes, his animated gestures nearly sending a piece of garlic bread flying across the table.

Jetta finds herself laughing—actually laughing—the sound almost startling after days of tension and fear. Beside her, Ethan's leg presses against hers beneath the table, a warm line of contact that feels both casual and deliberate.

"Pass the salt?" he asks, and when she hands it to him, his fingers linger against her wrist for a heartbeat longer than necessary. The small contact sends warmth spreading up her arm, a quiet reminder that they're connected even in these mundane moments.

Brandi watches them with barely concealed delight, her eyes bright with affection as she refills wine glasses without being asked. When all plates are nearly empty, she raises her glass, crystal catching light as she holds it aloft.

"To new beginnings," she says, her voice suddenly thick with emotion. "And to the strength that carries us through endings we didn't choose."

The glasses clink together, the sound clear and bright in the warm air. Jetta's eyes meet Ethan's over the rim of her glass, and the understanding that passes between them feels like its own kind of intimacy—deeper than the physical closeness they've shared, more fundamental than the words they've exchanged.

AFTER DINNER, they migrate to the living room, dishes abandoned to soak despite Jetta's halfhearted offers to help clean. Owen rummages through a cabinet beside the entertainment centre, emerging triumphantly with a board game box.

"PANDEMIC?" Brandi suggests, already arranging cushions on the floor around the coffee table.

"TOO REAL," Owen counters, setting down the box. "Let's go with something less apocalyptic."

THEY SETTLE on a strategy game involving territorial conquest, colored pieces spreading across the board like competing empires. As the game progresses, Jetta feels something unfurling inside her chest—a competitive spirit that had been buried beneath layers of vigilance and fear.

"YOU CAN'T JUST MARCH into Australia like that," she protests when Ethan makes a particularly aggressive move. "I had plans for that continent."

"ALL'S FAIR in love and board games," he replies, eyes glinting with challenge.

. . .

"We'll see about that," Jetta says, leaning forward to study the board with newfound intensity. She makes a calculated move that cuts off his advance, then sits back with undisguised satisfaction. "Checkmate."

"Wrong game," Owen points out, but he's grinning at the flash of the old Jetta breaking through—the woman who once organised cutthroat trivia nights at the bookshop, who never let anyone win just to be nice.

When she successfully defends her territory for the third time, Jetta can't resist a small victory dance in her seat. "And that's how it's done, security consultant. All your tactical training, and you still can't outmaneuver a bookshop owner."

Ethan's response is to pull her close, his lips pressing against her temple in a kiss that's both congratulatory and possessive. "I love seeing that fire back in your eyes," he whispers, his voice low enough that only she can hear. The words send heat rising to her cheeks, a blush that has nothing to do with wine.

The game concludes with Brandi's surprise victory —"While you two were flirting, I was conquering Asia"—and as they help clean up game pieces, Owen mentions a beachfront cottage his family owns.

"We should go this weekend," he suggests, the casual offer hanging in the air like a test balloon. "Get out of the city, breathe some ocean air. The place has three bedrooms, a massive deck overlooking the water."

"AND A FIREPIT FOR S'MORES," Brandi adds, her eyes carefully watching Jetta's reaction.

IN THE PAST WEEKS, the thought of leaving the city—of being in an unfamiliar place without immediate access to police—would have sent anxiety spiralling through Jetta's chest. But tonight, surrounded by friends and with Ethan's solid presence beside her, the idea feels not just possible but appealing.

"I'D LIKE THAT," she says, and means it.

LATER, as they gather their few belongings to leave, Jetta notices the change in her own behaviour. Where once she would have asked Ethan to check outside first, would have scanned the parking lot with hypervigilant attention, now she simply slides her hand into his and walks toward the door with steady steps.

"TEXT WHEN YOU GET HOME," Brandi calls after them, her mother-hen instincts never fully suppressed.

OUTSIDE, their shadows stretch long and joined beneath the streetlights. Jetta breathes in the night air, her fingers interlaced with Ethan's, and feels something like peace settling into the spaces where fear once lived. Not complete healing—not yet—but the beginning of it, taking root in soil made fertile by friendship, by justice served, by love carefully tended despite the harshest conditions.

LAMPLIGHT POOLS in golden circles on either side of the bed, casting the rest of the bedroom in gentle shadow. Jetta stands at the dresser, removing her earrings—borrowed from Brandi after the police took her own as evidence—and places them in a small ceramic dish shaped like a curled leaf. The room still feels new to her; this temporary apartment they found after the investigation team finished processing their old place. The walls are a different shade of blue, the windows face east instead of west, but Ethan's books line the makeshift shelves, and her plants cluster near the windows—small anchors of familiarity in this transitional space they're cautiously making their own.

BEHIND HER REFLECTION in the mirror, she watches Ethan pull back the covers, his movements easy and domestic in a way that still surprises her. His shirt hangs loose at his waist, revealing a sliver of skin as he stretches. The sight sends a pleasant warmth through her belly, different from the desperate need that characterised their early intimacy—gentler, more sustainable, built for long nights and lazy mornings.

"YOU DIDN'T CHECK THE LOCKS," he says, the observation casual as he fluffs a pillow. "That's new."

JETTA'S HANDS go still on the buttons of her blouse. He's right. The realisation washes over her with quiet significance

—she'd walked straight to the bedroom without performing the ritual that has governed her evenings since Alice broke in. Three checks of the deadbolt, two of the chain, testing the doorknob with a sharp tug to ensure its resistance. The compulsion had become so automatic she'd stopped noticing it—until now, when its absence suddenly feels monumental.

"I DIDN'T EVEN THINK about it," she admits, turning from the dresser to face him.

ETHAN SITS on the edge of the bed, the mattress dipping slightly beneath his weight. He extends a hand toward her, an invitation rather than a demand. When she joins him, the springs creak softly as she settles beside him, their thighs touching through the fabric of their clothes.

"I THINK I'm starting to feel safe again," she says, her voice barely above a whisper, as if speaking the words too loudly might jinx their fragile truth. "Not completely. But enough that I forgot to be afraid, at least for a little while."

ETHAN'S FINGERS find a strand of her hair, tucking it gently behind her ear. His touch lingers against her cheek, thumb tracing the curve of her cheekbone with careful precision. In the soft lamplight, his eyes hold both relief and lingering concern, the protective instinct that defines him still evident beneath his calmer exterior.

"I CHECKED my phone only twice today to see if you'd texted," he confesses, the admission carrying its own weight.

"Once after your lunch meeting, and once when you were late getting to Brandi's."

THE VULNERABILITY IN HIS VOICE—UNUSUAL for someone whose default is strength and protection—creates a moment of profound connection between them. Jetta reaches up to cover his hand with her own, pressing his palm more firmly against her cheek.

"THAT'S PROGRESS," she says softly. "Considering you were checking every twenty minutes last week."

HIS SMILE REACHES HIS EYES, crinkling the corners in a way she's come to cherish. "Baby steps, right? That's what the therapist keeps saying."

THE MENTION OF THERAPY—ANOTHER new element in their lives, sessions attended both separately and together—reminds Jetta how far they've come in the weeks since Alice's arrest. How much work they've put into rebuilding, into transforming their trauma-forged connection into something that can thrive in peacetime.

"I WAS THINKING about the bookshop expansion today," she says, the topic shift deliberate but not jarring. Future plans —once impossible to contemplate while living under Alice's shadow—now flow more easily between them. "Brandi found a contractor who specialises in historic buildings. He thinks we can open up the wall into the vacant space next door without compromising the structure."

. . .

ETHAN'S EYES light with interest, his hand moving to rest on her knee. "The café idea? With the reading nooks in the back?"

"AND DISPLAYS FEATURING LOCAL ARTISTS," she adds, warming to the subject. "A true community space, not just a store."

"I LIKE IT," he says, thumb tracing small circles on her kneecap. "And what about the apartment upstairs? Still thinking about converting it?"

"MAYBE." Jetta leans her head against his shoulder, breathing in the clean scent of his skin. "Or maybe we should look for a place with a yard. Something with space for a dog."

THE SUGGESTION HANGS BETWEEN THEM, loaded with implications about permanence, about shared futures extending beyond their current circumstances. Ethan's hand stills on her knee, his body tensing slightly beside her.

"A DOG?" he repeats, voice carefully neutral.

"TOO MUCH?" she asks, suddenly uncertain. "Too soon?"

HIS LAUGH VIBRATES through his chest against her cheek. "No. God, no. I was just thinking we'd have to find one big enough to keep up with my running schedule but calm enough for your reading time." He turns to face her more fully, his expression open with wonder. "You're thinking long-term. With me."

THE SURPRISE in his voice catches at something in her chest. "Of course I am," she says simply. "Aren't you?"

IN ANSWER, he pulls her close, arms wrapping around her with gentle strength. The embrace carries none of the desperate intensity that characterised their earlier connections —none of the frantic need to confirm survival, to feel alive amid fear. Instead, it holds the steady warmth of deepening trust, of roots finding purchase in soil once thought too damaged to sustain growth.

"EVERY DAY," he murmurs against her hair. "In every way."

LATER, after they've brushed teeth and changed into sleep clothes, they settle beneath the covers with practised ease. The mattress accepts their weight, shapes itself around their bodies as Jetta's head finds its place on Ethan's chest, her ear pressed against the spot where his heartbeat is strongest. His arm curves around her shoulders, fingers trailing lazy patterns along her arm.

"THANK YOU," she whispers into the dimness, the lamps now extinguished except for the small nightlight in the bath-room—another concession to healing that's not yet complete.

. . .

"For what?" His voice rumbles beneath her ear, a pleasant vibration against her cheek.

"For staying. For fighting. For..." She searches for words adequate to encompass everything he's been through with her, everything he's helped her reclaim. "For seeing me through to the other side."

His arms tighten around her, his lips pressing a kiss to the crown of her head. "We saw each other through," he corrects gently. "That's how this works."

Outside, a car door slams somewhere in the parking lot. The sound reaches them clearly through the window left partially open to catch the spring breeze. Six weeks ago, such a noise would have sent Jetta bolt upright, heart racing, body flooding with fight-or-flight chemicals. Three weeks ago, she would have tensed, waiting for Ethan's reassurance that they were safe.

Tonight, she registers the sound with calm awareness, categorising it as ordinary, non-threatening. Her body remains relaxed against Ethan's, her breathing steady and deep. His hand continues its gentle stroking along her arm, neither of them feeling the need to comment on the noise or its harm-lessness.

As sleep approaches, softening the edges of consciousness, Jetta allows herself to drift toward it without resistance. Her limbs grow heavy against Ethan's, her thoughts slowing to a peaceful crawl. The knowledge settles over her like the blanket he's tucked around her shoulders—their shared trauma has forged something unbreakable between them, a bond tempered in fire but flourishing now in gentler light.

NOT HEALED COMPLETELY. Not yet. But healing, day by day, breath by breath, heartbeat by steady heartbeat beneath her ear.

CHAPTER 18

Bookshop Bliss

MORNING LIGHT STREAMS through the tall windows of Bound Together, painting golden rectangles across the hardwood floor. Jetta trails her fingers along the spines of newly arrived novels as she moves toward the front display table. The touch of paper and binding cloth against her skin feels like a greeting from old friends. Six months ago, such a simple pleasure would have been overshadowed by hypervigilance, by the constant looking-over-her-shoulder that dominated her every waking moment. Now, she breathes in the mingled scents of books and coffee, allowing herself to fully inhabit this moment of ordinary grace.

THE SHOP HUMS with mid-morning energy—a mother and daughter huddle together in the children's corner, an elderly man with reading glasses perched on his nose examines first editions with scholarly attention, three college students sprawl across the new reading nooks, textbooks balanced on their knees. The renovation has transformed Bound Together from a charming bookshop into a community haven, exactly as Jetta had envisioned during those late-night planning sessions with Brandi.

SHE ADJUSTS the angle of a literary prize winner, creating a cascade effect with the surrounding novels. The bestseller display has become her particular domain—arranging covers to catch the light just so, ensuring that each book beckons with its own distinct personality. Her fingers work with practised precision, no longer trembling when the bell above the door announces a new arrival.

ACROSS THE SHOP, Ethan moves with fluid efficiency behind the counter. His security training manifests in subtle ways now—the casual pivot that keeps his back to the wall, the swift visual sweep each time the door chimes, the way he positions himself with clear sightlines to all entrances. But these habits no longer seem born of fear. They've evolved into something protective rather than defensive, a strength directed outward rather than a shield held close.

"THIS EDITION HAS THE ORIGINAL FOREWORD," he explains to an older woman clutching a leather-bound volume of poetry. His voice carries to Jetta, warm and assured. "The publisher restored it for the centennial printing. You won't find it in the mass-market versions."

JETTA CATCHES his eye across the room, and the smile he sends her way still carries the power to warm her from within. Between customers, his gaze finds her with such regularity that she can almost time it—a silent check-in that once felt like anxious monitoring but now registers as a gentle connection, a thread of awareness stretching between them.

Her attention shifts to the back wall, where the new vintage deadbolt gleams on the storage room door—Ethan's most recent "security upgrade." He'd installed it last Sunday, his movements methodical and focused as he explained the mechanism's superior design. "It's the same model they use in historical museums," he'd told her, the pride in his voice unmistakable. "Beautiful craftsmanship, but practically unpickable." She hadn't pointed out that no ordinary thief would bother with such a complicated lock when the front door used a standard commercial system. The installation had given him tangible purpose, a concrete way to protect what they'd built together.

The stockroom door swings open, and Brandi emerges with a stack of inventory sheets clutched in one hand, her other arm guiding a young woman who looks like she might dissolve into the floorboards at any moment. The new employee—Maya or Mira, Jetta can't quite recall—clutches a tablet with white-knuckled intensity, her eyes wide with the particular anxiety of someone determined not to make mistakes.

"The inventory system looks complicated, but it's actually intuitive once you get the hang of it," Brandi explains, her voice carrying the gentle patience she reserves for nervous creatures—new staff, skittish children browsing the shop, the one-eyed cat that sometimes visits the back alley. "See how the categories are colour-coded? Fiction in blue, non-fiction in green..."

. . .

THE EMPLOYEE NODS with the rapid-fire movement of someone absorbing too much information too quickly. Her shoulders hunch slightly beneath her cardigan, a posture Jetta recognises from her own days of recovery—the physical manifestation of expecting criticism from all directions.

"AND DON'T WORRY about memorising everything today," Brandi continues, her hand settling briefly on the girl's shoulder. "It took me three months to learn all our systems, and I co-own the place." She winks, coaxing a tentative smile from the young woman. "We'll go as slowly as you need."

JETTA WATCHES the interaction with quiet appreciation. Brandi's nurturing nature has always been her superpower, but since the events with Alice, it's gained a new dimension of perceptiveness—as if surviving that shared trauma has finetuned her ability to recognise pain in others.

THE SHOP DOOR SWINGS OPEN, and a booming laugh announces Owen's arrival before he's fully visible. The sound reverberates through the shop—rich and uninhibited, drawing smiles from nearby browsers as if happiness were contagious.

"GOOD MORNING, LITERARY LUMINARIES!" he calls, weaving between bookshelves with the confident grace of someone now intimately familiar with the space. He pauses to right a tilting stack of paperbacks, smooths a rumpled bookmark display, then makes a beeline for Brandi.

. . .

"HI, BEAUTIFUL," he murmurs, pressing a kiss to her temple. His hand settles at the small of her back with such natural ease that Jetta feels a twinge of envy—not for Owen himself, but for the unself-conscious way they inhabit their connection. She and Ethan are still working toward that effortlessness, still occasionally second-guessing the boundaries between protection and possession.

OWEN'S ATTENTION shifts to the young employee, his smile warming without intensifying—the careful modulation of charm that makes him so effective with nervous customers. "You must be our new book wizard," he says, extending his hand. "Welcome to the best place in the city."

BEFORE THE CONVERSATION CAN CONTINUE, a small voice interrupts from nearby. "Excuse me?" A boy of perhaps seven or eight stands clutching a well-worn library card, his gaze flicking between Owen and the towering shelves of the children's section. "Do you have books about dragons that aren't too scary? My mom says I can get one today."

OWEN DROPS IMMEDIATELY to one knee, bringing himself to eye level with the child. The transition from adult conversation to childhood earnestness happens without a ripple of hesitation. "Dragons that aren't too scary? You've come to the right expert." He leans in conspiratorially. "Between you and me, I'm something of a dragon specialist."

THE BOY'S eyes widen with cautious hope. "Really?"

· · ·

"ABSOLUTELY. I can introduce you to dragons who bake cookies, dragons who can't control their hiccups, even dragons who are afraid of the dark themselves." Owen rises, offering his hand to the child. "Shall we explore together?"

AS OWEN LEADS the boy toward the children's corner, his voice drops to a gentle rumble of storytelling cadence. Jetta watches them go, a profound contentment settling in her chest. Six months ago, such ordinary interactions seemed impossibly distant—happiness viewed through frosted glass, visible but untouchable. Now, surrounded by the gentle chaos of a thriving bookshop and the friends who became her fortress when everything else crumbled, she finds herself fully present in a life rebuilt from the ground up—stronger at the broken places, more precious for having nearly been lost.

THE MID-MORNING RUSH ebbs like a retreating tide, leaving behind a momentary stillness in its wake. Jetta glances at her watch—eleven thirty, the brief lull before the lunch crowd arrives seeking literary companions for their midday breaks. She catches Brandi's eye across the shop and tilts her head toward the coffee corner, a wordless invitation that needs no explanation after years of friendship. Ethan notices the gesture and finishes ringing up a customer's purchase with efficient courtesy before making his way over. Owen, sensing the gathering, extracts himself from a spirited debate about science fiction with a professor from the local university, promising to continue their discussion of interstellar politics another day.

THE COFFEE CORNER stands as testament to their collective vision—copper fixtures gleaming above a reclaimed wood counter, local pottery mugs hanging from iron hooks, the small espresso machine that Ethan researched for weeks before declaring it "the perfect balance of quality and maintainability." Jetta leans against the counter, surveying their domain with quiet satisfaction. Sunlight catches on the dust motes dancing in the air, transforming ordinary particles into tiny constellations that drift and disappear.

"WE NEED MORE of those chocolate biscotti," Brandi notes, reaching past Jetta to straighten a stack of napkins. "The Tuesday morning book club demolished the last batch."

"ALREADY ORDERED," Jetta replies, accepting the cup of tea Owen passes her with a grateful nod. "Double quantity this time."

HER BODY SETTLES NATURALLY against the counter, weight distributed with the easy balance of someone fully inhabiting her physical space. Six months ago, she would have positioned herself with her back to the wall, hyperaware of exit routes, muscles tensed for flight. Now, she stands with open posture, her eyes no longer darting to every new movement, her smile coming easily rather than being consciously constructed. The change feels like shedding a heavy coat she'd worn so long she'd forgotten it wasn't part of her body.

ETHAN TAKES up position beside her, close enough that their shoulders brush with comfortable familiarity. His posture maintains that security consultant readiness—weight balanced, sight lines clear—but the vigilance no longer consumes him. Instead, it forms a background habit that allows his personality to occupy the foreground.

"TELL them what you just told me," he prompts Owen, amusement playing at the corners of his mouth. "About the book you're looking for."

OWEN GROANS DRAMATICALLY, running both hands through his hair until it stands in haphazard peaks. "I was just saying I read this amazing book last year, and I want to recommend it to a client, but I can't remember the title."

"OR THE AUTHOR," Ethan adds, his eyebrow raising with practised scepticism.

"I REMEMBER THE IMPORTANT PARTS," Owen protests, reaching for a chocolate chip cookie from the display plate. "It had a blue cover. Dark blue, like the ocean at night."

"AH, yes, the rare and elusive blue-covered book," Ethan deadpans. "Narrows it down to roughly thirty per cent of our inventory."

JETTA HIDES her smile behind her teacup. The playful sparring between the men has evolved over months of friendship, their natural competitiveness transforming into something more akin to brotherly ribbing. Ethan's dry wit, once deployed primarily as a defensive mechanism, now serves to draw others closer rather than keeping them at arm's length.

. . .

"It was about that guy," Owen continues, undeterred, "the one who did the thing with the boat. Or maybe it was a plane? Some kind of vehicle definitely featured prominently."

Ethan rolls his eyes with such exaggerated patience that Brandi snorts into her coffee. "That narrows it down to roughly every adventure novel ever written. Was there perhaps a conflict of some kind? Maybe even a resolution? Revolutionary concepts in storytelling, I know."

"You're not helping," Owen says, lobbing a crumpled napkin at Ethan's head. Ethan catches it mid-air without looking, his security reflexes repurposed for mundane playfulness. "It had that really good quote about the stars. Something about how they're memories or witnesses or... something philosophical."

"'The stars are not just witnesses to history; they are its memory,'" Jetta offers, the line surfacing from her mental catalogue. "From 'Midnight Crossing' by Teresa Liu. Dark blue cover with silver constellations. Published last spring."

Owen points at her triumphantly. "Yes! That's it! You're a genius."

"No, she's a bookseller," Ethan corrects, his hand finding the small of Jetta's back with natural ease. "And you're hopeless."

· · ·

"I PREFER to think of myself as charmingly reliant on the expertise of others," Owen counters with a grin.

BRANDI WATCHES their exchange with knowing eyes, her gaze lingering on the casual way Ethan's thumb traces small circles against Jetta's sweater. Jetta recognises that look—the gentle assessment of someone whose intuition runs bone-deep, who reads the unspoken currents between people as easily as others read street signs.

"YOU TWO SHOULD COME to dinner Saturday," Brandi says, her invitation seemingly spontaneous yet perfectly timed to bridge the conversation. "I'm trying that new pasta recipe, and Owen's been insufferable about wanting to show off his wine pairing skills."

"INSUFFERABLE BUT ACCURATE," Owen interjects. "My palate is exquisite."

"YOUR PALATE THOUGHT Sour Patch Kids paired well with chardonnay last month," Ethan reminds him.

"AN EXPERIMENTAL PHASE," Owen dismisses with a wave. "Every artist has one."

THEIR LAUGHTER MINGLES with the ambient sounds of the bookshop—pages turning, quiet conversations between browsers, the gentle hiss of the espresso machine. Jetta feels herself fully present in this moment, anchored by friendship that weathered the worst storm and emerged stronger for it.

THE BELL above the door chimes, and they all turn to see Mrs. Harrington enter, her silver hair impeccably styled as always, her expression bearing the particular determination of a reader on a mission. A regular since the shop opened, she makes straight for their gathering with purposeful strides.

"GOOD MORNING, MRS. HARRINGTON," Jetta greets her. "How are you today?"

"FRUSTRATED," the older woman announces without preamble. "My granddaughter's birthday is next week. She's turning eleven and has suddenly developed very specific literary tastes that have stymied my usual gift-giving prowess. She wants books with—and I quote—'strong female characters who aren't princesses or chosen ones, preferably involving science or history, no dead parents as plot devices, and absolutely no talking animals wearing clothes.'"

OWEN CHOKES slightly on his cookie. "Sounds like a discerning young reader."

"SHE'S IMPOSSIBLE," Mrs. Harrington says with the fond exasperation unique to grandparents. "But I refuse to give her a gift card. It lacks personal touch."

. . .

THE FOUR EXCHANGE QUICK GLANCES, a silent coordination born of months working side by side. Brandi steps forward first, her nurturing instincts perfectly suited to understanding a child's needs. "Has she mentioned any subjects in school she particularly enjoys?"

"ASTRONOMY AND ANCIENT EGYPT," Mrs. Harrington replies promptly. "She has stars on her ceiling and a mummy costume from Halloween she still wears around the house."

OWEN TAPS HIS CHIN THOUGHTFULLY. "I know just the historical fiction series with an eleven-year-old girl who becomes an apprentice to a female astronomer in 1800s London. No talking animals whatsoever."

"SECOND SHELF IN HISTORICAL FICTION," Ethan confirms, already moving in that direction. "I'll grab it."

"AND FOR THE EGYPT INTEREST," Jetta adds, "we just got in that new middle-grade mystery set in the Cairo Museum. The protagonist is a curator's daughter who solves archaeological puzzles."

"PERFECT," Brandi says, heading toward the children's section. "I'll find our copy."

MRS. HARRINGTON WATCHES with visible delight as the four of them move with coordinated purpose, each retrieving suggestions, building a curated stack tailored to her granddaughter's exacting specifications. Jetta feels a quiet pride bloom in her chest as she observes their seamless teamwork—Ethan's methodical efficiency, Brandi's intuitive understanding of what might capture a young girl's imagination, Owen's enthusiastic descriptions of each plot without revealing too much.

THIS, perhaps, is the most profound change of all—how their individual strengths have woven together into something greater than the sum of its parts. Not just colleagues or friends but a unit forged in shared purpose, in survived trauma, in the daily work of rebuilding what was broken. Watching them move around each other with practised coordination, Jetta realises they've created something rare and precious: a chosen family bound by more than blood or circumstance, connected by threads strong enough to withstand even the fiercest storms.

THE AFTERNOON light shifts to the golden hue of approaching evening, shadows lengthening across the shop floor like gentle reminders of time passing. Jetta flips the door sign to "Closed," the familiar wooden placard worn smooth at the edges from years of daily turning. The last customer—a college student who spent three hours in the poetry corner with a notepad and cooling tea—gathers her belongings with reluctant movements, as if leaving a warm hearth on a winter night. Jetta offers her a smile tinged with understanding; the shop has become that kind of place—a sanctuary not easily abandoned for the harsher rhythms of the outside world.

"TAKE THIS," she says, pressing a bookmark into the young

woman's hand. "It's from our new collection. Handmade by a local artist."

THE STUDENT'S fingers close around the laminated paper with its pressed flower design, her eyes brightening with unexpected pleasure. "Thank you. I'll be back tomorrow, if that's okay."

"WE'LL SAVE YOUR CORNER," Jetta promises, holding the door as the woman steps into the fading daylight.

WITH THE SHOP empty of customers, a different kind of energy settles over the space—the intimate familiarity of a place returning to itself after hours of public performance. Jetta moves through the aisles with practised steps, straightening books nudged out of alignment, gathering abandoned bookmarks, rescuing tea mugs from precarious perches atop stacked novels. Her hands know this work so well they could perform it blindfolded, yet she takes her time, allowing her fingertips to linger on leather bindings and paper edges.

SIX MONTHS AGO, closing time brought a spike of anxiety— the dread of leaving a secure space for the unpredictable outside world, the hypervigilant scanning of shadows and corners. Now, the ritual carries a meditative quality; each book returned to its proper place a small act of order in a universe that once seemed chaotically threatening.

THE SHOP itself has transformed alongside its owners. What began as Jetta and Brandi's modest dream has expanded both physically and spiritually—the wall opened to the adjacent space, the café corner humming with its own gentle life, the reading nooks that invite lingering rather than mere transaction. Even the lighting has evolved; the harsh fluorescents replaced with warm fixtures that cast a honeyed glow over the wooden shelves.

BUT THE MOST profound transformation lies in what the space represents. No longer merely a business, Bound Together has become a physical manifestation of their collective healing—a testament to resilience, to the possibility of rebuilding after destruction. Every shelf Ethan reinforced with his careful hands, every corner Brandi brightened with cushions and plants, every rare edition Owen tracked down through his extensive network—each element represents a piece of themselves invested in this shared future.

NEAR THE BACK DOOR, Ethan moves with methodical precision through his closing routine. His fingers test each window latch twice, eyes scanning the frames for imperfections that might compromise security. He checks the vintage deadbolt with particular attention, the brass mechanism gleaming under his careful maintenance. There's something almost tender in the way he secures each potential entry point —not the clinical efficiency of a security professional but the devoted care of someone protecting what he loves.

"ALL CLEAR BY THE STOREROOM," he calls, his voice carrying the particular timbre of satisfaction that comes from completed protective rituals.

. . .

JETTA WATCHES him from between the shelves, noting the subtle differences between now and before. His movements still carry that hyperaware precision, but the tension that once rode his shoulders like an invisible weight has dissipated. He secures their space not from fear but from love—a crucial distinction that transformed his vigilance from burden to gift.

NEAR THE FRONT COUNTER, Brandi and Owen huddle together over the events calendar, their heads bent close enough that her blonde hair occasionally brushes his cheek. Their voices rise and fall in the particular rhythm of long partnership—sentences left half-finished because the other already knows the conclusion, small sounds of agreement that replace the need for words, the occasional synchronised reach for the same pen.

"IF WE MOVE the children's author to eleven instead of ten," Brandi suggests, tapping the schedule with a polished fingernail, "we could offer that breakfast pastry thing from the café. Might draw a bigger crowd."

OWEN NODS, already jotting notes in the margin. "And we should display those new illustrated editions next to the signing table. The watercolour dragons would complement her reading perfectly."

"I WAS JUST THINKING THAT," Brandi says, her smile carrying a note of pleased surprise despite the frequency with which their thoughts align.

. . .

JETTA APPROACHES, drawn to their comfortable synchronicity. "Need any help with tomorrow's setup?"

"I THINK WE'RE COVERED," Brandi answers, glancing up from the calendar. "Though we might need to rearrange the centre displays to create more seating. The response to the event announcement was bigger than expected."

"I CAN COME IN EARLY," Ethan offers, joining their circle by the counter. His hand finds Jetta's lower back with that now-familiar touch—gentle pressure that communicates presence without possession.

"WE'LL ALL COME IN EARLY," Owen decides, closing the planner with definitive movement. "Division of labour, maximum efficiency."

"NOW YOU SOUND LIKE ETHAN," Brandi teases, pressing a quick kiss to Owen's cheek before gathering her belongings from beneath the counter.

THEY MOVE TOGETHER toward the front door, falling into the familiar pattern of their closing ritual. Owen checks the café equipment one last time, ensuring everything is unplugged and clean. Brandi adjusts tomorrow's feature display, making one final tweak to the arrangement of covers. Ethan programs the security system with practised efficiency, his fingers moving across the keypad in a blur of muscle memory.

. . .

JETTA PAUSES in the centre of the shop, allowing herself a moment of quiet appreciation. The warm wooden shelves stretch around her like embracing arms, each book a brick in this fortress they've built together. The reading nooks with their overstuffed chairs invite comfort and lingering. The framed photograph of the four of them—taken at the shop's grand reopening three months ago—sits on the counter beside the register, their smiles genuine in a way that once seemed impossible to recapture.

HER GAZE TRAVELS over these details, collecting them like precious stones to be examined later in private moments. The sense of safety and belonging that permeates this space feels miraculous after months when nowhere felt secure, when danger seemed to lurk in every shadow. They've created not just a successful business but a testament to the possibility of healing, of moving forward without forgetting, of building something beautiful from the broken pieces of what came before.

"READY?" Ethan asks, standing by the door with keys in hand, the others waiting beside him.

JETTA NODS, taking one final glance around the shop before joining them. As Ethan locks the door from outside, testing the handle with that extra tug of security, Jetta feels the now-familiar sense of certainty settle in her chest. The shop will be here tomorrow, waiting for their return. This life they've built together will continue, each day adding another layer of distance between themselves and the trauma that once defined them.

. . .

THEY STEP into the evening air together, the spring breeze carrying the scent of blooming trees from the park across the street. Ethan's hand finds hers naturally, their fingers interlacing with practised ease. On her other side, Brandi links arms with Owen, the four of them forming a small procession down the sidewalk. The movement feels ceremonial somehow —a daily ritual affirming that they've chosen to move forward together, that the bonds forged in crisis have transformed into connections strong enough to sustain them through ordinary days.

"DINNER at that new place on Fourth?" Owen suggests, his voice carrying in the quiet evening air.

"PERFECT," Jetta agrees, squeezing Ethan's hand as they walk toward the setting sun, four shadows stretching behind them, connected and unbroken in the golden light.

CHAPTER 19

Full Circle

THE HIGH SCHOOL looms against the cloudless spring sky, brick and mortar transformed into something monumental by the weight of memory. Jetta sits motionless in the passenger seat after Ethan cuts the engine, her eyes tracing the familiar contours of the building she once fled in tears, never expecting to return. Time has weathered the facade, ivy creeping higher up the walls than she remembers, but the essential structure remains unchanged—just like the memories preserved within its walls.

"WE DON'T HAVE to do this," Ethan says, his voice gentle in the car's cocoon-like silence. His hand hovers near hers on the centre console, offering connection without demanding it.

JETTA PULLS her gaze from the building to meet his eyes. "Yes, we do." She reaches for the door handle, surprised to find her fingers steady despite the thundering pulse at her throat. "Some ghosts don't rest until they're acknowledged."

. . .

THE PARKING LOT stretches empty before them, Saturday afternoon sunshine baking the asphalt where teenage dramas once unfolded in chaotic clusters. Her boots make soft tapping sounds against the pavement, each step carrying her closer to a past she's spent years trying to outrun. Beside her, Ethan matches her pace precisely—close enough to reach if needed, not so close as to crowd.

AS THEY APPROACH the main entrance, Jetta's breathing shifts, growing shallow against her will. Her fingers find Ethan's hand, gripping with an intensity that betrays the calm expression she's carefully constructed. His thumb brushes across her knuckles in silent acknowledgment.

"THE VICE PRINCIPAL said she'd leave the front door unlocked," Ethan murmurs, reaching for the handle.

THE HEAVY DOOR yields with a familiar creak that slices through time, transporting Jetta instantly to her last day here —racing down these same steps with tears blurring her vision, laughter echoing behind her, the weight of public humiliation crushing her chest until breathing seemed impossible. She'd sworn never to set foot in this building again, a promise kept for ten long years until Alice's reappearance forced them to confront the roots of their tangled history.

ETHAN STEPS slightly ahead as they cross the threshold, his body angling subtly between Jetta and whatever might await inside—a protective stance evolved from his security training but softened by months of therapy, no longer smothering but simply present. She notices the shift in his shoulders, the alertness that never fully leaves him, but appreciates how he's learned to modulate his vigilance to support rather than control.

THE SMELL HITS HER FIRST—INDUSTRIAL floor polish layered over decades of adolescent passage, chalk dust suspended in still air, the faint metallic tang of aging lockers. Her diaphragm constricts, lungs seizing momentarily as her body remembers before her mind can intervene. Ethan's hand tightens around hers, anchoring her to the present as her free palm presses against her sternum.

"BREATHE WITH ME," he whispers, demonstrating the pattern they've practised—four counts in, seven held, eight released slowly through pursed lips. She follows his lead, grateful for the concrete technique that pulls her back from the edge of spiralling memories.

FLUORESCENT LIGHTS FLICKER OVERHEAD, the familiar electric hum providing uncomfortable soundtrack to their slow advance down the main corridor. Some bulbs buzz and stutter, casting shifting shadows across worn linoleum floors buffed to a dull shine. Their footsteps echo in the emptiness, unnaturally loud without the crush of teenage bodies and voices to absorb the sound.

"THEY STILL HAVEN'T FIXED that light," Jetta observes, pointing to a panel near the office that blinks in erratic rhythm. The mundane observation grounds her, offering safe entry into engagement with this space.

· · ·

THEY PASS THE MAIN OFFICE, glass walls revealing desks arranged in the same configuration Jetta remembers, though the ancient desktop computers have been replaced with sleek monitors. A poster about bullying prevention hangs prominently near the entrance—terminology and graphics updated for a new generation but addressing problems as old as education itself.

THE TROPHY CASES lining the next hallway capture their attention, drawing them closer with the gravitational pull of shared history. New names gleam on polished plaques, championships and records set by students who weren't even born when Jetta last walked these halls. Yet the cases themselves remain unchanged, the same dusty corners unreachable by cleaning staff, the same slight warp in the leftmost glass panel.

"YOUR NAME'S STILL HERE," Ethan notes, pointing to a small plaque listing debate team captains. "They never removed it."

JETTA LEANS CLOSER, finding her seventeen-year-old self preserved in engraved lettering. The sight sends an unexpected warmth through her chest—a piece of her remains here that isn't defined by humiliation or flight, something she earned through intellect and determination before Alice's machinations tore her from this world.

THEY CONTINUE their journey deeper into the building, passing classrooms with doors propped open for weekend cleaning. Through the windows, Jetta glimpses interactive whiteboards where chalkboards once hung, sleek tablets replacing the clunky textbooks of her era. A science lab glows with equipment she doesn't recognise, though the black-topped lab tables remain exactly as she remembers.

"SO MUCH HAS CHANGED," she murmurs, pausing to peer into the library where rows of computers have replaced card catalogues.

"AND SO MUCH HASN'T," Ethan responds, nodding toward a display of student artwork that could have been created in any decade, timeless in its teenage expression of identity and emotion.

AS THEY ROUND the corner toward the east wing, Jetta realizes her breathing has deepened, her grip on Ethan's hand relaxed from desperate clutching to comfortable connection. The initial shock of reentry has faded, allowing her to observe with greater clarity. She notes this shift with quiet wonder—how the body can recalibrate, even in spaces once associated with pain.

ETHAN NOTICES TOO, his eyes meeting hers with silent understanding. The distance between their bodies has decreased gradually since entering the building, shoulders now brushing occasionally as they walk side by side rather than in his earlier protective formation. This physical evolution mirrors their emotional journey of the past months—moving from hypervigilant positioning to natural proximity, from fear-based calculation to trust-based presence.

. . .

The hallway stretches before them, leading toward the gymnasium where their story truly began. Jetta feels her heart rate increase slightly at the prospect, but the panic that would have overwhelmed her months ago remains at manageable levels. She's no longer the wounded girl who fled this building, nor is Ethan the thoughtless boy who participated in her humiliation. They are walking this path as the people they've become—scarred but healing, connected by choice rather than circumstance.

"Ready?" Ethan asks as they pause at the intersection that will take them toward the gym.

Jetta looks up at him, finding strength in the steady presence that has become her cornerstone. "As ready as I'll ever be."

Their footsteps resume in synchronised rhythm, moving forward into the heart of their shared past.

The gymnasium doors stand before them like sentinels guarding the epicentre of their shared trauma. Jetta's steps slow as they approach, her breath catching at the faded blue paint, chipped at the edges but still bearing the school mascot —a snarling wildcat that seems to mock her hesitation. Through the small wire-reinforced windows, she glimpses the polished wooden floor where her life unravelled in twenty devastating minutes a decade ago. Her palm grows damp against Ethan's, but she doesn't pull away.

. . .

"LET ME," he says softly, pushing the door open with his free hand.

THE GYMNASIUM YAWNS BEFORE THEM, cavernous yet somehow smaller than the colosseum of her memory. Afternoon light filters through high windows, dust motes dancing in the beams that stripe the wooden floor. The bleachers sit folded against the walls like sleeping accordions, the basketball hoops retracted toward the ceiling, the space stripped to its essence without the chaos of bodies and voices that once filled it.

"IT LOOKS SO ORDINARY," Jetta whispers, the observation catching in her throat. In her nightmares, this room had grown to mythic proportions, the scene of her undoing preserved in perfect, terrible detail. The reality before her—just wood and metal and empty space—feels almost anticlimactic.

THEY MOVE TOGETHER across the floor, their footsteps creating hollow echoes that bounce between walls. A faint squeak of Ethan's shoe against polished wood makes her flinch, the sound too reminiscent of sneakers on court, of the basketball team's approach that day, of laughter that cut deeper than knives.

THE LOCKER ROOM entrance appears on their left, its metal door propped slightly open. Jetta stops abruptly, her body going rigid beside Ethan's. Her hand hovers over the handle without touching it, suspended in the space between present courage and past terror.

. . .

"THIS IS WHERE IT HAPPENED," she says quietly, her voice steadier than she expected. "Behind this door."

ETHAN STANDS BESIDE HER, close but not touching, his presence solid yet unimposing. The careful distance he maintains speaks volumes—respecting her space while offering silent support, a balance they've worked months to perfect.

"I'VE WANTED to tell you something," he says after a long silence, his voice low and rough with emotion. "About that day." He shifts his weight, eyes fixed on the door rather than her face. "The team—they pressured me to take your clothes. Said it was an initiation, that I needed to prove myself." His jaw works beneath his skin. "But that's not the whole truth."

JETTA TURNS TO HIM, surprised by the direction of his confession.

"THE TRUTH IS, I wanted your attention," he continues, the words emerging with obvious difficulty. "I had for months. But I was too much of a coward to just talk to you, too afraid of rejection to approach you directly." He meets her eyes at last. "I participated not because I wanted to hurt you, but because I thought it would be a harmless prank that might make you notice me. I was stupid and selfish and so, so wrong."

. . .

403

THE ADMISSION HANGS BETWEEN THEM, unexpected in its vulnerability. Jetta feels something shift beneath her ribs, a piece of old pain dislodging to make room for this new understanding.

"I HAD A CRUSH ON YOU TOO," she reveals, her voice barely audible even in the empty gymnasium. "Since chemistry class the previous semester. That's why the humiliation cut so deep—because it came from someone I'd built up in my imagination." A bitter laugh escapes her. "I'd actually written your name in my notebook like some cliché lovesick teenager."

ETHAN'S EXPRESSION CRUMPLES, the full impact of what might have been—what was stolen from them both—registering in the pained lines around his eyes.

"ALICE KNEW," Jetta continues, the pieces clicking into place even as she speaks. "She must have seen my notebook, realised I was competition. That's why she chose that specific humiliation—to ensure I'd never be able to look at you again without feeling that shame."

THEY STAND TOGETHER in weighted silence, the locker room door between them and the past it contains. Jetta doesn't reach for the handle; some thresholds don't need to be physically crossed to be confronted.

"LET'S KEEP GOING," she says finally, taking a deliberate step away from the door.

. . .

THEY MOVE through the gymnasium and back into the main hallway, continuing their pilgrimage of painful places. The familiar route leads them to the senior hallway where Ethan's locker once stood in a row of identical metal boxes.

"NUMBER 219," he says, stopping before a locker that now bears a different combination lock. "This was mine."

JETTA STUDIES THE METAL DOOR, her fingertips reaching out to trace what's barely visible beneath years of repainted surface—the faint outline of letters scratched deep into the metal. J-E-R-K. Her handiwork, preserved like a fossil beneath layers of institutional paint.

"I SPENT THREE AFTERNOONS ON THIS," she admits, a reluctant smile tugging at her lips. "Borrowed my dad's pocket knife. Nearly got caught twice. Worth it, though."

ETHAN'S LAUGH holds genuine amusement. "I deserved worse." His fingers join hers, tracing the ghostly letters. "I never requested a different locker. Felt like appropriate punishment."

THEY CONTINUE THEIR JOURNEY, stopping next at the chemistry lab where they were once partners before the incident. Through the door window, twin lab stations sit in precise rows, the black surfaces gleaming beneath overhead lights. Jetta remembers Ethan's careful measurements, his surprisingly meticulous notes, the way their hands occasionally brushed when reaching for the same beaker.

. . .

"You were a good lab partner," she says, the admission coming easier now. "I used to deliberately miscalculate just so you'd have to lean closer to check my work."

Ethan's eyebrows lift in surprise. "And I used to deliberately volunteer to get supplies just so I could walk past your table."

The revelation brings matching smiles, these glimpses of innocent attraction emerging from beneath the darker history that buried them.

The cafeteria doors stand open, weekend cleaning evident in the smell of disinfectant that overtakes the usual scent of institutional food. Jetta pauses at the entrance, her eyes finding the exact table where she once sat surrounded by friends who scattered like startled birds after the incident, unwilling to be associated with the target of such concentrated cruelty.

"I couldn't eat in public for months after transferring schools," she says, the memory still sharp enough to cut. "Took my lunch to the library every day."

Ethan's hand finds the small of her back, a gentle pressure that offers support without restraint. "I stopped sitting with the team. Couldn't stomach their jokes, their complete lack of remorse."

. . .

"Really?" Jetta turns to him, genuinely surprised. "I always imagined you all laughing about it for weeks."

"No." The single word contains volumes of regret. "I ate alone for the rest of the year. It seemed like appropriate penance, though nowhere near enough."

As they move from space to space, Jetta notices a gradual change in their physical bearing. Her shoulders have dropped from their defensive hunch, her breathing deepened to normal rhythm. Beside her, Ethan's movements have lost their cautious edge, his stride matching hers in relaxed synchronicity. The distance between their bodies has decreased with each revelation, each shared memory building a bridge across the chasm that once separated them.

"It's strange," she says as they pause in a quiet corner of the library. "I remembered everything as so much worse. Not that it wasn't terrible," she clarifies quickly, "but in my mind, this place became entirely evil. Nothing good could have possibly happened here."

"And now?" Ethan asks.

"Now I remember other things too. Winning the debate tournament. That ridiculous school play where you forgot all your lines. The time Mr. Bennet caught us passing notes and read them aloud, not realising they were chemistry formulas."

ETHAN LAUGHS, the sound warming the space between them. "Balance, I guess. Not erasing the bad, but making room for the good too."

HIS FINGERS BRUSH AGAINST HERS, a question rather than a demand. Jetta answers by taking his hand, their palms fitting together with practised ease. As they continue walking, their bodies draw closer, shoulders touching, steps synchronised—physical manifestations of the emotional distance they've crossed since entering this building.

THE PRINCIPAL'S office sits at the end of the administrative wing, its frosted glass door bearing a nameplate different from the one in Jetta's memory. She hesitates before it, her fingers fidgeting with the hem of her sweater. The last time she stood here, tear-stained and wrapped in borrowed gym clothes, she'd been told that "these things happen" and perhaps she should consider "not drawing so much attention" to herself. Today, she returns not as a victim seeking protection that never came, but as a woman confronting the institutional failures that compounded her pain.

"YOU OKAY?" Ethan asks, his voice low enough that only she can hear.

SHE NODS, squaring her shoulders. "Let's do this."

. . .

THE CURRENT PRINCIPAL had arranged everything via email—a brief, efficient exchange that culminated in this appointment with Mr. Harrington, retired now but still connected to the school. Jetta had been surprised by how readily the administration accommodated their unusual request, wondering if perhaps the institutional conscience had evolved in the decade since her departure.

ETHAN KNOCKS, three precise taps that sound unnaturally loud in the empty hallway. A muffled "Come in" responds from the other side.

THE OFFICE APPEARS SMALLER than Jetta remembers, its walls now painted a warmer beige instead of institutional white, decorated with student artwork and motivational quotes about inclusion and respect. Behind the desk sits Mr. Harrington, older and greyer but instantly recognisable. His silver hair has thinned, his face creased with additional lines, but the wire-rimmed glasses perched on his nose remain exactly as she recalls.

HIS EYES WIDEN when they enter, hand freezing in the act of rising from his chair. The shock of seeing them together registers in the subtle parting of his lips, the quick adjustment of his glasses, the momentary rigidity of his shoulders before he recovers his professional demeanour.

"MS. KINSLEY, MR. COLE," he says, voice raspier than in her memory. "Please, sit down."

. . .

Two visitors' chairs face the desk, their wooden frames worn smooth by generations of anxious students and concerned parents. Jetta takes the left one, Ethan the right, the familiar arrangement of authority and supplicants momentarily disorienting after years of adult autonomy.

"Thank you for agreeing to meet with us," Ethan begins, his tone formal but not cold.

Mr. Harrington adjusts his glasses again, a nervous tic Jetta now recognises. "I must admit, I was surprised by the request. It's not often former students seek me out, particularly not..." He trails off, clearly uncertain how to characterise their relationship.

"Particularly not two people with our history," Jetta completes for him, her voice steadier than the flutter in her stomach would suggest.

A heavy silence fills the room, thick with unspoken recriminations and decade-old regrets. Mr. Harrington breaks it with a halting attempt at pleasantry.

"I understand you own a bookshop now, Ms. Kinsley. And Mr. Cole, the current principal mentioned you've been working in security consulting after military service." His hands fold and unfold on the desk. "You've both built impressive lives."

. . .

"Despite what happened here," Jetta says quietly, the words emerging without the bite she might once have intended. "That's partly why we've come. To close a chapter that's remained unfinished for too long."

Mr. Harrington's shoulders slump slightly, his professional facade cracking to reveal the human beneath. "I suspected as much."

Jetta feels Ethan's attention on her, his silent support giving her the courage to continue. She meets Mr. Harrington's gaze directly, her voice calm despite the acceleration of her pulse.

"After the incident in the gymnasium, I transferred schools," she begins, laying out the facts like items on an inventory sheet. "I spent two years in therapy. I developed panic attacks in social situations, stopped participating in debate competitions despite previous success. I graduated with honours but skipped the ceremony because I couldn't bear being in a gymnasium filled with peers."

Each sentence lands in the quiet room with precise impact. Mr. Harrington's hands tremble slightly against the desktop.

"College was better, but the trust issues followed me. Every friendship was suspect, every romantic interest a potential trap." She pauses, gathering herself. "Even now, a decade later, I sometimes wake from nightmares where I'm standing in that gym, exposed and humiliated while everyone watches."

ETHAN REMAINS SILENT BESIDE HER, his presence solid but unobtrusive, allowing her voice to fill the space it deserves.

"THE SYSTEM WAS DIFFERENT THEN," Mr. Harrington says finally, his voice rough with emotion. "But that's no excuse. I should have done more." His hands press flat against the desk as if seeking stability. "We failed you, Ms. Kinsley. I failed you personally."

THE ADMISSION HANGS in the air between them, unexpected in its directness. Jetta feels something loosen in her chest—a knot of resentment beginning to unravel after being held tight for so long.

"YES," she agrees simply. "You did."

MR. HARRINGTON NODS, accepting the truth without deflection. "We knew about the social hierarchy, the way certain students were targeted. We saw the patterns. But we approached it as normal teenage behaviour, character-building experiences rather than what it truly was—abuse that adults had a responsibility to stop." He removes his glasses, pinching the bridge of his nose. "I've carried that regret throughout my career."

. . .

ETHAN LEANS FORWARD, his elbows resting on his knees. "I've carried my own regrets as well," he says, his voice steady with the confidence of a man who has done the difficult work of accountability. "It took years for me to understand what real strength looks like, what protection actually means."

"MILITARY SERVICE TAUGHT me that leadership isn't about power over others, but responsibility for their welfare." His gaze shifts briefly to Jetta before returning to Mr. Harrington. "I participated in something cruel because I was too weak to stand against peer pressure, too cowardly to express genuine interest respectfully. I've spent years working to become someone worthy of trust rather than fear."

MR. HARRINGTON LISTENS INTENTLY, his hands clasped tightly before him. When Ethan finishes, the older man's eyes glisten behind his replaced glasses.

"I WANT to offer you both an apology," he says, the words emerging with obvious effort. "Not as an administrator fulfilling a policy requirement, but as a human being who recognises the harm caused by my failures. I am truly, deeply sorry for not protecting you, Ms. Kinsley, and for not providing better guidance to students like Mr. Cole." His hands tighten visibly, knuckles whitening. "If I could go back and change my response, I would do so without hesitation."

THE SINCERITY in his voice is unmistakable, his regret palpable in the slight tremor of his chin, the deepened lines around his mouth. Jetta feels the impact of his words physically, like a key turning in a lock she hadn't realised was still secured.

"THANK YOU," she says simply, finding that the elaborate speech she'd mentally prepared has become unnecessary in the face of genuine remorse.

MR. HARRINGTON REACHES for a drawer in his desk, withdrawing a small manila envelope. "I thought you might want these," he says, sliding it across the polished surface. "When the current principal mentioned your visit, I requested them from the archives."

JETTA OPENS the envelope with curious fingers, Ethan leaning closer to see its contents. Inside lie two plastic cards, their edges slightly worn, the photos on their surfaces capturing versions of themselves long outgrown—her with awkwardly straightened hair and hesitant smile, him with a cocky grin and a haircut he'd clearly styled with excessive gel. Their student ID cards, preserved in the school's records like artifacts from another lifetime.

THE UNEXPECTED GESTURE—THIS tangible connection to who they were before their lives collided and separated— brings sudden tears to Jetta's eyes. Not the painful kind that burned her cheeks as she fled this building a decade ago, but a different sort entirely—the releasing kind that accompanies recognition, acknowledgment, the first tentative steps toward resolution.

. . .

ETHAN'S ARM slides around her waist, supportive rather than possessive, his touch communicating understanding without words. She leans slightly into his side, allowing herself to accept the comfort he offers.

"I CAN'T CHANGE WHAT HAPPENED," Mr. Harrington says softly. "None of us can. But I want you both to know that your experience changed how I approached my remaining years as an educator. The anti-bullying programs implemented after your departure, the new reporting systems, the staff training—all of it stemmed from my determination that no student should ever feel as abandoned by this institution as you were."

JETTA WIPES at her cheek with the back of her hand, the tears continuing despite her attempt to contain them. These, too, feel like release—water breaking through a dam long maintained by necessity but no longer required.

"SOMETIMES," she says, her voice wavering slightly, "the most meaningful apology isn't words, but action that ensures others don't suffer the same harm."

MR. HARRINGTON NODS, understanding passing between them. "Precisely."

THEY RISE TO LEAVE, the meeting having accomplished more than formal words could fully capture. As Ethan holds the door, Jetta turns back one last time.

· · ·

"THANK YOU," she says, clutching the envelope containing their former selves. "For remembering. For changing. For seeing us—then and now."

MR. HARRINGTON'S smile holds sadness but also genuine warmth. "The privilege has been entirely mine."

THE ADMINISTRATIVE WING empties into the main corridor, their footsteps echoing differently now—lighter somehow, as if the weight of unspoken words has been lifted from their shoulders. Jetta's eyes still feel warm from tears shed in Mr. Harrington's office, but the tightness in her chest has eased, replaced by a hollow sensation that isn't entirely unpleasant. Empty spaces can be filled anew, she thinks, glancing at the student IDs now tucked safely in her pocket, physical reminders of younger selves finally acknowledged and, perhaps, forgiven.

THEY NAVIGATE the hallways toward the front entrance, retracing their earlier path through the silent building. The institutional green walls, the scuffed floor tiles, the metal lockers lined like soldiers—all seem less oppressive now, stripped of the power they once held over her memories. Light slants through windows at a lower angle, afternoon shifting toward evening, casting long golden rectangles across their path.

JETTA NOTICES the change in her own body with quiet wonder—her shoulders have dropped from their defensive hunch, her breathing comes deep and even, her steps fall with confident purpose rather than hesitant dread. The hypervigilance that accompanied their arrival has softened to simple awareness; her senses no longer scanning for threats but simply experiencing the space around her.

BESIDE HER, Ethan matches her pace perfectly, their strides synchronised without conscious effort. His hand rests at the small of her back, the touch neither guiding nor controlling but simply present—a warm anchor connecting them as they complete this pilgrimage through their shared past. His body curves slightly toward hers, protective without hovering, a posture they've refined through months of mutual growth.

THE FRONT DOORS appear before them, daylight visible through the wire-reinforced glass panels. Ethan reaches for the handle but pauses, turning to her with a question in his eyes.

"READY TO LEAVE?"

JETTA NODS, but then stops, her gaze drawn back down the empty corridor one last time. "Wait," she says softly. "Just a moment."

TOGETHER THEY STAND at the threshold, looking back at the building that shaped them in ways both painful and profound. From this vantage point, the school appears almost benign—just brick and tile and metal, a container for thousands of individual stories, hers and Ethan's just two among countless others played out within these walls.

. . .

"STRANGE," she murmurs, the word escaping on an exhaled breath.

ETHAN'S EYEBROWS lift in silent question.

"I NEVER THOUGHT I'd feel anything but dread looking at this place," she admits, her voice steady despite the vulnerability of the confession. "For years, I couldn't even drive past without my stomach turning. But now..." She searches for words adequate to the complex emotions swirling beneath her breastbone. "It's just a building. Important because of what happened here, but not inherently threatening."

ETHAN NODS IN UNDERSTANDING, his eyes reflecting similar recognition. "Some ghosts are meant to be faced," he says, his voice low but clear in the empty entryway. "Not because they lose their power completely, but because we gain perspective on them."

HIS SIMPLE ARTICULATION of what she's feeling sends warmth spreading through her chest. This is the gift of their hard-won connection—being truly seen, truly understood by someone who has witnessed both her wounds and her healing.

THEY SHARE a moment of quiet acknowledgment, standing together in the space between past and future, neither rushing toward nor fleeing from what lies on either side. The silence between them feels companionable rather than heavy, a shared breath in the ongoing conversation of their lives.

· · ·

"TIME TO GO?" Ethan asks after a minute passes, his tone suggesting neither impatience nor pressure.

"YES," Jetta says with certainty, turning toward the doors. "We've done what we came to do."

THEY STEP into the afternoon sunlight together, the contrast between the institutional dimness and natural light momentarily dazzling. Jetta blinks against the brightness, her eyes adjusting to the shift. The warmth against her skin feels symbolic somehow, a physical manifestation of the emotional illumination this journey has provided.

STANDING ON THE FRONT STEPS, she takes a deep breath of spring air untainted by floor polish and chalk dust. Ethan's hand finds hers, their fingers interlacing with practised ease as they descend toward the parking lot. Their steps remain perfectly aligned, bodies moving in the unconscious harmony of people attuned to each other's rhythms.

"I WAS THINKING ABOUT DINNER," Jetta says as they approach the car, the mundane topic a deliberate pivot toward ordinary life. "We still have that pasta sauce I made yesterday."

ETHAN NODS, fishing keys from his pocket. "And those garlic knots from the bakery." He unlocks her door first, the small courtesy now a familiar habit rather than a calculated gesture. "Though we could always call Brandi and Owen, see if they want to join us at that new place on Maple Street."

· · ·

THE CASUAL DISCUSSION of evening plans feels like its own kind of victory—proof that they can walk through the epicentre of their shared trauma and emerge still capable of thinking about garlic knots and dinner reservations. Life continuing, ordinary and precious in its mundanity.

"LET'S DO THAT," Jetta decides, sliding into the passenger seat. "I'm in the mood to celebrate."

ETHAN SETTLES BEHIND THE WHEEL, glancing at her with a raised eyebrow. "Celebrate what specifically?"

SHE CONSIDERS THE QUESTION, her fingers touching the pocket where their student IDs rest. "Moving forward," she says finally. "Not being defined by what happened here. Choosing our own story instead of the one others tried to write for us."

HIS SMILE REACHES HIS EYES, creating the crinkles at the corners that she's come to cherish. "I like that," he says, starting the engine. "Though I'm pretty sure Owen will insist on ordering that weird octopus appetiser again."

"AND BRANDI WILL PRETEND to be adventurous and then fill up on bread," Jetta adds with a laugh, the sound emerging naturally from her chest without the strained quality it might have held hours earlier.

. . .

As they pull away from the curb, Jetta finds herself not looking back at the building receding behind them. Instead, her attention focuses forward—on the road ahead, on Ethan's profile against the passenger window, on the evening waiting to unfold with friends who helped carry them through their darkest moments.

The high school diminishes in the rearview mirror, growing smaller with each turn of the wheels. It remains a part of their history, a chapter in their shared story, but no longer the defining feature of their landscape. They drive toward the setting sun, their shadows stretching behind them, joined and unbroken in the golden light.

"Call Brandi," Ethan suggests, passing his phone to Jetta. "Tell her we have something to share."

Jetta takes the phone, her finger hovering over Brandi's contact information. "Not everything," she clarifies. "Some parts of today are just for us."

Ethan nods in understanding, his hand briefly leaving the wheel to squeeze hers. "Just for us," he agrees.

They continue down the road, the school now completely out of sight, existing only in memory—no longer a monument to pain but simply a place they once were, a foundation for who they have become together. Jetta makes the call, her voice light with the freedom of someone who has set down a burden carried too long. The future stretches before them, unwritten and bright with possibility.

Epilogue – Love and Literature

AMBER LIGHT POOLS across the polished wooden floors of Bound Together, transforming the familiar space into something magical and new. Jetta stands at the edge of the signing table, her fingers tracing the embossed lettering on the cover of her debut novel – "The Art of Surrender." The stack of books, her name emblazoned across each spine, still doesn't feel quite real beneath her touch. A year of early mornings and late nights, of memories transmuted into fiction, of pain rewritten into something beautiful – all of it culminating in this evening, this gathering, this tangible proof of how far she's come.

THE SHOP she knows by heart now wears its finest attire – cream linen tablecloths drape over display tables, strategically placed stands hold promotional posters featuring the book's cover art, and fairy lights strung between bookshelves cast a warm glow over everything. The café corner has been transformed into a refreshment station, champagne flutes catching light beside artful platters of hors d'oeuvres. Even the air feels different, charged with anticipation and the mingled scents of wine, flowers, and the particular comforting smell of books that has become synonymous with home.

Jetta smooths her emerald dress, the silk cool beneath her nervous fingers. She tucks a strand of hair behind her ear for perhaps the twentieth time, then stops herself, trying to channel the confident protagonist she created rather than the anxious author she feels like. Her reflection catches in the bookshop window – a woman transformed from the frightened person who once checked locks three times, who startled at sudden noises, who feared shadows. The woman looking back at her stands taller, her eyes clearer, though tonight they hold the particular brightness of contained emotion.

Across the room, Ethan navigates between gathering clusters of guests with practised ease. His dark suit fits his shoulders perfectly, the burgundy tie a deliberate match to the accent colour on her book cover – a detail he'd insisted on with surprising sentimentality. Despite his casual conversation with a local bookstore owner, his eyes find her every thirty seconds or so, a pattern she's come to recognise and rely upon. It's no longer the hypervigilant scanning of months past but something warmer – check-ins that say simply, I see you, I'm here, we're connected even across a crowded room.

When their gazes meet, his smile shifts subtly – a private expression meant only for her. She returns it, drawing strength from the silent exchange.

. . .

NEAR THE ENTRANCE, Brandi orchestrates final arrangements with the efficiency of someone born to manage events. Her blonde hair falls in styled waves around her shoulders, her hand gestures animated as she directs a server with a tray of champagne. The diamond engagement ring catches light as she moves, still new enough that Jetta notices how Brandi's other hand occasionally touches it, as if confirming its reality. Three months since Owen's proposal, and her best friend still glows with happiness that radiates outward, warming everyone in her orbit.

"NO, THE SIGNING PENS GO HERE," Brandi instructs, adjusting the placement of a cup filled with elegant black pens bearing the bookshop's gold logo. "And keep the water bottle discreetly beneath the table where Jetta can reach it."

HER ATTENTION TO DETAIL – born of friendship rather than obligation – brings a lump to Jetta's throat. This celebration is as much Brandi's creation as the book is Jetta's, months of planning channelled into creating the perfect stage for this moment of triumph.

OWEN HOLDS court near the café counter, his natural charm amplified by the pride evident in his animated gestures. He's surrounded by three people with press badges, leaning in to catch his enthusiastic description of the book's journey from concept to publication.

"—AND when she got the acceptance from the publisher, we opened that bottle of Dom Pérignon I'd been saving," he tells them, his storytelling talents on full display. "The cork hit the ceiling fan and sprayed everyone. Brandi was picking glitter out of her hair for days afterward, but it was worth it."

THE JOURNALISTS LAUGH, enchanted, and Jetta realises with a start that he's been doing this all evening – building anticipation, creating narrative around her book, wielding his professional networking skills on her behalf with such natural ease that no one would suspect the deliberate strategy behind it.

THE SHOP DOOR OPENS AGAIN, admitting another wave of attendees – local readers, fellow writers, book club members who've supported Bound Together since its beginning. The space fills with conversations that rise and fall like music, the occasional burst of laughter punctuating the general hum of excitement. Jetta's chest tightens with the sudden awareness that all these people have come for her, for her words, for the story she finally found the courage to tell.

BRANDI APPEARS AT HER ELBOW, gentle pressure guiding her toward the small podium set up near the signing table. "Ready?" she asks, her eyes searching Jetta's face with the particular attentiveness that has deepened since their shared trauma. "Everyone's here. It's time."

JETTA NODS, her throat suddenly dry. As she steps toward the podium, Ethan materialises on her other side, his hand finding the small of her back in that familiar, grounding touch.

. . .

"You've got this," he murmurs, his voice pitched for her ears alone. "They're already yours."

The room quiets as Jetta takes her place, faces turning toward her with expectant smiles. She takes a deep breath, finding her centre in the moment before speaking.

"Thank you all for coming tonight," she begins, her voice steadier than she expected. "A year ago, I couldn't have imagined standing here with a published novel. Back then, I was still learning how to feel safe again, how to trust again." Her eyes find Ethan's in the crowd, drawing strength from his unwavering gaze. "Some of you know parts of my story – how fear became a constant companion, how healing sometimes feels like two steps forward and one step back."

The room has gone completely silent, the collective attention almost tangible against her skin.

"What many of you don't know is that 'The Art of Surrender' began as personal therapy – a way to process my own journey from fear to trust, from isolation to connection." Her fingers rest lightly on the stack of books beside the podium. "I never intended to share it with anyone. But sometimes, the stories we need most are the ones we're most afraid to tell."

She pauses, gathering herself for the next acknowledgment. "I need to thank someone special – someone who taught me that enemies can become allies, that allies can become friends, and that friends can become..." Her voice catches unexpectedly, emotion rising like a wave. "...everything."

THE SLIGHT BREAK in her composure draws a ripple of empathetic murmurs from the crowd. Ethan's eyes never leave her face, his expression a complex blend of pride and tenderness that makes her heart swell against her ribs.

"ETHAN," she continues after a steadying breath, "thank you for showing me that our past doesn't have to define our future. Our story – from high school adversaries to where we stand today – gave me the courage to write Elise and Marcus's journey in these pages."

THE REST of her speech flows more easily – thanking Brandi and Owen for their unwavering support, acknowledging her publisher, expressing gratitude to the readers who have already pre-ordered and reviewed. When she finishes, the applause washes over her like a warm tide, buoying her toward the signing table where her journey as a published author truly begins.

THE FIRST READER approaches with a copy of "The Art of Surrender" clutched against her chest, eyes bright with the particular excitement of meeting a creator whose work has touched something within her. Jetta takes the book with slightly trembling hands, uncapping the pen Brandi has placed beside her.

. . .

"I STAYED up all night finishing it," the woman confesses as Jetta opens to the title page. "The scene where Elise finally confronts her fears – I cried. It felt so real."

JETTA'S HAND steadies as she writes, the inscription flowing from a place of genuine connection rather than obligation. With each reader who follows, each book signed, each personal moment of exchange, her confidence grows. She is no longer just the woman who survived, who healed, who loved – she is now also the author who transformed that journey into something others can hold in their hands, something that might help them navigate their own dark passages toward light.

TWO HOURS INTO THE SIGNING, Jetta's hand has found its rhythm. The initial tremor has vanished, replaced by the fluid motion of her signature flowing across page after page. She's stopped overthinking her inscriptions, allowing genuine connections to form with each reader who approaches – the woman who clutches the book like a talisman, the shy teenager who whispers that Elise's journey helped her find her voice, the elderly man who admits romance isn't his usual genre but something about the cover caught his eye. Each interaction fills another corner of the hollow space that once held fear, replacing it with the quiet certainty that her words matter, that sharing her story was worth the risk.

THE SHOP HAS SETTLED into a pleasant hum of conversation, the initial rush giving way to a steady stream of attendees moving between the refreshment table, browsing shelves, and joining the signing line. Warm light bathes everything in amber and gold, softening edges and creating pockets of intimacy within the larger gathering. Jetta glances up between signings, her gaze automatically seeking Ethan across the room. He stands near the mystery section, engaged in conversation with one of their regular customers, but his attention shifts to her the moment she looks his way – that sixth sense they've developed, knowing when the other needs connection.

A SMALL SMILE passes between them, laden with meaning invisible to anyone else. In that brief exchange lies a year of building trust, of nightmares weathered together, of learning each other's silences as fluently as their words. They no longer need constant physical proximity to feel secure; the awareness of each other's presence in the room is enough – a tether that stretches without breaking, flexible but unbreakable.

ETHAN EXCUSES himself from his conversation and approaches the signing table with a fresh bottle of water. He uncaps it before placing it beside her, his fingers brushing against her shoulder in a touch so light it might seem accidental to observers. But Jetta feels the deliberate care in it, the communication embedded in this small gesture – I'm watching, I notice what you need, I'm here.

"HOLDING UP OKAY?" he asks, his voice low enough that only she can hear.

SHE NODS, tilting her head briefly against his hand before he withdraws it. "Better than okay," she answers truthfully. "It feels real now."

· · ·

HIS EYES CRINKLE at the corners, that particular expression of pride he reserves for her accomplishments. "It's been real since that morning I found you typing at 4 AM, so lost in the story you didn't hear me call your name three times."

THE MEMORY BRINGS warmth to her cheeks – how he'd eventually approached with coffee, reading over her shoulder without comment until she reached a natural pause. How instead of urging her back to bed, he'd simply asked questions about the characters, engaging with her world until the sun rose.

"NEXT, PLEASE," she says to the waiting reader, but her smile remains influenced by the recollection, by Ethan's continuing presence at the edge of her peripheral vision as he returns to circulating among guests.

THE LINE THINS TEMPORARILY, giving Jetta a moment to flex her fingers and take a sip of water. She surveys the room, pride swelling in her chest at the sight of readers already immersed in her book, sitting in the café corners or leaning against bookshelves, pages open in their hands. Several are checking their phones, likely posting photos from the event, spreading ripples of this evening outward into the world.

"I THINK we can call this a success," Brandi declares, appearing at Jetta's side with four champagne flutes balanced expertly between her hands. The engagement ring on her finger catches the light, sending tiny prisms dancing across the signing table. "A well-deserved celebration is in order."

· · ·

SHE PLACES the glasses on the table just as Owen joins them, his timing impeccable as always. His arm slides around Brandi's waist with that casual possessiveness that somehow never edges into control – just connection, belonging, the physical manifestation of their deepened bond. Ethan completes their circle, moving to stand beside Jetta, close enough that she can feel the warmth radiating from his body.

"TO NEW BEGINNINGS," Brandi says, raising her glass with a meaningful glance between Jetta and Ethan. The simple toast carries layers of significance for their small group – not just the book, but everything it represents: healing, growth, futures reclaimed from the shadow of trauma.

"TO WORDS THAT HEAL," Owen adds, his natural charisma momentarily softened by genuine emotion. "And to the courage it takes to share them."

THEY CLINK GLASSES, the crystal sound bright and clear above the ambient noise of the party. The champagne fizzes on Jetta's tongue, bubbles that seem to match the effervescent feeling expanding in her chest. Looking at these three faces – Ethan, Brandi, Owen – she's struck by how fundamentally they've changed each other, how their individual journeys have become inextricably intertwined.

"REMEMBER OUR FIRST DOUBLE DATE?" she asks, laughter threading through her voice at the memory. "When Owen knocked over an entire bottle of wine trying to impress Brandi with his sommelier knowledge?"

. . .

"AND ETHAN SPENT the entire night looking over his shoulder because he was convinced Alice might show up," Brandi adds, her free hand finding Owen's where it rests at her waist.

"TO BE FAIR," Ethan says, his tone light despite the subject, "it was only two weeks after her arraignment. But yes, not my most relaxed evening."

"I WAS STILL CHECKING my locks three times every night," Jetta admits, the confession easy now in a way it never could have been then. "And jumping at every noise."

OWEN SHAKES HIS HEAD, wonder evident in his expression. "Look at us now. Engaged, published, planning international vacations without second-guessing every detail."

"WE EARNED THIS," Brandi says simply, and they all fall silent, acknowledging the truth in those three words. Nothing about their journey has been easy or given – each step forward claimed through persistent effort, through confronting fears rather than surrendering to them, through choosing trust when every instinct screamed for walls.

JETTA'S GAZE drifts across the renovated shop to the poetry section tucked in the far corner, its intimate arrangement of armchairs and reading lamps creating a sanctuary within the larger space. The memory surfaces with vivid clarity – she and Ethan arguing over a rare first edition Dickinson, their literary disagreement escalating until the tension between them transformed into something else entirely. How his voice had dropped mid-sentence, how the book had been forgotten between them, how the months of simmering attraction had finally boiled over into that first, hesitant kiss. It had tasted of coffee and uncertainty and possibility – a beginning disguised as an ending to their perpetual opposition.

SHE RETURNS to the present to find Ethan watching her, his eyes following the direction of her gaze with perfect understanding. No words pass between them, none needed for this shared recollection. His lips curve in the hint of a smile that tells her he's remembering too – the awkward bump of noses, the startled laugh against his mouth, the way they'd pulled apart only to come together again with greater certainty.

"YOU TWO ARE DOING that thing again," Owen observes, amusement colouring his tone. "The telepathic communication that makes everyone else feel like they're interrupting something."

BRANDI ELBOWS HIM GENTLY. "Says the man who can order for me at restaurants without asking what I want."

"THAT'S NOT TELEPATHY," Owen protests. "That's just paying attention."

"SAME THING," Ethan says, his eyes never leaving Jetta's face. "Just paying very close attention."

. . .

THE WEIGHT of his gaze carries warmth that spreads through Jetta's chest, a sense of being truly seen that once terrified her but now feels like coming home. The journey from that first adversarial kiss to this moment of complete understanding stretches between them – a path marked by small triumphs, by nightmares confronted together, by the daily choice to build something lasting from what began in brokenness.

THE CROWD THINS as evening deepens, leaving behind scattered conversations and the comfortable disorder of a successful event. Empty champagne flutes gather on the café counter, bookmark confetti dusts the wooden floors, and the stack of Jetta's novels has dwindled to the final few copies. She caps her signing pen with a sense of completion, rolling her wrist to ease the pleasant ache of hours spent inscribing her name. The bookshop feels different now – as if the walls have absorbed the evening's celebration, adding another layer to the accumulated history of this space that has witnessed so much of her transformation.

ETHAN APPROACHES from where he's been thanking departing guests, his tie loosened slightly, a hint of nervousness visible only to someone who knows the subtle tells of his body language – the way his right hand brushes his pocket, the slight intensification of his gaze, the almost imperceptible quickening of his step.

"I NEED YOUR HELP WITH SOMETHING," he says, his voice carrying an undercurrent she can't quite identify. "In the poetry section. Something seems off with the Dickinson display."

· · ·

SHE RAISES AN EYEBROW, suspicion flickering at the edges of her awareness. "Dickinson emergency at eleven PM? That seems very on-brand for us."

HIS LAUGH CARRIES a thread of tension that further piques her curiosity. "Let's just say some things come full circle."

HE EXTENDS HIS HAND, and she takes it without hesitation, their fingers interlacing with the practised ease of bodies that have learned each other's contours. His palm feels warmer than usual against hers, his pulse a rapid flutter that transmits through the point of contact. Jetta glances toward Brandi, catching a too-innocent expression that confirms something is definitely happening beyond bookshelf maintenance.

THEY WEAVE through the renovated shop, past the local authors section they expanded last spring, around the children's nook with its miniature chairs and plush reading cushions, beneath the wrought-iron staircase that leads to the new rare books loft. The space has evolved alongside their relationship – walls opened, corners softened, light invited in where shadows once gathered. Like their journey together, the shop has been transformed not by erasing its history but by building something new that honours what came before.

THE POETRY SECTION occupies the back corner of the store, its shelves arranged in a semicircle that creates a secluded alcove separate from the main floor. Even from the approach, Jetta notices something different about the space – the ambient lighting seems softer, more focused, casting a warm glow that doesn't match the standard evening settings. As they round the final shelf, her breath catches in her throat.

ROSE PETALS SCATTER across the hardwood floor, their deep crimson forming a path to the exact spot where they shared their first kiss. The scent rises to meet her – not the overwhelming sweetness of a dozen roses, but the subtle fragrance of just a few blooms, carefully selected and placed. A small reading lamp has been positioned to illuminate a specific shelf, drawing her eye to where a velvet box sits nestled between volumes of poetry.

"ETHAN," she whispers, his name half question, half realisation.

HE GUIDES her forward until they stand in the precise location of their literary argument turned first kiss, where months of tension had finally broken over the correct interpretation of Dickinson's metaphors. The memory feels simultaneously distant and immediate – another lifetime but also the beginning of this one.

"I HAD THIS WHOLE SPEECH PREPARED," Ethan says, his voice steadier now that the moment has arrived. "About time and second chances and how books brought us together." His thumb traces circles against her palm, the familiar gesture grounding them both. "But standing here, I keep thinking about that day – how we were fighting over Dickinson's meaning, both so certain we were right."

. . .

JETTA SMILES, remembering. "You said she was writing about immortality. I insisted it was about the limitations of language."

"AND WE WERE BOTH RIGHT, in our ways." He reaches for the velvet box with his free hand, the movement careful as if handling something infinitely precious. "That's what I love about us, Jetta. We can see different truths and still find our way to understanding."

HER HEART ACCELERATES as the significance of this moment crystallises fully. The rose petals, the secluded corner, the meaningful location – all of it coalescing into a perfect symmetry of ending and beginning.

ETHAN RELEASES her hand to open the box, revealing a vintage-style ring nestled against dark velvet. The centre stone catches light from the reading lamp, sending tiny prisms dancing across the book spines surrounding them. It's not ostentatiously large or flashy – instead, it carries an elegant simplicity that speaks to his understanding of her, his attention to what she would truly love rather than what tradition might dictate.

HE SINKS TO ONE KNEE, the motion fluid despite the emotion evident in his eyes. The box rests in his upturned palm, the ring catching light like a captured star.

"A YEAR AGO, we stood in this exact spot, arguing about poetry and trying to ignore what was really happening between us," he says, voice low and intimate, meant only for her ears. "But our story started long before that – back in high school, through all those dark years apart, and in every moment since we found our way back to each other."

His free hand reaches for hers, and she gives it willingly, her fingers trembling slightly in his steady grasp.

"From the moment you keyed my car, I should have known you'd leave a permanent mark on my life," he continues, a smile playing at the corners of his mouth despite the seriousness of the moment. "That angry girl with fire in her eyes, ready to fight the world – she scared me then, but God, Jetta, I love the woman she became. The one who faced her fears, who rebuilt her life, who taught me what real strength looks like."

Tears gather at the edges of her vision, blurring the image of him kneeling before her – this man who has witnessed her at her most broken and her most triumphant, who has learned the language of her nightmares and her dreams with equal attentiveness.

"We've walked through fire together," he says, his voice roughening with emotion. "And I want to walk through whatever comes next – the beautiful and the difficult, the ordinary days and the extraordinary ones – side by side, hand in hand." He takes a breath, eyes never leaving hers. "Jetta Kinsley, will you marry me?"

. . .

THE QUESTION HANGS in the air between them, though they both know its answer has been written in every choice they've made since finding each other again. Jetta reaches down, pulling him to his feet, unwilling to have any distance between them for this moment.

"YES," she whispers against his lips, the word a breath, a promise, a future condensed into a single syllable. "Yes."

THEIR KISS TASTES of champagne and tears and certainty, his arms encircling her waist as hers wind around his neck. The ring box presses against her back where he holds it, still open, waiting to complete its journey. When they finally separate, just enough for him to slide the ring onto her finger, its weight feels significant yet natural, as if her hand has been waiting for this particular completion.

"PERFECT FIT," she murmurs, watching how the stone catches light as she flexes her fingers.

"I HAD HELP," Ethan admits, nodding toward the end of the poetry section where Brandi and Owen stand partially concealed behind a display, champagne glasses already in hand. They step forward now, Brandi's eyes brimming with happy tears, Owen's smile wide and genuine.

"ABOUT TIME," Brandi says, her voice thick with emotion despite the teasing words. "I've been carrying that ring around in my purse for two weeks waiting for him to find the perfect moment."

. . .

"THE SUSPENSE WAS KILLING HER," Owen adds, passing out the champagne flutes. "She almost proposed to you herself out of sheer impatience."

THEY LAUGH TOGETHER, the sound rising toward the shop's high ceilings, mingling with the lingering energy of the evening's celebration. Their small circle tightens as glasses clink in toast, the four of them connected by more than friendship now – by shared survival, by futures deliberately intertwined, by the choice to build family from what began as refuge.

AS OWEN LAUNCHES into an impromptu engagement toast, his storytelling gift transforming even this small moment into something memorable, Jetta leans into Ethan's side, her head finding that perfect spot against his shoulder. His arm curves around her waist, pulling her closer with gentle pressure. The books surround them like silent witnesses – volumes of poetry and prose that contain countless love stories, none quite like their own but all sharing the universal language of transformation.

SHE FEELS the steady rhythm of his heartbeat against her cheek, the solid presence of him beside her no longer a safety measure but simply home. They've travelled so far from that first antagonistic kiss, from the frightened people who approached love through the lens of past wounds. The journey hasn't erased their scars – they remain, testament to what they've survived – but it has transformed them into something beautiful, proof that broken places can become the strongest when properly healed.

"To us," Ethan murmurs against her hair, the words meant only for her despite the continuing conversation around them. "Past, present, and future."

Jetta's fingers find his, the new ring catching light between them. "To us," she echoes, feeling the truth of it settle in her chest like the final piece of a puzzle long in the solving. "All of it. Always."

Also by Laci Mae Wyld

Texting Fate

In the glittering world of Hollywood, he's the enigmatic heartthrob whose every move makes headlines. She's a refreshingly unfiltered woman who just wants to survive an epic Tinder disaster. But when a chance encounter lures them into a whirlwind of mistaken identities and electric chemistry, their lives are about to collide in the most unexpected way.

When a sassy text message meant for a Tinder date gone wrong lands in the hands of A-list actor Charlie Benton, it sparks a digital dance of wit and warmth with a mystery woman known only as Bee. Little do they know that amidst the virtual sparks lies the beginning of an uncharted romance that transcends fame and fortune.

As their playful banter deepens into a magnetic pull, Charlie and Bee find themselves entangled in a hot and steamy connection. But can they navigate the treacherous waters of stardom's spotlight without losing themselves in its glare? With paparazzi lurking and fans clamouring for every detail, their connection is put to the ultimate test.

Amidst the chaos of Hollywood whispers, Charlie and Bee search for authenticity in a world defined by illusions, and they must choose: embrace the unpredictable journey of love despite the odds or retreat to the safety of their separate worlds. Will their hearts find solace in each other's embrace, or will fame's cruel glare shatter their fairy tale dreams?

Haunted Memories of a Broken Girl

Haunted by visions of a violent crime, Kelly's melodic voice offers solace amidst the chaos of her past. Lawyer Michael Lawson is captivated by her singing, his own memories stirred by her haunting presence. When he rescues her from danger, a chilling realisation sets in - Kelly bears an uncanny resemblance to a long-lost childhood friend's deceased wife.

As their connection deepens, Kelly's fragmented past unravels. Each revelation brings them closer to a shocking reality: Kelly is Helayna Cook, the missing daughter of arms tycoon Richard Cook.

Navigating the treacherous waters of truth and deception, their unexpected romance blossoms. But sinister forces lurk in the shadows, determined to keep buried what should never see the light of day. Threats loom and loyalties are tested as Kelly and Michael find themselves ensnared in a dangerous game of obsession and vengeance.

To survive, they must confront the ghosts of their pasts and unearth the secrets shrouding Kelly's mother's untimely demise - before a malevolent force silences them forever.

You Will See Me

When the lifeless body of Louise Mansfield is found on the bustling Chicago River Walk, seasoned detective Samuel Barron is thrust into a macabre investigation that unravels a web of dark secrets and chilling connections. Louise, daughter of the influential Senator James Mansfield, had been striving to escape her turbulent past as an exotic dancer and reconcile with her powerful father before she became the target of a sadistic killer's wrath.

As Samuel delves deeper into the case, he uncovers a sinister pattern linking Louise to five other tormented women, all tied to the charismatic senator. The discovery hints at a twisted serial killer fixated on beautiful victims associated with the prominent politician. The tension escalates when the primary suspect meets a gruesome demise in a manner mirroring the previous murders, pushing Samuel to confront a ruthless and calculating murderer with a disturbing agenda.

The investigation takes an alarming turn when someone they least expected, is driven by a volatile obsession to protect the Senator's reputation, escalating their vendetta by targeting the Mansfield family. In a heart-pounding race against time, Samuel finds himself in a deadly showdown with the killer, unearthing the depths of their malevolent rage. Their harrowing clash culminates in an intense confrontation of wits and wills, revealing a tapestry of hidden truths, envy, and intricate familial bonds.

Haunted by the specter of this chilling case and facing a new wave of brutal crimes, Samuel realizes that history has a way of resurfacing when least expected. To thwart the cycle of violence and deceit, he must confront his own demons and navigate through treacherous waters to prevent further tragedy. In this riveting tale of suspense and redemption, Samuel grapples with the enduring legacy of past sins in his relentless quest for justice amid shadows that refuse to fade.

Betrayal of Blood

In a whirlwind of betrayal, Sarsha Mitchell's once-promising future implodes when she catches her fiancé, James, entangled with her very own sister. Reeling from the heartbreak, Sarsha takes flight, leaving the shards of her shattered dreams behind. With her picture-perfect life in ruins, she seeks solace on an impromptu getaway to their abandoned honeymoon destination with her loyal confidante, Jess.

From the sun-kissed shores of Perth to the dazzling allure of the Gold Coast, Sarsha attempts to outrun her anguish amidst carefree escapades and electrifying nights out. Just as the shadows of her past threaten to engulf her present, a chance encounter at a club propels Sarsha into an unexpected charade with a mysterious stranger named Riley.

As sparks ignite between Sarsha and Riley during their fabricated romance, healing begins to seep into her wounded soul. However, upon their return to Melbourne, old wounds are ripped open anew as James refuses to relinquish his hold on her heart while envious desires stir chaos within her own family.

Supported by Riley's unwavering presence and unwavering gallantry, Sarsha finds the courage to confront the toxicity suffusing her familial bonds. Yet just as hope blossoms for a brighter tomorrow, a cruel act of revenge orchestrated by James and Megan threatens to shatter everything they hold dear.

In a race against time and treachery, Sarsha stands vigil by Riley's bedside, clinging to hope amidst the turmoil. Together, they uncover the depths of deceit woven by those she once trusted most. With Riley's love paving the way towards redemption and renewal, Sarsha severs the ties that bind her to darkness and steps boldly into a future brimming with promise

From Broken Roads to Healing Hearts

When Natalie's car breaks down on a secluded Tasmanian road, little does she know it will lead her to a ruggedly handsome stranger named Kai and his highland cow farm. Far from the city bustle, Natalie and Kai find themselves tangled in a web of past heartbreaks and hidden scars.

Amidst the picturesque countryside, they form an unexpected bond, discovering solace and passion in each other's arms under the starlit sky. But as secrets unravel and old flames flicker back to life, they must confront their demons together or risk losing everything they've found.

A Dark Descent into Chaos

Caught in the sinister grip of Sydney's underworld, at just 23, she becomes Diego's pawn, a mere facade of a girlfriend to the heartless crime lord. Imprisoned in opulence at Diego's Rose Bay mansion with no way out, Mila endures a life of torment and manipulation. Joe Sullivan is no stranger to shadows and secrets. With a steely gaze that betrays his hidden motives, he infiltrates Diego's inner circle on a covert mission for the authorities. Witnessing Diego's brutal nature firsthand, Joe risks everything to shield Mila from the savagery that lurks within their glamorous facade.

Bound by a dangerous game of deception and desire, Mila and Joe must join forces to uncover the truth amidst a battlefield of power-hungry adversaries. As their partnership deepens, forbidden attraction ignites, threatening to consume them both. With danger closing in and lives hanging in the balance, Joe is determined to protect Mila at any cost, even if it means forsaking everything he holds dear.

In a whirlwind of perilous escapades, high-stakes confrontations, Mila and Joe must navigate a treacherous path towards freedom and justice. But in a world where loyalties shift like shadows and love teeters on the edge of ruin, will they emerge unscathed from the dark empire they're entwined in?

Friend or Foe weaves a tale of passion, loyalty, and sacrifice against the backdrop of Sydney's underworld glamour and danger. In a battle where survival could mean surrendering to love's embrace, will Mila and Joe triumph over the sinister forces that seek to tear them apart?

When We Close Our Eyes

After tragedy strands Casey and Kirk in separate worlds of longing, an unlikely encounter entwines them in a slow dance toward solace. Their love, a tender construction of two battered hearts, finds a tenuous rhythm until a specter from Kirk's past tears through the fragile façade. Obsessed and ruthless, Layla—his ex-wife—emerges from shadow with a plan to reclaim what she believes is hers. As threats mount, Casey and Kirk must fight not only for their love but for their lives, finding strength in their scars and shelter in each other.

Lucky in Love and Bullets

Kitty and Peter are madly in love. Kitty, a successful hair stylist, and Peter, a partner in a prestigious law firm, celebrate a lavish wedding in Hawaii. Their perfect day turns tragic when a gunman appears. Kitty is shot in the head. She regains consciousness in the hospital with no memory of Peter, though she recalls everything else. Kitty struggles to reconnect with Peter, who moves into a separate bedroom. Suspecting he is hiding something, she returns to work and meets Fynn, a handsome new client.

Kitty and Fynn find themselves in dangerous territory with criminals as they try to uncover the truth about why she was shot on her wedding day, with each discovery they see how involved Peter was with the wrong kind of people

Twisted Obsession In the shadows of a seemingly perfect life, Anya Willows discovers that the past she thought she'd escaped is about to collide with her present in the most terrifying way imaginable. After years of uncertainty, Anya finally finds stability with a loving boyfriend, a loyal best friend, and a newfound relationship with the father she never knew. But when tragedy strikes and her world begins to crumble, Anya finds herself at the centre of a twisted web of obsession, deceit, and murder. As the body count rises and the lines between friend and foe blur, Anya must confront a darkness that has been stalking her since childhood. With each shocking revelation, she's forced to question everything and everyone she thought she knew. Who can she trust when the very foundations of her life prove to be built on lies? In this heart-pounding psychological thriller, love becomes a weapon, trust becomes a liability, and the truth becomes the most dangerous thing of all.